"Mapson is one of those fortunate writers able to spin an absorbing yarn without neglecting the underpinnings of character and theme . . . a gifted new novelist likely to be entertaining readers for many years to come."

—*Newsday*

"This is a love story with a salsa bite and a winning heart."

—Barbara Kingsolver

"A funny, harsh, visceral novel. . . . Mapson's finesse with both detail and the big picture, and her appreciation for the eloquence and explosiveness of silence between lovers, make this novel an engrossing, sensuous, resonant read."

—*Publishers Weekly* (starred)

"[T]he perfect dessert for women—and men!—who like *The Bridges of Madison County* then found they were hungry two hours later: hungry for character development, believable plot, dialogue and language at once controlled, mature, romantic, subtle, and memorable."

—*Los Angeles Times Book Review*

Praise for previous works by Jo-Ann Mapson

"*Along Came Mary* is a wonderful novel, filled with women so real and honest you feel you've known them all of your life. It is an absolute joy to read this book; you won't be able to put it down. You'll find yourself thinking about these characters, wishing them well, long after you've closed the last page. *Along Came Mary* is another sparkling gem from Jo-Ann Mapson, a novel about women who laugh through hard times and survive whatever comes their way. Bittersweet, poignant, and ultimately triumphant."

—Kristin Hannah, author of *Distant Shore* and *On Mystic Lake*

"The feisty characters and rueful emotional wisdom of this sequel will win over all but the hardest-hearted reader."

—*Kirkus Reviews*

"A valentine to oceans of good women who survive bad beginnings and worse men. . . . A well-crafted novel."

—*USA Today*

"What do you say about a book that makes you start checking maps to see if you can go live in Bad Girl Creek yourself? I fell head over heels in love with each of the four distinct women in this book, characters so indelible, so alive, the pages literally breathe. Written with prose as clear and sparkling as lake water, this is truly a heart-stunning novel about bonding friendship, abiding love (the friendly and the amorous kinds), loss, regret, and the faint glimmerings of hope that can spark and lead to a future."

—Caroline Leavitt, author of *Coming Back to Me*

"Jo-Ann Mapson has long been a wizard of words, and in her newest novel she makes magic—a literary potion mixed with brilliant characterizations, sweet emotional resonance, second chances, and a dash of laughter. This story of starting over is told through four women so real they'll live within you; their heartaches are heartaches we've all felt; and the redeeming strength of their sisterhood will have you calling up your own best friends late in the night, urging them to read *Bad Girl Creek,* too. Don't miss this one."

—Jodi Picoult, author of *Salem Falls*

"An absorbing story and quirky, appealing characters (a given with Mapson), deepened by honest grappling with a whole slew of messy emotions and issues."

—*Kirkus Reviews* (starred)

"Well-drawn settings and interesting characters . . . a pleasant diversion."

—*Library Journal*

"There's not a woman alive who wouldn't want to spend time with the ladies down at Bad Girl Creek. Mapson's women are complex and caring, funny and fierce, strong and fragile; in short, fully evolved characters you'd want to know in real life."

—*Booklist*

Books by Jo-Ann Mapson

Along Came Mary
Bad Girl Creek
The Wilder Sisters
Loving Chloe
Shadow Ranch
Blue Rodeo
Hank & Chloe
Fault Line *(stories)*

Goodbye, Earl

A Bad Girl Creek Novel

Jo-Ann Mapson

SIMON & SCHUSTER PAPERBACKS
New York • London • Toronto • Sydney

SIMON & SCHUSTER PAPERBACKS
Rockefeller Center
1230 Avenue of the Americas
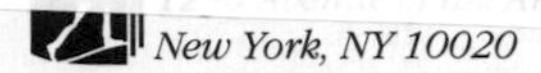
New York, NY 10020

This book is a work of fiction. Names, characters, places, and incidents either are products of the author's imagination or are used fictitiously. Any resemblance to actual events or locales or persons, living or dead, is entirely coincidental.

First Simon & Schuster paperback edition 2005

Simon & Schuster Paperbacks and colophon are registered trademarks of Simon & Schuster, Inc.

For information about special discounts for bulk purchases, please contact Simon & Schuster Special Sales: 1-800-456-6798 or business@simonandschuster.com.

Designed by Lauren Simonetti

Manufactured in the United States of America

10 9 8 7 6 5 4 3 2 1

The Library of Congress has cataloged the hardcover edition as follows:
Mapson, Jo-Ann.
Goodbye, Earl : a Bad Girl Creek novel / Jo-Ann Mapson.
p. cm.
Sequel to: Along came Mary.
1. Women—Alaska—Fiction. 2. Female friendship—Fiction.
3. Alaska—Fiction. I. Title.

PS3563.A62G66 2004
813'.54—dc22 *2003190064*

ISBN 0-7432-2463-9
0-7432-2464-7 (Pbk)

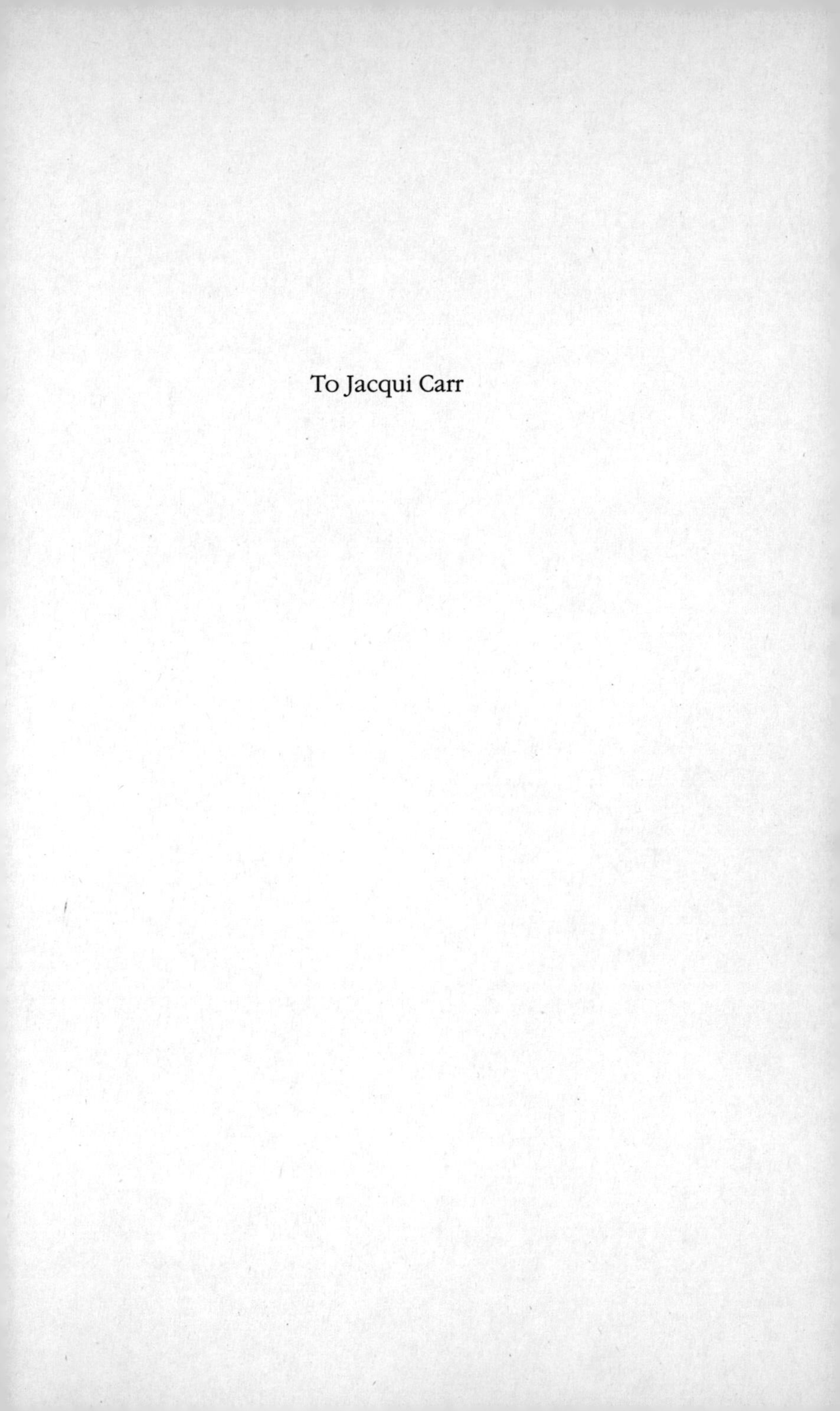

To Jacqui Carr

Sometimes, when one person is missing,
The whole world seems depopulated.

—Lamartine,
Premières Méditations poétiques, 1820

Goodbye, Earl

Several myths surround the aster, a fall flower available in both large and dwarf varieties. Virgo is reported to have sprinkled stardust over bare ground, causing the earth to bloom with the very first asters. The goddess Asterea, upon finding no stars in the heavenly firmament, cried such voluminous tears that every drop caused a flower to bloom. Other names for the aster include starwort, the eye of Christ, and *kallistos stephos,* Greek for "most beautiful crown." Greeks believed that burning aster leaves repelled evil spirits. Aster salve was alleged to cure rabies. Strangely enough, it's the violet aster that produces green dye suitable for wool. The poet Virgil boiled asters in wine and placed the tea near a beehive to sweeten the flavor of the honey. In China, asters are planted systematically, one shade blending to the next, to create a rainbow.

Beryl Anne

1

Peter Jennings and the Bear

THAT SEPTEMBER, Anchorage had more moods than a menopausal woman. The sun shone one day and disappeared the next. The leaves began to turn russet and gold, but instead of falling hung on to branches, unwilling to let go. When the first frost came, and the last of the columbines shriveled, people sighed with relief at the return of what seemed like normal autumn weather. Then, a week later, it was warm again, and pansies close to the earth shamelessly opened their petals to take in the shine. Perhaps most troubling of this out-of-season business was the bears. By the end of the month they were usually bedded down for the winter, and stayed that way until spring. This year, however, bears ventured out long past their usual hibernation dates. Programmed to fill their bellies in preparation for sleep, they got into trash, foraging like ravens, and were seen taking dog food from dishes left out for retired huskies. The newspaper's gardening column warned bird lovers like Beryl Reilly to hold off filling feeders with thistle and sunflower seeds for the chickadees for fear of attracting ursine visitors. A bear encounter was the last thing Beryl wanted. Life was hard enough already.

She sat on the leather living room couch with her journal in her lap. It was a small book, its cover a map of the world. For the last five years she had marked in red pen every place she and Earl had traveled. The western United States, their slow drive through the South and up to New York and Canada, and then beyond the Atlantic, where the line stopped, and they'd flown to Europe. Earl wasn't the "see the British Isles tour" kind of traveler. Despite his casual clothes and fondness for diners, he flew first class wherever he went. He knew cutting-edge places to eat, where to shop for French jeans, and most of all, where to listen to the best live music to be found. He had friends in far-flung places, places he often traveled to on a moment's notice. But since the middle of summer, when he'd announced that he wanted to stay home for a while, Earl had spent most of his time in the basement, which he'd converted to a music studio.

Beryl uncapped her pen and wrote down exactly what she was thinking:

> Earl's going to leave me. He thinks I don't know, but a woman can tell. When I walk into the kitchen and he's reading the paper, he tucks the sports section under his arm and heads downstairs to the studio. A shrink would call that "cave time," and advise me to "take care of my needs myself," but a shrink doesn't live with Earl, I do. He spends more time down there with the guitars and recording equipment than he does with me. Clear through the kitchen floor I hear him teasing notes from his guitars and keyboards. I imagine him adjusting the knobs and plunking the strings with the tenderness and attention he used to shower on me. With the flick of a switch he can loop a chord progression into a never-ending spiral, infuse an electronic drumbeat without a drummer within a hundred miles. Just the other day I heard the chugging sound of a locomotive passing underneath me sounding so real I ran to the window to look for a runaway train.
>
> An extra inch separates us in bed. My lover, who has always turned to me in his sleep, now sleeps on his left side, turned away. When I ask, "Do you want spaghetti for dinner," he looks at me as if I've asked

him to account for every single day of his life. No matter what I say, it puts him on edge.

Okay, so I've skipped a few periods. Maybe I *am* in menopause, the practical joke nature sics on woman so fiercely we wish our cramps and embarrassing accidents and water weight back again. Does he think I'm happy about hot flashes, mood swings, and my faltering libido? And lately I admit I cry at television commercials showing a tender family moment, and the one-legged chickadee hopping around our deck hoping for some crumbs tears my heart as if it's made of tissue paper, but is that necessarily a bad thing? I've been around the block. I know that in a man's world problems exist to be solved. What if I don't know what the problem is? "Just let me be sad," I say, and off he goes, alone, to the studio, to the bookstore, or to hike away from me, and I'm afraid he's never coming back. Yet sometimes we have sweet reunions. He whispers in my ear as he undresses me, and I feel the very pores of my skin open to take him in. And I want to say it doesn't matter, but it does, because I know Earl's going to leave me.

Five years back, when Earl had bought her the house, Beryl had imagined growing old there, the two of them, their life worn to softness by the years they'd weathered. Bohemian Waxwing, the oddly constructed house, was an Anchorage landmark high on the Hillside with its curving roads and occasional seventy-five-miles-per-hour winds. The builder had been a sculptor, married to a woman who was a serious bird-watcher. He'd set down his chisels to design a house that embodied his beloved's favorite bird. The roofline made up the arch of the bird's spine and connected two window-filled wings. To be sure, it was an unconventional dwelling, but the bank of windows struck Beryl as particularly illogical, since a week didn't go by without her hearing a fatal thump and finding a cooling feathered body lying on the deck. The house's story had its dark side as well. When the artist's wife developed a particularly aggressive form of breast cancer and died, the husband left town, and for years the house sat empty. Apparently nobody wanted to take a chance on hand-hewn beams if they came with the specter of love cut short.

But after walking through the empty rooms, Beryl told Earl she didn't believe in curses. She'd never thought she'd own a home, but she began to warm to the idea of decorating with earth tones and soft linens, making this place a reflection of the two of them. "Every house has a history," she said, "and every history holds its measure of sorrow." It was a house, for Pete's sake; Earl had put it in her name. Real estate, like lingerie, wasn't returnable.

Many nights she stood on the balcony wrapped in a blanket watching the northern lights shimmy across the evening sky. The aurora rippled and waned, varying from green to purple to—on rare occasions—nearly red. Supposedly, way out in the bush, if the conditions were right, you could hear it hum and whistle, but Beryl had never been that lucky. The lights almost made her believe in God again, but come daytime her confirmed distrust of the Creator of the universe came rushing back. There was too much sorrow on earth to believe that a Supreme Being would allow that kind of pain. Beryl told herself she believed in concrete details, in evolution, in matter she could touch, like the rich, dark earth, and her foul-mouthed parrot. Now that she lived where she could experience seasons, she believed in the earth all the more strongly.

Beryl studied the Alaskan landscape, the names of the mountains and glaciers—Sleeping Lady, Denali, the Knik, and Matanuska. She memorized the names of flowers like the periwinkle blue forget-me-not, assorted columbines, and the frankly yellow butter-and-eggs. She cooked reindeer sausage and tried salmon jerky, but Earl preferred plain old meat loaf, mashed potatoes with a puddle of butter in the center, and lima beans straight from the can. When he said thank you—like a man who after years of unwrapping ties and leather wallets finally receives the big red tool chest from Sears—that was enough for her. They sat together at the kitchen table eating while Hester Prynne, Earl's tabby cat, peered down from atop the fridge, and Beryl's parrot Verde muttered obscenities to himself from his elaborate, toy-filled cage. She loved her life, even if her boyfriend didn't love her.

The morning she'd decided to confront Earl, he was up before she was. She washed her face, ran her fingers through her curly hair, and poked at the bags beneath her eyes, which, like unclaimed luggage, appeared to be there to stay. She heard the downstairs television switch on, and sat on the end of her bed, tying the belt of her pale pink chenille robe while gathering her nerve.

I will get through this, she told herself. *It's time I took control of my life anyway. I'll learn to drive a car. Make an effort to find new friends. I'll let my emotions out instead of filing them away for that rainy day that never comes. I'll*—what was it her friend Maddy had said the last time they talked on the phone? "Fake it until you make it." A mantra for recovering alcoholics, it would work for newly single women as well.

Downstairs she stood in the kitchen and called his name. Her knees shook and she felt her stomach turn over. "Earl? Honey? We both know things can't go on like this. Can't we talk about it?"

For a long time he didn't answer. Rather than ask again she stared at the screen and watched Peter Jennings narrate in his strong, clear anchorman's voice over footage of whatever the latest world crisis was—teenage mothers stuck in the welfare system, drug cartels financed by unwitting Americans, a war that was always brewing someplace—oh, the specifics didn't really matter. Beryl stood at the kitchen table holding on to her elbows while Earl, on the living room couch, leaned forward concentrating on any news but hers. When he didn't answer her question, she sighed, swallowed against her nausea, and went upstairs to take her shower.

Later she could hear Earl bumping around in his studio, but she didn't go after him. She tried to work on some embroidery, but she had a headache, so she took a nap. She dreamed of her friends in California on the flower farm where she'd once lived.

It was a typical, sunny autumn day, and the smell of chrysanthemums was thick in the air. Phoebe, who had inherited the farm from her aunt Sadie, was telling them all something Sadie had said about growing roses, and Beryl couldn't help but smell the soft, dusty petals even deep in her subconscious. When she woke, the September sun was waning outside her bedroom window, bathing the birches in failing light.

Downstairs the kitchen lay half in shadow. While she could have turned on any number of lights, she didn't want the scene to have sharp edges. Earl was bent over the kitchen table writing checks from one of those enormous checkbooks, four of them to a page. He paid all their bills, and every month he gave Beryl more money than she knew what to do with for "household expenses." She hardly ever spent it unless she was buying him a gift. After all this time she had a bank account well into the mid–six figures, which didn't seem quite real when she opened her statement and examined the balance. "My buddy," she said as she rubbed his shoulders, "buddy" being her term of endearment for this skinny, gray-haired virtuoso who collected signed first editions and traveled to Europe as easily as people around here drove to the Kenai Peninsula for the weekend. "Tell me what's wrong."

Earl reached up and patted her hand. "Nothing's wrong."

Beryl took a breath, let it out, and spoke before she lost her courage. "Earl, don't do this."

"Do what?"

"Retreat from me," she said. "Go all icy and distant and pull away when I go to touch you. If there's something wrong, let's talk about it. Fix it. You know I love you, right?"

He stamped the envelopes and stacked the bills in a neat pile before he answered. "Beryl, I'm as fine as anybody is these days," he said. "The economy's in the toilet, and Bush is in the White House. Ask me again in four years." He closed the checkbook and stretched his arms above his head, neatly moving away from her in the same movement. "I need to get out. Winter's coming. It makes everyone feel a little claustrophobic."

Just then Verde squawked from the front room. Beryl's severe macaw didn't appreciate being left out of any conversation, and this one was no exception. Beryl opened a cupboard to get him some peanuts. "There's still some light. We could hike Powerline Pass trail if we hurry," she said. The hike wasn't exactly challenging for someone like Earl, but it wore Beryl out. The views were stunning, but unless you were looking inside a Wal-Mart, gorgeous scenery pretty much set the standard for south central Alaska.

The set of Earl's shoulders was stiff. Maybe this *was* all about impending winter. Maybe she was, as her stepmother used to say, "borrowing trouble." But deep down she felt sure he was trying to figure out how to leave—how a man could do that after promising a woman "forever." It gutted her legs, but she took a breath and forged ahead. "Look. I can tell you want to leave, and not just for a little while. So let's get it out in the open. Be grateful we had five years."

He stared at her, measuring her words.

"This isn't a trick," she said. "I'm sad, but I won't fall apart. Why don't you go take your hike? I'll stay here and make some bread. That rye you like. And soup. When you get home, we'll work this out like adults."

Earl smiled in such plain relief that Beryl fell for him all over again—the shy, reluctant grin, the slightly overlapping front teeth, and the crinkly lines near his eyes that smoothed out when they made love. "Are you sure?" he asked.

Sure? About dismantling her life? Well, it wouldn't be the first time she'd done it. "Why would I lie to you?"

"No reason. Okay, then. I think *I will* go. On the hike."

As if she'd signed his permission slip, Earl was out the door in twenty minutes. No perfunctory goodbye kiss, just him grabbing his daypack and jacket and a terse "See you later." Beryl glimpsed a wave of the hand with the callused fingertips she loved to feel travel across her skin—though she hadn't in quite some time, and now she was going to have to say goodbye to all that. He'd return less burdened. They'd eat dinner and push their plates aside and open their mouths and behave like civilized people. *You love that couch, so you keep it. I know how important your books are to you, so I'll help you pack them up so they won't get damaged,* when all she wanted was to sidle up close, unbutton the top of his Henley and run her hands over his chest until he got the idea that using bodies instead of words was a much better form of communication—and medicine to heal most rifts.

Instead she put on her winter jacket and gloves and set out for her own walk. A spattering of rain, typical of the autumn season, darkened the tarmac. Soon, enough moisture would collect in the graveled places and turn to frost. They lived too far up the Hillside to have streetlights, but it was still a fairly spendy neighborhood, complete with a homeowner's association she continually worried would discover her past felony conviction and boot her out as undesirable. Beryl tried to imagine who lived in the houses on the acre-plus lots. Some were styled in a postmodern box shape, with paned windows like staring eyes. Others were massive log-home forts, and when Beryl looked at them she pictured entire forests giving their lives to become pretty lumber. Rarely on her walks did she encounter a neighbor. Oh, sometimes a dog walker would give her a brief nod, but nobody spoke beyond "Hi," or "Cold, isn't it?" If you lived this far up the hill, people figured you didn't want to be bothered. She had her hands in her pockets, her head down, the posture of brooding, and was trying to reconcile what had happened in her kitchen half an hour ago with what would happen when Earl came home. Menopause had delivered her a unique method of reasoning, such as, "If Hollywood can make such authentic love stories, films that make a person cry time after time, then why can't human beings stay in love for longer than five years?" Furthermore, was the whole idea of finding one's soul mate doomed to failure? A beautiful pipe dream with a hairline crack? Could anybody sustain a relationship and maintain a sense of herself? Phoebe had nearly lost herself when Juan died. The love of Ness's life had left her with HIV. And why couldn't Nance, who would make the best mother, have her baby instead of three miscarriages?

After she'd thoroughly depressed herself, she pictured Peter Jennings, his handsome face, the dark hair graying at the temples, his professional calm, and wondered if he was like that in real life, if he was married, and who the lucky woman might be.

In fact, she was so caught up in her thoughts she didn't see the bear. To her it looked as if her neighbor's front-yard spruce tree had suddenly sprouted a goiter. What the hell, this was Alaska. Anything could and did happen, people falling into glaciers, the legalization of marijuana, the mayor shutting down a harmless library exhibit because he wanted to pretend there was no such thing as gay pride. But in the next instant, the tree goiter was on the ground on all fours, breath steaming from his nostrils, looking as surprised by Beryl as she was by him.

She tried to remember bear etiquette—were you supposed to run, like you did with moose, hauling ass as quick as possible from those deadly hooves? Bear claws were huge and thick, scar makers of the highest order. Maybe she was supposed to stand absolutely still, or was she supposed to make noise? Bear bells and pepper spray—just about every Alaskan store had them for sale—and a joke to tell along with them—but it didn't take a rocket scientist to know they wouldn't do diddly against a pissed-off bear. Should she back away? She didn't see a cub. Sows with cubs were the most dangerous. Was it a black bear or a brown one? It was hard to tell in the shadows. She remembered a Tlingit tale she'd read in a book she'd bought at Title Wave Books.

> "A woman is out gathering berries with her family. Surprised by a bear, she drops her basket. The bear takes her away. He becomes her husband. She makes his dinner. From their passion, children are born. Her husband treats her well. It's a good life, except for her occasional wondering about her life before this one."

Then, depending on the version, her brothers return for her and kill the bear, which by now she loves with all her heart or, seeing how bearlike she's become, they kill her, too.

Beryl closed her eyes and thought of the people who might possibly miss her should this bear take her life—her girlfriends back in California, definitely. Earl? Of course he would, for a while anyway. She smelled the bear's harsh odor, or maybe it was her own fear rising. All she knew for certain was that when she opened her eyes, she was home, having run all the way and seeing nothing. But even standing on her own front porch the feeling of safety eluded her. Peter Jennings, she thought. Peter would have known what to do.

To calm herself she would make bread. First she sifted the rye flour with wheat, shook anise seeds from the spice tin into the mix, and in another bowl she stirred blackstrap molasses with melted butter and warm milk. Then she spaced out for a moment, staring at the bowls, trying to figure out what was missing. Her mind returned to the bear. She remembered that her neighbors had hung a bird feeder in the tree. The poor bear was hungry, that's all. He was looking for something to fill his stomach before hibernation. Maybe he didn't like the taste of fifty-three-year-old women. Maybe he had a good laugh at her running down the street like her hair was on fire. Oh my God! Yeast! How could a baker forget the leavening? Outside it had begun to rain.

The six-burner restaurant stove was so powerful and efficient at baking that the bread was done and cooling on the wire rack in three hours. Its perfume filled the kitchen, and made Beryl so hungry she went to work on a white bean soup, taking time to chop shallots and then to lightly caramelize them before adding them to the soup. Such careful attention made the difference between an okay soup and a meal so wonderful that she knew Earl would ask for seconds. There was sour cream to dollop on top of the soup, and chopped green onions to sprinkle across. Why not put as much care into this dinner as all the others? She had just finished washing her hands when the phone rang.

"Are you channeling Martha Stewart?" her friend Phoebe asked when Beryl explained the dinner menu.

"I hope not," Beryl said. "Didn't she run over her neighbor or get really fat?"

"According to the rumors," Phoebe said. "At least you aren't being investigated for stock shenanigans."

Beryl could hear Phoebe's five-year-old daughter, Sally, screaming in the background. "What's wrong with the little princess?"

Phoebe sighed. "Her highness is making sure everyone

knows that she is not pleased with her dinner menu. How can any child of mine hate vegetables, I ask you? Suddenly all she wants is bacon or cheeseburgers, even for breakfast."

Beryl thought about how a change in appetite could be an omen, and how the words *omen* and *ominous* and were so obviously related, but how did the English language go from there to the word *augury,* or the queen of them all, *portentous?* She got so distracted that Phoebe had to startle her back into joining the conversation. "Beryl Anne? Are you still there?"

Hormones. The answer had to be hormones. She'd find a doctor and get a prescription and start taking them immediately. "I'm sure picky eating's just a phase, Pheebs. Sally won't perish if she eats a hamburger now and again."

"Over my dead body. They put all those nasty growth hormones in meat nowadays," Phoebe argued. "I don't want this child needing a bra by second grade. Oh, my God, Beryl. Think about it. My daughter is going to have bigger tits than me by the time she's thirteen years old! Probably even before that."

Now the rain had turned to snow—the first flakes of the season. They'd melt before they hit the ground, Beryl thought. She and Phoebe laughed, and for the moment things were so nearly like the year Beryl had lived at Bad Girl Creek that she felt as if Phoebe were down the street, or in the next room, even, instead of a six-hour plane ride away. She flew down to see them twice a year, but this winter she'd asked Earl if they could stay home. Winter in Alaska was slow and quiet, cozy. Beryl wanted to read, play with Verde, and cross-country ski along the Coastal Trail. If they traveled at all, she wanted to head back to New Mexico, where Earl performed music in out-of-the-way bars, tried out his new material, and where Beryl had first met Maddy, who was now living in Nashville, sans Rick, whom Beryl never thought was good enough for her anyway. When Earl left she would be alone for winter. Well, alone wasn't necessarily a bad thing. She took a breath and decided not tell Phoebe about the breakup. The last thing she wanted was to add to her friend's burdens.

"The reason I called," Phoebe said, "is my love life."

"You have a love life? That's wonderful, Phoebe. Who's the lucky guy?"

"Hang on. It's not what you think. I went on a movie date with my Rolfer, Grant. He's very nice, and he's handsome, and the movie was pretty good, too, but Beryl, am I nuts? The whole time we're sitting there in the theater all I can think is I'm sitting next to the man who knows my misbehaving muscles intimately. Not to mention he's seen my"—she paused and lowered her voice—"my bird's nest peeking out from my underwear a time or two. Honestly, I was so nervous I couldn't eat my popcorn."

"Your bird's *what*?" Beryl asked.

"Think metaphor," Phoebe said. "Precocious little pitchers have big ears, remember. Well, anyway, it was a tense evening. And he asked me to go again next week. Do you think that means something? Or is he just lonesome? I wonder if maybe he parked in a handicapped space and got assigned community service and I'm the service? Oh, enough about boring old me. How's the love of your life, you luckout?"

"Earl's fine," Beryl said.

"Pass the phone so I can say hi."

"He's out for a little hike, otherwise I would."

"He goes for hikes a lot, doesn't he?" Phoebe said.

"Well," Beryl said, looking out the kitchen window at the fat flakes illuminated in the porch lights and wondering where he was, if this would be the last time she had a right to feel this way. "Hiking's a religion up here. If it's a nice day, you go fifteen miles. If it's a crappy day, you only do seven."

"Wait. Isn't it dark all the time now?"

Beryl craned her neck to see if she could catch a glimpse of the driveway. Earl was probably in his truck, driving up the hill this very minute. She'd explained Alaska's light-and-dark peculiarities a thousand times, but her friends in the Lower Forty-eight persisted in believing that Alaska had two seasons, light and dark, so she'd finally quit trying. "How's Nance doing?" she asked. "Ness? Mimi and Dayle? David? Anyone heard from Maddy?"

"Maddy sent us a CD," Phoebe said. "Mostly cover songs, but man, she can really belt it out when she wants to. Did you hear that Rotten Rick had to go back to work? He got a job writing for that retirement newsletter! Ha. Everyone else is fine. Mimi and Dayle are currently broken up, however."

"That's too bad."

"It's a stalemate with those two. Dayle misses Alaska and wants Mimi to move there with her. Mimi refuses to leave Bayborough because her grandkids are here. Of course, her daughter-in-law still won't let her be a part of their lives, but Mimi persists in thinking that will change."

"Tell Dayle she can come stay here if she wants. There are whole rooms I haven't explored. Sometimes I feel like I live in Manderley."

"I loved *Rebecca,*" Phoebe said. "I was maybe ten when I read it for the first time. It was so creepy and romantic all at the same time. Kind of like love, actually."

Beryl said, "I think I read it in prison."

Both were silent a moment, and Beryl felt the shift in tension even before Phoebe spoke. Prison had ended ten years ago, and her friends loved her through and through, but every time Beryl made a reference to it, there was this momentary awkward hush. "There is one thing I wanted to tell you," Phoebe said. "Before you hear it from someone else."

The receiver suddenly felt leaden in Beryl's hand. "Oh, God, Pheebs. Save the worst news for last. Tell me what happened."

"Nance lost the baby."

"No. Oh, not again."

"Yeah, she did. Yesterday."

In her nearly five years of marriage to Phoebe's brother, James, Nance had been pregnant three times and miscarried three times. This made attempt number four. Beryl had watched Phoebe make the transformation from "Eh, who needs a baby" to a darned good mother, but Nance's maternal impulse ran clear to the core. Beryl'd never known anyone who wanted a child so badly.

"And she made it so far this time," Phoebe said.

"What's the doctor say?" Beryl asked.

"Time to give her body a rest."

"How long a break does she have to take?"

"Actually he said to stop trying altogether."

"Does that mean they're going to adopt?"

"Sally, you put that video down this minute!" Phoebe

sighed. "Sorry to sound like such a crab, but I cannot bear one more viewing of *The Little Mermaid* today. I should probably hang up. Poor Nance. They really thought this time was going to be the charm. The ultrasound looked good. It was a boy."

Beryl didn't want to think about it, but now the picture was in her mind, a tiny boy waving from across the creek that ran behind the flower farm. His face was in shadow, and he pressed his palms together and dived into the water. "Is she eating okay?" Beryl asked. Nance was anorectic, and too much stress could potentially send her back to the days of apple skins and half-cup cottage cheese entrées.

"James says she is. He made her go back to the shrink. Says she just needs time to grieve the loss. That's the one thing I suck at, you know? I'm just not a patient person. Never have been, never will be."

Beryl understood that, probably better than any of the other women who lived at the farm, but they had no idea why, and she hadn't gone out of her way to tell them. All Beryl'd revealed of her past was hints that a series of long-ago obstacles had kept her from having a career as a teacher. She'd closed off that portal, kept it from the world, and living in Alaska had only reinforced the wall. "I'll write her a card," Beryl said, hearing the sound of a car pulling up. "I have to hang up now, Phoebe. Earl's back. I have dinner ready."

"Keep in touch, Martha," Phoebe said. In the background there was a crash, and she sighed again. "I'd better go sweep up before one of the animals cuts a paw. Love you, Beryl."

"Love you back," she said, and hung up. In the time they'd talked, the weather had turned bad, one of those freezing rainstorms that made Alaskans stay indoors and light the woodstove.

Beryl waited for Earl's whistle as he took the stairs, the familiar clink of his key in the front lock, which generally triggered Verde's explosive greetings—a cussing parrot never ran out of things to say—and for Hester Prynne to jump from her perch atop the refrigerator, but instead, the someone rang the doorbell. Who would it be at this time of night? Maybe Airborne Express. Earl was always getting packages. She answered the door and instead of her true love, she met a state trooper. Snow and rain had dampened the shoulders of his extra-large jacket. He looked so young for someone that tall, his face unlined, his cheeks as smooth as a boy's. "Yes?" she said. "May I help you?"

The trooper removed his hat. "Ma'am, does an Earl Houghton live here?"

"He does," Beryl said. "But he's not in at the moment. Is there something I can do for you?"

The trooper had one of those military-short haircuts. Beryl invited him in to the foyer, where true Alaskans took off their shoes without a moment's thought as to the state of their socks. Only a *cheechako*—a newcomer, like she had once been—would stand there shod and dripping. But even though this man clearly wasn't a *cheechako,* water puddled around his boots on the slate tile. "I'm sorry to tell you, but we found his truck by Eklutna Lake."

Beryl looked at him. "Eklutna Lake?" No one went there after summer's end. The roads were impassable in snow. "No, he went for a hike up the Powerline trail."

"Ma'am, we found his truck off the road in the trees. Keys in the ignition, motor running, no sign of him. What with this ice storm—"

Beryl shook her head no. "You're mistaken. He'll be back any second."

The trooper looked at her sadly, as if his mouth were brimming with a speech he'd memorized from training, only to realize it was not going to make things any easier for either side of the equation. Beryl's knees began to buckle. "Ma'am," he said, catching her by the arm to steady her. "Is there someone I can call for you?"

However long it took to fall, Beryl had time to remember when she had been the one delivering bad news, six years back, on Phoebe's wedding day. Her fiancé, Juan, had been killed in a multiple car wreck on his way to their wedding. The pain of seeing the mangled cars and the devastation of Phoebe's life lay right below the surface, and if Beryl thought about it for longer than five minutes, she broke down. But now other memories began crowding in, demanding time and attention and recognition. Right then she would have given both her arms if that state trooper would just put his Smokey the Bear hat back on and go deliver his bad news to the house next door. He held her upright, struggling to maintain eye contact, to let her know just how serious this was.

He could have gone to Eklutna, Beryl reasoned. It was a beautiful lake. In the summer they'd kayaked there. Portaged their gear to a quiet spot, made love on grass so green it seemed to glow beneath their flesh. The trooper helped her to the kitchen table and got her a glass of water.

After she drank, Beryl pulled herself together. She could hear the soup bubbling on the stove. "Tell me," she said. "Even if it's really bad. Don't leave anything out."

Thomas Jack

2

The Bird Whisperer

During the winter months, Raptor Rehab's frenetic pace slowed to a dawdle. Summer volunteers returned to university to further their studies, found jobs at big box stores that paid minimum wage, went to two-dollar shows at the Bear Tooth Theater, or drank more than usual and waited for spring. Life wasn't nearly so interesting outside the center. Where else could a person bask in the good feeling that he'd done something positive for the winged residents of Alaska? Treatment continued with a skeleton crew of three salaried employees and a handful of longtime volunteers, some of whom'd worked there for as long as a decade. Thomas Jack had done both jobs. Now he was paid a small salary and had his own key to the place. He showed up for work before eight and stayed until things got done, and when they didn't he sacked out on the office floor by the cages of Mr. Jay and the resident redpoll, Lipstick.

Thomas could remove a fishhook from an eagle's beak, though somehow in doing so, his cleft palate scar always began to tingle. He performed physical therapy on ravens' wings, and doctored eagles too weak to try to bite him. He stood by the vets who volunteered their surgery skills, and sometimes he knew which way they were going to probe before they did. He scrubbed guano out of Astroturf cage liners; handpicked grub worms from the canvas littered with sawdust and potato slices, and chopped donated salmon into bird-bite-size chunks. Then he weighed them in kilograms, injected each piece with Lactated Ringers Solution, and dusted the lot with vitamins before setting the tray inside a cage to tempt a sick bird. Birds responded well to him. He knew not to try to catch an eagle without backup. He accepted the fact that no matter what a person tried, some birds did not get well; yet when he was on watch, it sometimes seemed they tried harder to heal. Of Thomas Jack, Dr. Simpson said, "That dude's got the mojo," and most everyone agreed.

Thomas Jack was who the vets called at three in the morning. They knew that he'd work a Saturday shift without complaint, and if a cage of baby swallows came in needing to be fed every twenty minutes, and Thomas said he'd do it, come morning every one of those swallows would be alive. Nearly everyone who passed through the double doors noticed that Thomas looked a little like an eagle himself, with those deep, hooded brown eyes and the hooked Roman nose. He was half Tlingit and half white, his skin the color of Starbucks latte, and his inky hair hung halfway down his back. A few years ago, when Raptor Rehab hosted an open house to raise funds, some *Daily News* reporter took it upon herself to bestow on Thomas the title "Native American Bird Whisperer." Since then he had suffered endless jokes regarding Robert Redford movies and how exactly was it one said "Thanks for the Oscar" in Eagle. Periodically, the paper ran a picture of whatever bird they had in-house that week, and made mention of Thomas Jack, "still whispering after all these years." When elementary school kids came to the clinic on a field trip, Thomas spun them stories of how in the old days, a Native man could speak to animals without moving his lips. He'd make his eyes go wide and his voice as steady as a metronome. It quieted the kids for long enough to get them past making jokes about bird scat and the stink of fish.

Today he was working with Alma Santangelo, who'd been there a month longer than he had and never let him forget it. Alma sometimes got a bug up her behind about the ravens' diets.

The weekend volunteers liked to fork out dog food for the ravens because it was easy and nutritious, and the food detail then took about thirty minutes and much less elbow grease. "It's downright laziness," Alma said, her voice getting that shrill tone to it. "Not to mention unhealthy. And these are the same individuals who buy organic bananas and granola for themselves. How hard is it to chop eggs, defrost fish, crumble birdy cornbread over a pie plate and sprinkle in a few berries?"

On this subject she could go on for hours. Thomas knew Alma just wanted to be heard. Her with that blowhard boyfriend sporting his mullet haircut, drunk half the time. When they did bother to come home, her daughters ran roughshod all over her. One of them had been busted for prostitution, and the other one was dancing at Showgirls. Raptor Rehab was about the only place where Alma felt in charge. This was the real miracle of listening, Thomas thought. Birds were walks in the park compared with Alma. Maynard, the other paid employee, sometimes referred to her as "Bitch and Game," but he didn't really mean it. Today Alma was particularly steamed because a Sunday volunteer had fed a convalescing raven McDonald's french fries.

"Junk food!" she wailed. "Would you feed a Big Mac to a cardiac patient? What the hell is wrong with those people? What do they do all day? Sit around and play cards? You'll notice nobody bothered to do a load of wash, either."

Thomas wanted to interrupt her. He wanted to say, *Look at the raven's chart, Alma. Bird hasn't eaten for a week, yet he scarfed the fries. The raven's a scavenger, food's food, and when somebody's given up, you tempt 'em however you can.* But his grandmother, full Tlingit and from a Raven clan, had brought him up to respect people and to listen politely. When the doorbell rang, Thomas offered to get it, leaving Alma in the food preparation room. She was probably telling her sad story to the twin freezers stacked high with rats and mice sorted according to size and color, alongside moose meat so old the gray surface was visible under the plastic wrap.

Far more interesting was the curly redhead at the door. She looked about forty, maybe a few years older. She held a powder blue bath towel in her arms. Inside the bath towel was a dazed looking magpie. "He flew into my window," she said as behind her a blue-and-white City taxi pulled away. "Can you help?"

"Bring him in, and I'll take a look." Thomas Jack opened the door so she could come inside. He gestured her past the display case filled with various sizes of eggs, an abandoned nest, and the taxidermied great horned owl that was losing its stuffing. Usual clinic procedure was to allow the rescuer to come in and watch the intake exam, but most of the time they dropped the bird and ran like hell. This one tied her jacket around her waist and slid on a pair of rubber gloves without Thomas asking her to.

"Has West Nile virus found its way up here yet?" she asked. "Do you quarantine all newcomers as a matter of policy?"

He sprayed the exam counter with Nolvasan disinfectant. "No and yes. You happen to know the approximate time of the bird's injury?"

She looked at her watch. "Twenty-six minutes ago. It takes the cab company ten minutes to get up the hill to my house, so twenty minutes there. Add in the four it took me to get the towel, call the cab, and a minute here talking with you. He's moving his head, so his neck's not broken, but he's in shock, and I'm sure he has a concussion. Do you guys use dex? I'd say he weighs—" and he watched her use her fingers gently to assess the bird's heft and tell him in kilograms.

He lifted the bird off the scale, leaving the towel and, mentally subtracting its weight, amazed at how close she was. "Dex" was short for dexamethasone, which was indeed their standard treatment for a shocky bird. Thomas Jack cocked his head. "How come you know all this? You got birds at home?"

"Just one," she answered, frowning. "A severe macaw that appears to be having a nervous breakdown."

"Really? Why do you suppose that is?"

"I don't have a clue. I'm about ready to call in the pet psychic lady on the Discovery Channel."

He laughed. "I love that show. So how come you know to glove up, worry about West Nile, et cetera?"

She folded the towel around the magpie while Thomas checked his wings. "A few years ago I worked at a bird rescue in

California. Probably by now all the procedures have changed. What I said—well, it just comes out automatically. I'll shut up now and let you get to work."

Thomas gently extended each of the magpie's wings. Mags were as hardy as tomcats, and just about as scruffy. Nothing broken. Alma came into the room, saw them at the table, and gathered up the intake papers. She laid them down on the edge of the exam counter and peered into the towel. "Want me to give the injection?" she asked.

Thomas said yes and recited the dosage. He and the redhead held the bird while Alma worked her fingers through breast feathers and with an alcohol rub, cleaned a patch of skin. The shot went in easily, and they rewrapped the magpie to take him to the quarantine cages. "I can take him," Alma said.

"I'll finish the paperwork," Thomas said, taking up the intake report. "You don't have to give your name," he said to the redhead. "But if you want me to call and let you know how the bird does, I'll need your phone number."

She was looking all around the building, and for a moment she didn't seem to hear him.

He tapped the pen on the counter. "Or I'll just put down 'anonymous.' It's up to you."

She let out her breath and told him her name. "That's *B-e-r-y-l,* like the stone, not the pickle barrel. Last name is Reilly."

"As in 'the life of'?" Thomas Jack said.

"Well, gosh. I've only heard that about ten million times before."

"Sorry. Soon as I finish this paperwork I'll give you the nickel tour. Then I'm going to talk you into volunteering here."

"Thanks, but I can't."

"Stay for the tour?"

"No. Volunteer."

"You work eighty hours a week or something?"

"Actually I don't have a job, but I still can't do it."

He watched her surveying the shelves of supplies, their pitiful boxes of outdated gauze pads and precious bottles of disinfectant. She would say no three more times, he figured, but in the end he'd get her to agree to at least come back.

"You think the magpie will make it?" she asked as he slid the paperwork into the half-full binder of records they kept on each bird.

"They're pretty hardy," he said. "Come on, let me introduce you to everyone."

Everyone meant the birds. Most of their patients weren't going anywhere except to a good home, where they'd live out their days in a nice roomy cage, get handled on a daily basis, and once a month or so, take a trip to a school or a bookstore to perform an education event. Thomas Jack watched Beryl-the-stone-not-the-pickle-barrel's face as she took in their haughty juvenile eagle, a study in brown feathers and royal attitude, despite having had half his beak shot off. Dr. Simpson was experimenting with fiberglass materials to create a prosthetic beak, and he figured she'd do it, too, if such a thing could be accomplished. Their goshawk was getting spoiled, but he was such a gorgeous bird that that seemed inevitable. They had a merlin that was on its way to Homer this very afternoon—Homer had been asking for one for five years. The cussed raven pair that came in a week before had already torn up the newspaper lining their cages and bitten one of the Sunday volunteers, probably for running out of french fries, Thomas imagined. Did she know about the statewide shortage of tetanus vaccine? Beryl nodded yes. She stood a long time looking in at the eagles. Seeing a wild bird up close was a darn good show. Thomas Jack took her into the baby bird room, opened the screen door, and led her inside. "That cage in the corner," he said. "I was just about to clean it. Would you mind holding Saint Francis while I do?"

"Saint who?"

Thomas Jack wrapped the pygmy owl in a flannel cloth and set the bird in her hands. He'd come to the center with his top feathers torn out, probably hit by a car, and a mild concussive injury that abated after a week. His tonsure made him look like a tiny pissed-off friar. The little guy was so enraged at being lifted from his secure cage and the spruce branch wedged inside for a perch that he clicked his beak furiously. The soft way Beryl cradled him in the flannel, the look she gave him, as if Thomas and the quail and the duck weren't even there—well, Thomas knew he had made a dent. Women and owls, he thought; there was a strange connection, sort of like women and horses. He'd long ago given up trying to understand such pairings. Usually he left the cleaning detail to the volunteers, but today he laid clean newspaper in the cage as slowly as he could get away with. He fetched six thawed mice, bloated to comic book roundness with the injection of Ringers, and set them in a clean recycled Lean Cuisine entrée dish.

"Even saints get antsy," Beryl said, "and I think this one wants back in his cage."

"Here. Give him to me. It's time for his breakfast anyway."

Thomas laid the mice on the Astroturf bottom of the cage. The owl immediately took one, neatly flipping it into his beak, and then worked his whole body in a series of shrugs to get the mouse down. Thomas bagged the bird's latest pellet and dated the label.

"You save their pellets?" she said.

"We recycle their recycling," he answered. "Science classes dissect the pellets, stuff like that."

"He's a beautiful bird," Beryl said.

"Yeah. We get a fair number of owls," he said. "Let's go see the water pens."

He took her through the maze of water pens where they sometimes had a swan or a variety of ducks, but today the pens were empty and drained. Summer had been an entirely different story. While the rest of Anchorage was out in the endless sunshine, wearing sandals and shorts, Thomas had worn hip boots and Carhartt overalls to work. To him summer smelled like the guano of a hundred screaming gulls.

Beryl stopped in front of the eagle cages again. "This probably sounds rude, but how do you get the money to maintain a place like this? In California, and I lived in a wealthy county filled with bird-watching retirees, we had a facility the size of a closet."

"The one good thing to come out of the oil spill," he said.

"This place exists in case of another one. Should that happen we have twenty-four hours to clear our birds out and get to work on theirs. That's a day I hope will never come."

"I take it you were in Valdez? That must have been hard."

He nodded. "It's still a mess. Go to the beach, turn a rock over, and dig down a few inches. You'll find oil. Shall we go see how the magpie's doing?"

"Yes, definitely."

The bird was perched in the corner of his crate, glowering at them, his food untouched. "Give him time," Thomas said. "It's like if you or me hit the windshield in a car wreck. Head's gotta ache."

"Yes," Beryl said. "I can relate. I started getting headaches this summer."

"Seen a doctor?"

She smiled at him. "From what I've read, it's all part of the dreaded 'change of life.'"

Thomas liked her face, the serious set of her jaw, and that she wasn't averse to laughing at herself. The way she studied things, taking in detail after detail until she had a clear picture of the whole, impressed him. Maybe she had come from California, but this was not your basic lunch-and-shop woman. In the front office he introduced her to Mr. Jay, possibly the oldest blue jay in captivity, blind in one eye, the other missing entirely, thanks to some boys and their rock-throwing abilities. Lipstick had an unfortunate feather disorder, and looked as if he were constantly molting. Both had been at the center so long that they knew the routine better than anyone. Lipstick liked the white mealworms, but he would not touch the brown ones. Mr. Jay wanted pine nuts and a pinecone to tuck them in to or he'd squawk up a storm. "So, Beryl," Thomas said. "That's all of it. What do I have to do to talk you into coming back, giving us a try? Buy you lunch?"

"Thanks, but this part of my life's over with. I'll always love birds, but I'm done with the rescue end of it. I just can't take it when they die. And the ones that respond and get released, I miss them too much. Not to mention the politics involved. A person gets tired of begging for money, you know?"

"Come on," Thomas said. "This isn't California, it's Alaska. We're easygoing."

She shook her head no. "I'll write you a big check. Think of all the medicines you can buy with it."

"I'll happily take the check, but why don't you come in tomorrow, just to hang out? Maynard will be in. He's a good guy, into falcons. He'd love to meet you. He's got a scarlet macaw at home. Plus you can monitor the magpie's progress."

She looked away. "You'll hate me if I take a pass."

"Not if you give me a good enough reason."

She touched the bars of the redpoll's cage, and Mr. Jay said, "Good bird."

Thomas noticed that made her smile. Figured, what with her owning a parrot.

"My life's sort of a mess right now. I don't know how much help I could be, really."

Boyfriend trouble, Thomas Jack figured. It was epidemic. He handed her a brochure. "Read this when you have a minute. Maybe you'll change your mind."

"Thanks. Is it okay if I use the phone to call a cab?"

"A cab? If you need a ride home it's no trouble for me to drop you off. This is about the time I go out for lunch, anyway. Who wants to spend ten bucks on a cab?"

"It's okay. I have the money."

Thomas Jack pointed to the donation box. "Then stick a tenner in there and let me drive you home. I love macaws, and it's been a while since I saw a severe, and you said he was having some kind of breakdown. Maybe I can help. Alma!" he called out. "I'll be back in an hour."

"I'll be damned," he said when he turned onto her street. "You live in the Nuthatch."

"Excuse me?"

"Your house. That's what people call it. On account of the man who built it poured hundreds of thousands of dollars into it, and it ended up looking . . . well, like this. He was . . . eccentric, I guess is the word for it."

Beryl gave him a look. "You mean a nut."

"Some people say so," Thomas allowed. "Funny thing is, the way it's built? The wings and so on, the red underneath the back end of it? It really does look like a nuthatch."

"Oh," she said softly. "I thought I was the only one who noticed."

"Nope. I saw that right away. So. Which way is in?"

"Just park in the driveway. The wall there? Behind it there's a stairway. You just can't see it from here."

No kidding. From where he sat in the front seat of his Subaru, it looked like there was no way in whatsoever. Thomas parked in the driveway, and she led him up the stairs to the front door, where spruce and birch leaned in close enough to touch. This monster of a dwelling was like nothing he'd ever seen. It beat all. The structure had enough wood in it to build maybe twenty houses. It looked like it was perching there on the lot, prepared to take flight for some other planet where a construction like this was considered a thing of beauty.

As he walked behind her, he noticed she was the same height as he was, five five, but he had close to sixty pounds on her. She was definitely older than him, but pretty the way some white girls can be, relaxed with themselves, forgoing the makeup.

Even before Thomas saw the bird he suspected it was a boyfriend-leaving thing. It was best to go into these situations with a clear mind, no prejudices, so he set his impressions aside. The problem could be as simple as the bird was tired of its diet or preferred its cage in a different corner. Really, when it came down to it, it didn't take much to make a bird happy, except to let it be a bird, throw a little consistent affection its way, and keep the rules clear. The cage was clean, roomy, and the toys looked worn from play. Looked as if Beryl spoiled him rotten, because on top of his cage was a parrot version of the Alaska Club gym. He noticed the TV was on. "You watch a lot of tube?" he asked.

"Not really," she said. "I leave it on for Verde when I'm not here. To keep him company. He gets lonely."

"Well, first off I'd change the channel. CNN's a little depressing," Thomas told her as he walked around the living room, taking the bird's-eye view and finding the place dark and cavernous. The bird needed more light, for sure. She had an odd mixture of nice things in the room, such as a leather couch that smelled like a saddle, but cheap things, too, like a crappy old lamp carved to look like a raven mask, only it was badly chipped and made of plaster. "That bad-news station has your bird in a world of worry."

"I keep the sound low," Beryl said defensively.

Thomas Jack took Beryl gently by the arm and steered her around to where the cage stood. After placing her just so, he took her place on the couch, facing the TV. He upped the volume and made a big show of enormous fake tears and wringing his hands. *"Bwaah,"* he said. "Oh me, oh my! The world is coming apart. The sun is a burning star. Any minute now there's going to be another earthquake. And a tsunami. Maybe even a nuclear bomb."

He watched Beryl Reilly fold her arms across her nice-size breasts and give him an irritated look. "I'm not a demonstrative person," she said. "Most of the time I don't even say a negative word."

He shook his head. Oh yeah, sure you don't. This was the hardest thing to explain to people. Any pet worth his salt would get to know his human's body language and moods. Where there was love there was intimacy, though where there was intimacy there wasn't always love. It was a sadly simple fact. "You may think you're projecting this calm air, but your little green friend here has the coping skills of a three-year-old. He's picking up on your fears. With all your worrying you're telling him the world's not a safe place."

"I feed him special treats all the time," she said.

Thomas nodded sympathetically. "I think that might be why so many kids are overweight these days. When they cry and act out, somebody stuffs chips in their mouths or hands them a soda. A treat isn't what he needs."

"Then what is?"

Thomas got up and walked to the cage. He took Beryl's hand and laid it on the cage bars. Verde was excited, and it didn't take ESP to know he was thinking, Openthecage, openthecage, openthecage, but Beryl was a million miles from hearing that. Maybe she was thinking about her boyfriend problems, or wondering if she could afford the taxes on the enormous house. She was not thinking, "Hello, birdie, come out to play," and that was the problem. When he finally undid the latch and opened the parrot's cage, Verde snapped blindly, but Thomas was ready for him and had placed his body between the bird and Beryl.

Beryl grasped Thomas's arm protectively. "I don't want him to bite you."

Thomas took out a pencil he carried in his pocket and gently pressed it into Verde's breast. "Knock off that shit and step up," he said, and Verde did. "What makes you think he'll bite me?"

"He doesn't know you. I heard you were never supposed to force a bird to do anything, that doing so was the quickest way to lose his trust. I mean, look how afraid Verde is."

The bird wasn't afraid; he was being a brat. Once Verde was on the pencil, Thomas transferred the bird to his right hand, which by now was gloved. Verde squawked and tried to bite him again, but Thomas moved his hand over the parrot's body, gently patting, vibrating his fingers, the same way a horse trainer would sack out an orphan foal to gain its trust. "I'm not going to hurt you, buddy. You can count on old Thomas Jack. I'm from a Raven clan, and I know from birds. Things are a little strange at the moment, but they are going to be A-okay." Thomas turned to Beryl. "A frightened bird clings to the bars or cowers in a corner. Yours is ticked off. He's waiting you out, Beryl. As long as he can make you give up, he's got the upper hand. Trust me. You sit down on the couch there and watch the clock. Verde and me, we're going from wild to mild in one hour or you don't have to pay me for my time."

Thomas said that knowing full well it wouldn't take him more than half an hour to get the bird to trust him. In five minutes he had him lying down in his hand, showing him his yellow feathers. He gave the joker a belly rub. Thomas held a sunflower seed between his teeth and bent his face down so the bird could take it.

Beryl was close to tears. "Maybe it would be for the best if you took him home. He obviously adores you."

Thomas stroked the bird's head. "Now, why would I want to do that? Every day at work I have a new bird. If I kept one at home, he'd be lonesome like Verde is. Come over here and put on the gloves. Ask him to step up, then transfer him to your left hand."

"I've never worn gloves with him. If I start now, won't he see that as me anticipating him biting me?"

"He doesn't want to bite you, but what if he does? It'll hurt and then it won't and it's not the end of the world, no matter what CNN says. Just put the gloves on every now and then. Be unpredictable in the glove department but consistent in everything else."

Clearly Verde loved Beryl. He fluffed up his feathers and trilled to her. His head feathers puffed up like he was trying to impress a lover. When he stretched his wings up, Beryl knew enough to mimic him. Watching these two was like reading a history book, Thomas thought. Hard times, a strong bond, Beryl leaning on the bird when a man let her down, Verde trying like hell to get her to listen to him, Beryl just missing hearing what the bird had to say because she was trying so hard to hold it together instead of letting herself be human. They'd enjoyed a stretch of good times, but not in Alaska. Verde didn't quite understand Alaska, and in particular the falling snow he could see from the living room window. Snow terrified him. Every night Beryl went upstairs. He couldn't see or hear her. If he called out, she didn't come. When Beryl left the house he screamed for her to come back. And why was that? The man had left, Beryl was terribly sad and afraid, and Thomas hated the fact that his initial impression was correct, not because it meant extra work with the bird, but because no matter what he did with him, the real problem lay with Beryl, and no man was trained to handle women.

Thomas talked to Verde, trying to communicate that women were emotional creatures, and that her crying and moodiness would pass in time. "I don't mean this in an unkind way," Thomas said to Beryl, "but are you by any chance a control freak?"

She looked at him. "What's that supposed to mean?"

Thomas grinned, flashing his white teeth, and the scar above his upper lip from his cleft palate surgery crinkled like it always did. "You know. Lay your clothes out for tomorrow before you go to sleep. Can't let dishes stand in the sink. Won't ride a roller coaster?"

"So what if I am? I don't see what that has to do with my parrot."

Now he'd ticked her off. He tried again. "Mrs. Reilly, I'm just trying to give you information."

"I'm not married, and I'd prefer that you call me Beryl." She looked him square in the face, waiting.

Huh. Maybe the boyfriend problem was a *big* problem. Time to change the subject. "What I do isn't magic, you know," Thomas said. "I'm not casting stones at your life, believe me. All I'm doing is being honest with you about what I sense is wrong."

Beryl went to the kitchen, which was just off the living room. It was decorated with those cupboards that look old because someone painted them that way, pale yellow, like winter sun peeking through a frosted window. She opened one, causing a stack of empty margarine tubs to topple onto the counter. Trailer-park Tupperware, that was what the people in his Muldoon trailer tract called that stuff. But she had Kaladi Brothers coffee and a fancy electric grinder on the counter. Thomas slipped a peanut from his pocket and watched Verde track it. As soon as the bird stopped complaining, Thomas gave him the nut. The bird muttered and cracked the shell open, happy to concentrate on his treat.

If he had been able to know a bird's thoughts, and if a bird thought like humans, he figured Verde would deliver a speech instead of the hysterical curse words he'd been flinging about. *Thanks for the peanut. She's hard to take care of. I'm about to start pulling out my feathers. Can I get you to pull that telephone cord there out of the wall? Maybe play some music? It's too quiet here since the guy left. At night I can hear her crying from clear up on the top floor.*

Thomas sat down on the leather couch and picked at a fleck of red paint on his faded Carhartts. Daily yoga kept his legs limber and muscled. He could chop wood and haul his own water, yet he'd never been successful with women. He had sort of quit thinking about them, but, meeting her, he was reminded of all the reasons it was worth getting your heart trampled on just to spend time with one. He took off his fleece-lined jacket and folded it on the cushion next to him. Underneath it he wore a black T-shirt that showed off his pecs, which were toned from doing handstands. Today he'd tied his hair back because he didn't want it in the way while he worked with the bird. The weight of it gave him a neck ache, and he wanted to undo the tie and let his hair fall loose around his shoulders, but he didn't. This woman who was more skittish than her bird might misunderstand such a gesture.

Beryl handed Thomas a cup of coffee and a coaster to put it on. "It's hazelnut," she said. "Someone gave it to me as a gift, and I'm out of Italian roast."

Her hands shook a little, and he could tell she felt ashamed for not considering how Verde felt about the television news. She stirred her own coffee but did not lift the cup to drink.

"Go easy on yourself," he said. "We're all in the same bowl of soup, you know? What's the point of sitting around feeling bad about a simple mistake? Time to snap out of it, I say. You're in charge here. Verde knows how to act around that kind of setup. Look at it his way. You're a hundred-and-twenty-pound lead bird, asking Verde to run the show."

Beryl stayed quiet. Thomas sipped his coffee. Frou-frou girl brand or not, it was tasty. They looked out the window together into the small yard surrounding the big house. There were tall spruce trees out there, one as wide around as a man. Birch trees, a Japanese maple, and some lilac bushes that looked newly planted and would make a lovely winter snack for passing moose. Snow was beginning to fall, fat white flakes tipping the spruce branches behind her strange house. Thomas noticed a moose path there between two birches. A place the cows came to rest, have babies, forage the fancy landscaping, and why not? "You know what Alaskans say about people who are together when the first snow of the season falls?"

She set her cup down on the table. "That they're destined to become ski partners?"

He laughed. "You don't make it easy on a guy, do you?"

"I can't think of a single reason why I should."

"Well, hell. Not all of us are bastards."

"Sorry." She looked down at her hands. He noticed they were freckled, the nails cut short, none of that lacquered crap. With all the pans hanging from the pot rack, he wondered if she liked to cook. Cooking for one was a dreadful thing. He wondered what it might be like to cook in a kitchen like that. Did she like smoked fish? He'd been craving it for a while now—salty smoked fish. He was pretty sure he could get the parrot sorted out in two visits, but Beryl, she was going to take a while longer.

Before his third visit—it was on the verge of becoming a habit; she showed up at the bird center around ten via taxi, walked around with him while he tended birds, and then he drove her home—she'd actually walked in to the center with a smile on her face. Alma called her the Hillside Debutante, and made fun of her taking taxis instead of driving herself. Thomas finished up his paperwork and handed her some feathers to log into the envelope where they kept a count that went straight to the Federal Government. Tribes needing eagle feathers for ceremonies could apply and receive them, but that was all. Anything sold to the public as an authentic eagle feather was most likely dyed turkey, he said. Beryl nodded politely like she already knew that, and once again he felt like a dope.

On the way home he asked her if she wanted pizza or burgers. "I'm not hungry," she said.

"Well, I'm buying one of each," he told her. They took them to her place. While Thomas ate he gave Verde another lesson in manners. The room had changed since his last visit, and he tried to put his finger on what was different about it. There was now very little in the way of personal objects out and about. No more framed snapshots, the decorative vase was missing, and a hanging plant that hadn't looked too good had been moved to the graveyard out on the deck. Verde, on the other hand, had a new parrot gym constructed out of PVC pipe and elbow joints.

"Look at that snow coming down," Beryl said, and Thomas

did. Just as it had for the last three days, it was snowing steadily, and all that had added up to a pretty good dump. Any minute now the snowplows would head out to scrape paths. "You'd better start for home or you're going to get stuck here."

Thomas looked at his boots sitting in a puddle on the entry floor tiles. He surprised himself when he realized he wouldn't have minded getting stuck. "See you tomorrow?" he asked at the door.

"Maybe," she said.

Which was what she always said.

She didn't show up for a week, and Thomas broke down and called her. "How's the bird?" he asked.

"Fine," she said listlessly.

"You sick? There's flu going around."

"No, just tired."

"How about I come by and bring you some soup?"

"I don't know," she said, and he was afraid he was losing her.

"I'm coming over," he said, and hung up before she could say no. "You can help me release the magpie."

Thomas never really got over how it felt to see a bird that had once been cage bound take off into the sky. Because the bird had been found at Beryl's, that was where he was being released. Thomas stood on the deck, snow underfoot and bird feeders behind him filled with seeds and suet. "You open the cage," he told her.

She undid the latch, and the magpie hopped out. He looked around, scolded them fiercely, grabbed a sunflower seed, and made for the upper branches of the spruce. "Oh," Beryl said. "He looks so beautiful back where he belongs."

Thomas squeezed her hand. "You know what they say about two people releasing a bird into the wild?" he asked.

She smirked. "That they'll never eat fried chicken again?"

"That they're destined to be friends for life."

On his day off he drove her to Russian Jack Park to eat sandwiches and watch the winter birds. Every now and then a sharp-shinned hawk in a spruce tree turned to watch them. "Hawks are regular Sherlock Holmeses when it comes to hunting," he told her. "I'll bet money that somewhere beneath the tree where the hawk's perching a mouse has a nest in the snow. Or maybe an Arctic hare's blending in with the snow."

Beryl watched but didn't say anything. Her roast beef sandwich had one bite out of it, and she was fishing in her purse for a couple of Tylenol. "Headache," she said, swallowing two with a sip of her Diet Coke.

"You shouldn't take those pills," he said. "They're bad for your liver."

"My liver doesn't have a headache," she said. "My head does."

"That's tension," he said. "You need to go dancing, knock the kinks out."

"I haven't danced in five years," she said.

"Why not?"

"I guess I just haven't felt like it."

Nearby two bald eagles watched the hawk. "They know we're here," Thomas said. "They're too nervous to go after prey with us watching. We should go dancing sometime. I'm a terrible dancer, but I make up for it by being enthusiastic."

They stayed quiet for an hour, pretending they were "like trees," which was what Thomas's grandmother had told him to do when bullies called him names. Just when Thomas felt himself about to doze off in the warmth of the car, his belly full, this pretty woman beside him, the sharp-shinned hawk quickly darted out to grab a smaller bird that Thomas had missed seeing entirely. "Well done," Thomas said. "Good catch."

"Don't you wonder?" Beryl said, turning to him, her hand closed around the soda cup, "what made him choose that exact moment to strike? Out of all the others?" she added. "How he knew?"

Thomas shrugged. "Who can tell what makes a bird do anything?" he answered, feeling reasonably sure they weren't talking about birds at all.

"I have to fly to Juneau next week," he said. "I'll be gone six days."

"What are you doing in Juneau?"

"Bird things. A lecture, a meeting." He wanted to ask her to come, but was afraid if he said so she'd run.

"Have a good time," she said.

"Beryl?"

"Yes?"

She looked at him calmly, the little wrinkle between her eyes the only imperfection on her otherwise pretty face. "Your headache better?"

"A little," she said.

"I could rub your neck."

"How about when we get home?"

And he drove her home.

Maynard said she hadn't showed up at the center while he was gone, and she stayed away another week before Thomas broke down and called her again. They'd pretty much gotten the parrot back on track, and he didn't really need to come back if she kept up the way he'd showed her. "I have this list," he said, referring to the troubleshooting agenda he'd typed up on a computer at the center. On it were twelve signs to watch for, and his standard lecture on biting. If the bird bit, and the handler pulled his hand away, and the next time you approached him you tensed up, expecting the bite, he'd learn that biting meant power. For that reason alone he suggested she keep up with the gloves, wearing them intermittently, just to keep Verde on his toes. "Okay if I bring it by this afternoon?"

"Sure," she said, without much enthusiasm.

Beryl offered him a plate of homemade chocolate chip cookies the minute he came in the door. She looked awful, like she'd quit eating since the last time he'd been there. He wondered why she made cookies if she wasn't going to eat them. "Those look real nice," he said, "but I don't eat sweets."

She looked crestfallen. "Oh. I made bread yesterday. You could take the second loaf home with you."

Thomas started to say something, but she held her hand up, and he could tell she was on the verge of tears.

"Please, Thomas. I'm not very good at saying thank you. Verde means the world to me. Money isn't enough for what you did."

"Verde's nuts about you," he said. "All I did was remind him of the fact. And I'd love to have some bread."

She cut him a slab and buttered it. He took a bite and mumbled, "Good."

"I learned to make it in prison," she said. "I was there five years."

"Five years is a long time," Thomas said measuredly.

"Five years is long in some places, but in there it's forever. It's part of why I'm not so good at being social."

He swallowed the bread. "Hell, Beryl. Everybody has something like that hanging them up. Why else do you think people move to Alaska? It's the end of the road. Anybody who's searching or has nothing but burned bridges behind him ends up here."

She laid the napkin she was holding down on the table. "Don't you want to know why I was sent to prison?"

Thomas shrugged and said what he'd come to say. "What I really want to know is if I have to keep on making excuses to come see you. I mean, I like your bird, but it's you I want to see."

Out of sheer relief, she laughed. "You're a terrible liar, Thomas Jack, and I am way too old for you."

She put her face in her hands and kept it there.

Thomas decided that so long as they were laying cards down on the table, he had a few things to say, too. "Verde is punishing you for something. You had some big changes recently. Am I right in thinking a man left?"

She looked up.

"Some people can fix a car lickety-split, some can paint polar bears to beat Fred Machetanz. With me it's birds. I know what affects them. Is there any chance you can get that boyfriend to come back and tell Verde a proper goodbye?"

Beryl got up and walked in to the kitchen. Thomas knew she was crying. Crying women didn't bother him so much. His grandmother cried when her hands bled from working at the cannery, when Thomas got in trouble at school, when Thomas's mother wrote from jail and asked for things his grandmother couldn't provide. He waited for her to run out of tears and sit back down.

"Earl didn't leave," she said. "He kind of . . . well, disappeared."

Even before she finished the sentence Thomas knew this Earl was the missing hiker from Eklutna Lake. He'd read the story on paper he'd lined the juvenile eagle's cage with. HIKER STILL MISSING. FOUL PLAY NOT RULED OUT. Your typical Alaskan headline—if there wasn't one like that in the paper it was a dead calm news day. The parrot thought it was his fault; Beryl thought it was her fault. Outside the snow was still dumping and now the wind was blowing, and Thomas would be back here in less than a month seeing to the bird unless Beryl opened up and talked about it. "You know, I could stand some dinner," Thomas said. "Why don't we cut up the rest of this fine bread and eat it right now? You got eggs in your fridge?"

He made her French toast, Tlingit style, with brown sugar and birch syrup and fried potatoes alongside. "The only thing missing is some salmon," he said, laughing at her face as she grimaced. She ate like a starving person. He took his time. "When's the last time you went to the market?"

"I don't have a driver's license," she confessed. "I rode my bike to the store before all this snow fell. This is the first winter I haven't gone Outside. I'm not used to it. Guess I'll have to break down and call a cab sometime in the next week or so."

"I could teach you to drive," he said. "I've been driving since I was eleven."

"Come on. Eleven?"

"My grandmother had cataracts. One day she just handed me the keys, and that was the end of her driving days and the start of mine."

Beryl folded her napkin. "Was she the kind of grandma that read you stories, made you oatmeal?"

He laughed. "She told me to mind my manners, to be as nice to old ladies as I was to young ones, and boxed my ears when I forgot. I learned some stories, but not all of them came from her. There was a cousin of hers that had gone to drinking. Old Ernest. Sometimes I went downtown to look for him. I'd bring him a sandwich, and he'd tell me stories."

She leaned against her upright arm, her plate clean. "Like what?"

"*Kukuweaq,* the ten-legged Polar bear, and how he taught *Kucirak* how to be generous. Why the owl dies with his wings outstretched. He was a pretty sad old guy. I don't know what he wanted me to learn from them stories. I make a mean pot of oatmeal, myself. Mostly my grandma worked in the canneries so she could keep me fed and dressed."

"Sounds like you had a pretty nice grandma."

Thomas Jack was bursting with questions about the missing man, but his grandmother had taught him it was impolite to ask questions, and it was rude to look directly at a person. Of course in the white world no one knew that, and most of the time Thomas tried to fit in, but when he really liked someone, the old manners came flooding back and he got tongue-tied. "What do the cops say about your boyfriend?" he asked as he folded his napkin by his plate. But what he was really saying was, *Forget him; how about we go for a walk right now*?

"They call once a week," she answered. "It's the same old story. He either left or something happened. They'll let me know if anything changes."

"Not knowing can be tough," Thomas said. He wondered if what she really meant to say was *I am so lonely since Earl left, I'm turning into an old-lady nun*.

"You're holding up fine," Thomas said, but in truth he was telling her, *You look damn fine to these eyes, and I'd happily take you out to look for him, any other place you want to go, even upstairs*.

She looked at him then, frank and firm, as if she was asking herself, *What would Thomas Jack think of me if he knew I lay around in my sweats all day on the days he doesn't come to see Verde? What would he think if he knew that at night after I cry about Earl, I imagine Thomas Jack taking me to bed and making me forget?*

Thomas looked back at her. You can dress up like Batman, he thought. Don't make no difference to me. Lady, I am smitten.

"I used to live with two women who were vegetarians," she said. "In California." What she didn't say was, *If you hadn't been here, I wouldn't have bothered with dinner.*

Thomas held out his cup for a refill of coffee. He took a breath and said, "I'd like to make you a proper dinner sometime. I'm a pretty good cook."

"It's more fun to cook for two, isn't it," Beryl said, switching knife and fork around so she made eating an aerobic exercise.

She ate and Thomas drank coffee and talked about birds, and the tension between them hummed and crackled, and Thomas looked at the pulse in her neck and wanted to kiss it. Verde watched from his cage, and every now and then he chattered his pleasure at hearing two voices instead of CNN and Beryl's crying.

Thomas had messed up with women so many times. Now this redhead. He thought about putting his arm around her, inhaling the fragrance of her hair, which he knew came from some kind of fruit-scented shampoo, and touching her white skin, soft and freckled and in some places so pale the blue veins showed through. He wanted to make her forget the man who disappeared, and hear her laugh again. But the name of the game was always restraint. He wiped his mouth and folded his napkin. As he got up, Beryl spoke.

"The roads have got to be bad," she blurted out, rising and peering out the window so she didn't have to face him, maybe. "I guess you could spend the night if you like. Any of the rooms on this floor are fine. The beds are made up, and there are towels in the bathroom. I'll say goodnight now. See you in the morning." And as she headed for the stairs, Thomas reached out and caught her by the arm.

"You didn't tell your bird goodnight. Verde's like a child. He needs a ritual as much as you do."

Chagrined, she returned to her bird's cage. Thomas watched as she sang him a little song with made-up lyrics, the kind of thing women do when they think no one is listening, and placed the sheet over his cage. Verde watched, too. Thomas knew the bird understood that this treatment meant that she loved him. Thomas was equally intrigued. He hadn't intended on staying so late, but she made such good coffee it was worth savoring. Now they were standing in her living room facing each other, the bird and all that heartbreak of the missing boyfriend between them, wanting to go somewhere.

Beryl took his hand and studied it, turning it this way and that, feeling the scars he had from fights and just being a man in the world. She touched his scar from the cleft palate surgery, and he reached up to take hold of her hand. She gave it a gentle tug, and they moved toward the stairs, walking up together, side by side. At the top there was her bedroom, the large bed made up with colorful wool blankets and six pillows. Thomas thought he would feel that man's presence here, but it was gone already. When he spied the French doors leading to a balcony, he gently steered Beryl to them. Outside the snow had stopped, and the moon glinted off the snow like it was one big field of crushed diamonds. They were treated to a magnificent boreal display, first green lights, like he was used to, and sometimes they paled to white, but then came these mesmerizing red trails. Down in Southeast, the northern lights were rare. His grandmother had taught him that they were an omen of change, and not necessarily good change. Sometimes, she'd said, they were the spirits of people who'd passed away, dancing and having a good time. Thomas Jack stood Beryl in front of him, his body just grazing the back of hers. She was warm; her muscles were tensed. He had a feeling that she'd never seen a thing like this. That somewhere inside she was smiling, shaking her head in wonder, that she wasn't thinking of anything else but this moment, and maybe the best present he could give her was this, time away from all the fretting, the not knowing. So tonight's lights were a good omen. He placed his arms around her, *to warm her up,* he told himself, almost but not quite believing it.

"You know what they say about two people who watch the northern lights?" he said.

"I'm afraid to ask."

"I could show you," he said.

"Okay," she said.

So he did.

Evergreen, the creamy white blossoms of the magnolia are highly fragrant. Fossil records show the magnolia tree to be an ancient species predating man. It was the Chinese who recognized the magnolia as helpful in seasoning rice and making bitter medicines palatable, and tea from the bark was once used to treat typhoid and malaria. Chewing the bark is said to aid in quitting smoking. Asians regard magnolia flowers as an emblem of purity, while according to the English language of flowers, the flowers signify a love of nature. Other names include big laurel, bullbay, and bat tree. One of the most impressive specimens of this tree grows outside the White House and was planted by President Andrew Jackson for his wife, Rachel. The Grateful Dead recorded a song called "Sugar Magnolia," a favorite they continued to play in concert until the death of Jerry Garcia.

Phoebe

3

The Terrible Forty-twos

OCTOBER BLENDED INTO November here in Bayborough Valley. Phoebe DeThomas sat on the edge of the tub watching her five-year-old daughter, Sally, steer a plastic yacht through the foam of bubble bath. The blue-and-white ship—a gift from Uncle James and Aunt Nancy—was on a collision course with a red rubber duck that sported horns—a gift from Uncle David and Auntie Ness. An entire crateful of other child-safe, water-friendly toys designed to stimulate the imagination sat on the floor beside the tub because Sally was bored with them. Her child lived the life of a princess, Phoebe thought, what with her roommates, relatives, and friends making up her adoring subjects. In a few short weeks Sally would turn six. She'd shrugged off toddlerhood long ago, and was clinging tightly to the lip of little girlhood, increasingly revealing an independence and will not in the least like her late father's. Juan had been a gentle, easygoing man. With each increment of Sally's growth, Phoebe thought about how, had Juan lived, he would have been a doting dad, endlessly patient. From there, however, Phoebe went straight to God and burned his ear off. *How could you let such a travesty take place?* In particular she wanted to know why God thought that leaving her, a forty-three-year-old handicapped woman with an iffy heart, in charge of this wonder child was a good idea. There were days she put Sally to bed, wheeled herself out onto the patio, stared at the gardens, and cried out of pure exhaustion. She couldn't afford a nanny, not that she wanted one. She was beyond grateful that Sally's aunts and uncles were so helpful. She wished she could shower them with luxurious gifts, sports cars, Picassos, and diamond bracelets, make their lives so comfortable that they'd always be there, because on bad days she handed her child off like the baton in a relay race.

"Mama?" Sally said, holding her devil duck under the water and letting it bob up again, "Why do you have a wheelchair?"

This, Phoebe noted, was Sally's favorite bath-time question. She asked it over and over, and Phoebe answered it over and over. "I've told you a million trillion jillion times, munchkin. Because my legs aren't as strong as yours."

The ends of Sally's glossy black hair were wet from the bubbles. "But I want a wheelchair."

"Sweetie, you don't need one."

Sally's full lower lip shot out. "But I *want* one."

Phoebe sighed. "Fine, I'll give you mine. Anything else I can get for you, your majesty?"

Sally smiled like she always did when she got her way, then was quiet while she thought it over. "Then how will you walk, Mama?"

"Well, maybe I won't walk. Maybe I'll just lie here on the bathroom rug and you can bring me dinner."

Sally giggled. "Okay. What do you want for dinner, Mama?"

"Oh, vegetables, of course. Lots of yummy green vegetables."

Out came the lower lip. "I hate vegetables, Mama."

"I don't see why. They certainly like you. They tell me so all the time. Why, just this morning I opened the fridge and the carrots said, 'We sure do love that Sally. We hope we can have dinner with her tonight.' Actually, I think the celery was a little jealous."

Sally scowled, returning to her yacht, driving it into the duck and making awful screeching noises. "They crashed," she said without inflection. "They crashed and the duck died and now he lives in the sky, the sky, the sky."

Phoebe felt her heart cleave. From the time of Sally's birth—or at least a few weeks after, since her daughter had spent that precious interval of time with her Uncle James and Aunt Nancy—Phoebe had periodically told her the story of her father's death. She didn't want the subject to be taboo, or Juan's brief life to loom like some awful mystery. She'd held Sally in her arms and said, "Your father was in a car crash before you were born. It was an accident. He may not have known you, but he loved you. Now he's up in heaven"—mad as she was at God, she knew this part was stretching things—"looking down at you and smiling. Look there. See that star? That's your daddy's smile. He's smiling at you."

Sally had the story memorized, but she wanted to hear it over and over, and she liked asking the same questions about it, too. According to all the kid psychology books, that was part of being five, and clear on up to thirteen, when they knew everything and the parent started asking the questions. Along with the repetition came stubbornness and the flat-out refusal to eat anything healthy. A mother could know it would pass in time—know all that logically and still have problems believing it. To Phoebe it was as if her once delightful child had turned into a pint-size dictator. Bath time was her only detente. In the warm water Sally mellowed, and Phoebe could gaze upon her daughter's perfect body and let her thoughts meander. Sally's skin was dusky olive, not as dark as Juan's, but darker than Phoebe's. Her hair was jet black, thick like Juan's, but lacked his natural curl. Sally's eyelashes were definitely her dad's, and her brown eyes loomed enormous in her little face, piercing and passionate, as if she'd gotten double the dose of Juan's genes in that department. When Sally looked up at her mother, Phoebe got chills. She swore it was Juan looking at her from the grave. Just when she thought she couldn't stand the stubbornness, just when the intensity threatened to give her a heart attack, Sally would do something magical—warble a high note, kiss the dog, arrange her magnetic letters on the refrigerator and spell a word—and Phoebe fell in love with her wild child all over again.

"Time to dry off," Phoebe said. "Do you want to pull the plug or should I do it?"

"I'll pull it!" Sally flung the boat and duck aside and reached down into the water.

"Find the chain and pull hard," Phoebe said.

"Mama, I *know* to pull hard," Sally said, and Phoebe caught a glimpse of her as a teenager. Oh, Lord. What will be popular then? Hopefully the piercing thing will have gone out of style. Will I live that long? Phoebe wondered. Or will Sally be raised by James and Nance, and along with Daddy in heaven, Mama will be just another star in the sky, a story to tell?

Just then Homer and Sumo, Mimi's cats, raced through the bedroom chasing each other. Sally squealed, and Phoebe knew she'd take off running after them if she let her out of the tub. It was hard enough to catch a slippery five-year-old without throwing cats into the mix. "Want me to paint your toenails?" she asked.

"Purple glitter!" Sally commanded.

"Okay." Phoebe wrapped her in a dry towel and daubed each tiny toe. The nails were so small, and her feet were still chubby with baby fat. Phoebe blew on the toes to make Sally giggle. They dried in nothing flat, and she let her go. "One lap around the house, then it's time to put on your jammies, okay? Promise, now. Auntie Mimi is waiting to read you a story."

Whether she heard her mother or not, Sally ran giddily across Phoebe's bedroom, her naked body a beautiful blur. Phoebe watched with admiration. She'd do that too, had her legs been capable. In fact it would probably do the whole world good to run naked after a bath. She heard Mimi scream, "Streaker alert!" and her hearty laugh. Phoebe's roommates—Mimi and Ness—made wonderful aunts. Sally had a good, rich life no matter low lonely her mother felt.

"You're always talking me into parties I don't want to go to," Phoebe told her sister-in-law, Nance. "Can't I just be a slob in my sweats? I worked hard today. I'm tired. I want to zone out and watch crap TV."

Nance switched off the television set, and *poof!* there went a perfectly good evening spent flipping between *Bonanza* reruns, *Survivor,* and probably an important bargain on the Home Shopping Network. "It's a dinner party, Pheebs. All you have to do is eat yummy catered food and talk to people."

"Talk about what?"

Nance sighed dramatically. "No one cares. Talk about the weather. It'll be over before you know it. Come on. I spent a long time working on this party. I want you to come."

Phoebe couldn't help but gawk at her sister-in-law. Nance had perfect blond hair cut in a short pageboy that lay perfectly against her perfect face and even more perfect neck (which was evenly tanned, and had no wrinkles either). Her clothing screamed designer labels and good taste; even the faded T-shirts she wore to work on the farm were Ralph Laurens. Her makeup was flawlessly applied, her lipstick glossy, and the one gold bracelet she always wore glinted from her wrist, which naturally led the eye to the enormous hunk of yellow-diamond-and-platinum engagement ring and matching diamond-studded platinum wedding band. Worst of all, she smelled good, like perfume instead of whatever Phoebe had spilled on herself in the course of the day while trying to keep up with Sally. All of them—Mimi, Ness, and Phoebe—looked at Nance as a level of womanly perfection to which only models could aspire. Once Ness had wondered aloud if Nance had maybe found a way to Scotchgard herself, since she never seemed to get dirty. Had Phoebe not known of Nance's continual struggle with anorexia, and the sad business with failing to stay pregnant, she could have felt jealousy. Instead she loved her dearly, but not quite enough to haul herself over to the party.

"I really don't want to go. Tell James I have a headache."

Nance checked her watch. "Nope. I'm not leaving until you come with me."

Phoebe picked up a *New Yorker*. Her late aunt must have renewed her subscription for life, because the damn thing just kept on coming, piling up next to the fireplace kindling, and they never once got a bill. She read the cartoons, the movie reviews, and sometimes a short story that made no sense and left her feeling strangely confused and depressed. "Why is it so important for me to be there? Is James planning some sort of coup to take over the farm? Tell him he needn't bother; I'll just give it to him. I'm tired of working. I want to marry rich like Jackie O. and lie in the sun all day while someone cleans my house and teaches my daughter impeccable French."

Nance tucked her hair behind her left ear, revealing a sparkling earring that looked expensive and new. "Quit being so stubborn. He's invited some new people, a couple who just moved to the Peninsula, your old pal Rebecca Roth, and this up-and-coming artist who apparently knows your work, because he asked to meet you specifically."

Phoebe arched an eyebrow. "Right."

"I swear on Christ our Lord Jesus I'm not making this up."

Phoebe laughed. "Anybody up-and-coming who knows my work has to be pretty hard up. What's his problem? Does he look like a gargoyle?"

Nance threw her hands up. "How should I know? James is the one who knows him. I'm just here to pass along the invitation."

Nance's face got that trembly look, and Phoebe felt bad for balking at what would probably turn out to be good eats and a laugh or two. Certainly it had to beat waking Sally up in the middle of the night so she could use the toilet instead of wetting her bed, which worked only about a third of the time. "I'll come, I'll come," she said. "But only if Mimi agrees to watch Sally, and I'm leaving right after dinner, agreed?"

Nance smiled, but the tremble look remained. Phoebe gave her a little hug.

"How about a quick washup and changing into your camel-colored wool slacks and that white crepe blouse I gave your for your birthday?" Nance said.

Phoebe stifled her inner protest. "Dress me up, take me home, introduce me to a gargoyle, feed me canapés, then please let me go home early enough to at least read a chapter of my new mystery club book."

"You read too much." Nance helped Phoebe from the couch into her wheelchair, and then pushed her toward the bedroom. "I was thinking your aunt's antique locket and the beaded earrings would be perfect accessories."

"Gee, wanna pick out my undies, too? Seriously, I think I can manage from here," Phoebe said, and Nance left her there in front of the walk-in closet, threatening to come back if Phoebe wasn't over in fifteen minutes. Phoebe dutifully donned the suggested clothes and took a long look at her reflection in the mirror as she slid the turquoise earrings into her pierced ears. They were a gift from Ness. Her roommate was in Tucson, Arizona, at the moment, with her close friend David Snow. David was in the advanced stages of HIV, and because the Central Coast winters of California were getting to be too damp for him, they'd gone to the desert. Ness, who had first tested positive for HIV five years ago, had undergone an experimental drug study, and ever since, though her tests had come back negative, no one, not even the doctors, knew what that meant. Phoebe missed her terribly. There was no one on earth besides Ness who understood Phoebe so well. They'd both get a craving for ginger and tofu, drive to Tillie Gort's in Sierra Grove, pig out, and then spend an hour watching the jellyfish tanks at the Aquarium without saying a word. They both liked Cadbury's Fruit & Nut bars, too. But Phoebe knew how devoted Ness was to David, and certainly didn't begrudge anyone a dry, warm winter, especially with David so frail.

She sat back in her chair and applied her makeup. Like spackling putty into a weathered windowsill, she thought. Can't hide every wrinkle, but you can fill in the gaps. The few gray hairs threaded through her dark brown glinted, and she tried to believe they were highlights, at the same time allowing that that notion might be midlife rationalizing. She held out her hands and looked at the diamond engagement ring Juan had given her, once upon a time long ago when happiness was there for the taking. Five years. Maybe it was time to take the ring off. Put it in the safe so that nothing would happen to it, and when Sally graduated high school or college, give it to her. Phoebe slid it off her finger into the apple green Depression glass dish that her aunt Sadie had always used for her baubles. *I wish you were here,* Phoebe mentally sent her aunt's way. *And I probably don't have to tell you that sometimes I wish I were there with you.*

"Mimi?" she called out. "I'm going now. Are you sure you're okay to take care of Sally?"

Mimi hollered back, "Already am. We're reading another story. Have fun, and don't worry about us, okay?"

Always easier said than done. Of course it was barely a five-minute roll from her house to James's, so if something happened, she could be back in time to fix it. James had built the pathway four years ago, a winding walk lined with bird's-nest spruce, bamboo, and deep purple coneflowers that bloomed like crazy in the spring and summer and were harvested for the echinacea tea the farm sold as part of their Herbal Comforts line. The path was easily negotiable for Phoebe, and took just long enough to make her feel grateful they'd quit being feuding siblings and become friends. After years of their childhood bickering, Aunt Sadie had died, leaving Phoebe this farm and James all her money. Phoebe had struggled to revive the farm, but there just wasn't enough cash to make a go of things. That had led to her taking in roommates in the first place, and to James meeting Nance. So many wonderful times but a host of hard times, too—not the least of which were her heart attack and losing Juan. She looked at the flowers and told herself her brother's world had been as rocked as her own. From a fast-talking day trader to a cautious investor, James had begun diversifying his investments into real estate, always a good move in pricey Bayborough-by-the-Sea and its surrounding environs. The farm expansion plans had once included buying a property across the road.

But the winery next to it had gotten there first, and from the rumors flying around the Valley, there was talk of them opening a plant nursery, too. What could a person do about that besides worry? Phoebe concentrated on growing her own flowers, keeping things running smoothly, expanding their line to include top-quality gift items, and raising Sally. Maybe that was putting on blinders, but a child was a child and deserved a happy childhood no matter what lay in her mother's future. Every month she and James sat down and looked over the books, hoping for profits, predicting expenses, trying to suss out problems before they started. After close study there came the interval of time when they'd exhausted the business talk, and each let out a collective sigh at the thought of all that had happened since Sadie died.

Do you think she had any idea? James would say, and Phoebe would feel the lump rise in her throat and wonder why it was that happiness, that miracle that had happened to her and James both, had to be tempered by so much sorrow. *I miss her,* she'd say, and for a long quiet spell each of them would remember a particularly fine moment, then lift their heads, sigh, and move on.

James loved Nance; Nance loved James. It was a strong match between strong individuals. They both wanted babies. They had the necessary financial stability to make a family, but Mother Nature apparently had other ideas. Nance's fourth miscarriage had happened late enough in the pregnancy that she had to be hospitalized, and a D & C performed. When the obstetrician found no clear answers, Nance went to see Lester, Phoebe's internist, longtime friend, and all around miracle-worker. Lester looked Nance in the eye and pronounced it time for her to give up on conception. "There are worse things in life than not giving birth," he said. "One of them is taxing your health. Right now, I want you to rest up and stop living your life by the ovulation predictor."

Nance had cried for days. "This is my fault," she said, as Phoebe sat beside her in the exam room, holding her hand. "My not eating. I know if I hadn't taken diet pills, I'd be a mother by now. I might even have two children. . . ." James had wrung his hands, wanting his cake and wanting the cupcake, afraid he'd end up with neither. Then he'd spent a day working the fields with Segundo and appeared to sweat it all out.

As Phoebe pushed the front door open to the soft noise of her brother's dinner party, she tried not to think about how Nance had maybe spoken the truth. James hurried over, dressed in his casual-but-elegant clothes, charcoal gray slacks and some silk long-sleeve black thing that looked like long underwear but undoubtedly cost a lot more, and she'd bet had a fancy label inside the collar.

He introduced her to the older couple, Snoop and Evie, and Phoebe promptly forgot their last name, which she blamed on her hormone depletion due to perimenopause, a subject she had read too much about to forget even though she was still having regular cycles. Then James steered her chair to the stereo alcove, and said, "Andrew, may I present my sister, Phoebe? Phoebe, this is Andrew Callahan. He's an artist, too. Moved here from Georgia a couple of years back."

Georgia? Phoebe tried to imagine the place and came up with clichés of Southern belles, wraparound porches; a mint julep in a glass covered with beads of sweat, and mosquitoes the size of Piper Cubs.

"That's right," this Andrew character said. "My parents moved out here to retire. I came for a visit, took one look at your little stretch of coastline, and not even all the peach cobbler in the world could drag me away."

James laughed his big, fake, nervous dinner-party laugh—the one that made Phoebe want to pinch him.

Phoebe rolled herself forward to shake Mr. Peaches' hand, trying not to fume openly at her brother. This Andrew, this "fellow artist" she was supposed to believe admired her work, who had been by the stereo studying a lapful of CDs, just happened to be in a wheelchair. What was this? Throw the cripples together, they'll have lots to talk about? "Nice to meet you," she said politely. "What medium do you work in?"

Andrew Callahan was as different from Juan Nava as zebras were from octopi. He was red haired, ruddy skinned, gray eyed, and did not have a wide smile. He had thin lips and a sharp chin, and his hair was so red it reminded her of the last time she made French toast for Sally's breakfast and spilled the cinnamon. When he spoke Phoebe noted how his Southern accent and idioms carried through the room, strange and compelling and just loud enough that people turned to look.

"I'm a potter, sugar," he said, taking Phoebe's hand in his.

"Sugar"? His fingers were rough and cool, and she didn't think much of him throwing out an endearment like that when they hadn't yet said ten words to each other. She couldn't wait to pull her hand back into her lap and warm it back up. "Really," she said, throwing as much acid into her voice as she could. "How do you manage to load up the kiln? Do you have an assistant or something?"

Andrew blanched, and then stammered. "M-most of my p-pieces are small. I lift weights to keep up my upper body strength. Looks like you do a little of that yourself. While it isn't my favorite pastime, what's the alternative? I suppose I could get one of those reaching tools they sell on infomercials. What is it called?"

"Oh, God," Phoebe said, and laughed. "'The Grabber'!" One night she had come close to ordering one for every room in the house. "When I saw that ad I had the very same idea."

"Hopefully that's a little ways off for both of us."

So, okay, maybe he wasn't entirely bad. Phoebe willed James to return, but his back was to her, and he was busy visiting and pouring wine from a vineyard he and Nance were currently in love with. Phoebe wished she could have the whole bottle of the pinot grigio to herself. She was sure the blouse she was wearing showed too much of her scrawny arms, that her aunt's jewelry appeared pretentious on someone under five feet tall and weighing a robust eighty-nine pounds (she'd put on weight since having Sally).

"So tell me about yourself," Andrew said. "What do you like to do for fun?"

"I'm a mother," Phoebe said, hoping to make clear that she wasn't interested in some pity-date-chatter this Andrew fellow might have felt forced into giving. "Mothers don't get to have fun because they are too busy organizing after school playdates, preparing nutritious meals, and thinking up good reasons why we can't have a pony."

"Oh, let her have a horse," Andrew said. "I grew up on the back of one."

"How many times did you fall off and crack your head?"

Andrew smiled. "Countless. I never told my mother, though. Just dusted myself off and got back on. I love kids with horses. Builds confidence, you know?"

Okay, she hated him again. No single man in his right mind loved a five-year-old unless he was related. "Got any of your own squirreled away?"

"'Fraid not. So where's her daddy?"

"Oh, dead," Phoebe said, not caring how bluntly the words came out.

"My goodness," Andrew said. "I'm so sorry. Please forgive me for asking such a personal question."

For no reason at all Phoebe felt the old flood of tears rising. After this many years a person was supposed to have moved beyond spontaneous outbursts of grief. Grief had wrecked her life for a while, but now it just made her angry, and without another thought, she began to take it out on Andrew Callahan. "No, you're not. How could you be? You didn't know him. You don't know the circumstances in which he died. Isn't that just something people say because they're supposed to?"

Andrew cocked his head and, soft as corn silk, his red hair fell over his temple, making him look twelve years old instead of middle aged. He studied her unblinking, as if her stinging words had fallen short of the target and now lay on the common ground between them, pathetic little paper darts someone was going to have to sweep up. Hell, they might even need a Grabber to do it. "Darlin', my fiancée stood by my bedside in the hospital one week after I learned I'd never walk again and told me we couldn't get married. Grief's an old bastard everyone spends a little time with. I'm afraid nobody's exempt."

As he spoke, his gray eyes fixed on her sympathetically. Phoebe looked down at her hands. "I'm sorry. James and Nance insisted I come. I'm tired today. And I really don't like it when they fib."

"What did they fib about?"

"Never mind, it's not important."

He gave that shy smile again. "So if it's not important, then it won't hurt to tell me, will it?"

She waved her hand as if trying to discourage a fly. "Some bullshit about you liking my art. Ha. It would have to be damn *old* art, since my daughter takes up a hundred and fifty percent of my time, and I can't remember the last time I held a hunk of clay in my hands. I'm *praying* Rebecca Roth doesn't come over here and ask me about it."

Andrew's smile widened. "That wasn't a fib, darlin'. I bought two of your pieces at her gallery. And I keep on pestering Becky, asking her when you're going to do another show. Ask her, she'll tell you. She's the one who put me in contact with your brother. I begged my invite to this party. Of course it helped that James and my father are doing a little business together."

"A-nuth-a show"? "Bru-tha"? Was this guy for real? Phoebe stared at him, waiting for her BS detector to redline, but the needle stayed remarkably still. She tried to glom on to the feelings of

pride she had when Rebecca had thrown a reception in honor of her first official show, hoping that would ease her over this awkwardness. One thing for sure, she would have remembered it if anybody else there was in a wheelchair, especially someone as good-looking as this character. She told Andrew as much.

"Oh, the old days. That was back when I was walking. But I remember meeting you."

"Maybe I'd had too much wine," she said, dying to ask what had happened to put him in his chair. "I kind of overdid things that night."

"On a night like that, I would think a person's entitled. Sugar, you want a Co-cola?"

Had she ever in her life heard it called that? "I guess," she said.

"You like yours with peanuts? That's a Southern tradition."

"I like mine with cherries. Lots of cherries."

Andrew fetched their drinks and they rolled to the picture window that overlooked the farm, lit up special for the evening. For a December night it was clear and crisp, and the greenhouses were filled with hanging baskets people had stored for the winter. There were a few straggly poinsettias left, but as usual, they'd sold out in their day-after-Thanksgiving sale, which they'd extended this year to two full days in order to let customers browse the craft items they'd begun carrying—baby quilts, ornaments, those tiny indulgent "gifties" women bought for each other and men did not understand. Until the Christmas holidays passed, there wouldn't be much activity on the farm other than regular maintenance. Segundo watched for the bulbs to come up, but really it was a quiet season. They worked a skeleton crew.

"That sure is one good-lookin' pony," Andrew said, pointing to the corral where Ness's black horse, Leroy Rogers lived. "I thought you said you didn't want your little girl to have a pony?"

Phoebe looked out the window. There in the corral with Leroy stood a palomino pony. James had gone ahead and bought one for Sally's birthday—over Phoebe's objections, as if they mattered. "Damn it all," Phoebe said. "My brother's ass is grass, and here comes the lawn mower." She wheeled across the room and grabbed James by the arm.

"Hello, sister," he said. "You and Andrew look like you're

finding something to talk about. Aren't you glad you decided to come?"

"We need a moment of privacy," Phoebe said to the couple James was chatting with. "Would you excuse us for a moment?"

"What's the matter?" James said as she pulled him toward the bathroom off the kitchen.

"I figure you'd rather have me rip you a new exit in private," she said. "What in the Sam Hill is that ratty little pony doing in the arena?"

"That pony," he said, "is a papered Pony of the Americas out of the dam that won damn near every class she was entered into before she retired. And her name is Penelope, and she is Sally's birthday present, and I'm not taking her back so you can just get used to it."

Phoebe blew out an angry breath. "James, if you give her every little thing she asks for she's going to grow into an awful person! That is, if she lives that long without falling off the pony and getting trampled to death."

James put his arm around her. "Kids need to fall off stuff. The pony comes with a trainer, Pheebs. And as many lessons as she needs. If Sally loses interest, I will find Penelope a new home. You have my word. Now can we get back to my party?"

"James, you went behind my back. After I said no."

"You didn't really mean it," he said. "Come on, Nance is laying out the food."

Phoebe wanted to throw the table of canapés out the window. She was Sally's mother. Didn't that count for anything? Even Leroy seemed to be colluding against her, nuzzling Penelope, and this trainer James had hired—well, how was she to fight all that? Phoebe liked the *idea* of her daughter on horseback. She imagined Sally all grown up, saying, *Yes, I was lucky enough to have a pony as a child, and it contributed greatly to my compassion for the world's creatures, not to mention I never went to therapy because I never needed it*. However, Sally was *not* grown, and Phoebe was scared to death that Sally was going to get stomped to death by dainty little pedigreed hooves. Phoebe had not let Sally ride so much as a rental horse, and unless James and Nance had taken her riding behind her back—oh, crap—she was certain now that they had, that they had let her pick out Penelope, and had already ordered Sally's hunt coat and whip. Phoebe sighed.

Across the room Andrew waved to her. He was talking to a pretty brunette who was wearing one of those short flowered dresses with hardly any back to them. He looked comfortable; maybe she was his new girlfriend, more tolerant of wheelchairs than the last one. Phoebe sneaked peeks at Andrew's legs, which were normal-size, the muscles in them not so noticeably atrophied under the baggy slacks, but if he'd been walking at her gallery reception, whatever put him in the chair had happened recently. It was the kind of question only one crip could ask another, but asking it—ooh, that was hard for anybody. She drained her Coke, chewed on her cherries, and glared at her brother. She had to pee, and worried about negotiating James's guest bathroom, with its extra-low toilet and the strange faucets she couldn't work without leaning over the countertop at a weird angle, which would no doubt soak her blouse and make her look like even more of a retard than she already felt. Forget it; she could wait until she got home, when she planned to grill Mimi about the pony, because if she was in on the secret, heads were going to roll.

When the brunette left, Phoebe wheeled over to Andrew, who was putting the CDs in order. He looked at her warily. "I take it the pony was a surprise. Sorry if I ruined it for you."

What could she say to that? *Oh, it's all right, no one ever listens to me?* How about, *I deserve to have my authority questioned since I'm the mother who wouldn't look at her daughter when she was born? Did you know I gave her to my brother? Yes, that's one for the record books, isn't it?* "I was born this way," she blurted out. "What's your excuse?"

Andrew laughed. "James told me you were a corker. He wasn't kidding."

"Wud'n kid'n"? "My God, with that accent, you could give Colonel Sanders a run for his money."

Andrew smiled. "On occasion I believe I have."

Phoebe covered her mouth with her hand. "Oh, hell. That didn't come out right. I'm curious, I blather, I have so many bad habits I can't count them all. Please, no more talk about the pony or I'll blow a gasket. I was wondering how you ended up in your chair. If I'm out of line, we can talk about the weather. I know a thousand adjectives for warm. Or you can ignore me and go back to the CDs. Just don't play the sound track to *The Little Mermaid* or I will self-immolate."

He looked at her squarely. "I broke three vertebrae body-surfing, dear heart. Pure pigheadedness, with a little macho nonsense thrown in. Not terribly interesting, I'm sorry to say. If your story's boring, they kick you out of the South. Which is how I come to live here now."

"We're definitely a more tolerant lot in California."

"Good to know. For a minute there you had me worried."

Now he was putting the CDs back into their alphabetized slots. His nostrils flared ever so slightly, like he was terribly amused, and Phoebe wondered whether he was amused by her, or at what she'd said, or the sad photo of Van Morrison in a black coat and hat trying to look cool instead of old and fat. Well, she couldn't leave now. She had to at least make polite conversation to apologize for strafing him like that with her rudeness. "That's a pretty nice chair, by the way. Custom made?"

He nodded. "I figured if I had to give up tennis and golf and ballroom dancing, I could afford to splurge on my wheels."

"Well," Phoebe said. "It's nice enough that I'm jealous."

"You should get one. I can give you the name of the company that made it."

"It looks kind of expensive." She clapped her hand over her mouth again. "There I go again. I shouldn't be allowed in public."

Andrew smiled. "That's all right. It was expensive."

"Dinner, everyone," Nance called. She had place cards set out, and linen napkins rolled inside polished silver rings engraved with James's initials. Andrew was seated clear at the other end of the table, between two gorgeous women, one blond and the other that brunette. Neither looked as if she had ever opened a cookbook, or any kind of book, for that matter. Phoebe was sure they'd undergone breast augmentation and Botox injections and worked out six hours a day to look that good. Did men really like that sort of thing? Did Andrew? Well, what kind of stupid question was that? His having legs that didn't work didn't change anything. And what the hell did it matter to her anyway? Paralysis from a sports injury was leagues apart from congenital disease. In the handicapped world there were distinct camps: the able-bodied who'd had accidents, and those poor, lifelong congenital cripples to be avoided at all costs. They had nothing in common besides the chair. He was probably lying about the potter business, too. Though not really her type, she had to admit this Andrew was conventionally handsome and had good manners, if a woman went for that southern-drawl, dripping-with-honey chitchat. He'd marry one of the women he met here tonight, Phoebe felt sure. The only mystery was which one it would be: blond or brunette? She tried to adjust her bra strap without calling attention to herself. It was held together with a safety pin that had a blue plastic duck head on it, left over from Sally's diaper days. Big deal. These days it wasn't like anyone was tearing off her clothes in a fit of passion.

Mimi stood at the counter buttering toast while Phoebe tried to get Sally to eat her breakfast. Mimi was dressed in her UPS uniform, and though she'd lived at the farm going on five years, Phoebe still felt that she didn't know her very well. Maybe it was her fault. The sight of that chocolate brown uniform still gave Phoebe a pang for missing Juan. "Come on, Sally. You can't have the cinnamon toast until you eat some fruit. You like fruit, remember?"

Sally pouted.

"Well, you liked it on ice cream the other night. How about some yogurt? I have strawberry yogurt. You want to try that?"

"No."

"I give up; eat sugar straight from bowl for all I care. Here," Phoebe said, and set the toast in front of her daughter. Sally picked it up and began eating.

"You might want to try not giving her more than two choices," Mimi said quietly. "That generally worked with my boys." She sat down at the table and wiped a smear of butter off

Sally's mouth. "Honey, I'm sorry, but I don't think you're old enough to eat that banana. Let me get a napkin and I'll take it away."

Mimi made a big show of turning her back, and the moment she was gone, Sally picked up the banana and took a defiant bite.

"Now where did that banana go? I thought I saw it right here," Mimi said, playacting in the way that made Sally giggle. "Oh boy. Now we're in trouble but good. Apples, bananas, I hope the food police don't come and arrest me."

Phoebe bit into her own toast, utterly weary at eight A.M. "Write me a script, will you, Mimi?"

Mimi laughed and stood behind Phoebe, rubbing her shoulders. "Make it a game, Phoebe. Don't take it so seriously. With my first, Carlos, I tackled him when he went to eat a blade of grass. When Julio came along, and Carlos was still in diapers, I figured he had to eat his peck of dirt one way or another, so I let him. Who turns out to have allergies? Carlos. Julio's never been sick a day in his life."

"I still want a script," Phoebe said again. "Something I can hold in my hand and read from. Have you heard from Dayle? Did she make up her mind?"

Mimi nodded. "She's going back to Alaska."

"And you're okay with that?"

"I have to be," Mimi answered, making herself smile. "I need to stay here in case my grandchildren need me."

Phoebe sighed. Mimi's ex-daughter-in-law had not let her see the kids in six years. It was a handy excuse, but not enough to give up happiness with a partner for. "There's always airplanes," Phoebe offered. "Beryl manages to come visit twice a year."

Mimi shrugged, and the phone rang.

"I wonder who's calling this early?" Phoebe said.

"Maybe it's Beryl," Mimi said. "Maybe she got your message."

"Nah, Alaska's one hour earlier than California. Ms. Reilly isn't a morning person." She reached for the phone. "Hello?"

"Mr. Callahan calling for Ms. DeThomas, please."

Phoebe pointed at the phone and mouthed, "It's him." "Ms. DeThomas speaking. What are you doing up this early, Mr. Callahan?"

"Oh, honey, I haven't slept past daybreak a day in my life. I figured you'd be up, what with your spoiled-rotten five-year-old daughter and the pony argument and all."

"Well, you figured right. Is there something I can do for you? Offer you breakfast so you can turn up your nose the same way my daughter does? Or can I interest you in an early morning Barney video? We have several to choose from, all featuring his purpleness in a variety of didactic story lines."

He laughed, and to Phoebe the sound was rumblingly deep, irritatingly so, and she felt it all the way to her belly. "Y'all want to go to a Christmas party? Tomorrow night, at the Links? Please forgive me for calling so late, but I only just now decided I want to go—that is, if you'll come with me."

"It's kind of short notice to get a baby-sitter," Phoebe started to say.

"I'll baby-sit!" Mimi yelled loud enough that Phoebe gave her the finger.

"Well, I hope you don't mind, but I took care of that before I called you. Your brother and Nancy will be happy to watch little Sally. So is it a yes?"

"I guess," Phoebe said, caught off-balance.

Sally was squeezing the banana in her hand, letting it gush out between her fingers. "Nice work, *hija,*" Mimi said. "Very nice. I bet you can't eat this blueberry. You see, blueberries are for grown-ups. *Ay,* I shouldn't even show it to you." She held the berry up and fed it to Sally like a mother bird feeds its young. "Wow, that's one for the record books," Mimi said. "We better get out the baby book and write this down."

"I don't need a baby book," Sally said. "I'm going to be six in two days and I'm going to get a cake and ride my new pony and have new dancing shoes."

Phoebe hung up the phone. "Damn you, Mimi."

Sally said, "Damn is a swear! Put a damn quarter in the swear jar."

"Yes, do that," Mimi said sweetly. "So what did he want?"

"Duh," Phoebe said. "Now I have to go to a party at the Links. Dress up and everything. Jesus, do I ever catch a break?"

"Jesus is a swear unless you're praying!" Sally yelled. "Another quarter!"

"Now look what you've started," Mimi said. "Give me five, Sallykins. Your mama has a hot date."

"I get to come, too," Sally said.

"Not this time," Mimi said.

"But I wanna go on a hot date!" Sally crowed.

"Oh, that would be no fun at all. You and me will raid the swear jar and go out for junk food. Sound good?"

"I love you, *Tía* Mimi!"

"I love you, too, *bebé."*

Phoebe sat there stunned. She didn't bother to lecture Sally or make sure she drank her juice. She handed her the cartoon character–shaped multivitamin, wiped her hands clean of banana, and let her go watch the goddamn Little Mermaid fall in true love for the millionth time, which was not only totally unrealistic, it was propaganda; indoctrination, really; an assurance she would one day need major therapy to outgrow. And the pony—she still hadn't dealt with the pony!

Mimi cleaned the table. "I have to go to work now," she said. "You okay?"

Phoebe looked up at her roommate as if it was the first time she'd noticed her there. *"'Y'all wanna go to uh Chrismess pahty?'* I'm fine," she said. "Just stunned by my life and irritated as hell at James for getting the pony."

"Nothing new there," Mimi said. "Bye-bye, Sally. *Tía* Mimi has to go to work and deliver important packages. You be nice today. Give your mama a break."

The door shut, and Sally ran from the table. "Under the Sea" came on loud and resonated through the gaps in Phoebe's brain. She pressed her fingertips into the cinnamon sugar and like a total slob, sucked them dry, thinking about the potential in bananas as a sculpting medium. She had the strangest desire to call Juan's relatives and ask their permission to date, but that was crazy thinking. Or was it? Certainly no crazier than going to the movies with her Rolfer, or a handsome Southerner asking her out.

"You talk funny," Sally said to Andrew when he arrived to collect Phoebe for the party.

"Sally, don't be rude," Phoebe said, holding her daughter in her lap. "Andrew's from the South. Remember, I showed you on the map? Everybody there talks like he does. To Southerners the way we talk sounds funny."

Sally slipped off her mother's lap and approached the man in the wheelchair. She stepped close enough to take a sniff. "You smell funny."

"That's cologne," he said. "Boys wear it to impress girls. You could be a detective, Sally. You're sure smart."

"Oh," Sally said. "I know. How come your chair is different than my mama's?"

Phoebe laughed. Inside, however, she was cringing. "Andrew, it seems my daughter has forgotten her manners. Sorry."

"It's okay," Andrew said. "She's engagingly forthright. Most people just pretend they don't see me."

Sally did a little spin. "I can dance," she said.

"And very nicely, I can see that," Andrew said. "Do you want to be a ballet dancer?"

"No. I'm going to be a horse-jumper. I'm going to win trophies and be on television and have new baby horses every spring."

"Those are noble goals."

Sally sighed. "I know." She looked up at her uncle James, who had just come into the room. "Uncle James? Andrew talks funny and he smells funny."

James nodded. "That he does, as do most boys, which is why you should steer clear of them. You ready to say goodnight and go see what Aunt Nance has for our dinner?"

Phoebe was cringing again. "We should go," she started to stay. "Sally, come give me a kiss."

Sally pulled away from her uncle and ignored her mother. This Andrew character was too interesting. "Do you like bananas?"

"Certainly. But the question is, do they like me?"

Sally's eyes went wide. "Do they?"

"Maybe you can ask them for me."

She placed one hand on her hip. "Can I see your penis?"

"I'm sorry, darlin'. My penis is very shy. In fact, it stayed home tonight."

Sally exploded in laughter, as did James. Phoebe shook her head and said evenly, "Sally, please go with Uncle James now. James, please take Sally to your house immediately."

Andrew, however, was laughing his rumbling laugh again.

Sally tried once more. "Is your penis all hairy like Homer's?"

"Sally," Phoebe said. "That's enough. Penises are private. It's bad manners to ask about them, especially people you don't know very well. Sorry, Andrew. We've been reading a book on body parts, and the child is fascinated with male anatomy. I showed her on the cat and now she's convinced all men have hair . . . there. Lord, can we just go?"

James was doubled over. "Better escape while you can. Come on, Sally. Aunt Nancy has a special treat for your dinner."

"I hope it's chocolate," Sally said.

"Of course it is," James said. "She has made you an entire meal consisting of chocolate beginning with a chocolate salad. Doesn't that sound yummy?"

"And then we can go see my pony!"

They disappeared through the foyer, and the worst part was, Phoebe knew he wasn't kidding. She shook her head. "She's five, spoiled rotten, she says whatever comes into her head—"

"You look beautiful in velvet," he said. "I can't wait to show you off. You ready?"

Never, Phoebe thought. I wasn't ready for Juan, and I sure as hell am not ready for this. It's like looking over the cliffs at Big Sur—such a long, long way down that the beauty hardly seems worth it.

Ness

4

Last Words

WHILE DAVID WAS SLEEPING, Ness named the cacti that grew in the earth behind the condo. Fishhook, barrel, jumping cholla, and saguaro. One old soldier of a saguaro held his arms upright, revealing his woody skeleton, frozen in time, like a bandit told decades ago to put up his hands in surrender. Ness wondered how old it was, how long it took for the flesh to fall from its limbs, what caused that to happen, whether the plant world had an AIDS equivalent, or it had simply lived its life span. A healthier specimen just her height, six feet nothing, had a round dark hole between its arms out of which spilled some kind of dried grass. At first Ness had thought that hole the result of some wild kids with guns, but then one day she'd seen a cactus wren fly inside and realized it was the wren's nest. She began to look for the bird, and on the days she caught sight of her, Ness felt a brush of luck. It wasn't the same thing as wishing on a star or buying a winning lottery ticket—just a quiet moment when she felt her heart leap up. A promise that somehow, somewhere, someday, life would be easier. David was her friend, and she was staying to help him so he wouldn't die alone. She wanted to be there, but sometimes she got lonely for the farm, for her friends, especially Phoebe, who understood things that other people had trouble with. Today was Sally's sixth birthday. Ness closed her eyes and pictured Sally's towering stack of birthday presents beside an enormous birthday cake decorated with the Little Mermaid swimming through a sea of flowers. She will always know she's loved, Ness thought. It doesn't get much better than that.

"DeThomas Farms. Can I help you?"

For a second Ness wondered if she'd dialed Nance by mistake. "James? Is that you? It's Ness calling to wish the birthday girl many happy returns."

"Hey, Ness. How's my favorite horse person?"

"Horse person?"

"Yeah. Tell me something. At what age did you begin riding?"

"Gosh, James, I can't remember. I think I was five, maybe four. Why?"

"Because the way Phoebe's acting, you'd think I'd given her child a machine gun instead of a pony. She won't even speak to me! It's not like I enrolled my niece in hang-gliding lessons. It's a damn pony, and it's what Sally wanted. Hey, I could use some support. Will you talk to her?"

Ness sighed. "James, did you ask her before you went and bought this pony, or did you surprise her?" The silence that followed gave her the answer. "Lord God, don't tell me you went and bought a horse without asking someone who knows about horses first."

"Okay, so I maybe should have asked first, but this is a registered POA, and she's out of some fancy-ass champion or other, and I have the papers to prove it. Not to mention you should see Sally on her. I mean, the kid's a natural. Already trotting. And I also hired a trainer."

"Excuse me?"

"Someone to teach her how to ride the pony. I swear, that sister of mine is behaving like a diva. She won't even cut me a piece of birthday cake! This is just how things were before Sadie left her the farm, you know. I was persona non grata, the black sheep of the family, a money-hungry social climber; if something went wrong, blame James—"

"James, you *are* to blame for this! What a fool thing to do! Of all people, don't you think your sister has a right to be afraid of the people she loves dying?" Ness pulled the telephone inside the condo. It was in the fifties but sunny and bright, the sky absolutely robin's-egg blue.

"Well, pardon me. Sally doesn't seem a bit scared. In fact, she's got this ear-to-ear grin on her that just brings tears to my eyes. I'm taking the time to videotape this historic event that will no doubt bring hours of joy over the years because I want to be a good uncle. Phoebe, however . . . "

God help us, Ness thought to herself as she watered the potted herbs on the windowsill. The warm sandy colors of the kitchen tile were a perfect complement to the green basil and the aromatic rosemary spilling out of their clay pots. "James, if I were you, I'd check into a Kevlar vest. Phoebe wouldn't be comfortable letting Sally ride a pony even if it came with rubber bumpers. You know what she went through to have that child, and what she lost. Whatever made you go and do a rash thing like that—well, get some therapy is all I can say."

"Sally is six years old!" James said. "It's the perfect age for a serious equestrian to get started. Nance said these days they start as young as four, which means she actually has some catching up to do. And she loves horses. Oh, God—she's cantering now. I wish you could see this. Hold on a sec while I sneak in for a close-up."

Ness heard the phone clatter to the porch and sighed. While she waited for James to remember he was talking to her, she studied the colors of the desert in winter so she could repaint her room at the farm in similar tones. Was there paint on earth to capture that breathtaking blood orange? She could find nearly every shade of green in the cacti, the cottonwoods, and her favorite, the lacy mesquite trees with their sharp, oily scent. Today she was in love with the sage green of the ocotillo's spindly branches; yesterday it had been the ground-hugging succulents that grew in a roseate pattern, just sprang up in the middle of stones and sand and grew like saxifrage, splitting rock. Every breath she took in felt cleansing. The quiet seemed endless. Her troubles felt miles away, when in actuality she knew they were sleeping fitfully in a rented hospital bed until it was time for the next dose of his medication. For a week now she'd had the nurse come twice a day to help her get David cleaned up and comfortable. Today she was coming by three times. She'd made noises about hospice care, and even suggested that Ness move David to the hospital in town, but that was the last thing David wanted. Still, something had to change.

She heard the sound of the phone being picked up. "Is there someone there?" she heard Mimi say. "Hello?"

"Hi, Mimi, it's Ness. I called up to say happy birthday to Sally. Sounds like things aren't going so well."

"Oh, Ness. You picked a good time to be away. What a mess. Sally's riding the pony. She's wearing her nightie, a bicycle helmet, and her new red dancing shoes. She won't even get off long enough to put on her riding clothes, sing 'Happy Birthday,' nothing. *Malcriada,* that one, spoiled rotten. Phoebe is spitting mad. Happy birthday? Forget it. It's more like war. There's nothing I can do to get those two to talk, and I'm afraid to leave them alone, but I have to go to work."

"But it's Saturday."

"I know. I'm picking up extra shifts so I can save money to go visit Dayle. Hang on, I'll find Phoebe for you."

Once again Ness heard the phone topple from the chaise to the porch, and after five minutes of waiting, she was certain Mimi'd failed to tell Phoebe. Things were like that at the farm—busy, changing every minute, exciting, sad, profitable, scary, hopes rising and falling as fast as the mercury in a thermometer. She should just hang up, try to figure out how to use the computer to send an email, but she wanted to speak to Sally, her little "niece," the light that shone on the farm twenty-four hours a day, the reason no one could stay depressed for more than a few self-indulgent moments. She remembered how Sally liked to perch on her lap and using her index fingers, turn Ness's sad mouth into a clown's grin. She'd sing "Don't Worry, Be Happy," or try to dance the robot, or get down on all fours and whinny like a horse and buck, this child who slept with a lasso under her pillow just in case a horse showed up in her dreams. David couldn't be around her without a mask, since, as Lester had put it, "children are the vectors of germs." From the moment Sally could walk she was a handful and a half, and now she was six, and things were heating up in a new way, and Ness wanted to be there to see it all firsthand so badly that she felt a sore place grow in her chest just thinking about it.

The phone clicked, and Ness heard the dial tone. She gave up and walked down the hall to check on David. He was still sleeping, his face terribly pale. The bones seemed to have risen another millimeter in his cheeks. His wrists and hands, once full and well manicured, now reminded her of the hands of a ninety-year-old man, skin thinned out to parchment, blue veins all ropy, and though she rubbed them with lotion three times a day, they remained dry and chapped. AIDS made her so angry she just wanted to scream, for David; for Jake, who'd infected her; for all the babies born with no chance of celebrating a sixth birthday, let alone enjoying a gift as fabulous and inappropriate as a pony.

"Hello, Precious," he whispered, trying to sound like Gollum in *Lord of the Rings,* which they'd watched the night before on DVD.

"Hello, yourself. Want a sip of water?"

"Mmm."

She bent the straw to his peeling lips. His complexion looked as grainy as a photograph. He needed to be shaved. When he finished drinking, she set the cup down on the bedside table.

"Heard you on the phone."

"I was trying to get hold of Sally, to tell her happy birthday. Didn't get her, but I spoke to James and to Mimi."

He smiled. "Come sit. Talk to me."

"What would you like me to talk about?"

"About yesterday."

"Yesterday yesterday, or yesterday in general?"

"General. Tell me about flowers."

Ness sat down in the rocker and took hold of his hand. She rubbed it softly. "Well, let's see. Once upon a time I thought the only bulb in the world was a lightbulb. Then I came to the farm, and I had to learn to identify their little wrinkly root balls and feed them special diets like they were horses. It seemed crazy dropping something that looked dead into the ground and watering it. I don't think I'll ever forget that first spring. Nothing could ever compare to seeing a field of color like that first spring."

David was breathing evenly, but she could hear a tiny rattle in there that worried her. An infection at this stage would do him in. Well, she'd make soup for dinner, and that would help. "The key to bulbs is keeping them cold for six weeks before you plant them. Cold and dark. If they don't get a good chill, they won't bloom. California's just too hot for them. I'll never forget how Duchess dug up row after row of tulips just so she could eat the bonemeal we'd fed the bulbs. Nance stood there stamping her foot, and Duchess wagged her tail like she expected a prize for all her hard work. Of course now I can look back and see that Nance didn't give two rips about a row of tulips. She missed Rotten Rick and was worried she'd made the wrong decision in leaving him. It turned out to be the right decision, though. The longer I live the less I understand about love, you know? Seems like the strongest force on earth should have a little more common sense to it, but then I think, look at you and me, and maybe it's better off things stay a mystery."

David smiled, and slept.

In the tiny kitchen of the rented condo there was room for one person to work. The pots and pans were cheap discount-store metal with nonstick insides. Ness steamed yellow squash, which was called *calabasitas* at the little market she'd been going to. The recipe for tortilla soup listed chicken broth as the main ingredient, but she figured vegetable broth would substitute just as well. While that simmered, she cooked sweet potatoes, pureed them, and made a pie like Granny Shirley used to make for Christmas. Even if he could manage only a teaspoon, she wanted David to taste it one last time.

Christmas morning David woke up early, and Ness brought all his gifts in and placed them on his bedside table. "Somebody was a good boy this year," she said. "Look at all these presents."

"You open them," he said, his watery eyes on her.

"Okay," she said, loosening the bow on the first one. "Oh, you're going to love this. Nance and James sent you a Dale Evans watch. In the original box and everything."

He held up his hand. "Put it on me."

She was surprised. David was a savvy collector, and she knew from his stash of cowboy memorabilia that things retained better value when kept intact. Nevertheless she lifted his wrist—bird bones—and strapped the watch on. The fact that it fit made her eyes tear up. "It looks wonderful," she said. "Very smart."

David smiled and laid his hand down on the quilt. "I want to see it one last time," he said.

"See what?" she asked. "Your watch?"

"No. The coastline."

"Sweetie, we're in Arizona, remember? There is no coastline."

"No, no," he said. "California. Home."

Ness weighed his words, trying to figure out whether he meant them or was just thinking out loud, which he did more and more these days. One moment they would be listening to music, the next David was rambling about the summer he was ten, and he'd fallen in love with the lifeguard at the country club his parents belonged to. Or he'd recount some Hollywood party where the stars paraded through, their faces tight with plastic surgery and their clothes so impossibly beautiful it was hard to look at them.

"I'm here," she said. "Any place we're together is home."

"Home," he said again, and turned his face to the wall.

Ness bent down to touch his face. "If you really want to go home, we should fly," she said softly. "I'm afraid the car trip could be too much for you."

He frowned, screwing his face up like Sally did when she was told to go to bed. "I want to see water. From the car."

"Okay," she said. "We'll see what we can do. Shall I leave the presents for later?"

"Open them."

"I'll do that." How did a person shop for someone who was dying? David was beyond the Get-Well card stage, and he certainly didn't need any more flowers. Ness stopped folding the paper so carefully and went through the presents quickly. "A special edition DVD of *The Wizard of Oz,* from Sally. And Mimi sent you bunny slippers. Two Erik Satie CDs, from Phoebe," she said. "Shall I put one on?"

He nodded. "The slippers," he said, so she removed his socks and slid the brown bunnies on his thin elegant feet. He wiggled his toes inside them, smiled, and said, "Now home."

"Okay," she said, trying not to let her voice betray her. "Just rest now. I'll make the arrangements." She kissed him on the forehead and then cupped his cheek in her hand. The bones were right there. Christmas in Arizona was over.

Ness called the nursing service first. "I need a couple of prescriptions filled, and I need to arrange for someone to pick up the rental bed. Yes, I can hold."

While she waited she looked around the rented condo, took note of the nondescript prints matted in peach tones, framed in rustic wood. The decorator magazines fanned across the glass coffee table. The fireplace was on a timer, like a heat lamp, and "burned" phony logs. There wasn't a single child's toy to be found, and outside, the patio furniture couldn't have been more than a year old. What was supposed to be an oasis felt more like a mirage. She decided she wanted to be home as much as David did.

The voice came back on the line. "I can sign for morphine," she said. "I have a note from his physician in California."

David didn't want dinner. She took a bowl of soup out to the patio to try to eat. She missed her granny and imagined what the old woman would say of the giant saguaro. *That old feller's losing his britches. That one looks to be a cousin to that Gumby fellow.* No. Granny Shirley would have said, *Child, look at our Lord's fine handiwork! The desert humbles me.* If somebody littered, she'd bend to pick up the wrapper and say, "Won't pass up a chance to bend my knees." She had been dead several years now, yet Ness missed her every day, just like she was going to miss David when he went—which, if she could trust her instincts, would be soon. She went indoors, poured the soup down the sink, and called the farm.

"DeThomas Farms, Merry Christmas!" James hollered into the phone.

"You sound jolly," Ness said. "Last time we talked things weren't so great. How's the pony?"

"Couldn't be better. I'll have you know Sally's in love."

"And Phoebe?"

"Any day now my sister is going to grudgingly admit I'm a genius. Hang on, and I'll get her for you."

"Ness? Merry Christmas. Why haven't you called? I've been worried sick. Didn't you get my messages?"

Ness twirled the cord around her hand. Yes, she'd gotten them. Sometimes when Phoebe had called she was in the middle of trying to get David comfortable, and sometimes she just sat there and listened to the phone ring because she didn't trust herself to say anything because she'd been cleaning up diarrhea or changing urine-soaked sheets, and trying hard to hold herself together. "Merry Christmas, Phoebe," she managed. "I wanted—so many times I've started—you can't know—" Her voice stuck on that syllable like her throat had rusted shut, and she could not say another word.

"Ness? Are you still there?"

Ness tried to clear her throat, but only a croak came out.

Phoebe said, "I understand. It's okay. I'm here. Let me tell you what the princess raked in so far today. A Crump saddle with a hunt seat. James again; remind me to kill him later. Barbie's English riding stable, which comes with several mares and foals; a wheelbarrow; plastic carrots, saddles and bridles; of course, those horse raincoats that don't come with hats; and these darling little miniature hay bales. I bought the stable stuff. I'm praying she'll get this equine business out of her system ASAP. And Mimi and Dayle had a life-size custom-made doll created using a photo of Sally. It's as tall as she is and can wear her clothes. The only thing it lacks is her smart mouth. Mother and Bert sent her a new nightie, robe, and slippers, and Segundo's wife made her a purple afghan with orange tassels. Let's see. What else? We've been cooking for days. Dinner is an organic vegetable casserole, and yes, I will freeze some for you. James is burning a roast for himself and Nance. Oh, Nance made your granny's sweet potato pie and the hard sauce. Did you know the frosting is basically powdered sugar mixed with Jim Beam? Doesn't sound very Baptist to me. Nance is eating, so don't worry about that. Mimi and Dayle are burning up the phone lines. Everyone misses you. It doesn't really feel like Christmas with you gone."

Ness heard her take a breath.

"Can I ask how David is? Think you're coming home anytime soon? Do you want me to fly over and stay with you guys for a few days? Ness? Jeez Louise, tap the phone once for no, twice for yes. Tell me what you need, and I'll do it."

Ness pressed her hand to her chest, where she felt things fluttering in panic. *I have to remember to tell David about the ribbon candy in the Carnival glass dish,* she told herself. The dish her grandmother had left her. And the fat oranges studded with cloves she put in each of her friends' Christmas stockings. It took no time at all. She would make him one. And she would spin out a long story about how she and her friends, though they all believed in different religions, usually went to midnight services at Ness's church and sang their hearts out—even Sally, who had been known to talk back to the minister. The choir group had a potluck with things like candied carrots and green Jell-O with marshmallows and mandarin oranges, and meatballs in sweet-and-sour sauce that was probably made from jelly. Someone always brought greens swimming in butter and vinegar, and someone else brought roasted chestnuts. Did David know the story of their first Christmas at the farm together, how Ness had tried to make chestnuts, how they'd blown up in her face, and she'd confessed that she was HIV positive, and now here she was, this Christmas six years later, David dying, and her own HIV status in a crazy no-man's-land of not testing positive since the drug trial, but no one could say it wouldn't return? She couldn't remember. But if it weren't for HIV, she never would have had the courage to leave Jake, she never would have met the girls or David, and she couldn't imagine how she could ever live without that.

"Shall I fly out?" Phoebe said. "Ness? Say something. You're scaring me."

"No," Ness answered, and the sharp feeling in her throat began to fade, and her nerves to settle down. "We're coming back. I can make the drive. Look for us tomorrow, maybe the next day. I'll call. Merry Christmas, Phoebe."

She hung up, sat down on the tile floor and sobbed until she was dizzy.

"Tell me about yesterday," David said that night, but once she gave him his pills, he'd gone right to sleep.

She stayed up late and cleaned out the fridge, throwing away food, including the uneaten pie. Lester had said the trip to Arizona would be good for David, that a lift in his spirits was helpful. Maybe it had helped. It was hard to say for sure. Every day he seemed a little frailer and took longer and longer rest periods. Ness knew that eventually the virus outsmarted the drug regimen, no matter what you threw at it. And David was never a good candidate for drug trials. For so long she'd told herself that he'd wake up stronger tomorrow, but here they were now on the downhill side of this mountain. She was so scared that her knees began knocking. She wiped the fridge clean and went to work on the counters until the tile gleamed.

She woke up just before dawn. David was still sleeping, so she slipped outside and sat on the patio staring at the cacti, looking for her wren. She gulped in deep breaths for David, tried to soak in the beauty of the desert so she could whisper it in his ear every night, and maybe if they were lucky what she said would find its way into his dreams. She knew it was a place where he was strong and happy and they were together, riding his horses.

Indoors she packed the cooler and went to get David ready, stopping for a moment to look around this place that had been their home for the last two months. There were magazines in the living room, but she figured she would leave them for whoever rented the place next. She went to David's room and stood at the end of his bed, staring at the telephone.

She knew she could have called Lester. He'd said when

things got to the end stage, David would let them know, and Lester was used to having his life interrupted with one crisis or another. But what was the point? David was making his wishes clear. Last summer he'd had Malcolm Colburn tidy up his legal business. Everything she needed to do was inside a manila envelope inside her suitcase. Important papers, addresses of people to notify, who he wanted to have his things—but she couldn't bring herself to open it—she felt if she did he'd die right then. She wanted this to all be some temporary backslide, and for David to rise up and tell her a joke or say they should drive to Patagonia for dinner at the Stagecoach Inn instead of home to Bayborough.

She went to his side and thought all the things she could not say aloud. David, you cannot die. I haven't known you long enough, and I've only just learned how to properly love another human being, so you simply are not allowed to go just yet. Selfish of me? Sure. But I'm not ready to imagine a world without you in it. I believe with all my heart that God will take you into his arms, that your voice will become a part of the heavenly choir, but I cannot help bargaining for time, and if that makes me a terrible person, so be it.

In the bathroom she washed her face, wrung out the facecloth, and began to pack up shampoo, the hair dryer, the few girly items she had come to believe she couldn't live without, and remembered the time in her life when she washed herself with horse soap and used that to wash her hair, too, and managed just fine. David asked about his horses every day. She'd taken care of them, boarded them at the winery that also sponsored trail rides. Ness had left explicit instructions: The bay mare needed pelleted feed, and the Morgan needed daily Bute, but he wouldn't take it unless it was ground into molasses and slathered way back on his tongue. David still asked about the horses. Every time she told him they were doing fine.

She heard the doorbell and hurried to answer it. The registry had sent her a male nurse, a big white guy with a shaved head and a gentle face. "Mrs. Snow?"

"Yes," Ness answered. "I need some help getting Mr. Snow ready to return to California. If you'll follow me, he's here in the first bedroom."

While the nurse checked David over, Ness decided that he would have looked downright scary if he hadn't been wearing a beaded stethoscope featuring Kermit the frog. He gave David a shot of morphine, disposed of the needle in a red plastic box, and turned to her. "This should hold him for five hours. I recommend you give him his pills with some Ensure, so there's something in his stomach. Are you spending the night in a motel?"

She shook her head. "No. I'm planning only to stop for gas, and that's it."

He unfolded a piece of paper. "Here's a list of hospitals along your way should you run into trouble."

Ness thanked the young man, and held onto the door of the PT Cruiser that David had bought and put in her name. "We're going to see the water in just a few hours," she assured David, because it was the only way she could get him to calm down and stop fighting the drugs. "Sleep, darling." The last thing she did before driving away was look at the saguaro with the wren nest, hoping for one last sight of her, but it wasn't meant to be.

When the landscape thinned out and the radio stations faded, Ness plugged in a Pavarotti CD. She put the car on cruise control and wondered about the strangeness of seeing a seagull all the way out in Yuma, and how maybe Beryl would say it was perfectly normal behavior for the gull because Beryl knew about birds, even though it had been a while since anyone had heard from her. She glanced in the mirror and looked at David, who was lying against three needlepoint throw pillows of her own making. She'd tried to capture the beauty of the cacti in wool but had fallen desperately short. She remembered how the señora she bought tortillas from at the Mercado told her that wren feathers were good luck. She'd wanted to find one to lay on David's pillow, but despite a daily walk hadn't gotten that lucky. At the chapel at San Xavier Mission she'd lighted five candles for Nance, one each for the lost babies, and one for the baby she felt she'd get. She had prayed nonstop for David, but she told herself that some things were simply in His hands. "You doing okay back there?" she called out when David stirred.

"Mmm."

"It won't be long now, honey. Just a few hours. Close your eyes."

At the second gas station she bought ice for the cooler, gave David his pain pill and a sip of Ensure. She rearranged his blankets, bought herself a soda, and checked to make sure the cell phone was plugged in. "Ready to hit the road?" she asked, and David nodded, a smile on his face. "Don't let me miss it," he said.

"It doesn't get pretty until Santa Barbara," she answered. "Think you can be patient a few more hours?"

"Wake me when you see water."

"I promise." She thought maybe she would take him to CHOP—the Community Hospital of the Peninsula—instead of home, and immediately hated herself for lying to David. How could they be at this stage already?

When they crossed the state line into California, David got fretful. "What's the matter, sweetheart?" she asked. "Do you need me to pull over?"

"I'm missing it."

"Missing what, David? Tell me."

"Mmm," he said, as if he were in pain. "Yesterday."

She took a breath and said everything she could think to say. "My love, we'll be at the water soon. I'll tell you a story until we get there. This is an old tale of Granny Shirley's. It's about how we rise from the dust and make our way. We must shake ourselves, throw off fear, the habit of oppression and bondage trained us in—those are the words of Brother Absalom Jones, born in the year 1786. We'll learn to walk the tightrope by putting one foot down, and then the other. We learn the rope of life by untying its knots—according to poet Jean Toomer, who would not be silenced. Did you know that Sojourner Truth could not read a book? Didn't stop her from reading her people. I'm your people, David. We're each other's people. A free man is the one who will not let one closed door stop him. In the words of Martin Luther King Jr., if you can't run, walk; and if you can't walk, crawl; and in my words, if you can't crawl, I will carry you; and I don't care if the song says you have to walk that lonesome valley by yourself because nobody else can walk it for you, I will follow you as long as I can. I will uphold the lantern of Diogenes, Carl Lewis, Joe Louis, and Pearl Bailey, and Michael Jackson had courage, and courage is all it takes. My ancestors led me on this path, and yours led you on yours, and against the odds we found each other. Our hearts are God's most precious gifts to us, and we have to use them even if it hurts as much as it feels good. Even Muhammad Ali knew there were better things to do than beat up people. Faith breeds courage and suffering breeds character, and when one is in the deepest trouble, that is when he remembers God, but bear in mind that God has remembered *you* all along, and God kept the African slave sane and the gay man sane and both will meet him though he is already here, in every place you look if you only look, and those who are dead are never gone, they are in the shadows watching over us. Rosa Parks didn't think about making history, she was just tired of giving up her seat. Oh, David. In my mind I know that if you need to go, if that is what will take away the pain and grant you peace, then I will drive us to your house, and then you can see all your beautiful things, but don't leave me just yet."

She checked the mirror, and he was smiling at her, and if he had had the energy to speak, she knew he would have said, "Don't look now, but she's getting 'alleluia' on me." He seemed to be sleeping peacefully, so the morphine must have done its job.

She made it through Los Angeles, and when she got to Santa Barbara and saw that David was sleeping, she decided to let him sleep. From here on the coastline was stunning, but his face was so unburdened when he slept she didn't have the heart to wake him. He looked like a child. And then just south of Big Sur it began to dawn on her that he wasn't sleeping anymore, he was gone; and then she remembered that in spite of all she'd said, she'd left out the most important thing: That in the beginning we have God, and in the end God is there waiting, but in the middle—that's the special time because we have each other.

Beryl

5

Spare Cats

On New Year's Eve, Detective Michael Stokes called Beryl, opening the conversation with an apology. "Wish I had some news for you, Mrs. Houghton, but I don't. That doesn't mean we won't solve this case. You've got to think of me like one of those drug-sniffing dogs at the airport. My nose is a well-tuned instrument. We'll get to the bottom of things. I'll bet you a steak dinner at Sullivan's on that. Speaking of dinner, what are you doing tonight?"

Was he going to ask her on a date? "I hadn't planned on anything."

"My recommendation is get yourself out there among them. Surely one of your neighbors is having an open house. Go, have a few drinks, but don't drive. You know what we cops say, drive hammered, get nailed."

Beryl exhaled, trying hard to muster enthusiasm for what, aside from the party comment, was essentially the same conversation as last week's. It had been nearly four months now since Earl had disappeared. She felt terrible that it had taken her so long to realize the cat was gone, too, but Hester had never been one to hang around and beg to be petted. Basically Beryl set out kibble, and the kibble disappeared. She changed the litter box every week without paying much attention to its contents.

Detective Stokes said she'd turn up, but Beryl knew poor old Hester Prynne had probably become eagle kabob a long time back. Just that day she'd seen a pair of bald eagles fly overhead.

"I'll probably just curl up with my parrot and watch HBO."

"Uh-oh," the detective said. "Sounds like you're isolating yourself."

Why shouldn't it? It was what she did every night that Thomas Jack didn't show up to take her mind off things. Suddenly she got a picture in her head of how that looked on New Year's Eve—miles beyond pathetic, the perfect illustration for a kid's book about an old lady hermit slowly turning into a dried-out crone. "Let's not bullshit ourselves here, Mike. If Earl is out there, he's hiding. And if he staged the whole disappearance thing, which I think is just the kind of crazy thing he might do, he's probably checked into some five-star hotel in Europe and is enjoying a glass of champagne surrounded by a bevy of ladies. As far as I'm concerned he's moose meat."

So why did her mind immediately conjure up a scrap of jacket material caught on a spruce branch, and spy the sole of a hiking boot buried under frozen leaves?

"Moose don't eat meat," Detective Stokes said. "Explain to me again why you think he'd stage a disappearance."

Beryl wished she hadn't said anything. She was tired of the cop's questions. How did a person summarize that after five years of cohabitation, she still couldn't say for certain that Earl was Buckethead, or why his money seemed to arrive from no particular work source, or that people like Eric Clapton sometimes stayed the night, sharing sections of the newspaper with you over breakfast? Since Earl's disappearance she'd felt like Alice going through the looking glass on a daily basis. "People knew him as Buckethead," she said. "It was a pseudonym he sometimes performed under. His guitar buddies and so on. Look it up on the Internet. You'll find a link from every outcast teenage male's website. But it won't tell you anything past that. I should go. I'm in a weird mood today."

"Do you have a light box? One of those ten-thousand-lumens things that fills your brain up with serotonin?"

"Sure," Beryl said. Anything to get him off her back.

"Mrs. Houghton," he said. "Lying to a cop is not a good habit to get into."

Beryl sighed and pushed her hair away from her face. She wanted to tell him, *Detective Stokes, I have been lying to someone just about every day of my life. I have more secrets than Harry freaking Houdini. It's going to take more than ten thousand lumens of light to put a smile on this old face, and I am not Mrs. Anything,* but what she said was, "So you've told me."

"Getting back to this Buckethead thing. I'll try digging a little deeper, see what I come up with. But so far as the cat goes, I think you're getting your feathers ruffled for nothing. After all, you do live on the Hillside. Stuff like that happens."

"Stuff like what? A bear coming out of hibernation and eating her, then going back into hibernation?"

He laughed. "Something that newsworthy would no doubt end up in the paper, Mrs. Houghton. Maybe she's camped out at a neighbor's where the eats are better."

"How many time do I have to tell you I'm not married! My last name is Reilly! You're a detective! If you can't remember these things, how on earth do you expect to find Earl?"

He was quiet a moment. "Have mercy, dear. I'm getting old."

She'd seen Detective Stokes in person once, the week Earl had first gone missing. He wasn't that old, maybe sixty. One of those tired looking men who dressed in Sears suits and bought his dress shirts three to a package. He looked like somebody's dad.

BERYL'S PRIVATE JOURNAL

Sometimes I dial Earl's cell phone and hang up before it rings. I remember the sound of his voice. It echoes inside my ear and I remember another life, the one I thought we were living, and now maybe I think didn't exist except in my mind. I don't want to grow old alone without anyone to hold me in the dark. Is that selfish? When we slept next to each other, I wasn't afraid of the dark anymore. So what if Earl kept his past to himself? So did I. Earl's cell phone bill arrives, and I think I should have the thing shut off, but I don't think I could stand not ever hearing his voice again. Wouldn't he have taken the phone with him if he were leaving me? No, something happened. It had to've. Something that I will never know the answer to. But what if he did stage all this, like Detective Stokes says? How do I live with that? You'd think by now I'd've gotten a letter. Something.

The reason I lie to my girlfriends is that they have more important problems—real, tangible issues. David died while Ness was driving him home. Phoebe said he *died in her car,* and I can't imagine the courage it took for her to keep on driving. How will Ness get over losing David? She was more devoted to him than any wife. Phoebe's trying so hard to do a good job mothering little Sally, who's a pistol; and Phoebe's health, while strong at the moment, is subject to change without warning. Nance losing so many babies—it's too unfair to imagine, and yet there she is, throwing dinner parties, working on the farm plans, nicely dressed, and not a hair out of place. I'd have a baby for her, if I weren't menopausal and my last few eggs so past their shelf date they're stinking up the fridge.

There's no way I can tell them, *Excuse me, please put all that life-and-death stuff on hold for a moment while I whine about my perfect world caving in on itself because (1) yet another man has decided he doesn't love me and hauled ass, or (2) the man I really, truly believed would love me forever staged this cruel disappearance because it was too hard to face me and say goodbye?* Or (3) maybe there was foul play and I should be hiring private investigators with all this money that's lying around, but I'm such a coward I don't want to know? (4) For sure I should tell them how the only man I truly count on to call me every week is Detective Stokes, who says Earl's leaving the truck at the lake smells a little fishy to him, and he's been with the department twenty-eight years. (5) And then there's the little issue of me sleeping with Thomas Jack—how do I explain that I can lie down with this perfect stranger and have wonderful sex all the more easily because of Earl's absence? Nance would say that's "reactive" sex and will never be making love. Ness would say, *Bullpuckey, it's revenge, plain and simple, just make sure you use a condom.* Only Phoebe would understand that when Thomas Jack is with me, the world spins a little less swiftly. After we use each other, then can I sleep a dreamless sleep, and for a little while after I wake up, pretend I have a normal life.

So when the girls call and ask how's Earl, I answer fine. On a hike. At the store. In Portland for the weekend. Playing a gig. Fine. My white lies have stacked up into a Great Wall of China. Sometimes, though, I just let the phone ring.

Beryl sat on the couch watching the snow come down. So many tiny flakes spiraled through the air that it seemed impossible they would amount to anything, but she knew that by morning she'd have to get out the shovel. What was love, anyway? she wondered. Fuel for Hallmark cards? Or a lacy veneer to pull over lust in order to make palatable a woman calling out, "I love you!" when what she really meant was, "This feels great"? She shut her eyes and listened to the muted sounds of the downtown fireworks going off. Fireworks in January because in July there wasn't enough darkness to appreciate them.

There was a time in her life she would have poked out her left eye if it meant that her husband, JW, would disappear. Sacred vows didn't stop murderous thoughts. Let him die in a car crash, she'd think. Get caught in the middle of some convenience-store robbery, the innocent bystander—*hah!* like he was ever innocent. Drown in his beer vomit, get brained in a fight, anything but come home and take his rage out on her. He slept with other women, took money from his boss, lost jobs because he couldn't be bothered to show up five days a week, bought a car on time they couldn't afford and had it repossessed, destroying their already pitiful credit. She remembered cooking up a huge pot of oatmeal and another of beans so there would be something to eat. How was it there was always enough money for beer? She'd wanted kids but kept on using birth control because bringing a child into any kind of world that included JW for a father was unthinkable. Worst of all, she loved him. She was terrified of life without him. She went to work; she sat on the floor and helped kindergarteners trace their letters, encouraging every crooked line and wobbly circle. After school she gave riding lessons, and cheered the daughters of the wealthy when they kept their backs straight as they posted the trot. At six she came home to heat up the beans, but often she'd stand there in the galley kitchen of the double-wide trailer and suddenly find herself unable to move. Maybe she hadn't challenged herself since she got out of prison. Maybe things were too easy. She'd gone from prison to the studio apartment to Bayborough Bird Rehab to Bad Girl Creek to Earl, and—oh God, was she doing it again with Thomas Jack? He was too young for her. She hardly knew him. He was Native, and she was white. Alaska was her one big risk, and look how that turned out. Alone, scared, angry, and unable to stop crying—that was the formula for domestic violence right there. Take primal emotions; fling them up into the air. Whatever falls to earth, you punch the shit out of, and whatever rubble remains, you build a life on.

She tried picturing Earl lying dead in some deep ravine, snow covering his beautiful, craggy face, his hands curled into icy claws, and she thought, Fine, be dead, just be *something*.

Beryl woke on the couch a few hours later, and reached for her journal before she forgot her dream.

Tuesday Night

I dreamed Bette was driving me to Saint Margaret's.

It's been years since I thought of life before prison. Now when I shut my eyes, all these memories pop to the surface. I told Phoebe and the girls I hated Bette, my stepmother, but she was the first one to call herself a poor excuse for a parent. *You don't have to say a word,* she'd tell me, one hand at her throat as if she were holding back a scream. *I know I'm no good at this. I'm sure your mother, bless her soul, would have done better. My own mother used to tell me, "I hope you get a child as sassy as you were," and what do you know? I got worse.*

But it wasn't me she meant. It was Morris, her son, who made everyone call him Moose, which now that I live in Alaska seems like cruelty to animals. Moose was two hundred pounds to my one-twenty. He stole Bette's cigarettes, shoplifted hard liquor, lived in an eternal state of school suspension, and mistreated anything that crossed his path and took joy in it. He'd been held back two grades while I skipped forward one. I got a plaque with my name engraved on it for perfect attendance. Moose broke the school record for truancy. From age eight to age sixteen, my bedroom was next to his, and we shared the bathroom down the hall. Eight years of holes punched in the plaster, him jumping out at me when I walked down there without checking first to see whether he was lurking. At night he'd whisper a constant flow of suggestive remarks. I slept with my pillow over my head. Nights were for threats, but daylight was the hard part. The moment Bette left the room, he'd hit me with his forefinger bent at the knuckle so I'd get a bruise. Three months after my sweet sixteen—Bette had given me a bouquet of daisies, apologizing that she couldn't afford roses—she was driving me to Saint Margaret's of Cortona, a couple hundred miles from Eureka, so I could hide out until it was time to have the baby. It happened the night she had car trouble and got home late from her secretary job. Bette walked in and I was lying there crumpled, too shocked to cover myself. Moose was zipping up his pants. "Hi, Mom. Didn't expect you so—" I didn't know Bette had that kind of punch in her. She even managed to make the bully cry. Even though she wasn't my real mother, I loved her for that.

I'd never heard the word "rape" spoken out loud—saying it was like cursing or telling a dirty joke—but I remembered thinking that it sounded exactly like what had happened. Something far worse than a scrape. One horrible syllable. Saying it out loud caused snickering, as if any girl who had that happen to her secretly wanted it to. It was my first time and the blood wouldn't stop, and I was torn up inside so I needed stitches. The doctor at the ER was businesslike, using Latin words for my injuries. He stitched quickly. When I cried and told him that what he was doing hurt me, he said, *There are no nerve endings in the vaginal canal,* and Bette clapped her hand on his forearm and said, *You give that girl more anesthetic right this second.* He did, and I went blessedly numb, but that was all. No counseling, no emergency birth control, and no words of reassurance, not even a sleeping pill to make it through that long and dark first night. But the next month I got something, all right. No period. I couldn't tell Bette. Maybe the blood would come next month. My cycle was out of whack because of the shock. When it didn't come the second month, I stole a vial of pills from the health food store that were supposed to bring on a period delayed because of stress: Humphrey's Eleven. I still remember the name, the black printing on the blue-and-white bottle. I had the money, but I couldn't pay for it or everyone would know. Then for a long time I pretended nothing had happened. I wanted my old life back. I wanted teachers to tell me facts that I could write down and memorize and work on chemistry experiments and read stories with important lessons, so I just didn't think about it.

December and January were dark. The Alaskan winter did things to people—tweaked their senses, pitched their moods around like a plastic bag in the wind—it brought out behavior that normally stayed dormant. New Year's Day morning Beryl made breakfast for her bird, lit an oil lamp, and flipped through her journal. The cover of the book was a blue-veined map of the world, the paper worn smooth in the places where her fingers fit. Some days she filled page after page; others she wrote only a sentence, but every day she wrote something, inspired by Aunt Sadie's farm journal, which wasn't entirely about plants. What a strange and wonderful gift the record of that woman's life had been—not just to Phoebe, but to each of them. From passionate entries about new men in her life to crushing disappointments most people would never admit, Sadie had recorded her version of the truth. From her notes Nance and Ness learned how to coax the poinsettias into blooming at the right time. Sometimes Phoebe read aloud to all of them, and they debated over what Sadie had meant; other times shared silence was comment enough. Occasionally it was a two A.M. kind of thing, a secret read on the couch because despite belonging to the sorority of Bad Girl Creek, Beryl had often felt alone in her confusion with all her untold secrets. Beryl didn't know why she kept her own journal, really. Obviously she didn't have a niece to hand it down to. And what kind of story would her life make? *Go Ask Beryl What Not to Do.* What she'd written in California wasn't earth shattering, but here in Alaska she was digging down to the bedrock of her life, and it was a stony parcel of land to till. What kind of idiot would voluntarily enter those caves? She couldn't explain the compulsion to herself, so how could she tell anyone else?

"Morning, Red," Thomas Jack said as he came out of the bathroom, a cloud of steam escaping behind him, the white bath towel a striking contrast against his dusky skin. "Got any coffee in this big old house?"

Beryl smiled at his simple beauty, the way his presence filled up the empty spaces of this house. "I thought you'd sleep late."

He grinned. "Yeah, this redhead kept waking me up and having her way with me, you know?"

She smiled. "We had fun." Thomas showing up put an entirely fresh start on New Year's Day. She switched the television off. Thomas's body was muscled and strong, his face far from perfect. The cleft palate scar was one thing. His terribly flat feet were another. He needed glasses, and he snored, though she would never tell him. The night before as they lay in her bed stroking each other and watching the fire in the fireplace, she noticed his heel as if for the first time. His skin color seemed most intense on the place where his ankle curved over the bone, and then lightened to a color that was almost rosy. She'd snaked her body down the bed until she could take his foot in her hand and lay her cheek against the missing arch of his foot. This is where the heart should be, she thought. People would be a lot more careful of it if it beat below that thin surface of skin, if you had to walk on it all the time. Everyone would buy these amazing handmade shoes that fit instead of mass-produced and punched out in narrow widths that pinched and didn't last. Another man might have said something awful, like *Suck my toes, baby* or *Don't waste your talents so far south,* but Thomas Jack only reached down to stroke her hair. When Thomas Jack was there, she didn't think about Earl. She put Earl on hold and tried to ignore the guilt that twisted her insides.

Beryl pointed her pen to the kitchen behind her. "Coffee's still hot. Want a big mug, or do you only have time for a little one?"

Thomas took the towel from around his middle and rubbed his hair with it. Wet, his hair was blacker and showed its true thickness. It took a long time to dry, but he looked at her like she was crazy when she suggested using a blow-dryer on it. She looked at his penis and decided it was probably one of the nicest ones she'd ever seen, no matter what state it was in.

"Sit. I got legs. I been pouring my own coffee for a while now." Then he whistled to Verde, who flapped his wing stubs and whistled back.

Beryl flushed a little when she saw that Thomas had brought *her* a cup. His kindness made her nervous. Earl had been like that in the beginning, letting her pick the restaurant, or saying he was fine with a chick flick instead of seeing the latest guy movie. She kept waiting for the bomb to drop with Thomas, for him to go off on a trip and speak vaguely about his return, and then she'd never see him again. He went everywhere people had birds in trouble, and up here people had parrots in the most unlikely places: Kodiak, Gustavus, Barrow, Little Diomede. She tried to make her voice casual as she said, "Thanks, Thomas," but he looked her in the eye, and they both knew it wasn't just for the coffee.

He set his mug on the table in front of her and reached out for Verde, who spraddle-walked willingly onto his hand, and then said something entirely X-rated. "Ooh. Kind of early in the day for that," Thomas told him. "Let's work on something nicer."

He pronounced a word that sounded to Beryl like it had a click hidden inside it, like one of those penny metal frogs she used to get in gumball machines as a kid. Verde cocked his head, and Beryl set her journal down. "What's that mean?"

"'Hello,' 'nice to see you.' Nothing much, really." He stroked Verde's back, and the bird was quiet. "You writing a book, Red?"

Beryl looked down at her journal, her place marked by an expensive fountain pen Earl had left behind. "Just thoughts. Nothing much, really."

Thomas put Verde back on top of his cage, and Verde screeched his unhappiness. "Settle down," Thomas told him. "You had your turn. Now your mama needs some sugar." He held his arms out to Beryl and wiggled his fingers. "Come on over here," he said. "Come on now."

Beryl sighed. Somehow at night it was easier to admit her needs. In the dark the way she and Thomas comforted each other felt human and necessary, and temporary, too. But throw daylight on sex, well, then she had to admit what she'd done—what they'd done—all that kissing and body parts against each other with this man who was very nearly a stranger—but then again, how well had she known Earl? She slid across the couch into Thomas's arms and he kissed her neck. For the jillionth time she said, "I'm too old for you."

"Trust me," Thomas said huskily, pulling her shirt down to kiss her bare shoulder. "You need a younger man to keep up with you."

They kissed a little, nothing deep, and then they held on to each other and closed their eyes. His skin was warm. Beryl smelled the coffee on the table, and Thomas's own smell, soap and his hair and a little of her own self on him deep enough that it couldn't be washed away with a single shower. In her fifty-some years, she'd slept with only a handful of men. Usually at the first hint of sex, she'd gone running, Moose partly to blame for her skittishness. The memory of her rape was encapsulated, a permanent cocoon that housed something too ugly to allow into the world. At the strangest times it thudded into her life, and no matter where she was, no matter how happy, she was forced to abandon everything to examine it. When she cried hard, or broke up with someone, or lost out on a job she wanted, the memory went dormant, as if it had extracted enough of a price to be satisfied. And when it was hungry again, it would shuck off all the good things she'd managed to accomplish and pass judgment. It had been a while, so she was expecting it. By writing about it in her journal, she hoped to head it off at the pass.

"What kind of stuff you write in there?" Thomas asked.

"What's happened to me over the course of my life."

"Your history?"

She nodded. "I guess."

"Most of the history books I've read are pure lies," Thomas said. "Myself, I'm waiting for a history book written by a Native. Then I'll believe it. Otherwise, I prefer mysteries."

"History has a lot of mystery to it," Beryl offered. "My friend Phoebe, she reads mysteries exclusively. She reads more than anyone I know—" Beryl stopped herself before she added, "except Earl." She'd moved his books to the basement recording studio.

Thomas blinked and rubbed her neck. "Got a lot of knots in here. Thought last night would have taken care of that. We better go back upstairs."

"The coffee—," she started to say.

Thomas shushed her. "Beryl, why else do folks get a microwave oven if not for times like this?"

They lay down on her bed, a rumpled mess of sheets from the previous evening's lovemaking. Now that Earl was gone, Beryl had made the bed hers alone. She'd bought the most expensive sheets Fred Meyer had to offer, and their high thread count provided a softness that was tremendously soothing. Thomas sighed happily as she undressed. Apparently he liked that, her doing it herself, because he didn't help until the very last, and when her shirt was over her head and she was at a disadvantage, he kissed her right there on her . . . what had Phoebe called it? Bird's nest. Beryl liked watching him watching her, and she thought how lucky he was that his body still had that youthful sense of springiness to it, the muscles staying firm even in winter. Thomas had very little body hair, but what he had was dark and straight and soft in her fingers. It seemed like all she had to do was step out of her sweats and let them fall to the floor and Thomas Jack was breathing shallow breaths and staring at her with desire that could only be described as flat-out want. She'd worn the sweats to sleep in, so there was nothing underneath them. She hadn't even had time to wash. Thomas looked at her nakedness and shook his head as if in awe.

"Don't," Beryl said. "I know my body's nothing special. It's old, and gravity's starting to win, so don't pretend with me, Thomas."

He gestured toward his penis. "Does it look like I'm pretending?"

Beryl didn't answer or smile. She'd kept her socks on, and Thomas shook his head. "Got to take care of that," he told her, pulling them off. "I want you good and naked."

Maybe it was a middle-age thing, but how that one gesture touched her. She felt the familiar warmth spread from the pit of her stomach to each of her nerve endings, but it was a faint fire, not yet burning strong. She wanted Thomas close, inside her, but at this time of her life it took her longer to reach the state of readiness that used to wash over her as quickly as a blush. Thomas ran his hand down her flank, cupped her bottom, and gently held her breast as his mouth closed over her nipple. They'd made love a dozen times; already he knew her places and what was off-limits. He knew never to press too hard with his hands, and not to push her into some position she wasn't comfortable with, and strangest of all, he seemed to understand how hard it was for her to begin things, that foreplay to Beryl was just about the scariest thing in the world. She hadn't told him about what had happened to her at sixteen, but she knew that somehow he could tell. And even though time had faded her stretch marks, she'd caught him looking, measuring with his eyes how old they might be, and whether or not he should ask her about children.

As Beryl reached out to touch him, she had to shut her eyes and think of nothing except Thomas in order for her body to make that final leap. Thomas Jack, in this small moment alone with her. Remember his soft voice as he spoke to her bird. How gently he explained Verde's troubles to her in his simple, straightforward way, over and over until she got it. The way he was grateful for her making him dinner, and how he shared the aurora with her and told her stories. How he seemed to live his life fully in the present, to tender himself to her in all of those ways and here, in her bed, too. How thrilling it was to pass that marker with someone, to feel free enough to tease a little bit, how exciting that could be. But all that wasn't enough this morning, so she pulled up from her subconscious a memory of the previous night, of Thomas slipping inside her so easily, the way he held himself so carefully above her, the slight frown on his face from concentrating on delaying his own pleasure in favor of hers. Finally she felt ready, calm enough for his touch, and she nodded to him okay, okay, now, don't hesitate, just take me with you wherever it is you want to go, and he kissed her. Palmed her nipples. Parted her flesh in that astonishing cleft, a finger here, the thumb there, and kissed her, not sloppy but gently, a light pressure, hardly touching, like you would a robin's nest filled with blue eggs, not wanting to disturb the fragile creation yet unable to walk away. He ran his hands up her body and took time to admire her, from her toes to her shoulders; all of it was important to Thomas. Then he knelt between her legs, and she gasped once, and he felt her resist, so he backed off until her breathing was steady, and then once again, he was inside her, and in her mind Beryl pictured this old rowboat, its red paint peeling, its hold teeming with tiny silver fish. The boat was tethered to a dock a man and his sons had constructed of wood from a tree they'd cut down in woods their family had been coming to for generations. Every board on the dock had started out the same size, firmly doweled into the pier—there wasn't a single nail to rust—but time and weather had brought out differences; like children of the same parents, some were handsome, others slightly plain, one or two warped, but all members of the tribe, and equally loved. She felt the boat moving on the tide, bumping gently against the dock. That small sound.

Now that Beryl was older, sex was different. While she moved in time with Thomas against the soft sheets, so many thoughts flitted in and out of her mind she couldn't keep track of them, so why try? She thought how it wasn't really possible to have one-night stands when you were middle aged. How there was the mandatory discussion of diseases, and the condom wrapper on the bed that ended up sticking one or the other of you in the side like a forged permission slip. And how women's bodies really did change with menopause. The slow narrowing of that swift river she'd taken for granted. This business of him inside her was wonderful, but there was another night when Thomas had shown her that so was lying side by side and touching each other, and when she needed to do it herself to show him how, that way was just as nice, if that's what it took to help her find her way. When she felt herself approaching orgasm, she imagined that the rope holding the boat to the dock had come loose, the old knot frayed and loosening, and now the boat was drifting out to its own destination, water lapping against its sides. Her eyes blinked open and looked out through a sheen of dampness as if rain fallen in the night but had stopped by morning. Slowly they took in this gentle man smiling above her, shyly watching her mouth open, and the sound came out of her with fevered reverence: *Oh!* She thought how like a natural pearl orgasm was, a hidden gift pried from the grip of the heart's muscle. And after all this time, and years of rushing toward the release that seemed to elevate the world's goodness and flush anything negative or sorry from the body, it was only now that she had learned not to hurry.

Outside the bare tree limbs sparkled in their blue-white crystalline coats. Thomas Jack dressed by the window, and Beryl delayed pulling her sweats on until he was tying his boots. Downstairs she poured fresh coffee into a mug with a wide bottom, and wrapped biscuits in a napkin for him to eat on the drive to work. "Looks like this here Indian won't starve today," he said, and gave her a kiss.

Outdoors Beryl gasped at the cold. The trees were covered with those white whiskers she liked. "Look at that," she said. "I wonder why we only get this frost sometimes. I wish the trees looked that way all through winter."

Thomas Jack explained. "Some people, they'll go on to tell you how interlocking ice crystals form on items of smaller diameter, like tree branches, in specific. That's history-book stuff. How it comes about the same way as dew collects on grass. Except in this case the branch is already freezing, so the cold air brings the freezing dew point to saturation. When it cools, you got yourself some serious hoarfrost."

"Hoarfrost. Doesn't sound very poetic."

Thomas shrugged. "Don't think science has run into poetry yet. If I think about it, I'm sure I can find you a prettier story, like maybe the frost is really tears from some lady who's so sad she should be spending part of her day crying."

"Very funny."

"Hey, just telling it like I see it." He chucked her under the chin, and Beryl made a face.

"Go feed your birds," she said. "You're not a shrink, but you are one wonderful lover."

"Huh, maybe I should put that in a Yellow Pages ad. Birds and babes a specialty." Thomas opened the Subaru's driver's-side door, then stopped and shut it again. He pushed his glasses up his nose, which was running a little in the cold air. He touched his scar as if the place had more nerve endings than the rest of his face. "What are you going to do all day, Red?"

"I don't know. Why?"

"I'm curious. I might want to think about you, and if I know what you're up to, I can get a clearer picture in my mind."

She laughed. "Well, probably I'll take a shower and wash my hair, and play with Verde, and do the yoga exercises you showed me. Then at some point I'm going to call a taxi and go to the market, since I'm out of paper towels and peanut butter."

Thomas Jack rubbed his nose with a gloved hand. "Beryl, even a poor guy like me has a car. I have to ask you. Why don't you get one?"

"I told you already. I don't know how to drive."

"You could learn," he said. "I said I'd teach you."

She hugged him close. "Thomas, I like you too much to put you through that."

"Your call," he said, and looked at her like he was fixing her image in his mind.

When he'd driven away, Beryl got busy with the shovel. Instead of a short pathway to the mailbox, she tackled the entire driveway. Soon she was stripping off her jacket, her heart racing, damp skin beneath her sweats, and when she stopped to catch her breath, she felt a tingle of exhilaration climb out of all that panic she lived with day in and out. She leaned on her shovel, fighting the urge to run along with some kids on their way down the hill with their sleds. The trees glistened, and when the light played over the snow covering her yard, it glittered like crystalline limestone.

While she showered, she thought of Thomas's suggestion. There were plenty of reasons not to drive: the environment, the cost, insurance. And there were obstacles she didn't want to think about. But suppose Earl never came back? What would she do? Hole up in the Bohemian Waxwing, taking in stray cats until the county descended on her and the newspaper published awful grainy pictures of her messy house?

While she was drying her hair, the phone rang. She grabbed it up and said hello in the same hopeful way she always did.

"Mike Stokes here," the detective said. "How you doing, Ms. Reilly? Notice I got your name right."

"You don't have any news for me today either, do you?" She could tell by the silence that he didn't. "Are we ready to call off this charade now? Stop wasting the city's money and have him declared dead? At some point we really do have to stop this."

He ignored her direct questions, same as always. "Actually,

I was hoping to get you to come pick up your husband's personal effects we found in the truck. We're done with them, and I thought you might want to have them."

She felt her jaw automatically clench. "He wasn't my husband. What personal effects?"

"Oh, you know. Some papers, the contents of the glove box. A cell phone missing the battery."

Beryl put a hand to her neck. "Oh," she said. That explained why no one ever answered.

"I know how it is," the detective went on. "Some women can't face this part. I'll drive the truck up and leave the envelope in the mailbox."

"But I don't—," she began, and Detective Stokes talked right over her.

"You live in that birdhouse, right?"

"Detective Stokes, you've been here at least five times that I know of. If that's a joke, it's getting old."

There was a pause. "Well, no one's ever accused me of being king of the ha-ha's. I'll be by in an hour or so. By the way, I'm bringing you a—"

The static on this phone drove her nuts. "A what?" she asked, but he'd hung up, and Beryl decided if he'd said "hat," he could take it back home with him.

She finished drying her hair, picked up the cups from the morning, washed and dried them, and then sat on the couch with Verde. Her bird was on good behavior, but she could tell he was looking for Thomas Jack. His life was like being the only child of an inept single mother, she imagined, always interviewing for a new daddy. It made her think of Moose, who'd seemed to like Beryl's father. And then she was in the thick of remembering the time she spent at Saint Margaret's.

And the incident with the butter lambs.

They were pure unsalted butter whipped from fresh cream, pressed by spatula into lamb-shaped metal molds. My God! She hadn't thought of them in years.

It was an old mansion turned into a home for unwed mothers. A place far from town where girls in trouble could rest and gestate, and when the time came, give the baby away discreetly. "Here at Saint Margaret's of Cortona," the nun with the pink cheeks told Beryl, "we have only one rule. To become a resident of the house, a girl must fully open her heart to Christ. Do you think you are capable of an open heart, young lady?"

It was a speech, Beryl knew, and all during the drive there, Bette had coached her in how to answer. "Just tell them yes," she said, wiping her eyes with a tissue as she drove. "It doesn't mean anything, really. And if they ask about the father of the baby, Beryl, I know this sounds hypocritical, but I want you to lie. Say it was too dark to see him clearly."

"Why?" Beryl said, her stomach lurching as it had been all morning, as if it couldn't make up its mind whether it was nauseous or hungry.

Bette glanced at her, and she could see the fear in her eyes. "Because people judge."

"Even nuns?"

"Oh, Beryl," Bette said. "Nuns especially."

"My heart is fully open to Christ's love," she said to the old biddy nun.

Bette looked at her, shocked.

"Don't be afraid, Mother," the nun said to Bette. "Christ's love for sinners is infinite. Once your daughter allows Jesus inside her heart, goodness and mercy will follow."

The nun's voice was soft and her body lightly scented, like Avon's lilac talcum powder, or a jasmine hedge in bloom, but too strong, or maybe it was being pregnant that made it seem too harsh to Beryl. "It's only for a few months," Bette said as she signed the necessary papers. The nun led them in the Lord's Prayer, and that was it. Bette drove away. Mother Superior shut the door to the office and then things changed.

"We expect you to use this time wisely," the pink-cheeked nun said. "To turn your life around from your current shame to a state of grace."

Beryl was used to wearing the mantle of shame. It wasn't like the nun could say anything to make her feel any worse. "What's your name?" Beryl asked.

The woman looked startled. "Why, I'm Sister Odilia, mother superior here at Saint Margaret's. However, I prefer that the girls call me Mother."

"Odilia. I've never heard that name before. Were you named after a relative?"

The nun smiled, and her face crinkled like tissue paper, filled with tiny wrinkles that stayed after the smile faded. "Odilia's my chosen name," she said. "I hold myself up to her example. I strive to be worthy of her name and all it means. Do you know the lives of the saints?"

Beryl shook her head no.

The nun looked at her pityingly. "No matter, child. You can read about the lives of the saints in our library."

A library! Now she was talking. Beryl could stand the place for a few months so long as she had something to read. "I will," she said. "I love to read."

"Now that you've mentioned names," Mother said, leafing through an ornately decorated leather book, "Let's settle on yours. I think . . . here you will be called Bee, in honor of Saint Bega, the patroness of labors."

Beryl waited. Was she supposed to say thank you for having her identity erased?

"Let's kneel for a moment, shall we?" Mother said, and Beryl did, though the hardwood floors were gritty from whatever her shoes had carried in, and it hurt her knees. Mother remained standing. She shut her eyes and smiled. "Like you, Bega was also Irish. She was quite radiant, I'm told, whereas you have squandered your beauty and now are paying the price."

Beryl opened her eyes and looked at her, shocked. What was this? All the kindness sloughing off to reveal rot within? Bette had told her Beryl was raped. Did she think they'd lie to a nun? "Excuse me?"

The nun continued as if she hadn't heard the question. "Bega was good. She loved our Lord faithfully. She held on to her chastity for dear life, as any woman betrothed to Christ must do. Many men tried to seduce her. She was forced into marriage vows with a prince who took her aboard ship and set sail for Norway, but Bee prayed to God to spare her a carnal life, and the angels heard her prayers. They blessed her with a bracelet marked with the sign of the cross, and gave her the courage to jump overboard, though she was miles from shore."

Beryl unfolded her hands and let them fall to her sides. "Come on. That's a folktale. How could a person stay alive in the ocean?"

The nun was ratcheted up now, her sentences spilling into one another and growing higher in pitch. "Gulls fed her. Gannets tended her. When she washed ashore in Cumberland, she covered her nakedness with a piece of sod and at once knelt on the very spot, making her vows. Bee built a monastery, taking in laundry and mending to gain the necessary funds . . ."

No wonder Bette quit going to church, Beryl thought. This stuff is worse than the brothers Grimm.

"Now, I'm sure you doubt me, don't you, Bee? You're thinking this is some kind of fairy story I'm telling you. But every word is true. Her bracelet still exists, a holy relic to which believers make pilgrimages. When someone swears an oath on the bracelet of Saint Bega, you can be sure they will keep that promise. I swear to you, Bee, that during your time with us we will teach you to scour your heart until it is as bright and shining and worthy a vessel for the Lord's love as was the saint you are now named after. Do you have any questions?"

The gravel beneath her knees was harder than diamonds. Beryl's legs shook, and she needed to pee. She wanted to know what a gannet was, but knew that was the wrong question. "Please help me," she said to mother superior, and she could tell by the nun's smile, that was exactly the right thing to say. After a few Hail Marys, Odilia allowed Bee to get up.

The molded butter lambs were made to sell, not for profit, but for the church that sponsored the home. They were made year-round, but apparently reserved for truly special occasions, and the girls weren't allowed to do anything besides whip the cream and ladle it into the molds which clamped shut with a latch mechanism that more often than not pinched a finger in the process. As a special treat for the priests, they were sent to the rectories around the holidays. Butter lambs for bishops and cardinals and whoever else was high and holy and not pregnant.

"I can't stand it," Dymphna, who used to be Debbie, said as she finished kitchen duty and joined the others in Bee's room. One thing the girls had agreed on was that the nuns were out to starve them. Instead of gobs of institutional starches like macaroni and cheese, they were served small portions of plain food. Rice, meat loaf, vegetables boiled into tasting all the same. Sometimes there was bread on the table, but rarely butter, and never a butter lamb. Outside on the windowsill Helena, who used to be Hayley, had hidden a pack of Winstons. Bee had stolen five Blue Tip matches—the kind that lit when you struck them against a rough surface—from the big box in the kitchen. She'd learned to flick the business end with her thumbnail so well she reminded herself of the tough girls who hung out in the high school rest rooms. Beryl would see them when she went in to use the john. Everyone else seemed to wait until gym class to pee, but Beryl didn't see why she should wreck her bladder just because someone was smoking in the stall next door.

"I spent the last hour ladling new butter into lamb tins," Dymphna said. "I had this plan that at the end, I'd at least get to lick my fingers, you know? So who comes along but Mother Odor herself, and stands there while I wash my hands. That dried-up old bitch! What does she need butter for? It would take a lake of cold cream to get any juice into her wrinkled old carcass."

Everyone laughed except Elly, who was due anytime now. She let out a shocked gasp. "Dymphny, you can't say things like that! God's listening."

"Like God cares," she said, placing her hands on her lower back and grimacing. "Somehow I doubt he gives a rat's ass about my evil thoughts."

"You shouldn't laugh," Elly said. "God hears everything."

"Everything but me begging not to be pregnant," Helena said, lighting a cigarette and blowing the smoke out the window.

Everyone laughed at that, but soon after, their faces resumed the bland resignation that got them through the days. Dymphna took a drag from Elly's smoke and exhaled. "Cigs just don't do much for me," she said. "I wish they did."

"At least they help keep me from being hungry," Helena countered.

Bee looked around the room. "How many in this room are hungry?"

All hands shot up, even Elly's.

"How many would like a butter lamb?"

All hands stayed where they were, but Elly's went down. "Quit being a pious little shit," Helena said. "You know you want one."

Elly raised her hand up, but she was near tears.

"All right," Bee said. "One butter lamb coming up. I'll bring back a loaf of bread with it."

"You wouldn't dare," Elly said. "If you got caught, they could send you home."

"And tell me how home could be any worse than this," Bee answered.

In the kitchen the tiles were clean, the stainless-steel food prep tables dry and tidy. The food cupboards had locks on them, the kind Beryl had used on her school locker. In the days before he became a rapist, Moose had taught her how to pick locks. But she didn't want to get caught over a box of cereal or leave cracker crumbs behind like evidence. She went to the industrial-size fridge and opened it. Gallons of milk. An enormous container of cream. The yellow plastic gallon tub of the cheapest, most awful margarine. Behind it, however, four butter lambs, released from their molds and wrapped in waxed paper, maybe for the nuns' own secret feast. It was Bee who stole them. Beryl would have gone hungry. But like Mother Odor had told her on the first day of her imprisonment, Bega was the bravest kind of woman, denying herself any kind of life to assure closeness with God. She wrapped the lambs in another sheet of waxed paper and tucked a loaf of Wonder Bread under her arm. She walked boldly up the stairs as if that was exactly what she was supposed to be doing. It was time for communion, all right. Past time.

Their faces when they saw what she brought made the theft worth it. They gorged and licked every last bit from their hands. Elly cried and worried about sinning, and Helena told her that was stupid; no God would ever fault a hungry pregnant woman for feeding her baby. Bee cut the waxed paper into small enough pieces to flush down the toilet. The bread bag was plastic, and harder to conceal. Then Dymphna told Bee, "Give it to me. If we get caught, I'll say I did it. My baby's due anytime now. I have nothing to lose."

It was a small crime, Bee told herself, as she lay in bed that night, waiting until morning to start the same boring routine all over again. The first of many crimes she would get away with at Saint Margaret's of Cortona. Every subsequent caper was easier. *I'm only trying to live up to my namesake,* she would say if anyone asked her. *This I swear on the bracelet of Saint Bega.*

That afternoon dusk came a few minutes later. Every day Alaska was gaining a few minutes more of light. Beryl picked up her mail and found a manila envelope from Detective Stokes tucked far back in the mailbox. She tore it open, and out fell Earl's house keys, grimy with fingerprint powder. The cell phone, its backside gaping. His hands had touched these. She threw them on the table as if they were filthy. There were receipts from Mammoth Music, Fred Meyer, faded credit-card receipts, and a guitar pick worn thin along the edges. She left it all on the table and unpacked the groceries. Detective Stokes had left a message on her answering machine. *Ms. Reilly, did you know you have mice in your garage? Don't feel bad; everybody on the Hillside has them. I've left you a spare cat inside the garage. Her name is Beatrice. Her mother was a champion mouser. Give me a call if she doesn't work out. Det. Mike Stokes.*

Mice. Why not? She fingered Earl's cell phone and tried to match up his voice-mail recording with this useless piece of equipment. She'd gotten so used to thinking the phone was with him. She had imagined that sooner or later he would pick up, and she could have her questions answered. Or if somebody else had the phone, sooner or later they'd try to use it, and then it was a matter of tracing calls, like those cop shows on television. She didn't need to be an FBI agent to think that up. Scratch that plan. Outside the window the snow was deep, the white mounds reminding her of meringue, of Bette making her famous lemon pie.

In nooks and crannies the snow was shadowy and creepy. She dialed the cell phone from her house phone, and when the out-of-range message tone chimed, she said, "Fuck you, Earl. What you did, leaving that way, it's cowardly," and she hung up.

The next morning Beryl got out the Yellow Pages and hefted them onto her lap. They weighed about as much as a baby, and she flashed on the time hers had been born, that unwanted child, conceived in violence yet innocent, and she hated herself for not loving it, for refusing to look at it. *Hold him once so you can say goodbye,* the nurse urged her, but Beryl had shut her eyes tight. Then he'd made this little noise, and she knew if she were ever to hear his voice, no matter how many years later, she'd be able to pick him out of any crowd. Suddenly every dark angel in the world was on her, picking at her skin, whispering in her ear all sorts of memories she'd banished when she left Saint Margaret's. She needed to talk to another person, but it had to be someone who didn't know her, someone who could listen and nod, but not judge what she'd done.

You could get a massage, she told herself. *Call a taxi; go downtown to the galleries, or the museum, just walk among the living. Join the bookstore group.* But she couldn't make herself take that first step. I'll call a crisis line, she decided, someplace where I can remain anonymous, and all they'll do is refer me to someone else after they hear what I have to say. But she flipped the pages too fast, bypassing the *C*'s, landing instead on Driving Schools. *Earn your Alaska Driver's License in Twelve Lessons or Your Money Back.* Earl's truck was just sitting there. She made the call, and scheduled her first lesson for Monday. The school was only a block south of the market. Her instructor's name, they said, was Zoë.

Then she went downstairs to let in the cat, which was sleeping on the hood of Earl's truck. She looked so much like Hester Prynne, Earl's cat, who'd either run off or been killed by a car, but whose welfare had seemed so unimportant at the time that Beryl began to cry all the tears Thomas said she needed to. She sat on the step that led upstairs and made noise and cussed almost as good as Verde. When she was finished, she let the cat in and they went upstairs. The cat explored, and Beryl lay down on the couch, covered herself with a blanket, and slept.

Phoebe

6

Just a Potter

"SEE HOW RELAXED SHE IS?" Nance said to Phoebe as they watched Sally taking her first official English riding lesson on Penelope. "That's half the trick to staying on. If she does fall, it's into soft sand. And the helmet will protect her little head. Not to worry, Phoebe. These days girls begin riding hunt seat as soon as they turn three."

"When Sally was three she was still peeing her pants. What kind of parent puts a three-year-old on top of a horse? If she wants a trophy, I can order her one from a jewelry store, for God's sake."

Nance turned and looked at her sister-in-law and in her face Phoebe saw only wonder. "Pheebs, Sally is plain horse-crazy. Give her a choice between talking and whinnying, she'll whinny. She carries her lunchbox by the handle, in her teeth. Wouldn't you rather have her riding a pony that's safe, and taking lessons with a trainer than sneaking across Valley Road to the winery horses, riding them without you knowing?"

"Sally would never do that. She knows she's not allowed to cross Valley Road by herself."

Nance pursed her lips. "I hate to burst your bubble—"

Phoebe gasped and gripped the armrests of her chair. "Tell me you're making that up."

"Honey, I wish I were. The only reason you didn't hear about it was that the foreman recognized her, called James directly, and you were already having such a bad day James and I decided you didn't need to know."

Phoebe sighed so long and so deep she felt as if her heart had hitchhiked out on her breath. She pulled her jacket closer around her neck. It was one of those gray winter days, and suddenly it had gotten a lot grayer. If she had to stick one more silk Valentine into one more decorative pot filled with crocus bulbs she was going to flip her lid. They'd had to lower the price by one whole dollar to stay even with the local florists. Yet there were orders stacked up, and the minute they finished Valentine's Day, they had to get going on the Saint Patrick's Day pots of oxalis, which featured a really ugly clay leprechaun that was also a device to make certain the plant had enough water, and Nance's new plan for the Easter basket delivery service was a monumental undertaking that made her think vile thoughts about rabbits and those marshmallow Peeps in particular. This riding business—now that she'd allowed Sally the lessons—had seemed like pure insanity. But if her wild daughter was crossing highways to slide under the winery's fence, then maybe she had to calm down and look at it differently. Wouldn't it just happen to be the same winery that had leased several acres to a new nursery just aching to give them competition? Oh, poop. Too many worries to fit in my head, she thought. It was easy for Nance to say her daughter would emerge intact.

No, it wasn't easy at all.

She couldn't blithely dismiss Nance keeping Sally's transgression secret—nothing was easy for Nance, really. The thing she wanted most in the world was out there riding a pony, getting private lessons guaranteed to instill a long-lived National Velvet complex. Phoebe guessed it beat a lot of things, growing up too fast one of them. Still, it would have been a lot easier to watch the lesson if she'd had a Valium in her. "Hey, *you're* originally Southern," she said to Nance, who was leaning against the fence watching Sally's every move. "Explain something to me."

"If I can," Nance said. "Remember, my biggest Southern influence came from a crazy alcoholic mother."

"Relax. I'm not asking you to get my daughter into Ole Miss." Phoebe admired her sister-in-law, clad in designer jeans and suede jacket that showed off her always-trim figure. Her hair was cut to neck length, curved gently under, and did not blow about in the wind into an unholy rat's nest like Phoebe's was currently doing. "It's about Andrew," she said.

"Oh, goodie!" Nance said. "I promised myself I wouldn't ask until you said something. I'm just dying to know how the Christmas thing went. Did he try to kiss you?"

Phoebe gave her a look. "Why is it everyone is so interested in my sex life? Especially a person who has one of her own?"

"James and I just want you to be happy," Nance said, so sincerely that Phoebe felt immediately sheepish.

"Okay, if you count a peck on the cheek, he ravished my blush powder. What do you think is the deal with him? Somebody that good looking, just moving to Bayborough and leaving behind generations of relatives and warm weather. Bad divorce? White-collar crime? Recently released from the sanatorium?"

Nance plucked a tiny errant hair from her lipsticked mouth. "I don't know any more than you do."

"Ha. Remember now, lying's a sin. What you don't tell me you'll have to confess. Come on, Nance. Spill. I don't want to get myself entangled with somebody who's using me for filler until he can get an able-bodied woman to look beyond his chair. I know he was engaged at one time."

Nance reached out and patted Phoebe's shoulder. Her enormous yellow diamond ring glinted in the sun and for a second Phoebe felt absurdly jealous. "That's true. He was engaged."

"And I know she broke it off."

"Look at me!" Sally yelled, and they turned to admire her posting the trot.

"Very nice, honey!" Phoebe called. Then under her breath, "If she falls and breaks something you are going to have to scrape me up with a putty knife."

"Your kid's a natural," Nance said. "Look at her leg. She rides like a sack of potatoes, which means she's learned how to keep her weight balanced. In no time she's going to be trotting over cavallettis and fences, Phoebe."

Phoebe ignored this comment meant to distract her from her mission. She did not know and did not wish to know what a cavalletti was, or how it was someone trotted over one. "Who did whom dirt in the breakup? Did she really tell him she couldn't marry him after his accident? Or did he tell me that so I'd feel sorry for him?"

Nance sighed. "The way I heard it—and this is gossip from Rebecca Roth, mind you—Andrea flew out, kept a vigil by his bedside, and then when the doctor broke the news that Andrew wasn't going to walk again, the lovely, well-bred Andrea waited until Andrew was asleep, left the ring on his bedside table, and hauled butt back to Atlanta. Andrew had to be sedated. I think they were engaged from age five on. Families the best of pals, et cetera."

"That's evil," Phoebe said. She watched Sally for a moment, taking note of her little hand reaching down to pat the pony's neck every time she did what Sally asked her to. "So how long ago was this breakup? I need to get a picture of the time frame, in order to rule out rebound romances, my handicap is your handicap, outright pity, and so on."

Nance laughed. "Good Lord, Phoebe! You have the most suspicious mind I've ever come across. You're right up there with Rotten Rick. With that devious a mind you're the one who should try to write books."

"Hey," Phoebe said. "Call me names until the cows come home, but don't compare me to that loser. I'm a mother. That's an automatic gold star. For all I know this Andrew fellow could be a child kidnapper, selling babies to the slave trade."

Nance let out an exasperated sigh. "Andrea was fourth-generation Southern debutante. Daddy a heart surgeon, mother an interior designer. What she did besides get herself engaged to Andrew I have no idea, but her leaving was hard on Andrew. Apparently he went a little nuts. Under the circumstances I believe he was entitled." She placed a palm on her stomach and looked sad. "Dammit."

"Damn what?"

She looked at Phoebe, and tears were gathered in her eyes. "I feel all crampy and cranky and I think I'm getting my goddamn period again and I just hate my goddamn reproductive system having a will of its own, goddammit." She stopped to look at Sally once more. "Sweetie," she called out. "You're looking aces up there. Anytime now you're going to be jumping fences. Come over after your lesson and we'll have us a Cherry Coke."

I am worse than Rotten Rick, Phoebe thought as she watched her sister-in-law slowly make her way to her own house, successfully avoiding puddles. It was hard for her to imagine this Andrea's leaving her fiancé simply because he'd lost the ability to walk, but on the other hand, at least she hadn't led him on. Perfectly visible people in the walking world sat down in a wheelchair and turned transparent, she knew. People just didn't see them anymore. Either way the breakup was a good thing. Andrea and Andrew—they sounded like matching dolls, for Pete's sake. She tried to reconcile Nance's information with the facts of Andrew's life, but certain parts didn't add up. Successful potter, at least doing well enough he could move to ultra-spendy Bayborough-by-the-Sea. How did he manage that? Did he make pots only for the rich and famous? Maybe he dealt drugs. Potter who bodysurfs his way into a wheelchair. Shows up at James's party, asks her out, clearly on a date. Fancy Christmas party with a jazz band, and a catered dinner she wouldn't soon forget. And what was the fuel behind all of it? Love of his life walked when he couldn't. Phoebe waved at Sally, who was now walking Penelope, this blasé look on her face that gave Phoebe a start. How could a six-year-old manage to look that jaded? She decided not to say anything about the dash across Valley Road just now. If she'd learned anything about raising this child, it was that she had a conscience, and if Phoebe gave her time, eventually Sally came to her and confessed. "You looked wonderful up there," she called to her daughter.

The horse trainer, a willowy Asian girl with a butch haircut she gelled to stick up in spikes, had been recommended by Ness. It had taken all of five minutes for Phoebe to trust her. When she walked in the barn, the horses blew and snorted and danced on their hooves, thrilled to death that someone who knew what she was doing had finally arrived. "You're hired," she had said. "Please don't quit on me until my daughter stops worshiping horses."

Sally took the pony into the barn and began grooming her. Without the trainer telling her to, Phoebe noted.

Mimi and Sally waved to Phoebe. "Adios," she said. "Munchkin, tell *Mamí* we're going to the aquarium to look at the seahorses, and out for dead cow burgers and ice cream after. Tell her she doesn't know what she's missing by staying home and eating vegetables."

"Bye, Mom! Take care of Penelope for me! Give her some carrots, okay?"

Phoebe waved. "I will guard her with my life. You two have fun." Sally looked thrilled at the possibility of so many mother-free hours, she thought. She'd meant to go along, but at the last minute, backed out because for the first time in months, she'd felt an urge to work with clay. As soon as the car pulled away, she wheeled herself across the flagstones to the small workshop James had built for her at the same time he was finishing his house. From the outside it looked like a fairy-tale dwelling, redwood siding weathering to a lovely gray, curvy slate roof, and a stone facade covering the chimney. The doorway was wide enough for her chair, the top of the door arched, its latch cast iron, ornately shaped, and easy for her to lift. Inside there was a low sink, a table just the right height, and shelves for drying pieces. Behind one door a full bathroom with a wheelchair-accessible shower for messy days. Behind another, a top-of-the-line kiln she'd never fired up. Never felt the need to, until she met Andrew.

"Tell me about your work," she'd asked him on the drive to the Christmas party. He was driving a late-model Thunderbird, a big black car fitted with hand controls. Their wheelchairs sat in the backseat, cozy as a couple of robots. "I want to know what you do with yourself besides drink Co-cola."

He waved his hand. "I told you, I'm a potter. My stuff is nowhere near as nice as yours. You're the artist. I'm only a craftsman."

"Craftsman in what way? Do you make ceramic mugs for the tourist trade? Terra-cotta flowerpots? I can't picture this unless you tell me the details. Or see your studio."

He smiled at her and lifted his eyebrows suggestively. "Well, well. Already you're asking me to show you my etchings. You California women are so forward."

"Hush," she said, blushing. "Can I help it if mysteries drive me crazy?"

He laughed. "After the party I'll show you my studio. No funny business, I promise. But I think you'll be disappointed. It's just a work space, that's all."

And then the party was so distracting she'd nearly forgotten. The house was *the* house—the Frank Lloyd Wright dwelling that sat on a bluff overlooking the costliest stretch of beach for miles around. The home was a landmark in Bayborough-by-the-Sea—there were postcards of it for sale in the tourist shops. It had been used in a couple of well-known movies, the most famous being *A Summer Place*. Phoebe could not look at the house without hearing Sandra Dee ask Troy Donahue if he was a "bad boy," if he did bad things with girls. Its copper roof had aged to a spotty green patina. All around the house were narrow windows at the same height, like half-closed eyes, as if they were so dazzled by the sea view that they couldn't take it all in at once. "How do you know the people who own this place?" Phoebe asked. "I've lived here for decades and I don't."

Andrew directed Phoebe inside and wheeled in behind her. Immediately he was shaking hands with people, while Phoebe just sat there entertaining thoughts about tandem bikes and the potential for tandem wheelchairs, and wondering if Andrew was one of those rare paraplegics who retained some sensation below the belt. When he'd finished schmoozing, he took her hand and introduced her to the same beautiful people Phoebe had met at James's party. They looked to be in their late seventies; the silver-haired man had silver bushy eyebrows, a lovely tan, and was dressed in a cream-colored suit with shirt and tie to match. He smiled broadly at her, his teeth so white and even Phoebe thought for a second about having hers bleached. He turned slightly to introduce his wife, and she was gorgeous, too, with long white hair pulled up into a Gibson girl bun, and pearl teardrop earrings the size of grapes. She wore a pale gray satin dress and a single strand of pearls that perfectly matched the earrings. The necklace lay evenly across the front of her dress, and she wasn't even five pounds overweight. "Phoebe," Andrew said, when the couple had finished introducing themselves—Snoop and Evie Callahan. "These are my parents. When they retired they bought this house. I was visiting them when I had my accident."

Not just rich, swimming in it, Phoebe thought, and they'd give every penny if it made Andrew walk again. She transferred herself from her chair to the window seat. It was covered in a blue-and-white flowered chintz, the cushions firm and just long enough to take a nap on. She stretched out her legs and did the breathing-stretching exercises her physical therapist had taught her. They really helped relax her cramped muscles, and as she limbered up, she felt warmth spread to her toes and fingers. Stretching five times a day, he'd told her, was the key to rejuvenating the long-dormant muscle beds, and while Phoebe could see the truth in his words, so was a day away from Miss Question Box. *How come you went out with that man, Mama? Did you see me brush Penny's mane? Mama, I need leather boots to ride. Mama, are you listening to me? Mama, why don't I have a daddy like Sabrina H. at gymnastics?*

The answers to every question were the same: Because Juan died; because Juan wanted me to be happy. As interchangeable as peas in the succotash she made and Sally refused to eat. *Mama, I can't eat the salad. It grew in the dirt!* Big crocodile tears on cue, and the little sneak had even figured out that Uncle James and Aunt Nancy were number two on the speed dial.

Phoebe needed to work on her clay ladies, even though they were beginning to bore her silly. People still bought them. Not just at Little People, which carried all kinds of statuary, but at the Roth Gallery as well. And after her date with Andrew—he'd sent her flowers the next day, roses, as if she needed flowers—she couldn't stop thinking of his so-called pots.

"So, you left out the part about your parents being billionaires," Phoebe said when they left the noise of the party and wheeled outside on the deck. Under the heat lamps she felt perfectly warm, and the smell of the ocean in her nose, the sound of the waves in her ears, was more intoxicating than champagne. "I guess you thought that wasn't worth mentioning."

"Well, gosh. I was just minding my manners. Does it matter to you whether a person has a set amount of money?"

"Not really, Andrew. It's just that I don't get invited to the Frank Lloyd Wright house every weekend. And didn't you tell me you got a last-minute invite to this party? I don't like liars, though I find myself telling all manner of lies now that I have Sally. 'Sure, honey, you can have a car when you turn sixteen, sure, you can wear makeup, sure, you can become a fashion model,' stuff like that, but those are harmless lies, not gapingly huge sins of omission like you just got the invitation."

Andrew cocked his head and smiled at her as if she were far more interesting than the jillion-dollar view. "You are the funniest woman I've ever met."

She tried to stamp her foot, but her legs were tired and her foot would only tap. "I am not funny. I am pissed off, and you might want to explain things to me if you want to go on a second date or kiss me or even get your potter's hands anywhere near me or my—oops. Where's the delete key for conversation? Never mind."

Andrew laughed and laughed, and pretty soon Phoebe had started laughing, too. In the background the ocean roared, and it was just another winter day for the water and the tides. The fish swam, the sand drifted, and somewhere in all of that Aunt Sadie's ashes traveled slowly over the ocean floor.

Andrew set his glass down on a teakwood table. "Sugar, this is my first Christmas without Andrea. I told my folks I didn't want a lot of fuss. You know how it can be. How angry it makes a person to see that the world hasn't held still for your own loss. I had the invitation all along. I just hadn't made up my mind about attending."

Phoebe felt bad that she'd hassled him at James's party. "I'm sorry. It took me four years to venture forth. And then it was to an Arnold Schwarzenegger movie with, of all people, my Rolfer! I couldn't tell you what that movie was about, I was so guilt stricken and nervous to be in public with someone other than . . ." She made herself say it. "Juan. Say you accept my apology or push my chair over the cliff, okay?"

Andrew took a sip of his drink. "No need to apologize. Isn't this one heck of a nice night? Not too cool. It's nothing like the South at this time of year. I'm sure glad I ventured forth. How about you, Miss DeThomas?"

"I will be as soon as I stop trying to shove my foot down my throat," Phoebe said. "So are your parents big fans of Frank Lloyd Wright or something?"

He nodded his head yes and looked out toward the water. "Daddy's got a thing for fancy houses. He'll hang on to it until he and Mummy miss the South, and then sell it for a ridiculous profit and give the money to charity. I hope you won't hold his money against us becoming friends."

She felt her throat constrict. That wasn't just money, it was *money*. "I think we can be friends," she said. "So long as you don't buy my daughter a horse."

He laughed. "Not to worry."

Phoebe opened Sadie's journal and leaned on one elbow to read just a few pages before she started to work the brown clay she'd set out. The oversize book was stuffed with newsprint clippings, pressed flowers, marginal notes, and drawings; her aunt's deepest worries and happiest moments. The only thing that wasn't there was photographs, and Phoebe was glad, because having to picture the people named in her mind was so damn much fun it had to beat old Kodak photos with crimped edges. Phoebe kept the journal in the studio so it would stay safe from Sally's sticky hands and scented marker pens. Despite care some of the pages were yellowing, and she worried the day would come when it would fall to pieces in her fingers. She read:

Phoebe's coming for the Labor Day weekend and I couldn't be more thrilled. I love that child as if she were my own. James, too, of course, but Phoebe, she's an old soul. I can see it in her eyes, all those past lives and loves, all that joyous full-fledged living. She's lonely right now, but I think she's going to have the most marvelous life. The day will come when she wakes up to the fact that she's a beautiful young woman, as capable of love as any of us. . . .

Phoebe thumbed through the pages, skipping ahead years. Here it was, the first mention of illness:

I hope this darn charley horse I've got in my lower back settles down so Phoebe and I can do some shopping. I swear, if it doesn't quit by Monday I'm going to have to call Lester and cajole him into prescribing more muscle relaxants. . . .

Of course the pain hadn't gone away, and had turned out to be not a charley horse but the cancer that had begun in her colon and cruelly spread to her bones. Phoebe remembered Lester saying that he was surprised Sadie had been able to withstand the discomfort, and Sadie telling him, *Oh, I've had worse. All I felt was a nagging pinch. I thought it was a sprain.* A sprain. A car wreck. A date. Life was filled with surprises, not all of them pleasant. She closed the book and got back in her chair, rolling over to the stereo to turn on some music to work by. She chose Van Morrison, whom she loved above all others. His voice offered the sexy Irish lilt, the occasional low growl, and long, strung-out notes that broke her heart in their earnestness. Van was the only one she could listen to sing love songs. Van was her man. He hadn't let her down yet.

Andrew's place was just up the road from his parents' place, and they had decided the night was nice, so why not roll over instead of drive? His house turned out to be one of those small cottages Phoebe referred to as a "one." One block from the water, it had one bedroom, a one-car garage, and cost well over one million. He'd made some conversions to accommodate his chair, Phoebe noticed. Small fridge placed down low, bars to grab onto in the bathroom, doorway thresholds planed flat, stuff that made life so much easier for crips like them, which the able-bodied rarely considered. Andrew had opened doors and showed her his place very briefly, then led her out on a small stone patio toward what looked like a guest house. The sky was wild from here, Phoebe thought, that indigo blue of winter with wispy gray clouds teasing across the moon. On first glimpse she decided that if Andrew's studio were a painting, it would have been van Gogh's *Starry Night*. The floor was concrete stained indigo; there were two walls of river rock, and two walls of concrete. Every window was leaded glass, screenless, and opened to let in the sea air along with the view of the Pacific. It was too dark to see the water, but in front of the window the sea fingered its way into the room, leaving a wonderful salt smell that lingered like costly perfume. There was a stone fire pit in the very middle of the enormous room, a chimney rising up from there through the roof, and beside the pit, a leather chaise and Pendleton blanket.

The walls that didn't have shelves filled with enormous bisque-fired vessels—some as tall as Sally—were covered with paintings, all of them at least three feet wide, a few scribbled sketches here and there, but mostly finished paintings of seascapes, yet far from the typical "sailboat on the water" fare. These were photorealist, such a close scrutiny of the shoreline that Phoebe was reminded of the way Edward Weston photos of tide pools made her think of moonscapes. "Jesus," Phoebe said.

"Nope, just early Andrew," he answered, and for just a moment she saw his mouth twist before returning to its usual grin. "You want some cocoa? I have one of those instant hot-water taps. Only take me a jiffy to make it."

Phoebe held on to the arms of her chair. "Got marshmallows?"

"Wouldn't be cocoa without them, now would it, darlin'?"

They had drunk cocoa and sat in the middle of all that intense art, neither one saying a word. For once, Phoebe thought, I'm keeping my mouth shut.

Phoebe had the rough shape of the figure in her hands, completed. The shoulders were broad, the hips narrow, the legs—she knew she was obsessed with them—bent slightly, the feet long and tapered, and just the suggestion of toes. She knew it was a man's body, but it wasn't Juan's. She set it down, wiped her hand on her smock, and picked up a tool to go to work on the face.

Sadie, she said to herself, *I could use a little advice. This An-*

drew character—is it real or is it a pastime until he accepts his handicap? Her aunt used to come to her in dreams; she used to feel her presence lingering. But when Sally arrived, all that had stopped, and Phoebe found she missed the visits the same way she missed alcohol, which Lester had forbidden her to drink more than once a week since her heart attack seven years earlier. *Your heart doesn't need any extra strain,* he said. Well, it doesn't need a lot of things, she mused, like Andrew Callahan and his stormy art. She forged ahead, telling Sadie her troubles, her hand moving smoothly across the clay, gently shaping, until it was his face beneath her thumb, and she could almost hear his Cracker voice, his deep rumbly laugh such a contrast to the dark paintings.

She thought of what Andrew had said to her on the drive home. She was sitting there, watching the magical world transform back to the ordinary, when Andrew switched off the radio. He cleared his throat, and she looked at him. "Before you say anything," he said. "I want to make something clear. I don't paint anymore. If I could get those in my studio down, I'd pitch them in the ocean. Do you understand?"

"No."

He made an irritated sound that came out like a groan. "What I mean is, can you accept it?"

She'd thought a while before answering. She'd taken into account all she knew about him—the Co-cola with peanuts, the fabulously rich family, the shallow fiancée, the easy laugh that seemed only to be hiding a very real and close-to-the-surface agony. "Andrew," she said. "Around here you can't just go throwing things into the ocean."

"Why not?"

"For one thing, it's littering. And for another, my aunt lives there."

The crocus arrives just when winter's grown so old that we've forgotten why it is we love our sweethearts. Through the snow it pushes its bud, a hardy harbinger of spring. Varieties include the well-known light purple, blue, white and a sunny, golden shade of yellow. Approximately four thousand crocus stigmas are required to produce a single ounce of saffron, the world's most expensive spice. But few know that saffron was also once used to gild the pages of prayer books. A delicacy to man and beast, the crocus is a favorite snack of mice and rats. *Krókos,* the Greek name for saffron, has a tender legend regarding its origin. It's said that Zeus and Hera, in a particularly passionate coupling, so heated the ground beneath them that on their leavetaking, the earth simply exploded with crocuses.

Beryl

7
Driving Lessons

It was late January in Anchorage, a time when Beryl felt sure the light was never coming back. She stood in her snowy driveway waiting for Zoë Pratt, her driving instructor, to pick her up for her first lesson. It was supposed to last an hour, but Beryl felt sure she would fail in less than half that time.

"Get out of town!" Zoë said. "You live in the Nuthatch?"

For a moment, Beryl hesitated in the snowy driveway she'd spent two hours clearing and, if the sky was any indication of weather, would soon need to do again. "The nuthatch is a wonderful little bird. He might be stout, and look as if he's wearing rust-colored underpants, but in the bird world, he's a marvel. If a person is lucky enough to have a nuthatch come to her yard, she might notice that unlike other birds, the nuthatch works his way headfirst down the trunk of a tree. It's an unusual approach, and probably to some it looks crazy, but in the long run, the bird catches more insects."

This Zoë person stared at her, trying not to smile. "You should be on that show *Jeopardy*. You'd rock in the bird category." She laughed, and then apologized. "Sorry, I can't help it. Do you teach high school biology or something?"

"No, I don't." Oh, what was the point of trying to learn to

drive? For that matter, did she really want to get in a car with a person who thought birds were a joke? Was learning to drive in snow and ice the best way to face her fear of automobiles? Thomas Jack had promised he would teach her, but he was either working at the bird center all hours of the night or flying to various places instate to help wayward birds get back on the straight and narrow. This woman's brassy hair looked as if she'd poured a bottle of hydrogen peroxide on it, and her makeup—even if the Cleopatra look was back, it was a travesty to muck up what were otherwise perfect Audrey Hepburn eyes. Beryl thought how Nance would have screeched at her tarty outfit and exposed cleavage. Not to mention that her electric blue nail polish had glitter in it. Or that on her right pinky nail there was what looked like a decal of the Grateful Dead dancing bear. "The house's name is Bohemian Waxwing," Beryl said. "The man who built it was married to a world-class bird-watcher whose favorite bird was the waxwing, which is why it's painted bright red under the wings and on the back. Do you have something against birds?"

"Well, I like fried chicken," Zoë said, and laughed a laugh that ended in a cigarette cough. "Hop in; I'm freezing my butt off with the door open."

Beryl got in the green Subaru, locked her seat belt, and took a breath. This was it. No turning back. She'd written a check. She would grit her teeth, master driving, and then—well, by the time she earned her license, surely she'd know what to do next. "What happens today?" she asked. "Is it mostly paperwork and learning the parts of the car?"

Zoë shook her head no. "Nope. ADD's policy is drive on day one. Relax, it's fun. I haven't lost a client yet."

Life was either extremely funny to this young woman or laughing was her personal form of punctuation. Beryl took note that Zoë's voice was not the soft, demure tones of a young woman in her thirties. She cackled, she hooted; even her giggle reminded Beryl of a saw blade. From there she let her mind drift. Here on the Hillside, where residents paid homeowner's fees to keep things pretty, construction was creeping in. To her right was an acre of trees felled for hasty construction. It made her think of the ongoing building in Central California; how as soon as a new resident secured his property, then suddenly he was dead set against development. She wondered if the contractors would reseed the trees, and at once she missed Phoebe's farm with all her heart. Maybe she should go back. At least there everyone knew her. They didn't laugh at her choice of dwelling or pester her with questions. But she loved Alaska. She'd wanted to come here since her first week in prison. "Ms. Pratt? Does everyone in Anchorage make fun of my house?"

"Jeez, call me Zoë, would you? 'Ms. Pratt' sounds like I'm getting arrested. We don't make fun of it per se, we just call it the Nuthatch."

"Why call it anything?"

She gestured while she drove, something Beryl could never imagine doing. "Same way you give somebody directions by using a Brown Jug liquor store or the giant roller skate on top of Skate World on Frontage Road. You know, 'If you turn left at the Nuthatch and keep going four-point-six miles, that's where the party is.'"

"But why not 'the wooden house on the hill,' or by its address?"

Zoë stopped at the corner and looked both ways, and Beryl took note of her actions. "It's just a story, you know? Alaska's full of them. I know a few myself. Maybe I'll tell you one as soon as you've mastered the left turn. How's that sound?"

Beryl felt annoyed. She stuck a finger into one of her curls and pulled. "How many lessons do you think it will take me to turn left?"

"Oh, a dozen or so. It might be less if you were a fast learner. But I can tell you're the type who's going to need all twelve. Not to be rude or anything, you just have that look like you're scared of driving. Am I right? Can you tell me what happened? Did you get in a bad wreck? Run over the family pet? Don't worry. I rule at helping scared drivers get over their phobias. Why, I once had a student who could back up great, but ask him to make a left turn, he turned green and had to breathe into a paper bag or he'd puke. It just takes some people longer than others. But nobody's quit on me yet. I plan to open my own driving school as soon as I can save up the money. Of course, there's no telling how long that might take."

Beryl thought back to her sixteenth birthday, and how she put off getting her license after Moose had hurt her. When she was at the convent she'd made a pact with God: Let the baby be born healthy and go to good parents and she'd skip the driving thing altogether. All during her labor she bit her lip rather than cry out. When she felt the baby slip from her body, and the doctor said he was okay, she reminded God of all the things she was willing to give up. When people asked, she told them that the last thing she wanted was the responsibility of driving around a ton of metal that could hurt someone else. Also, she didn't relish being alone in the car. But now things were different. The child she gave up for adoption was thirty-six years old and didn't even know she existed. He could have been driving for twenty years already. She had to face her fears, because how else could she make a new game plan?

Zoë made a right on Main Tree and hit a shady spot where the ground was icy. She fishtailed for a minute and then turned into the skid, and the car straightened out. *"Woo-hoo!"* she cried. "That was close. We almost ended up in the ditch."

"But how do you know?" Beryl asked. "When to do that, which way to turn the wheel?"

"With skids, just remember to turn into them. You'll learn, Beryl. It's kind of like having an orgasm. Think too hard about it, you lose it." She switched on the defroster to defog the windows. "I am so tired of this damn snow I could hold the weatherman for ransom."

Beryl was still getting over the orgasm comment. The boldest person she'd ever met was Mary Madigan Caringella, and Zoë Pratt made Maddy look like a Girl Scout. "You think spring will ever get here?" she said, trying to change the subject.

"It usually does," Zoë continued. "We have to get your driving permit first. So it's on to the DMV, home of the crazies, the homeless, and the just plain shit out of luck. I'm telling you, that building's a real gathering place. A person should be able to take care of car stuff via the Internet, in my humble opinion."

"I don't have a computer," Beryl confessed.

Zoë gave her a surprised look. "Really? You should get one for surfing the Net, if anything. It's the greatest way to meet guys who pretend they're handsome and turn out to have comb-overs and wear elevator shoes." She laughed hard at her own joke. "Thankfully the driving-school cars still have snow tires on. We're not supposed to get snow this late in the year. This last storm broke all the rules. " She rolled down the window and hollered in the direction of the Hilltop ski area. "No more winter, you hear me?"

Beryl clutched the seat-belt strap. An hour—that's all she'd paid for—would pass quickly. She looked out the window at the sloppy snow and bare trees. Anchorage might be having a lingering winter, but what was that compared to mood swings, night sweats, crying jags, and feeling about as sexy as a spayed cat most of the time?

After the DMV, and only three wrong on her written test, Beryl sat in the driver's seat and learned where everything was. Like a pilot doing his flight check, she rattled off the names of the instruments to Zoë's satisfaction: "Ignition. Shifter. Signals. Pedals. Emergency brake. Emergency light flasher. Gas gauge. Oil pressure. Battery light. Lights. Brights. Turn signals. Oh, I already said those. Let's see. Door locks. Rearview mirror," she said breathlessly, certain the terms would leak out of her head in the middle of the night. Forgetfulness was part of The Change, too, which explained things like her putting the cereal box in the linen closet a few days back.

"You're doing great," Zoë said. "Now let's change places and you can start the car."

During lesson two, while Beryl was making right turns in the driving school parking lot, it occurred to her that the three-foot-tall red plastic letters ADD (Alaska Defensive Driving) read like Attention Deficit Disorder to passersby. Next door was an AM radio station. Parked out front was one of those PT Cruisers, painted with the radio station's call numbers and some awful pink-and-lime-green color scheme. When Beryl was instructed to stop, put the car in reverse, and back into a parking space, she got a better look at the Cruiser. Before he'd passed away, David Snow had bought one for Ness. While it didn't seem like typical Alaskan transportation, it looked fun to drive. I could buy one, Beryl told herself, and felt a little thrill bubble up. Maybe even get enough money from selling Earl's truck so I wouldn't have to dip into my bank account. But the truck wasn't in her name. To understand the legalities, she'd have to ask Detective Stokes, and she liked talking to him about as much as getting her teeth cleaned. *This won't hurt,* the dental assistant always said, but it did.

For months she'd pictured Earl's truck sitting out by that lake. But it turned out the police had it all that time, parked in an impound lot so they could go over it looking for some kind of explanation. When Detective Stokes brought it back to her, he had very kindly parked it in the garage, where it sat now, gathering dust. Beryl had no reason to go out there, but sometimes she thought about it. When Stokes called her, he reminded her to start the truck once a week so the battery would stay charged. She never outright lied to him since he'd caught her fibbing about the light box, but she didn't volunteer details. His determination to solve the mystery kind of broke her heart, actually. "When spring arrives we'll have more to go on," he'd say, then start in with the personal questions. "I have to go," Beryl would say, over and over, while he phrased the same old questions in slightly different ways. He wouldn't rest until he had his answers. She figured by now he'd gotten wind of her prison term for accidentally killing JW, and that he felt it was his duty to make certain she hadn't had a hand in all this. Once a husband killer, always a husband killer, she imagined him thinking. As if she'd driven Earl's truck to Eklutna, made her way home to fix that last meal nobody ate, and then delivered an Academy Award–worthy performance of shock when the trooper came to the door.

The thing was, maybe Earl wasn't dead. She didn't believe he was a keeper of secrets. Look at all that real estate he owned in California, and what about the company he kept? She had been pretty sure he wasn't Buckethead, the anonymous guitar legend, but more than once she'd seen him play a concert in that particular getup. It was something they didn't discuss. The mystery. She'd fallen in love with his quietness, his inability to articulate his feelings. He'd called her for months and played the guitar over the phone. When she said, "I love you," he said it back, but hardly ever using words.

When they traveled in the States, he preferred Best Western motels; the pared-down, nothing-special room was his personal favorite. But in Europe it was first-class accommodations. And how often did a person living in Anchorage come downstairs to find Eric Clapton sitting at the breakfast table eating Fred Meyer oatmeal?

"Straighten your wheels," Zoë said. "Come on, Beryl, hop to it. You did this fine ten minutes ago. Where's your brain?"

Beryl learned to back up the driving school car arrow-straight, even though she had to crane her neck unnaturally to do it. The car seemed designed for making right turns, which she loved. Right turns made her feel powerful, successful—if only life could be a series of right turns! Turning left, however, felt worse than backing up, and she vowed that if she managed to get her license, she'd avoid left turns whenever possible. Life was one big spiral anyway; all right turns inevitably led to the desired destination. She remembered from the earlier lessons not to forget to click on the turn signals so that the car behind knew what you were doing, and not to forget to turn them off so the car behind you wouldn't get pissed off, but it was news to Beryl that the glove compartment where you kept the car registration and proof of insurance contained long sticks that looked like dynamite but were really flares. Unlike fireworks, thankfully outlawed in Anchorage, flares were red and waxy and only to be used in really bad accidents where there was debris or bodies on the road. Bodies? "Come on," she'd asked Zoë. "Wouldn't the last thing on a person's mind in that bad a wreck be flares?"

"Are you morbid or something?" Zoë asked her back.

Beryl couldn't help the dark thoughts creeping in. In prison she'd been conditioned to constantly think in terms of what-if.

"You're doing great," Zoë said, staring at her clipboard and checking boxes, even when Beryl did something wrong, like stop too far back from the crosswalk, or park so close to the curb Zoë couldn't open her door. At the end of lesson two Beryl knew the following things about her instructor: She was born in Soldotna, a town whose claim to fame was having the state's only Dairy Queen. Her mother lived in Muldoon in a single-wide trailer with a man Zoë couldn't stand. Her biological dad had skedaddled when Zoë was a baby, and nobody knew his whereabouts. Her boyfriend was named Cleveland Douglass, two *s*'s, who was in the military, and yes, he just happened to be black, and did Beryl have a problem with that, because Zoë didn't. Her dream life was to build a log cabin on enough land that she could grow vegetables in the summer, not to eat, but to sell. That and Cleveland, plus winning some lottery somewhere and getting to stay home instead of work, but that wasn't in the cards for at least ten years because first she wanted to establish her driving school, and maybe start a day care next door, so then she could work one job and pop next door to check on the other.

When she talked like that Beryl felt excited for her. Part of her wanted to tell Zoë about Phoebe and Ness and Nance, about how they'd taken the dilapidated farm from rubble into profit. She wished she could explain how they sat around and tossed out ideas that seemed crazy and silly but actually ended up working into real efforts. Convey how that felt. But part of her didn't have any right to say those things, and maybe she didn't even belong there anymore, so she stayed quiet.

Driving was mostly boring unless you were in traffic. When they took the highway down to the Turnagain Arm, Beryl's mind wandered. Suppose Earl's body was frozen far in the woods, buried deep enough under leaves and so on that a hiker passing by would miss it? What if animals checked out his corpse on a daily basis, waiting for the snow to melt so they could have Earl for dinner? One of his songs had the craziest line: *You know your life's in flames, of course, but my God, you make such a beautiful corpse*. . . . No, he was alive, in bed with a Swedish supermodel. He could have opened another used bookstore in another seaside town—the world had such places to spare. He could be sitting behind the counter looking so cute that right this minute another bookish woman was falling for him. But no decent man would ever pull a stunt like this. And the house—the money—the Nuthatch in her name, it just didn't make sense. She looked hard at her life—it wasn't all bad. Thomas Jack was fixing Verde, and they had a nice little friendship going with sex on the side. She was learning to drive, and after that—

"Beryl!" Zoë hollered. "What the hell are you doing stopping in the middle of the intersection! Go! Never hesitate."

Daydreaming. You could do that on a bike and no one cared. But here, surrounded by honking horns and bearded men mouthing "asshole" behind their truck windshields, all the nice Alaskans who'd stop for you if you got caught in the snow instantly turned into Californians.

Lessons three though five went well.

Lesson six, she learned about moose as obstacles the hard way. Things started out fine. Now that the snow was melting, left turns seemed easier. She'd done so well that Zoe actually complimented her. "See? I knew you could do it. Okay, you can drive through Kincaid Park as your reward."

Beryl was thrilled. Finally, driving slowly enough to appreciate the scenery. There were only two left turns, and both of them without any cross traffic. Then the moose cow came out of nowhere. One minute there were spruce trees, some of the branches still tipped with snow. The next the moose was in front of her, her ears flattened like an angry horse, her ruff up and spiky, everything but steam issuing forth from her nostrils. Beryl slammed on the brakes, and the clipboard went flying. Zoë swore, and the mama moose pawed the ground while her twins crossed the road. When they were safe, she followed them into the brush on the other side.

Beryl had to pull over and cry. Zoë's sympathy was brief. "Listen, if I had a dollar for every moose I nearly hit I'd be living on Maui sucking down piña coladas and working on my tan."

"But Zoë, I could have killed her!"

Zoë snorted. "You should be more worried about her killing you. This buddy of Cleveland's hit a moose on the road down to Seward. Unfortunately he screamed on impact and got a mouthful of moose guts and glass. That'll put you off your feed."

Beryl turned to look at her instructor, who in honor of breakup—Alaska's never-ending thaw and freeze process that was supposed to end in summer—was wearing a pink halter-top with a glitter heart on the front and a fleece vest over that. "Is that supposed to make me feel better?"

Zoë picked the clipboard up from the floor of the Subaru. "Say the worst thing is you hit a moose and kill it. Well, okay. What do you do? You call the cops or Fish and Game or whoever the hell else it is that has to know, they dress the fucker out and give the meat to some people who'll really appreciate it."

Beryl stopped sniffling. She couldn't fathom the fact that people really ate moose. "That's horrible," she said.

"There you go again," Zoë said. "Those are the kinds of comments that let people know you're from California."

That day Zoë had dark-green-painted nails with bright red tips. Her fingers looked like some South American rain-forest lizard's toes. She tapped them on her clipboard, *click-click-click,* and stared out the window at two guys riding mountain bikes alongside the road until they could pick up the trail into the trees where, no doubt, the terrified moose had fled to tell her fellow gang members to be on the lookout for a green Subaru with a terrorized former Californian at the wheel. "I just love those wetsuit kind of shorts they wear, don't you? Shows everything, and I mean the whole package." Without waiting for Beryl's reply, she forged on. "One bite of moose burger and you'll tell McDonald's to kiss your ass. It's low in fat, too, so you can have extra fries."

Beryl tucked her Kleenex into her pants pocket.

"Let me see you execute a three-point turn," Zoë said. "Then head downtown so we can do some parallel parking."

Lesson seven, things were bad from the get-go. First off Zoë was in an obviously foul mood. Her jaw was clenched, and she wasn't saying anything besides, "Drive north, and remember to keep a safe distance between you and the vehicle in front of you," while staring out the window.

"What's the matter?" Beryl asked the minute she slid into the driver's seat.

"Nothing."

"That usually means everything," Beryl said, starting the car and checking her rearview mirror. "Come on, Zoë. We've gotten to be friends, haven't we? Tell me what happened."

Zoë turned her head and looked out the window of the passenger's seat. "If you must know, I've been put on probation at work."

"Probation?" Beryl echoed, merging nicely with the flow of traffic on New Seward Highway. "What does that mean?"

"Don't ask, Beryl. Just drive."

They meandered along the flattest, most unoccupied streets Anchorage had to offer, through the part of the city called Fairview, by Alaska Regional Hospital, and then down to the Sullivan Arena, where the marquee advertised that the World Wrestling Federation was coming to Anchorage. That'll have them lined up, Beryl thought. February may be the shortest month on the calendar, but try telling that to a light-deprived, chilled-to-the-bone Alaskan. She tried to think of various ways to get the usually chatty girl to talk to her.

Zoë ordered her to drive up such a ridiculously steep hill that Beryl balked and pulled the car to the curb—maybe there *was* a curb in all that disgusting brown-and-gray accumulated snow—she couldn't be sure. "Not the hill, Zoë. I have nightmares about the car flipping over backwards. I'm not kidding."

"Huh. Sounds like a sex dream to me," Zoë said. "Are you getting any?"

Beryl thought of Thomas Jack. He'd paid her a visit last night, whispered some kind of lullaby to her parrot, and then he'd taken Beryl to bed for a solid hour of breathless fun. In the morning he'd woken her early, made love to her again, then slipped out the door and said he'd call. No, she was doing just fine in the meaningless sex department, so long as she didn't think about the moral aspects of what she was doing sleeping with one man and not sure what had happened to the other one. "What kind of question is that?" she asked.

Zoë snapped her gum. "All I know is if I go three days without an orgasm I can't concentrate on jack shit."

Beryl decided it was a good thing she'd skipped the gum when Zoë offered it earlier, or by now it would be stuck in her throat. "There you go again, talking about orgasms with complete strangers. I'm old enough to be your mother. Speaking of mothers, what would yours say if she heard you talking about orgasms?"

"She'd agree with me. Besides, you're no stranger," Zoë said. "This is your sixth lesson. I could practically write your autobiography."

"Biography," Beryl corrected. "'Auto' means you write about yourself. And it's my seventh."

"Well, nothing's auto in your case," Zoë said and gave one of her short, harsh laughs. "Relax, Beryl. One hill won't kill you."

Beryl felt the sweat gathering between her breasts, a signal a hot flash was coming on. Now it felt as if someone had thrown a hot scarf around her neck. She cracked her window and sucked in air. "All right," she said. "I'll do it. But when I get to the top you tell me what happened at work. No more nonsense about orgasms, deal?"

"Fine. Now do the hill."

Beryl took a deep breath, let it out, and then another. She pressed the accelerator, the car surged forward, then balked. Under her foot it felt like the engine was weakening, like one of those awful takeoffs out of airports with noise abatement policies, which made her worry the engines would never rev up enough to move the plane through so much sky. Her heart pounded, her skin went prickly with fear, and she was in the throes of the biggest hot flash ever, one that made her underwear go damp and her shirt stick to her back, and any minute now she expected to steam up the windshield. At the top of the hill, she let out a scream of survival. "That was harder than prison!"

Zoë checked another box on her clipboard. "Keep talking, and I can write that biography," she said.

Beryl pulled to the curb. "Okay. Tell me what happened."

For all her youthful attempts at fashion, despite the shockingly long nails, under that overdone makeup, Zoë's chin trembled. "My boss is mad because he found out about Cleveland."

"I take it you don't mean Ohio."

"What is the big deal about me dating a black man?"

"Are you sure that's what it's about?"

Zoë sighed. "Oh, I'm sure, all right. Delbert has been asking me out since I started work here. See, if he asks and I say okay, then whatever happens isn't sexual harassment, he's just a geek who wears gold chains and satin shirts. I wouldn't date him if he were the only man left breathing. Cleveland picked me up the other day, and Delbert saw us kissing. Some people just can't take interracial dating."

"You don't have to explain it to me. Let's go have lunch somewhere that serves really good burgers. There's a diner on Old Seward. Shall I drive us?"

Zoë looked at her watch. "Can't do it on work time. Plus we only get a half hour for lunch."

"So call this Delbert up, and tell him I'm paying extra for a longer lesson."

"Really?"

"Really," Beryl said.

They got the last free table in Judy's Diner. Beryl sat at the table sipping a cup of hot chocolate while Zoë stood outside in the cold and smoked a cigarette. Beryl'd never smoked, never understood what felt good about taking anything but air into your lungs, but Zoë looked like she was calming down. She ground the butt into the grimy snow and came back inside, stamping her feet to dislodge any snow. "Thanks," she said at the table. "If we time this just right, I can drop you at home, get the car back just in time for Delbert to go on his lesson, finish my paperwork, and escape before he figures out something else to blame on me. What did you order?"

"A salad," Beryl said.

Zoë took hold of the menu, one of those cards encased in

plastic worn from years of handling. "I want a three-egg omelet stuffed with hash browns and bacon," she told the waitress. "And to drink I want a chocolate milkshake."

Beryl shook her head when the waitress looked at her. "I'll just stick with the salad."

"You should eat more. This is Alaska, you don't want to go through the winter underweight or you'll fall apart the second you get a cold."

Beryl ignored her. Clearly Zoë was one of those people who could ingest five thousand calories a day and burn them all off. "Tell me about Cleveland," she said, leaning back in her chair to get comfortable. "How long have you known each other?"

It was never a good idea to badmouth another woman's man, even if he had picked your friend up at a bar and the two of them had had sex the same night. Beryl listened, nodding when appropriate, pressing her lips together when she heard how Cleveland Douglass had a daughter with another woman in town but hadn't married her. Zoë and Cleveland had dated for six months now, on and off. Cleveland serviced cargo planes. It was a high-pressure job, and being in the air force was intense. He inspected engines, repaired the parts that were reusable, and whatever time he could carve out, he and Zoë filled up dancing at bars like Chilkoot Charlie's, where the music was loud even if it wasn't any good.

"What's his long-term plan?" Beryl asked. "Will he stay in Alaska when his enlistment is up so he can be near his daughter?"

"I don't know," Zoë said, smiling shyly. "I don't want to put pressure on him. This is the first guy I've managed to get to stick around, so I kind of let him run the show."

Beryl's salad arrived, and a minute later, Zoë's omelet, the plate so enormous the waitress used both hands. "How does he feel about your plans for opening a driving school? Is he behind that?"

"Oh, that's just a dream I had," she said, lifting her fork. "I'd like to have kids and stuff, too. If we had a kid together, then he'd feel responsible, you know? If it was a boy, I could probably get him to marry me." She filled her fork and dipped the mess into ketchup. She smiled around the bite, and Beryl tried to imagine being hungry enough that something like that would taste good.

The waitress refilled Beryl's cocoa. After spooning out the whipped cream onto the saucer, Beryl sipped. Her son would be about the same age Zoë was now. Maybe he had his own family, a job he took pride in, and a baby on the way; it wasn't so impossible an idea. When she was Zoë's age, she'd felt the same hopeful way about JW that Zoë felt about this Cleveland fellow, only JW was smacking her around, while Cleveland just seemed to be using Zoë for an excuse not to grow up. How could he have a child with someone else and take up with another woman? What the hell was wrong with people lucky enough to have babies, anyway?

Zoë cleaned her plate and mopped up what was left with a piece of toast. "You know, Beryl, I can't help but notice that this place is five-point-two miles from the Nuthatch. How did a hermit like you ever find it?"

Beryl laid her fork alongside the half-eaten salad. She and Earl had eaten here a number of times. The diner fitted his needs—plain food, unassuming decor, and the other patrons left him alone. *Don't cook,* he'd said. *Let me take you somewhere people will wait on you.* Inside it made her laugh—any other woman would expect fine dining, a bottle of wine, and candlelight—all he meant was she didn't have to do the dishes. He used to kiss her in the truck sometimes, take hold of her like they were teenagers and couldn't wait to get home. She remembered how sexy it felt when his foot touched hers under the table. How did she get things so wrong that he would want to leave her, want to fake his death and get everyone so worked up? "I used to come here sometimes with a friend," she said. "Back to Cleveland for a minute. Zoë, your driving school plan is a good plan. Don't base your happiness on what the guy wants, ever. Trust me, that's the shortest route to unhappiness."

"Oh, and what's the best way to find happiness?" Zoë asked, her eyes flashing. "Sit around and wait for it to fall out of the sky? What have I got to pick from? My mom's boyfriend is moody when he drinks and psycho when he's sober. Half the guys I meet are more in love with killing animals to make themselves a hat with eyes and a tail than building a career. I don't make a ton of money at ADD, I'm no raving beauty, and I have credit-card bills up the yin-yang, so what if it isn't true love? So what? At least I have somebody to sleep with."

Beryl looked down at her plate. "Sorry. I've made some monumental mistakes in my life. I like you, and I was trying to spare you some heartache by giving you advice you didn't ask for. Would you mind taking me back home now? I don't want you to get in trouble with Delbert."

Zoë got up and went out the door first.

Beryl sighed. Phoebe had a knack for seeing deep inside a person's soul, telling who was a potential friend and who needed to be shown the door. Ness used to say Phoebe could get a stone to open up. But Beryl wasn't Phoebe.

Zoë dropped Beryl back at the Nuthatch, waved, stuck a fresh stick of gum in her mouth, and sped off to her future. Beryl stood watching long after the Subaru disappeared around the corner. Then, for the first time since Detective Stokes had returned the truck, she opened the garage and stared at it, circled it like it was prey, kicked the tires, and swore worse than Verde on his worst day. She wished she had a penis for as long as it would take to properly christen the vehicle in the name of unreliable men everywhere. Then she opened the driver's door, slid inside, and laid her head down on the steering wheel, the last place Earl's hands had been, and breathed in deep breaths, hoping to catch whatever molecules he'd left behind. Earl's scent was a recipe she knew by heart: A little of that green deodorant soap, the ghost of Kaladi Brothers coffee, and his own sharp tang. She caught a whiff every time she opened a book, which was another reason not to join the monthly discussion group at Chapter One, where surely the talk would veer easily from books to their own lives, and discussion of their children.

But somehow, since Thomas Jack, Earl's smell stayed in the truck.

Phoebe

8

"You Must Remember This"

BUCKETS OF CUT ROSES FILLED the greenhouse. They were red, pink, white, and yellow; long-stemmed, miniature, and tea roses, and that only included the fresh cut flowers. There was also a worktable covered with silk and satin sachet packets filled with dried petals, and chocolate roses wrapped in red foil, their long stems wrapped in pale green ribbon. The silk-wire-ribbon roses came in bouquets and single stems, and the tiniest ones could be worn as lapel pins. DeThomas Farms was ready to cover every possible Valentine eventuality. With everyone working in shifts it took a solid week to create all the arrangements. This afternoon Phoebe and Segundo sat side by side, plugging into florist's foam leafy mother fern, a smattering of baby's breath, and a lace-edged glazed white ceramic Victorian heart on a pick that read, in old-fashioned gold script, "My Valentine." The picks had been shipped from overseas—insured, thankfully—because they were costly and one box had arrived shattered. Costing a mint compared to last year's red plastic hearts outlined in gilt, Phoebe had to admit Nance was once again right to make this change. The porcelain classed up the arrangements something fierce, allowing them to up their prices. Little touches like these counted now that the nursery across Valley Road was open. The roses themselves were always a gamble. Would they arrive too late, and wilt? Too early, and never open? Endurance was the name of the game. The women constructed the arrangements with precision, carefully placing the roses last of all with a fresh cut to the stem so they would drink up water.

Phoebe preferred daisies, calla lilies, purple iris, coneflowers, zinnias, or for elegance, there was always the peony. Aunt Sadie had once told her a true story about roses back in Roman times, a lesson on wealth and gluttony handed down from king to servant. It seemed that when feasts and celebrations called for luxury, servants were enlisted to pluck rose petals from every blooming flower, and to gather them together in an enormous cloth. At the height of the party, they dropped the petals from above, so as to shower special guests like confetti. Well, apparently once the host of the party wanted more and more petals, until there wasn't a single flower left for miles around except for what was in the cloth. Gallons of sweet-smelling petals, more than any party guest had ever seen. His party would be the most memorable, and it was, but not for the reasons he expected. The effect of so many petals was that an entire party had been suffocated, crushed under the roses.

There in the humid greenhouse Phoebe cocked her head. She could hear her aunt's voice speaking to her—after Sadie's death, so many things she'd said seemed eerie, almost premonitory. She poked the dethorned rose stems into green florist's foam and tried to imagine how happy the flowers would make the recipient. Valentine's Day was one of those holidays that caused single people to feel more alone than ever, yet it gave couples an excuse to snuggle up and feel grateful. The only romantic Valentine Phoebe had ever received was from Juan—a store-bought card he signed with his name. It wasn't gushy or particularly elegant, but she kept it tucked in the recesses of her panties drawer, a treasure for all time. Yet she had to admit her steadfast Valentines were her girlfriends. "Happy Valentine's Day," one or the other of them would sigh, and immediately unleash a chocolate-and-old-movies binge.

Nobody was feeling very lovey around the farm this year. Nance had a stomach bug that kept her hugging the toilet, and

James was in Texas brokering some land deal. Mimi and Dayle were on the outs, so Mimi's trip to Alaska was postponed. Ness was trying to straighten out the latest wrinkle in David's estate, which involved some ticked-off cousins who thought they were going to inherit. Nobody had heard from Beryl, the only one besides Nance who had a steady beau. Phoebe'd left Sally a big lacy Valentine featuring a puffy satin heart held in the delicate lips of a stuffed horse, asking, "Will you be mine?" No dummy, she'd signed it "Penny," and managed to find a chocolate horseshoe wrapped in gold paper to place on Sally's pillow. As soon as the munchkin got home from school, they would take some carrots out to the horses, have a cup of cocoa, and Phoebe would listen to the details of Sally's day, serialized like a soap opera. What had the little boy who ate paste done today? Who got picked to help Mrs. Shiazaka pass out art supplies? Did they have a good midmorning snack, or had somebody's mother sent apple slices instead of granola bars? After that installment they'd deliver their homemade Valentines to everyone at the farm. At bedtime Sally would find her Valentine and so would end another day in the life of Juan's daughter. At breakfast that morning, Sally had asked, "Mama, who made up Valentine's Day?"

"Hallmark," Phoebe had answered.

"*Mama,*" Sally had said skeptically. "Really."

"Oh, all right. Saint Valentine made it up. But Hallmark bought the rights to it."

Her daughter played with her toast crusts, fashioning them into the shape of a star. "Did he just one day go, 'From this day on everyone gets hearts'?"

Phoebe paused. "You know what? That sounds like a very good question for Uncle James." She relished sending Sally armed with her most difficult questions out to the Great Giver of Ponies. She laughed, thinking of how James would handle this one.

"What's funny?" Segundo asked grumpily. "Or are you drunk on roses?"

"Hammered," Phoebe said. "How about you?"

He parted some ferns to insert curly willow branches on one of the custom arrangements. "I can't even smell them anymore. At this point I think I prefer ragweed."

Phoebe set down a handful of baby's breath and looked at his arrangement. "Me, too, pal. Hey, where did you learn to do flowers, Segundo? That's really beautiful."

"My mother," he said. "She liked to make centerpieces for holidays. I watched and learned. Youngest child, you know. She kept me a baby as long as she could. Wouldn't cut my hair, made me wear shorts and suspenders, took me with her everywhere she went. All that crazy last child stuff."

"Aw, I think it sounds sweet."

He looked at her frankly. "How sweet is it when you get the crap beat out of you by the neighborhood boys every day for being a mama's boy? Man, I wouldn't go back to those years for a million bucks."

"Me, either," Phoebe said. "Especially since I can watch Sally's. Be sure you take some roses for your girlfriend."

He smiled. "Already made her an arrangement."

"Well, then, I have to see it."

Segundo opened the newly purchased cold case and rummaged around, emerging with one of those Martha Stewart–type bouquets—a squat, fat vase crammed with two dozen utterly perfect cream-colored roses. A silk ribbon tied around the neck of the vase was its only decoration, but somehow the simplicity was what made it sensual, rich, and downright seductive. "Wow," Phoebe said. "Getting something like that would make me extremely grateful in extremely demonstrative ways."

He winked and put it back. "That's what I'm counting on."

"You old heartbreaker," she said, and smiled, reaching into the ceramic heart pick box and finding only packing material. "Grab me that last box of picks, will you?"

"Sorry, *guapa*. It's empty."

"No way. How can we be out of these? I have more orders to finish. Didn't the replacement box arrive?"

"Appears not," Segundo said.

"Crap! What are we going to do?"

He shrugged. "You got me. We could use the plastic picks from last year, but they're kind of faded."

Phoebe sighed. She took her cell phone out of her overall pocket and called the florists she did custom work for. "Hey, Lily.

Phoebe here. We're short on picks. Any chance we can buy some from you guys? Oh. Thanks anyway." She went down her list calling until all that was left was the new place across the road that was giving them competition. "Segundo, what do you think? Should we call first or just show up?"

He set aside the willow arrangement. "Let's go over," he said. "But take something with us, a peace offering, a trade."

"Like what?"

He looked around the greenhouse, where stock for holidays from Saint Patrick's Day to Easter to Memorial Day was already lined up. The ubiquitous oxalis in small, medium, and large pots. If a customer knew how hard it was to kill one, how easy it was to cut the wilted stems back and encourage new growth, they'd never buy another plant. Fortunately this knowledge was still a secret. "Face it. We got more shamrocks than we'll ever sell. Take them a case."

"Did I ever tell you that you're brilliant?" she asked.

"*Si,* but I don't think you mentioned that to my paycheck," he said, smiling.

Phoebe felt a pang. She paid her workers as well as she could, but Segundo wasn't a worker, he was like Florencio had been—the backbone of the farm, the true tender of the earth. "You haven't had a raise in a long time," she said. "I'll see what I can do. Let's go now. I want to be back before Sally gets home from school."

They parked near the winery stables, and Phoebe recognized David's horses in among the rental stock and the gorgeous draft horses. They looked happy and well fed despite the last couple of weeks' rain and chill. Phoebe wondered if she could score a pickup load full of manure to take home and add to their compost heap. Nothing like horse poop to make good fertilizer. Leroy and Penny simply did not produce in great enough amounts to feed the whole farm, but that didn't mean she wanted another horse to care for.

Segundo helped her unfold her chair and guided it up the cobbled walkway to the flower shop. The building was new, built in the mission-style architecture that echoed the winery's design. The arched windows featured leaded panes, and the tile floors were that wonderful salmon color with a diamond of cobalt glass every now and then. Just outside the building a fountain dripped water into a pool thick with water plants—papyrus, rushes, horsetails in miniature and full size. Water plants were something Phoebe hadn't even considered, but the moment she saw them she knew they would sell, as would the more profitable idea of installing fountains and water features. She made a note to tell Nance. Their cold case was the size of a movie star's walk-in closet. It was packed with flower arrangements—roses, mostly, but also exotic flowers, like bromeliads and Hawaiian bird-of-paradise. She had to look away from the cards and gift section. It was like something out of Bayborough-by-the-Sea, upscale toiletries with French labels, the finest stationery, one-of-a-kind sculptures, and glass whatnot boxes. In comparison, DeThomas Farms' products looked hodgepodge, as if made by hippies toiling only to earn money to buy dope. "Hi there," Phoebe said to the older woman working the register, mustering up her cheeriest voice. She looked as if she spent her days off in the gym and eating right, and maybe swimming in the ocean, even on cold days. "I'm Phoebe DeThomas, from the farm across the road."

"I know who you are," the woman said, turning to look at her. "I'm Dolores Doheny."

"Doheny?" Phoebe echoed. She studied the woman's Irish knit sweater, her tartan scarf draped decoratively around her neck, and the Celtic knot hair clip that held her silver hair gathered neatly in a short ponytail. "Gosh, you look familiar. Do I know you from somewhere?"

Mrs. Doheny smiled. "I wondered if you'd remember. A long time ago I knew your aunt very well. I was sorry to hear she'd passed away. If I hadn't been out of the country, I would have come to her service."

"Oh," Phoebe said, feeling oddly like she'd walked into the middle of someone else's conversation. "We didn't have a service. Just following her wishes." She grasped the pots of oxalis, already wrapped in green foil printed with silver and gold shamrocks. Segundo nudged her. "Well," she said. "It's nice to meet you again. We were wondering—we're running low—I don't suppose—"

Segundo lifted the pot from Phoebe and set it on the counter. "Good afternoon, Mrs. Doheny. We over ordered on these shamrocks for Saint Paddy's," he said. "Wondered if you might like to trade us for some heart picks so we can finish our Valentine's Day arrangements. Any chance you have extra? We'd be happy to pay you for them. We only need fifty or so."

"Of course," Mrs. Doheny said, reaching beneath the counter for a key ring.

Phoebe had the urge to take this woman's hands into her own, that in doing so she might feel a flesh-and-blood connection to Sadie. "This is very kind of you," she said when the box of picks was brought forth from the supply closet. She noticed that these picks were bisque-fired with a matte surface, and how beautiful they looked compared to the glazed variety. Mrs. Doheny might be new to this particular flower business, but she had mastered the details that spoke of years of experience. Suddenly Phoebe realized that—*duh*—with her studio and kiln, she should just *make her own* heart picks for next year. Fancier ones. Unique and one-of-a-kind. She burned with questions for Mrs. Doheny. *How much are you charging for your standard arrangement? Why the hell did you have to move into the Valley just when I was starting to feel calm about my business? Were you friends with my aunt?* But she just sat there staring until Segundo muttered about getting back to meet Sally.

"Come for tea sometime," Mrs. Doheny said. "Rain or shine, I take it every afternoon at four-thirty. Bring that sassy little daughter of yours. Caught her riding my horses a while back. No, no, don't you dare apologize. It did my heart good to see that little girl out there. Reminded me of Sadie, don't you know."

"That was weird," Phoebe said as they finished up the last arrangements. "It felt like she knew everything there is to know about me."

"She does," Segundo said. "She's your competition. I gotta get this stuff loaded in the truck, Pheebs. See you *mañana*."

"Bye, Segundo. I'll have a chat with your paycheck as soon as James gets back from Texas."

When the arrangements were loaded into the delivery truck, Phoebe tidied up the table and made mental notes on what had gone well and what could be improved for the next season. She surprised herself, thinking in terms of next year so blithely. She looked up, scanning the rows upon rows of plants that paid the bills. So much had changed in the last eight years. Would Sadie have been proud of her? Or would she have felt, like Phoebe did, that Mrs. Doheny's shop crowded the waters just a bit?

"Mama!" Phoebe heard Sally hollering as she raced up the driveway. "Mama! Look how many Valentines I got! And candy! Mama, look!"

Phoebe rolled herself out of the greenhouse onto the paving stones that made up the walkway. There she was—Juan's daughter—a ring of red from Kool-Aid circling her lips, her leopard-print leggings dusty from play, and her black sweater with the fake fur cuffs and collar splattered with paint and paste stains. What did you do with a six-year-old whose favorite color last week had been pink and now suddenly was black? Nance said the right answer to that question was, "Buy her colorful hair scrunchies, a little black dress, and wait for her to grow out of it."

"I'm right here," she said. "Now let's see all those Valentines."

Sally dropped the loot right where she stood. "In a minute. First I have to feed Penny."

Phoebe watched her go into the barn. Motherhood was endlessly challenging, but she would never cease to be impressed at how quickly things could change. What was life-and-death important a moment ago could disappear in the time it took to take a breath. Be it favorite colors, the politics of recess, or upcoming holidays, none of it could compete with Sally's larger love, which was that dang horse.

That night at dinner, Ness showed up looking haggard. She plopped her legal envelopes down on the counter and came to sit at the table where Phoebe was toying with her salad while

Sally used her fork to mush together everything she didn't want to eat. "Hi, Auntie Ness," Sally said. "How many Valentines did you get? I got eleven so far and one from Segundo that's all in Spanish. Maybe tomorrow Saint Valentine will bring me another one because he's very busy and I think I have been pretty good and I already ate my chocolate from school when we had our class party."

Ness smiled. "You little bundle of energy, I want what you're having," she said as she sat down at the table and poured herself a glass of iced tea. Sally began to inch her plate toward Ness.

Phoebe passed Ness the sugar and scooted Sally's plate back to her. "How'd it go at the lawyer's?"

"What was it Shakespeare said? First kill all the lawyers? Well, he got it wrong. First off we need to kill all the homophobic relatives who suddenly are broken up that they've lost their estranged cousin and what do you know, it seems like only cash will alleviate their suffering."

"What's 'homophobic'?" Sally asked.

"Someone who doesn't like perfectly nice people for no particular reason," Phoebe said. "Please eat some of your dinner, Sally. You can't watch TV unless you eat one bite of everything, and that includes the salad."

Sally folded her arms across her chest and began pouting.

Phoebe ignored her. "Anything I can do? Run over someone with my chair?"

Ness stirred her tea. "Come with me to the thing tomorrow."

"What thing?" Sally asked.

"A memorial service for David, sweet cheeks," Ness said. "Unfortunately it's just for grown-ups. The lawyer reads the will, stuff like that. Believe me, you'll be happier in school."

"But I *want* to go to the memorial," Sally whined.

"You can go," Phoebe said. "By the way, did you know that this memorial is also a luncheon with vegetables?"

Sally made a face. "I could stay home with Penny. Mama, I want to save my dinner for later, okay?"

Phoebe looked at the clock. Seven-thirty. She'd been trying to coax Sally to eat for a solid hour. "Sure," Phoebe said, defeated. When her daughter ran from the room, she looked at her friend. "You seem really down tonight, Precious. What can I do? Open some wine? A bag of M&Ms? I'll stay up watching *Parent Trap* with you. Tell me what I can do."

Ness picked up a fork and began eating Sally's salad. Phoebe knew that everyone was relieved David was no longer suffering. But his absence was like the hothouse roses, so pervasive it seemed to overpower the room. Ness, always stoic, hadn't cried, at least in Phoebe's presence. Phoebe wanted to wring the necks of those evil cousins, but if anything, their appearance had made Ness even calmer. When Phoebe had called to check on Nance this evening, her sister-in-law had gone so far as to say, "Ness could give a robot a run for his money," before she had to hang up. They all waited on tenterhooks for the first crack in the plaster. She placed her hand on her friend's shoulder and gently kneaded the knots.

"I'm fine," Ness said. "Just exhausted. I think I'll take a bath and hit the sack." She picked up Sally's plate and took it to the sink. Phoebe tidied the kitchen, waiting for Ness to come out of the bedroom and say something about the construction-paper Valentine she and Sally had left on Ness's pillow, but the door stayed shut. Sally was awestruck over the Valentine from Penny. "But I didn't make *her* one!" she wailed.

"You brought her carrots," Phoebe pointed out.

"I bring her carrots every day! Carrots aren't special!"

Phoebe stroked her daughter's hair and settled her in bed. "Tomorrow you can bring her apple slices, okay?"

When Lester Ullman, M.D., walked in the door and shook out his jacket, Phoebe smiled at her old friend, thinking this must have been how Sadie felt when she saw her doctor outside the office. Out of the white coat, Lester was still someone she wanted to know. As he aged, his hair was graying over his temples just like Gregory Peck's. He reminded her of Atticus Finch in *To Kill a Mockingbird,* every girl on the planet's idea of the perfect dad.

"The rain is trying my nerves," he said. "I'm starting to wonder if Noah's not far behind."

"Rain's good for the flower business," Phoebe said softly, not wanting to appear too casual. All around her the people who'd gathered at David's house to remember him told stories, wiped their eyes, and waited for the tray of snacks to empty.

Lester speared a cheese cube and took a chocolate-covered strawberry. "I love these things," he said.

"Ness hasn't cried yet," Phoebe whispered.

"Every person grieves differently," he reminded her. "She'll fall apart when she feels it's safe to do so. And you'll be there for her the same way she was there for you."

Phoebe had a hard time articulating her deepest feelings to Lester. They joked and parried like fencing partners. She thought of Shriners Hospital, how she'd spent years in that horrid-smelling place, how the volunteers were so nice to the patients, but they came and went so fast it seemed like just when you got to know one, they had to take a job, move out of the area, get a divorce, or something. The nuns were aliens so far as Phoebe was concerned. The doctors were curt. Who knew? Maybe they tried to make contact as brief as possible, since it took even the dumbest kid about five minutes to connect doctor with pain/shot/operation. What a crazy childhood she'd had, spending years in that place. How different Lester was from the orthopedic surgeons. She could call him in the middle of the night, and he'd calmly talk her through Sally's spiking fever. When she confided that she feared her daughter would grow up spoiled rotten, overdosing on aunts, her every whim indulged, Lester listened soberly. *This is how dictators are born,* Phoebe had gasped, and Lester, without missing a beat, said, *Either that or Leona Helmsley.* Well, brat or not, Phoebe would lie down and let a train run over her before she let anyone lay a hand on Sally. She knew Lester felt the same way.

After the memorial part of the day, most everyone had left except for the girls, Lester, and some snotty second cousins who appeared out of the woodwork. Three of them sat on his couch, waiting to hear what they gained from the death of a relative they'd ignored in everyday life. Phoebe glared at them, trying to fix them with a hate ray, but she had to stop when Malcolm began to read the will.

David had a lot of things to say in his will, most of them boring, but he'd left amounts in six figures to AIDS research and Project Angel Food. He outlined a scholarship he wanted put together in his name for college students studying film. The cousins looked crestfallen when Malcolm read the part about him leaving trusts to their children to be used for education only, and paid directly to the institution. They left in a huff. Phoebe studied the last sandwich on the silver platter. Someone had taken a bite out of it and put it down. It was a perfect bite, like whoever had done it had really good orthodontia, and she wondered how tacky it would be to pick it up, cut away the bite and eat it. When she looked up, everyone was staring at her. "Huh?" she said. "Did I miss something?"

Malcolm read it again. "The Big Sur property I leave to Sarah Juanita DeThomas, to be held in trust for her by her mother, Phoebe DeThomas, to use in any way she likes until her daughter comes of legal age, or her mother judges her to be mature enough to care for such property."

Andrew, who had apparently arrived sometime after Lester, smiled at her.

"As to the matter of the Valley house," Malcolm said, clearing his throat, "the Valley house and any remaining assets including stocks, bank accounts, and personal property, I leave to my wife, Ness Butler Snow."

That was the moment Phoebe realized that silence had its own unique gravity. Here she was, picturing a falling-down log cabin overgrown with weeds, a rickety structure where a person had to stand on tiptoe to glimpse the Pacific, and the next moment she was hearing that Ness had gotten *married* without anyone knowing it, to a gay man, on top of that, and now she was his *widow,* and standing in the house she had just inherited along with the vintage Fiesta ware, the framed movie posters, the kidney-shaped ashtrays, the books, the barn, and the bedroom decorated in Roy Rogers memorabilia. Ness looked timidly over at Phoebe, and Phoebe felt her face flush. "When did all this take place?" she blurted out. "Were you ever going to tell me? Seems to me you have some explaining to do."

Ness looked down at her lap, and then up at David's friends

gathered here in his living room, and promptly burst into the long postponed tears.

James stood up and put on his jacket. "Way to go, Phoebe," he said. "Way to effing go."

"You must think I'm a terrible person," Phoebe said in Andrew's car on the way home. "How could I upset my best friend like that? How could I say that to her in front of total strangers? But marrying David? Why didn't she tell me? Did she think I wouldn't approve? All I want is for everyone to be happy. But also to tell the truth, you know? I mean, when I was a kid at Shriners, all they did was lie to me. *This won't hurt, this operation will straighten your spine, if you lie still and let the medicine work, you can one day walk out of here as strong as anyone else. You're not going to throw up from the anesthetic, the pudding is good, and your mom will be here tomorrow.* So I get out of Shriner's and then my mom takes over. *If you eat too much chocolate you'll get pimples, if you dress in skin-tight jeans boys will think you're cheap.* Hah! As if any boy ever looked at me. All they did was look through me. I was the GE Transparent Teenager, a virgin for life."

"The part about the blue jeans sounds good," Andrew said. "Will you wear some on our next date?"

Phoebe gave him the finger. "Assuming there *is* a next date."

He laughed. "Sugar, I cannot believe your spirit. If you'd been in charge way back when, we could have beaten those Yankees into a sorry pulp and made notebook paper out of them. Relax, why don't you? You're tired. It was a difficult day. No one's going to remember what you said. Put your seat back and snooze."

Phoebe shut her eyes. Part of her felt bad for upsetting Ness, and part of her was entirely jealous of Nance, who'd taken Ness into the bedroom to help her calm down. Did that mean that Nance had known about the marriage? Then Mimi went into the bedroom, and Mimi had known Ness the least amount of time of all of them! Did she know about the marriage, too? Why in the hell was everyone keeping secrets from her? What else didn't they tell her? The bedroom door had closed, they didn't come back out, and people began leaving. Soon it was just Andrew and Phoebe, and the caterers cleaning up David's—no, *Ness*'s—kitchen. Phoebe sighed. She'd just rest her eyes for a while. At home she had work to do. There was no downtime with a six-year-old. She could hear Andrew humming as she dozed off.

For the first time in a long while, she dreamed of her aunt Sadie. They were traveling by ship, some sort of cruise thing, standing on deck watching a series of gates open. They cleverly flooded below the ship, so that it was gently lifted to the surface of the sea, and Phoebe realized they were in some sort of canal. Once level, the last gate lifted, and the powerful ship motored away. Where was this place? Panama? Did it matter? Then on the ship, the sky opened up, and warm rain began to fall. Phoebe held Sadie's hand, and turned her face up to the sky. She smiled, happy to be somewhere new, where things she'd never seen were happening, and the person she loved best in the whole wide world was beside her and alive and loved her, too. "I love you," Sadie said. "Now say it back."

"You know I love you," she said.

"I know. It's just nice to hear it," Sadie said, and the dream slipped away into the dark water, and Phoebe slept the hard, dreamless kind of rest that renews the entire package, body and soul.

When Phoebe woke up, she knew where she was—her own bed—but had to struggle to remember that Andrew had driven her there. She'd flopped down on the coverlet and cried, and she vaguely recalled him rubbing her shoulders. The room was dark, and while the bed beneath her was soft and familiar, her room had changed. The view out the French doors could have been a painting—dusky blues and those ghostly gray clouds that hadn't departed even though night had arrived. She rolled to her side, and there was Andrew, lying next to her. "You talk in your sleep," he said. "Whole sentences and everything."

She bolted upright. "Did you slip me a Sominex or something? Criminy, where's Sally? Give me the phone; I have to call her sitter. I'm hours late to pick her up."

Andrew put his hand on her shoulder. "It's eleven o'clock, Phoebe. Sally's in bed fast asleep. By the time I got you home you were dead to the world. James fetched Sally. Thinking you'd wake up and panic; I stuck around to explain things. But you didn't and I was tired, so being the mannerless cad I am, I just invited myself. You don't have to worry. No hanky panky. But as I said, you talk in your sleep."

"What the hell did I say?"

Andrew smiled. "You must have a lot of fun in those dreams of yours. Who's Sadie?"

"My aunt who died."

He reached over and touched a finger to her lips. At first Phoebe wanted to bite it. She lay back down and stared at the ceiling. It made her crazy that he'd been here with her and she didn't even know it. The last man who'd slept in this room, the only man who'd slept with her, was Juan. That side of the bed was her little sanctuary, her portal to the past. She remembered back to their early days. How she'd asked him, Why me when there are tons of able-bodied women out there that would kill to be yours? How he'd laughed and said he'd had his eye on her for a long time. She wondered what Southern witticism Andrew would dredge up if she asked him the same question. But Andrew was a cripple, too. She had plenty of live nerve endings below the waist. There was nothing wrong with her in that way. Did Andrew think maybe she was paralyzed down there, and that would take the pressure off him?

"Okay, Andrew," she said. "Plain unvarnished truth. No cornbread, no flattery, and no Co-cola with peanuts, okay?"

"Yes'm."

"There are plenty of women out there who find you studly and a catch. Willing to polish your wheelchair, or just go to fancy parties and spend the rest of their lives looking married and happy and inheriting your dough. What I mean is, there's not a cripple alive who hasn't seen *Coming Home* and watched Jon Voight give Jane Fonda the business. So what the hell are you doing trying to insert yourself into my life? I'm a single mother, I'm not very nice, and I make widows cry. Tell the truth."

She could feel him laughing because it was making the bed shake. She felt his hand squeeze hers, and his fingers tickling up her arms to her neck, which gave her entire body a shiver she couldn't hold back. "Simply put," he said, "I believe I'm falling in love with you."

"Horse poop. You hardly know me."

"*Au contraire,* dear heart. I know your art. And that, my beautiful, cussed friend, is ten times more intimate than what Jon did to Jane."

"I have a brat for a daughter."

"I love her, too."

"I'm not over Juan."

"I'm not over Andrea."

"My finances are in terrible shape."

"I have money, Phoebe. I'm certainly not after yours."

Phoebe's mind raced. "Well, then how about this? I'm cranky, and I don't want to get my heart broken again."

Andrew was quiet, and Phoebe shocked herself by wishing she could take that last part back. She felt him rise up on his arm. Suddenly he pulled her to him and kissed her, so hard and deep and mystifyingly different than any other kiss she'd ever had that in the process, he woke up everything that had been asleep for the last five years. When he let her go Phoebe gasped, and Andrew laughed, and said, "How about that, Phoebe?"

For once Phoebe, Miss Smart Remark of the Central Coast, didn't have an answer.

Thomas Jack

9

Owl Soup

WHILE HE WAS WORKING WITH BIRDS, Thomas Jack knew how to live his life. "Imping" feathers, a way of training a damaged feather to grow straight, stopping a bleed, giving pills to the unwilling; you name it, he could do it. In his hands the crankiest of eagles eventually calmed down and accepted whatever he was trying to do in the name of their continued health. The thing about injured birds was they didn't drink too much and make a scene in public, sleep with other men just to get his attention, or crave diamonds and wedding dresses just because they saw pictures of them in magazines. Which was why Thomas Jack would rather have been in the middle of some unpleasant task like cleaning out a maggot-filled wound instead of witnessing Beryl's current behavior. His Red, slow and thoughtful, gentle and mild, now stood in front of the refrigerator throwing out food as fast as she could pick things from the shelves.

"Babe?" he said. "What are you doing?"

In answer, she tossed out jars of mustard, a package of salami, and what looked like a bottle of vitamins. They crashed into the sink with an awful noise.

He watched for a while, then went to her and took hold of her hands. "Stop it."

She wouldn't meet his eyes. "Don't you see? I have to get rid of his things. I'll never be free of him with all this crap around."

Thomas Jack shook his head. "Let's back up for a minute. Ten minutes ago we were making sandwiches. Now all of a sudden we have to get rid of food?"

She reached into her jeans pocket and pulled out a credit-card bill, waving the white paper like it was a parking ticket unjustly tucked behind her windshield wiper while there were still ten minutes on the meter. "Don't you see? This proves he's still alive," she said. "There are hotel charges in Denmark, airfare in Norway; I have to call Detective Stokes and tell him not to waste any more of the department's time. How could he do this? How could he do this to me? Did he think so little of what we had that he thought it was fine for me to think he was dead? Bastard!"

Right before his eyes, *boom!* normal person to crazy person. One minute she had been making him a halibut sandwich, and the next the mail lady knocked at the door because all the letters wouldn't fit in the box. Verde started in cussing, and that new cat Beryl kept trying to pawn off on him ran under the couch and started making a terrible racket. Thomas didn't know much about cats, but he could tell this one had never seen a parrot in its life and thought it had landed in the seventh circle of hell. Beryl had opened one envelope and immediately gone nuts. "So call the detective," Thomas Jack said. "Nobody's stopping you."

Instead, she sat down hard at the table and tossed the bill down in the middle of the sandwich makings. The knife with the mayonnaise was just touching the edge of the paper, which immediately began soaking up oil. Beryl began to cry. Thomas decided maybe she was entitled to it. After all, she'd been with the guy five years, and it *was* kind of a chickenshit thing he did, leaving her like that without saying where or why or what have you, and now this bill his cowardly way of telling the world he was alive. "Tell me what I can do to help," he said, but Beryl was so wigged out she didn't hear him.

"Wait," she said, as if he were about to leave when he hadn't moved. "Is this any of my business? Is it? We'd said the words, we'd agreed we were breaking up, he'd done everything but pack his suitcases. I knew he was going, and he knew I knew.

Maybe I should call the credit-card company, make sure it's Earl using the card. I mean, the card could have been stolen, couldn't it? Don't you think I should check?"

Thomas did not think she should check. It wasn't her bill, he didn't believe in credit cards, and the idea that some magnetic strip on the back of a piece of plastic could reveal information about you made him nervous. But he kept his mouth shut.

"He was always going to Sweden or Norway or one of those Scandinavian places. What are the chances a credit-card thief would go there, too? Earl always said one day he'd take me to Stockholm. Do they have Best Western hotels there? Once in New York we had to stay in some skanky place near his heroin-chic jazz buddy's club. Not that I'm some prima donna who needs buttered scones every morning, it's just that there were bugs, and the whole thing seemed so out of character—but I really didn't know his character, did I? How could I waste five years of my life on a stranger? How do I know you won't skip out on me when you get tired of me?"

Thomas Jack sighed. "Beryl, I'm your friend and I love you. I won't skip out on you."

She gave him a hard look. "You do *not* love me. We agreed to have a simple relationship, so you do not love me, understood?"

He threw up his hands. "Okay, fine. I don't love you. Are you happy now?"

She began sobbing.

"Holy cow, woman! I'm trying to reassure you, not piss you off."

She grabbed the bill back up, went to the telephone and pressed in numbers for the help line. Thomas Jack watched as she waded through the voice mail on the other end, and then, amazingly, caught a real live operator. "Ma'am, I know I'm not on the account, I just want to make sure you verify it's his signature. Because he's missing. Yes, missing, as in no one knows where he is. There's a police report. I can give you the number of the detective in charge. No, I don't know his mother's maiden name. Or his social security number. Are you serious? Well, fine, then. I hope your company policy can afford to pay all these international charges, because you're sending the bill here and he's not here and I'm not on the account so I'm not the one who has to pay for it!"

She slammed the phone down and turned to Thomas, her face starting to crumple. He tried to put his arms around her, but she pushed him away.

He wondered if drama was a specialty of white women. He'd had girlfriends from all walks of life, mostly Native girls, some biracial, but only a few white, and Beryl Anne's mood swings had them all beat. He remembered a Hudson Bay woman who got loud when she drank too much, and once took her bra off in the Salty Dog Tavern down on the Homer spit. She didn't really need a bra, and bars made people do stupid things all the time, so it hadn't bothered him too much, but he would have drawn the line if she'd gone for her panties. His stomach growled. Beryl's crying was getting old, and he was hungry. He reckoned that if he finished making his sandwich, Beryl would tip over into full-blown hysteria, but the thing was, he needed to get to midtown ASAP. More than an hour ago Alma had called him about a couple of owls coming in. She was counting on him to help.

He moved closer to Beryl, took the bill off the table, crumpled it, and threw it into the trash. Then he hauled her in close to his flannel shirt, a blue-and-black check that he'd found for three bucks at Value Village. People moved to Alaska expecting that the radical change would wipe clean the cluttered slates of their lives. They expected to see the aurora every single night, to wake up to fluffy white Christmas-card snow, but they wanted the streets magically clear and easy to negotiate, and the temperatures to stay a nice comfortable forty and above. When day-to-day Alaska turned out to be much like any other place, they ran back to wherever they'd come from, abandoning perfectly good stuff like the shirt. Beryl's face was blotchy, and her breath was coming fast and shallow like she'd been running. "I have such a headache," she said. "Would you please get some aspirin?"

"You don't need aspirin," he muttered, kissing her on the top of her head. "Come with me to see these owls, Red. Alma said one of them's a snowy. Come on, it'll take your mind off your troubles. That bill isn't going anywhere. Whatever's happened has already happened. Just give that old credit-card bill the Alaskan *mañana*."

She pulled loose, stepped back from him, and tried to smile. "I'm too old for you," she said.

"Oh, Jesus. That story again?"

"It's a true story, Thomas. You should go find a nice young fertile thing and make a family. You'd be such a good father. You should have kids. Daughters. You'd be a good father to a daughter."

He smiled. "I like things right where I am, Red. If I don't, you'll hear about it."

"I'm still too old for you."

"Fine, you're too old. Let's worry about that later."

Thomas Jack admired Beryl's toughness. He'd never said so, but he thought she would make a good fishing partner, able to withstand the wind and salt spray and the boat's rocking without whining. Get all excited about catching a fish. Wouldn't flinch when it came time to gut them. She didn't wear makeup or a lot of jewelry or paint her nails. She did cry a lot, sometimes even during sex, but she was a natural redhead, so he chalked that up to excess passion. Though, there were times he wished he could push her off button.

Beryl went into the bathroom and ran water in the sink. He finished making the sandwiches and wrapped them in foil. If Beryl didn't want hers, he would eat it for her. He stood outside the closed door and talked to her so she wouldn't change her mind. "Did you know that the snowy owl is twenty-four inches tall? Well, he is. No color on him but white. His eyes are yellow, his ears don't have tufts, and he hunts during the daylight hours while all his buddies are snoozing."

She opened the door and shook her head at him. He held up her jacket. She slipped her arms into her sleeves and stomped her feet into her boots. "How you can talk calmly about birds at a time like this—well, I wish I had your inner strength, Thomas."

"You need to get out, that's all. Now that the snow's beginning to melt and the days are getting warmer, you'll do better."

Once they were in his car, she looked up at the house appraisingly. "I used to think this was what I wanted," she said, gesturing toward the house and yard. "Big house, nice things, the so-called space to live my life. But it turned out that wasn't what I wanted at all."

Thomas waited for her to go on. When she didn't, he checked to be sure Beryl had her seat belt on, and then backed out of her driveway and circled around O'Malley, eventually making a right onto Dimond, where a few intersections later, he'd pick up C Street. Seward Highway was backed up again. Every year the tourist season started earlier. He didn't know what they expected to see in the dregs of winter besides the Iditarod, and even then, what they did in Anchorage was a ceremonial start, not the real thing.

In the treatment room, a *Daily News* reporter was interviewing Doctor Simpson regarding the prosthetic eagle beaks. A photographer was taking pictures of the prostheses, lined up in a row of varying shapes and sizes. Baba Yaga, the first eagle to receive such a beak, sat quietly in Dr. Simpson's arms, but Thomas Jack had held her and knew she was the kind of bird to explode when you least expected it. "Do you feel like Michael Jackson's plastic surgeon?" the reporter said, pinching a prosthetic beak between her fingers.

"No, I pretty much feel like a veterinarian who doesn't make any money," Dr. Simpson replied.

"How do you attach the beaks?" the reporter continued.

"Glue," the vet said. "Eastman makes a special bonding adhesive."

"And do you really think the beaks are a feasible enterprise? That it's worth your time to experiment on birds and potentially prolong their suffering?"

Thomas couldn't stand it any longer. "It'll work," he said. "I use this material in making masks. It dries hard as rock, but it's got some flex."

The reporter turned from Dr. Simpson and looked at him, recognition showing in her eyes. "Hey, aren't you the bird whisperer?" she said. "Mind if I ask you a few questions?"

He didn't miss a beat, simply said, "Yes, I do mind," and walked over to Alma, who was standing by the freezers next to two dog crates.

"Does that happen all the time?" Beryl asked.

Thomas shrugged. "Occasionally. The owls are waiting. Let's talk about it later. Hey, Alma."

Alma kept her face impassive, but Thomas knew she wasn't happy to see Beryl there with him. Alma liked to be the center of attention, the authority, the one who came up with the clever solution to the impossible problem. Thomas thought she should go back to college and get her veterinary degree. Only then would she have a chance of being nice for two minutes. Beryl slid past him to walk alongside Alma, and surprised him by initiating conversation.

"Thomas said one of the owls was a snowy. What's the other one? And how's Saint Francis doing?"

"A great horned," Alma said, her voice steely. "The pygmy died." When the phone rang, she ran to answer it, calling out, "Don't open the cages until I get back!"

"Saint Francis died?" Beryl said to Thomas. "But he looked so strong."

"Come on, Beryl. You know it happens."

"I expected to see him again." Her voice trailed off, and Thomas hoped the tears wouldn't start until they'd done what they came for and left.

In the center of the warehouse two large dog crates sat on pallets, covered everywhere except for the front grate. One cage had padding sticking out the side grates, which meant there was a feisty customer inside. Usually the birds that needed the most help were past trying to escape, but sometimes there were those wild-at-heart ones that refused to let anyone come near. Thomas squatted down and pulled the towel back so Beryl could look in. The sound of the old brown washer and dryer chugged along, pumping out the soft, warm scent of detergent. The steps up to the eagles' cages were in the process of being scrubbed by a pair of teenagers wearing East High sweatshirts, probably there on some kind of work-study thing. At the cleaning station longtime volunteer Elise Reese sprayed artificial turf with a spray bottle of antiseptic cleaner, and then hosed it down, directing the water to a drain in the cement floor. Dr. Simpson's drilling started up, and then ceased, and Thomas heard Lipstick scolding her for making noise. Before the day ended, who knew what birds would come in the front door? The ones that got well enough to fly were sent to the flight center at Fort Richardson. Others stayed here. Those that could be were adopted out as education birds, and some, like Saint Francis, died no matter what you did, but no bird suffered when a human being could ease that suffering. The trouble with owls was there was a surplus of them, and not enough homes.

"The first time you took me here I felt like I was back in California," Beryl said. "I remembered the time when my life had structure, when I felt in control of things. I kind of missed it."

"That's because you hardly ever venture off the Hillside. I don't know why you won't come work here. You know more than Alma does, for Pete's sake."

"I know that's true," she whispered. "Unfortunately, so does Alma."

"Thomas," Alma called. "Can you come here a minute?"

He left Beryl by the owl cages to take a look at the eagle Alma was holding. Alma had pulled her long, dark hair back into a knot at the nape of her neck. Elise had put down her hose and come to hold the bird's feet, and Thomas turned back the blanket to reveal what was left of the amputated wing. "Dr. Simpson operated four days ago," Alma said. "The bird's been on antibiotics and seemed to be improving, but today she hasn't touched her salmon. What do you think?"

It was times like this that Thomas Jack wished he could whisper to birds, and hear what they had to say back. How did he know if the bird wanted to live? For all he could tell, she might want to be set free so she could die with a semblance of dignity—and dignity to a bird was probably 180 degrees from a human's idea of it.

Beryl came up behind them and cleared her throat. "I just don't get how it's a kindness to save her when she won't fly again."

Alma bristled. "Both Homer and Kenai are anxious to get an

education bird. Homer's been waiting the longest. Even with one wing this is a gorgeous eagle. Putting her down is one option, and we will if she gets any worse, but life as an education bird is better than no life at all."

Before Beryl could argue, the eagle shook herself and in the process, dropped a feather. "Give that to me," Alma said as Beryl bent and picked it up.

She put it into the plastic Baggie on the eagle's clipboard chart.

"We keep count," Alma said. "Owls and eagles, it's illegal to keep the feathers unless you're Native, which clearly you're not."

"I'm aware of that," Beryl said, ice in her voice.

Thomas Jack wondered whether she was disgusted by the law, or wanted to get into it with Alma, or if she was thinking about the credit-card bill again. For sure she and Alma did not like each other.

Alma said, "Now that's settled, can we go ahead and move the owl?"

Ordinarily it would take two or three people to retrieve a bird this large from its carrier, one to bravely stick a gloved hand in with a towel, and another to stand behind the first with a blanket. The idea was to cover the bird and simultaneously get hold of its legs just above the talons. If a leg got loose, one of those claws could sink into your flesh and snap a bone, not to mention give you a nasty infection. Thomas wondered if Beryl knew the language they used in the process: "Do you have this leg?" one person asked and the other answered, "I have this leg." It was a choreographed, careful dance. Only then did they transfer the bird to the treatment room, lay him down on the table, and work fast to get the procedures done as quickly as possible. The minimal amount of contact, the minimal amount of stress was essential in a bird that was potentially releasable.

The owl offered very little resistance, which Thomas took as a bad sign. As soon as they got her to the table, she clicked her beak rapidly, wanting to go back to the crate. "Okay," Alma said. "Let's lay her down bandaged wing stump up."

The snowy's eyes inner eyelids were closed. "Beryl, can you tuck that blanket around her head?" Thomas asked.

"Got it," she said.

Thomas stood at the owl's head, one hand deep in the feathers that covered her neck, the other at her legs, also being held by Alma. The owl was restrained, but there were no free hands to give her the injection. "Elise," Thomas called, but she had the water on, and didn't hear them.

"I can go ahead and give her the shot," Beryl said. "I've done it millions of times."

"You cannot," Alma said. "You have to be trained, checked out by a senior staffer, and then there's the matter of liability—"

"Oh, for fuck's sake, Alma, let her give the shot already," Thomas said.

Beryl looked at them both. "The bird rehab in California didn't get owls too often, but I've handled a few."

Alma looked at Thomas. "It's against our policies—"

Thomas looked at Alma. "We can put the owl back in her cage and start all over, or do this and only stress her once. Your call."

Alma looked up at Beryl skeptically. "Well, give the shot then, but be careful." She began narrating the process, and Beryl pretended to listen.

Beryl used her index finger gently to rake through the breast feathers until she found skin. Holding the syringe in her teeth, she tore open an alcohol wipe, daubed the place she'd bared, and stuck the bird without so much as a moment's hesitation. Alma started to say, "Don't forget to pull back on the syringe to check for blood to make sure you haven't hit a vein," but by the time her words were out, Beryl had already done so, given the shot, and disposed of the syringe in the red sharps container behind the table. "This bird's starving," she said. "I can feel every bone in her body. She hasn't got so much as an ounce of fat on her. And she's dehydrated. Are you hydrating her mice with Ringers? Are there rocks in her water so she can drink without getting too wet? Somebody might sit by her cage and hand-feed her. If her wing stub pains as much as I think it does, the act of bending down to get the mouse must be agony. I bet I can get her to eat if you leave me alone with her for a couple of hours. Do you ever try homeopathic medicines? Sometimes they'll help a bird in this kind of shape turn the corner. I like Rescue Remedy. We used that a lot on lost causes. And Noni. It's available at the health food store."

"I have a question for you," Alma said. "If you can read this owl so well, how come you have so much trouble with your parrot?"

Beryl looked at her, chastened. "Congratulations. What you said just became horrible thing number three in my otherwise stellar day." She walked to the sink and stuck her hands under the tap.

Thomas and Alma got the owl back into the crate, and Elise went to the food prep room to hydrate some mice. "That was mean, Alma," he said as she fastened the cage latch.

She looked at Thomas. "It's a legitimate question."

He sighed. "You don't even know her."

"I know her kind."

Beryl wiped her hands on a paper towel and headed toward the front office. Thomas Jack followed. "I'm sorry about Alma," he said.

She shrugged. "Alma's her own punishment. You know, that owl reminds me of Verde. There isn't a day that goes by that I don't try to put myself in his place, imagine the day he lost his wings. How much that hurt. It must have been like being a poet in Chile when Pinochet was in power. In comes the fascist general to chop off your hands so you won't write another word. It flat-out breaks my heart worse than anything Alma could say about me."

Thomas Jack sighed. All this had begun as some girl's pissing contest, intellectual more than physical. He had no doubt that Beryl was going to win, but did that mean their personal business had to include Alma?

Inside the food prep room Beryl and Alma were conferring hotly over thawing mice, "discussing" their shared passion for all things winged. Thomas watched them moving around the room, Alma standing taller than usual; Beryl's chin jutting out when she wanted to make a point. From across the room the two women were more alike than they'd ever admit. Good looking, funny, fierce in their hopes. Alma lived for the reversal of odds; Beryl lived for the odds of reversal. One he liked to sleep with, one would have made a good traditional wife and mother, had he taken that path.

He checked on the snowy owl, her breathing noisy. Maybe pneumonia. She didn't bother to hiss. She'd likely die sometime in the night, he figured, but she'd wait until Alma had gone home, after the last volunteer had done a bed check. It was just something that was going to happen, like a flower dropping petals. They put great horned owls down all the time that were in better shape. Too many birds, too few homes.

"I'd like to see Saint Francis," Beryl told him. "Elise said he's in the freezer. Will you get him for me?"

Thomas set down the pen and did as she asked, unwrapping the small owl and setting him down on the exam table. Beryl touched his wings, ran her fingers lightly over his feathers. He hadn't lived long enough to grow his top feathers back. "What did he die of?" she asked.

"Chart says infection."

"Thanks," she said, and turned from the table to wash her hands at the sink. Thomas rewrapped the owl and put him back in the freezer. Beryl came to him and took hold of his arm. "Stay," she said. "They need you here. I'll call a cab to take me home."

As she kissed him goodbye he wondered what she was thinking, what she'd do when she left here, whether she'd go back home and take the credit-card bill from the trash can, or if she'd sit and write in her journal. For a moment, when they were working on the owl, the two women had their heads bent so closely that their foreheads nearly touched. They looked like schoolgirls telling secrets. Women hoped harder than men, he thought, sometimes hard enough to change the outcome of things.

That night he went home instead of to Beryl's. He heated a pizza and checked his mail. He went to work carving a mask. Carving took listening. A carver had to know the wood he was using. Knowing the wood took a lot of handling, studying the way the grain traveled, trying to sense what lay beneath the surface. Not many carvers made clay maquettes, but Thomas Jack liked to use plastic clay, warmed by his hands to softness, then roll it into coils, join it with a flat tool, and carve away clay until he had a rough idea of what was in this wood: dog spirit, raven, bear, frog. He banked the fire in the woodstove and bent over his clay, the chunk of spruce to his left atop a piece of checkered oilcloth. The clay had a mind of its own today. He was thinking maybe he'd give up, give in to the urge that the fine spring day was sending him, the soft smells and textures of woods, that a long walk would be just the ticket, but then his thumb moved a smear of clay to the left, and then his index finger pinched it just so, and there, under his fingers was Beryl's mouth, the lips he liked to catch in his teeth ever so gently, the mouth that told him over and over he was too young for her, the shape of it always changing so that she was speaking or whistling or making the sweet sounds of a satisfied woman as he cupped her chin in his hand and moved inside her in the ways that he knew she liked. He caught his breath and felt the spike of adrenaline rush his skin.

Ness

10

Like Trying to Fence the Ocean

THE MARCH WIND BLEW GRIT across the parking lot of Cecile's Comb-out. The salon was where Ness went when she was feeling sad and too ashamed of her selfishness to go to church. There nobody expected her to smile, and talk skated on the surface of things like a skittering water bug teasing a trout. Ness's skin was sallow from lack of sleep and a diet of coffee. Her eyes were puffy from crying, and her mouth was surrounded by those fine wrinkles that just *love* to trap lipstick and make a girl's smile look pathetic. Rubber lips, she thought, biting them. And crooked teeth behind them. Rusty elbows, she thought, and Lord, if I don't stop now I will be laid out and crying. While she waited for Gabby, she held the magazine she was reading up high so that it covered her cheekbones. Like plow blades, they poked through her skin, the first place to show when she lost five pounds. Losing weight made her think of David, never-coming-back, dear dead David, and once again see in her mind how the flesh had practically fallen away from him the last few months he was alive. No matter how much butter and fat she sneaked into the foods he could manage, he'd grown thinner and thinner.

She turned the page, came face-to-face with a perfume ad

featuring two beautiful models looking at each other hungrily, and sighed. It didn't matter how much time passed; every day the first thing she thought of was David. Even Phoebe not talking to her made her think of him. She heard the echo of David's voice, how it would dwindle off when he was tired. *No matter,* she'd said so many times. *I know what you're trying to say, love.* They had loved each other a lifetime's worth. But David was a quart of ashes, waiting to be picked up at the funeral home and spread over the ocean so he could float off in all directions. Ness wanted to keep the urn. Hide it in her dresser drawer, lug it out to talk to, sleep with, read like a cereal box so she wouldn't have to be alone in the mornings. Why couldn't Phoebe understand that?

"It's been three weeks since we've talked," Ness told Gabriella as she sat down in the hairdresser's chair. "Starting to feel like the Hatfields and the McCoys around the farm."

"The two of you must stop this feuding at once," Gabriella said, dropping a comb into the jar of blue disinfectant that sat on her station's counter alongside Afro-Sheen, mink oil, and a neon pink jar filled with "Rock Star" wax. "What good can come of prideful anger? Look at Rwanda, Precious. The Hutu and the Tutsi killing each other with machetes. A million dead, and for what? You're a Christian; it's your duty to make the first move." She held out her leopard-print cell phone. "Call Phoebe and tell her you love her. Already both your lives have more loss than most folks."

Ness looked at the phone, but didn't reach for it. She and Phoebe usually came to Cecile's Comb-out together. Gabby used the pink Lanza shampoo and the matching conditioner on Phoebe. For Ness she used baby shampoo and five kinds of conditioner, all mixed up together like a parfait. Gabriella was a hairdresser, not a shrink, but she sure listened well.

"Phoebe knows I love her. She's my best friend. But that doesn't give her the right to be angry with me because I married David."

Gabriella clucked and undid another tiny braid. She shook her head and said things in a language Ness might have known if she'd grown up in Africa, where tall black women wrapped themselves in bright cloth and sang and rocked one another's babies instead of in Oakland, where a black woman could spend a lifetime slouching and wanting things she couldn't have and end up bitter. She had a nice neutral wardrobe; she could hum on key, but the only baby she'd come close to having was Phoebe's.

"Well, then, don't call. I haven't got all day," Gabby said. "Lie back and let me get to work."

Ness leaned back, a warm towel on her shoulders. She didn't really expect Phoebe to apologize. It wasn't that she was waiting for. But she was tired of saying, "I'm fine," when she wasn't. What did she want? "How about we cut my hair short? Maybe what I need to snap me out of all this is a drastic change. Something I can just run my hands through and go."

Gabriella, a six-foot-tall West African with waist-length red hair, bent close so that their faces were visible side by side in the mirror. "We look like a pair of drama masks," Ness said. "Happy and sad."

"You hush," Gabby said. "Close your eyes."

Ness did as she was told. Gabby finished taking out Ness's braids and gently fluffing her hair until it looked like a soft, dark cloud filling the sky of Cecile's Comb-out, a salon with four chairs and an entire wall of beauty products, some so arcane they bore typewritten labels. But for all that softness and womanly comfort, all Ness could see was sharp edges, broken fingernails, and bad dye jobs that left hair looking like straw.

"Sweetheart," Gabby said. "When your life is in a mess, the *last* thing you do is cut your hair. Paint your nails gold, or buy yourself expensive shoes you'll never wear. Some lacy panties, or even a nice piece of jewelry. Hair, you leave alone. Now lean back and let me go to work. I'll give you a little trim, and then we'll see how you feel."

Ness felt like crying from the kindness. Gabby's hands were strong but gentle as she rubbed Ness's neck. She clucked when she came across a knot, massaging gently until the muscle surrendered, and Ness thought that if she ever felt like quitting hair, she could make a living giving neck rubs. Ness felt herself slip into that drowsy state near sleep, that in-between country she longed to visit. These days she wasn't sleeping through the night.

When she stayed at David's—her house, she had to keep telling herself—she was up half the night touching his things, wondering what she was supposed to do with art books and South American masks and majolica pottery. With the horses gone, the place felt deserted. At least at the farm Sally was available to jump in bed and snuggle with you. The child smelled like cotton candy, and she always had something interesting to say.

Life went on in the most ordinary of ways, and somehow that hurt even more than sympathy cards covered with pastel flowers and filled with catch phrases. Ness had been at the farm for six years now. Six *years*. She'd gone from horse thief to death sentence to the miracle of medical management and back to grief again. Along the way she'd learned the dainty act flowers put on was a fable. Forget the soft petals and the seeming magic where the stem ended and flower began. All tricks. According to Sadie's journals, people had given their lives to bring flowers into the world. Smugglers, kings, peasants laboring over a cutting to nurture it into a species. All that made a person think about what kind of mark they left on the planet. David made movies for television. After-school specials. So it wasn't Pulitzer Prize material. Somewhere out there in the world there was a little girl who watched one and made it through her parents' divorce because of it. And there was a deaf boy—he'd written David a letter—who thanked him for his movie about the boy who lost his hearing and had to learn to talk all over again using his hands. Too late for me to do anything important, she thought. The best I can hope for is being a good friend. But how to get through to Phoebe? Sally, that's what will do it. After my hair's done, I'll go to the toy store, and find the perfect olive branch. She felt the tickle of warm water against her neck as Gabriella rinsed the conditioner from her hair, and she smiled.

Gabriella sang while she patted dry, hummed as she braided, ran the blow-dryer on the lowest setting, and wove small yellow beads into the many new braids. Ness's hair was two inches shorter and much livelier now that the dead ends had been trimmed away. "You and I should go to Africa," she told Ness. "See our homeland. It puts things in perspective. You can't help but feel a connection."

“Africa,” Ness said, nodding. “Maybe we should. Thanks for talking me out of the haircut.”

“That’s what I’m here for. Go tell Phoebe you love her,” she said. “Start there, and you two will work this out.”

Ness left Gabby a twenty-dollar tip folded inside the thirty-five for the haircut. It was a lot of money, but a therapist would have cost more. The wind against her neck as she made her way to the car had a hint of warmth to it, promising a brief spring and long, hot summer.

Sally was leading Penelope around the property when Ness drove into the driveway and parked next to the Land Cruiser. A cooling-out walk following her riding lesson, she figured. The riding teacher was a stickler for making Sally tend her own horse, pick Penny’s feet, and brush her clean before and after the lesson. Ness admired her. Sometimes the sight of the skinny girl in her chaps and windbreaker made Ness ache for the old days, the times when she could have bounced a dime off her thigh muscles and shoed four horses without breaking a sweat. Now the muscles were soft. She had a soft body and a hard heart. “Hello, munchkin,” she said as Sally headed in her direction. “I think there’s a surprise for you in my purse.”

Sally’s hair was done up in ponytails that stuck out the sides of her helmet. She insisted on riding in the habit Nance and James had bought her, replete with English boots and spurs there entirely for show. It cracked Ness up to look at her and see the future there. She was going to be even tougher as a teenager than she was as a six-year-old. Poor Phoebe.

“What is it?”

Ness took her bag from her shoulder and set it on the ground. “A surprise. Why don’t you look for yourself?”

“Will you hold Penny?”

“Be happy to.”

Ness relished the feel of leather reins in her hand, and took in a deep breath of horse—mares smelled sharper than geldings—savoring the perfume. Sally examined each item and set it aside until she came to a small white plastic bag. Inside, wrapped in tissue paper, was a family of porcelain horses, glued by their hooves to a square of cardboard. They were made by an artist in Laguna Beach, and had been around since Ness could remember wanting them herself as a child. "Appys," Sally said. "They have spotted butts."

"Do you like them, honey?"

She looked up solemnly. "Oh, yeah. I'll put them in my Barbie barn. Want to help me name them?"

"I'd like that. Why don't you let me put them inside while you take care of Penny? And do you happen to know where your mom is?"

Sally used her riding crop to point to the studio. "Mama's in there making clay things and having *lots* of fun while I'm stuck here walking in circles when I will probably die before I get a Co-cola."

"A what?"

"You know. A Co-cola. With peanuts. Andrew taught me to drink it that way. It's Southern. I might decide to grow up to be Southern."

Ness grinned. She didn't know about Phoebe, but Andrew certainly had this child under his spell. "You don't *have* to walk Penny in circles. You *get* to walk Penny out. Look how much that pony loves you, Sally. Look at her big brown eyes blinking at you with love. Why, I think this might be her favorite part of the day. Don't you love Penny?"

Sally pulled an exasperated face. "*Duh!* Penny is my bestest friend in the whole wide world, universe, planet, and galaxy!"

"Hmm. I suspected as much. Well, Penny doesn't have arms and hands to get her treats or fill up her water. You do. And believe me, she's grateful to have you make sure she gets everything she needs."

Sally stuck a finger in her left nostril and dug. Ness didn't bother to correct her. She wished she could do that without the entire world, planet, and galaxy thinking she'd flipped out. Sally inspected her fingers and wiped them on her horse. That's something I would have done if I'd had a pony at her age, Ness thought. Horse as Kleenex. I certainly spent enough time sobbing into the side of one.

"Did you know you have yellow beads in your hair, Auntie Ness?"

"I do know that."

"Where'd you get 'em?"

"From Auntie Gabriella."

"I could have yellow beads if my mom wasn't so mean."

"If you want yellow beads, I'll take you to get them. But you have to sit still for a couple of hours to get them. Can you do that?"

"How long is a coupla hours?"

Ness thought. "Well, it's like three *Sesame Street*s in a row. Two *Little Mermaids*. One and a half *Toy Stories*. It's a long time to sit still."

Sally pursed her lips, looking so much like her mother that Ness felt her heart tug. "Penny can sit still while I braid her mane. Only I'm not very good at braids."

"Maybe we can put beads in Penny's mane. Would you like to do that someday soon?"

The horse trainer whistled. "Sally, you have five minutes left to get that horse cooled out. Keep walking."

Sally sighed dramatically. "I *have* to *go*."

"I'll see you later, baby," Ness said. "Give Penny a horse cookie for me."

Spring weather provided perfect growing conditions. The Central Coast's mild mornings gently eased flowers into opening. When the sun heated things up, they flourished, and ocean breezes tempered the heat. New grasses sprouted so quickly that Ness thought if she stared at them closely, she could see them grow. Around the perimeter of the house, where the garden was simply for looks, ranunculuses bloomed in vivid shades of yellow and orange. Not too many red ones this year. The flowers were lush and thickly planted, and Ness bent and fingered the fine petals, so thin and soft they reminded her of her granny Shirley's cheeks, paper-thin, full of kindness, and how one day she had lain down to take a nap and gone instead to visit with the Lord. Ness smiled at the idea of it—her grandmother pouring out tea from celestial china, nearby a Carnival glass dish—for sure they had it in Granny Shirley's heaven—filled with ribbon candy. She noticed one flower that was getting crowded out by its neighbors, so she picked it and headed to the studio.

Outside she could hear music. Phoebe had the Indigo Girls cranked up. They were singing about telling someone they loved them. This was a love song to the rest of the world, but Ness suspected all love songs, at their core, were singing to Jesus Christ. When Van Morrison kicked in next, another of Phoebe's favorites, her argument proved itself. The Irishman lived in a country torn by poverty, politics, and terrorism. The only antidote for that was turning one's heart over to the Lord. She recalled the day five years ago when she had opened her heart to Him, and how every day since, no matter what it held, was a gift. Every time she thought of it, she felt rebaptized. Why did some people have such a hard time with God? It wasn't like he lay in wait for them, some annoying Hare Krishna rattling his can of coins. Yet Ness knew that Phoebe had been irked by Ness's return to church. She would have bet money on it. Thinking about God made Phoebe sad and sorry and so angry it was a little scary. Ness wanted to tell her that was okay, that God could take it, but she had a feeling if she did Phoebe would scoop out her eyeballs. She thought of Ephesians 4:26, "Let not the sun go down upon your wrath," and how she had been doing just that for weeks. She lifted her hand to knock on the handcrafted door that looked like it belonged in Hobbitland rather than Bayborough Valley, and forced herself to say, "May I come in?"

Immediately the stereo went quiet. "Come in," Phoebe said.

Ness could hear that carefulness in her voice. Still angry. "Hello," she said when she stepped into the room.

Phoebe looked away and then back. "Better put on an apron if you don't want to get clay on your clothes, Mrs. Snow. I'm working."

Ness, trying not to sting from the "Mrs. Snow" remark, declined. "Can we talk a minute? Would you be willing to set down your clay long enough to hear me out?"

Phoebe didn't look up from the clay she was pounding free of bubbles, a technique she referred to as "wedging." "I don't know if that's possible."

Still furious about the secret marriage, that barbed wire

strung between them. Ness tacked around that first barrier and went for common ground. "Phoebe, you are being unreasonable. We farm girls are batting pretty low averages in the marriage department. Although I guess I can't include Beryl in the statistics since she's technically not married to Earl. But you have got to stop this and forgive me."

Phoebe said nothing.

"It's mighty peculiar to me, Pheebs. Out of everyone, I thought you would be the one person who'd understand why I married David. Maybe I should have told you when we did it, but you were so sad for so long, and then Nance and James got married, and Beryl and Earl were still going strong, and I guess I was afraid you'd feel the odd one out if you heard we'd done the deed." She sighed. "Once again I try to spare someone's feelings, and it blows up in my face."

Phoebe stared at the clay in front of her. Her mouth was drawn into a tight line, like she was tasting what she thought was sweet pickles only to discover they'd been so liberally seasoned with dill that she might as well have grazed her way through the herb garden. When she looked up, Ness was alarmed at the hopelessness she saw in her friend's face. "What happened to us, Ness? You and me, we were like sisters. I told you everything. When you kept your HIV a secret, I forgave you. You promised no more secrets."

"I know, honey. You must feel like you can't trust me at all."

Phoebe gave a dry laugh. "I'm still trying to figure out what happened."

Ness moved closer to the table between them, so close she could smell the earthy damp clay. Van was turned down so low that the song, one that sounded like drunken mumblings, was merely whispering in the corner. God forgive her, she wished she could reach the boom box from here, pick it up and throw it out the window. "You want to know what happened to us? Juan happened. Sally happened. David stopped surviving and started dying. It's not any one thing. Don't you think it's the nature of human beings to wander around trying to find out what's missing from ourselves? That it's partly biological?"

"Maybe, but—"

"But what? You don't think I had a right to that?"

"He was gay, Ness."

"So what? Come on, Phoebe, look at Mimi and Dayle. Siegfried and Roy. Amos and Andy or whoever. David and I weren't such a stretch."

"Tell me how I'm supposed to understand why my best friend felt compelled to keep secret from me the most important thing a girl can do with her life? What was that about, Ness?"

Ness looked into the fireplace, where half-burned logs lay gathering dust. Instead of a fire crackling and hissing, their barely repressed feelings provided the heat for the room. On the cushions lay Phoebe's barn jacket, and on the table, fixings for tea were laid out. Phoebe was like that—thinking ahead, the second thing already in place, since it was so hard for her to do the first. Ness was suddenly hungry for scones and butter and big gobs of blackberry jam. "It was all happening so fast. I didn't want it to be happening at all. David was so worried about his money going to his homophobic relatives. You saw those creeps. Malcolm said he had to make a living will. He asked could he make me executor—you know, put in writing that I could control his money and make sure it went to the college and so on—and when we talked to Malcolm he explained the pros and cons of everything, and suggested that if we were married, things would be more secure, so we did it. We got married."

"That's the reason? To help him manage his estate?"

Ness fidgeted. "Well, there was some of that other thing going on."

"Define other thing," Phoebe said.

"Oh, Phoebe. Doesn't the love thing go without saying?"

"It most certainly does not."

Ness sighed. "How can I explain this to you? There's sexual love and there's friendship love and out of nowhere came this other thing, this communion, I guess, for lack of a better term. It was right there, beyond sex, beyond friends, a kind of love I never dreamed I'd experience. We both had the virus. David was like my unwilling mentor. He loved horses. When I was with him, lying next to him in his bed talking about the afterlife, trying to figure out how I was going to go on living after he died, something happened to my heart. I loved him enough that when he asked I didn't hesitate for a second. I wanted to marry him. He's probably the only man I ever could marry. Why, why, *why* can't you understand that and forgive me?"

Already the surface of the clay was turning white, drying out in the warm air of the studio. Ness longed to spritz it with the water bottle Phoebe kept handy, to send it back to its great, soft lump of potential.

"But I was your best friend, Ness. You couldn't have told me all this when it was happening?"

Ness crossed the room to the wedging table. She dipped a cheesecloth rag in a bowl of water and covered the gray lump. "Phoebe, you *are* my best friend. I like to think you loved me enough to let me be brave enough to marry a man with a death sentence hanging over his head. I like to think that you above everyone else would know that no matter how short a union it was, it was pretty important—that for while it lasted, I needed to make it my first priority—and another thing—Lord, I don't know if I should say this."

"Just say it, Ness."

"Sweetie, after Juan died you were a mess. So angry at having him torn from your life there were days you spit on me just for the crime of bringing you your oatmeal. But I knew the grief was devastating you, pushing you into corners that made you show your claws to everyone. I let you say awful things to me because you knew I was safe. I never stopped loving you. Now it's my turn. I'm a wreck, and maybe I don't show my pain the way you did, but trust me, inside, I'm a raw wound, and if I didn't have the kindness of friends, I'd swallow the pills in David's medicine chest and drive my damn PT Cruiser over the cliffs at Big Sur."

Phoebe, who'd been leaning on her crutches against the worktable, moved back to sit in her wheelchair. She wheeled herself to the sink and rinsed her hands, flicking on the electric teakettle. Calmly and deliberately Phoebe said, "I know you loved David. We all did. He was an amazing person. If I learned anything of worth from losing Juan, it's that you don't have to stop loving that person. I mean, nowhere is it written that thou shalt not feel love for someone who's gone. Maybe I'm a selfish brat just like my daughter. Immature. I never really had friends before you. I had hospital wardmates, and my aunt, and the occasional well-meaning stranger. Deep down I'm terrified I'm replaceable. How awful to be so petty."

Ness went to her side. She wanted to bend down to hug her friend, but she knew if she did Phoebe might throw her arm up to keep the distance. "Pettiness is human. We all have it. I could never discard you, Pheebs. For one thing, I'd have to give up on Sally, and I need that little dickens around. She is an angel on earth. Thank God you brought her into all our lives."

Phoebe gave a short laugh. It was all that was needed to shift things back to normal. "Angel, my butt. That child is more of a workout than my Pilates tape. Thankfully she's too young to understand that she inherited a house. Otherwise she'd probably move out today, hire herself a cook and cleaning person, and lie around giving orders while she watched the *Powerpuff Girls* and gorged on Gummi Worms. I am doomed, Ness. And it has nothing to do with the wheelchair, my heart, or her eventual adolescence. It's her brain I fear the most. I think her IQ might be higher than Ask Marilyn."

"Ask who?"

"Marilyn vos Savant. She writes that genius column in *Parade* magazine. Solves brainteasers and breaks military codes and generally makes the Mensa Society people look like Dick and Jane in the slow readers' group." Phoebe shuddered. "And Sally already reads and tells time. Why did she have to be so freaking smart?"

"God has a sense of humor."

Phoebe looked at her and said nothing, but Ness could tell she was meeting her halfway. She made tea for both of them. They lay down on the cushions near the fireplace and said nothing for a long time. Ness didn't know about Phoebe, but she herself slept hard and dreamless, one less thing to worry about weighing on her no longer.

Ness drove back to David's—her—house the next morning, several boxes of trash bags in the backseat. She thought she might tackle David's wardrobe, but the minute she opened his dresser drawers she knew she could never lay cashmere and silk against Hefty plastic. She stacked the clothes on the sofa and sat on the floor looking at them, trying to imagine someone coming across his suit jackets and button-down shirts, wearing something of his to a job interview, or loving one shirt so much it became the thing he wanted to put on the second he got home from work. She called the *Blue Jay,* Bayborough's weekly newspaper, and placed an ad for an estate sale: *Men's clothing, lovely furniture, many collectibles including Western and Indian artifacts. Saturday, nine A.M. to four P.M. No early birds.*

She put on his raincoat and went outside, climbed the fence, and sat looking into the empty corral. Men and horses. Horses and men. They came and went and cost a lot to keep, and when either died, it was like a redwood falling. She vowed never to fall that deeply in love again.

The Saturday of the estate sale Nance showed up early with a bag full of croissants and some tangerines. "You want coffee?" Ness hollered as she heard the door open. "I made it extra strong."

Then she heard another door open and the unmistakable sound of retching. Setting down the stickers and marker, she went to the bathroom and gently rapped on the door. "Nance? Are you getting sick again? That flu bug bit you hard, didn't it? Listen, you didn't have to come down here when you're feeling bad. Go on home. I can handle the hordes."

Nance emerged from the bathroom looking pale and puffy.

"Goodness, you look like you were up all night slamming body shots. You need to slow down, girl. Stop living that high life."

"This isn't a hangover or the flu," Nance said. "I'm pregnant."

"You're *what*? I thought Lester said you had to stop trying."

Nance reapplied her lipstick and primped the ends of her hair. "Lester did. He just didn't explain it to my ovaries. And voilà! just when I'd given up on them, they surprised me. I'm four months gone."

"But you don't look pregnant."

Nance gave a weak smile. "I know. But I've gained five pounds."

"Whoopee! All that does is make you look normal." Ness held on to her friend, her hands weighing the solidness of Nance's bones, assessing the amount of flesh there, constantly checking to make sure she wasn't slipping into her eating problems, which she had a tendency to do under stress. "Oh, Nancy. What's James think about all this?"

Nance's smile disappeared. "James is furious. He thinks it was irresponsible of me to get pregnant—like he had nothing to do with it! And he's certain it's going to end in disaster, like every time before. The worst part is he says I have to have an amnio. Lester hasn't said anything, because Lester does not know. I've been seeing a midwife in Sierra Grove. She put me on a vegetarian diet and herbs and has me doing yoga. When I'm not throwing up, I feel just great."

Ness was still standing there, openmouthed. "But—," she started to say, and Nance interrupted her.

"Ness, I am forty-five years old, and I have a snowball's chance in hell of carrying this baby to term. I am sick and tired of tests and lying in bed with my legs up in the air, and I am beyond tired of the dreaded spotting that means it's all over again. So until six months have passed, and this baby has a viable chance, I am going to throw up in private and take vitamins and eat right, and if James can't live with that then I will move back into the house with you and Phoebe."

Ness sucked in a breath. "I don't know if you can put Phoebe in that position. James is her brother. And whatever you do, don't keep this a secret from her. I'm walking proof of just how bad an idea that is."

"Well," Nance said, "I guess that means I should call her now, because if she can't deal with me pregnant, I have to get the hell out of Dodge before James has me committed."

"You know what, Nance? Let's erase that conversation. Think you can keep some tea down?"

Nance shook her head. "Never liked that stuff. But Seven-Up works. I have a six-pack in the car. If I sip on that and eat little bits of croissant, I do okay. It's worst in the morning, but after I upchuck, I'm good to go."

They heard a car drive up and Ness pulled aside the curtain. "Damn early birds," she said. "I told them in the ad I wasn't going to open a minute before nine."

Nance stood by her and looked out the window. A tall black man stepped out of one of those new retro T-birds Ford had come out with last year. He was dressed in faded blue jeans and a long-sleeved white T-shirt. "Be still my heart," Nance said. "Now isn't that a sight to jump-start the heart first thing in the morning?"

Ness shushed her friend and continued sticking price tags on David's things.

The early bird waited until nine, sitting on the fender of his car and reading a newspaper.

Nance studied him. "He's polite," she said. "And easy on the eyes. Wonder if he's single?"

"Hush up," Ness told her. "Fine talk for a mother-to-be. So this midwife, the one in Sierra Grove. What's she say about your pregnancy? Does she think things are going okay so far?"

Nance smiled and touched her belly. "That's just it, Ness. She thinks things are going fine. I heard the heartbeat. It's fast, so maybe it's a girl."

"What's her opinion on the amnio?"

"She's for it but agrees it's up to me." Nance shrugged. "And that's what has James so angry. He says an amnio is mandatory—that with my age and history, it's a crime not to have the test, and if the baby is Down's I must have an abortion. He says the risk of harm to the baby is minimal, and blah, blah, blah. But I don't want to take even a minimal risk, you know? And while I do believe in a woman's right to choose, I myself could never abort a child. Let's say I carry this baby to term, and it's born with Down's. Does that mean I wouldn't love it to the best of my abilities?"

Ness closed up the package of price stickers. "Of course not. But God gave us minds, Nance. We came up with tests like that to help better children's lives."

"Would you do it?"

Ness bit her fingernail. "Honestly?" she said. "I wouldn't. Follow your heart, Nance. I'll pray for the baby. We all will. I'll make a call and get my prayer group at church working on it. And Nance?"

"Yes?"

"Congratulations. I hope this time everything goes okay."

All day the Bayboroughites came and picked up things, tried to bargain on the unbargainable, *ooh*ed over the odd piece of Baccarat, questioned the authenticity of the Lichtenstein print, generally behaved as if they thought Ness was some kind of hayseed who didn't know from designer labels. When they became annoying, Nance stepped in, removed the item, and told them no. Ness admired how she could smile and slip something out of a grubby hand while at the same time explaining its market value. She flat-out refused to sell the Navajo baskets to this heavily made-up matron with a Kate Spade pony bag in hand. "Now, I'm not one to ban leather," she said, "but that purse did not come from a cow, which is one of God's more simple-minded creatures. Horses and ponies have *souls,* as do these baskets, and I think we're going to donate them to the museum, so you can set them down now."

Ness ducked into the kitchen and made the two of them a cheese-and-fruit plate. She had stuck some 7UP in the freezer until it turned to slush. Nance scooped it into her mouth and looked about to cry from relief. "Oh, this is wonderful! What made you think of freezing it?"

Ness shrugged as she wrapped Murano glass pheasants in newspaper. "Granny Shirley used to give it to me like that when I had a stomach bug. Figured it couldn't hurt a pregnant woman."

Nance grinned. "Pregnant! I say that to myself twenty-five hours a day."

They had made an arrangement with Rebecca Roth to consign David's considerable art collection. She in turn had sent over some serious buyers interested in the collectibles. The price they offered for the Roy Rogers furniture was absurdly low, and

Rebecca told them to get the hell out of the house if they were going to behave like tourists bargaining in Mexico. Ness laughed. "I can't believe you, girl. You just open your mouth and *va-voom!* the room is cleared."

"I don't care. Freaking cheapskates! Life is too short for jerking chains and besides, I plan to use my commission from this to take a nice trip to Mexico where I can lie on the sand and drink myself to sleep while avoiding the whatever holiday is coming up next. Look at me, I'm as pale as mushroom soup."

"That's Central Coast living for you," Ness said. "The only tan you're going to get up here is in a tanning parlor."

Rebecca waved hello to a little old lady who was walking up up the drive. "Oh, don't get me wrong," she said, "I love Bayborough-by-the-Sea. The parties, the houses, the art scene, and so forth, but it's these nouveau riche intruders I can do without. I mean, this isn't LA, for God's sake."

The handsome guy was leaning against the fence, surveying the corral, apparently. Ness nodded in his direction. "Any idea who that is?"

Rebecca shook her head. "But I can find out."

Before Ness could say a word, she was halfway across the yard, and then he was turning to talk to her. She shook his hand, and then went into typical Rebecca mode, gesturing, laughing, and her long blond hair splayed out beautifully against her back. The man put his hands into his jeans pockets, and Ness could tell he was trying to keep Rebecca at a distance, from thinking he was interested, that he was doing it as a kindness. Then he turned his head and looked directly at her. Eye contact. At once Ness knew that he'd tracked her the entire time, that he was waiting for four o'clock, so he could come and ask her for something that hadn't sold. She wondered if he was a Roy Rogers freak like David had been, or if he liked art books, because despite pricing them at a very reasonable twenty dollars apiece, not a single one had sold. Then it hit her—he wanted to buy the property. New car, deliberate casual air, the handsome African-American man realtor who knew that in order to find the properties his clients wanted, he had to be there yesterday to get the listing.

Disappointment flooded her veins, and she went to help the

little old lady who apparently wanted the Baccarat vases, because she was waving her ancient pocketbook and pointing to the glass Ness had polished that morning.

Ness was in the kitchen wrapping the set of dishes the old lady decided she wanted, too. Turned out they were Homer Laughlin, when all Ness had thought was that they were funky fifties restaurant china. She wrapped the cups last, and the woman tottered off to get someone to help her carry the three boxes to the car.

"I understand you need some muscle in here," a voice said, and Ness looked up to see the realtor standing three feet away. He had hazel-colored eyes that reminded her of a fox's.

"Thanks," she said. "These boxes are ready to go."

He hefted them under his arms. "Just out of curiosity, how much did you get for these?"

"Two-fifty."

"Good. It's a fair price."

"How do you know that?"

He nodded toward the box under his right arm. "Antiques dealer. I come from a family of them. You priced things just right here."

"I looked a lot of it up on the Internet."

"That's a good way to check prices. Well, nice talking to you."

Nance came out of the bathroom.

"Are you sick again?" Ness asked.

"No. I just have to pee a lot. Also I figured I'd leave you alone with the handsome guy. I thought maybe he was Rebecca's squeeze, but I guess not, considering how he was looking at you."

"Stop it," Ness said. "He's an antiques dealer. As soon as everyone leaves he'll probably turn into a scavenger and hammer at me until I give him the Roy Rogers stuff."

"Oh, I doubt that. How much money have you made so far?"

"I haven't counted."

"*Ooh,* let me," Nance said. "I just love stacking lovely green bills into piles."

Ness looked at her friend, smoothing out twenties and singles, working the day with her in order to make sure nobody took advantage, and smiling all the while, even though she was in this fragile state, this last-chance pregnancy that most likely would end in miscarriage. Beneath all the designer labels and costly makeup, Nance was a steel magnolia, and deep inside that steel was one of the biggest hearts Ness had ever known. There was no end to her list of things to love: her ex-lover, Rotten Rick; her husband, James; all the farm girls; Sally, quite possibly to excess; horses, her yellow lab, Duchess, to the point that when the old girl was dying, Nance held her in her arms until she took her last breath, whispering "I love you, I love you," until the dog sighed her last. Ness felt her eyes well up as she looked around the house, the shelves half empty, the place looking ransacked, and for a moment, she considered taking the pills in David's medicine cabinet. God knew there were enough.

"How much for the mosaic table?" the antique man said, an hour later when she was ready to call it a day.

Ness dropped the dish towel she'd been wringing. "It's not an antique."

"I didn't say it was. I just wanted to know how much you would take for it."

Ness eyed him. Maybe he meant it. Maybe he was a Realtor in addition to being an antiques dealer. "It's not for sale, actually. I made it. It was a gift to my late husband. Sentimental value and so forth. I'm afraid I really can't part with it."

He nodded. "Mind if I sit for a minute?"

Ness laughed. The only piece of furniture left in the room was a red velvet fainting couch, and the idea of this leggy black man on it was beyond comprehension. "Suit yourself. But it's almost four. I'm kicking everyone out as soon as the last customer finishes loading his car."

He nodded. "I just need a minute of your time."

She sighed. "I'm not interested in dating, selling this house, or giving you a deal on the cowboy stuff. I'm thinking I might hang on to it, actually."

He laughed. "Direct. I like that. I'm not interested in the house or the cowboy stuff, but I would sure like to take you out for a cup of coffee and a doughnut. What kind's your favorite? I'm betting you're a jelly-doughnut gal. Raspberry jelly."

"I like lemon."

"Hey, I was in the right category, wasn't I?"

She looked at him. So handsome. His high-wattage smile. This is how it starts. A dance, a doughnut, a kiss, and then you're in the thick of things. She couldn't go there. Not now, maybe not ever. As handsome as this man was, she felt no chemistry. "You seem like a nice man. But I can't eat a doughnut with anyone right now."

He looked at her levelly. "What *can* you do?"

"Grieve, I guess. Pray when I can stop being mad at God for long enough to say a few words. Clean up this house and figure out what to do with it."

He stood up, took hold of her hand, and gave it a squeeze. "You're going to feel better soon," he said.

"Why did you come here today?" she asked. "You didn't buy anything."

"I wanted to see the Navajo baskets," he said. "Though one of them's Apache. Well. You take care now."

"Goodbye." She watched his back, the way his shoulders squared up, the long legs in his jeans, legs that would need a horse seventeen hands or taller, and how easily he folded his body into the T-bird, backed up, and drove away.

She felt Nance come up beside her and put her arms around her, then lay her head against Ness's shoulder. "We made almost two thousand dollars," she said. "But I think the real bargain of the day just drove off in a T-bird."

"Oh, you," Ness said. "Enough already. He's just another handsome man."

"Right," Nance said. "California has them to spare. You know, I think I might want to buy the Roy Rogers stuff. Do you think you can hang on to it for a few months?"

Until we see if this baby sticks, she did not say, but Ness heard it all the same. "I'll tell you what, Nance. We'll put that furniture in storage, and if things work out, it'll be my present to you, okay?"

Nance clung to her arm. "I'm afraid to hope, Ness."

Ness patted her hand. "I know, sweetie. Believe me, I know."

Phoebe

11

Big Sur for Lunch

WHEN NESS CAME HOME the night of the estate sale, she went directly to Phoebe's room, and found her already in bed, just about to crack her March mystery novel book club offering. It was titled *Beware the Ides*. "I thought you'd be staying at David's," she said.

"Can't," Ness said. "The place feels so empty. I'm going to sell it."

"Uh-oh," Phoebe said. "You have that look on your face. Did something happen? Why can't we go a week without a crisis?"

Ness shoved her hands into her jacket pockets. "You wanted to be kept up-to-date on things," she said. "Well, I've got breaking news. Brace yourself. Nance is pregnant again. Just entering her second trimester."

Phoebe listened while Ness explained about how Nance had waited three months to tell James in the first place. How the beef-eating protein cheerleader among them was now filling her plate with organic veggies and lecturing on the merits of antioxidants and yoga exercises. She saved for last the fact that James was none too happy over Nance refusing to have an amniocentesis. "Four months," Phoebe said, remembering lying in this very bed at that stage, sure the nausea would be with her forever. "That's a good long while. It seems kind of pointless for James to get all huffy at this late date. Think I should I go talk to him?"

"Yes," Ness said. "Absolutely I think you should. What Nance needs now is to be supported, not stressed. And while I think it's great she's finally eating properly, is during pregnancy the time to make such a drastic dietary change? I hate meat as much as you do, but if it meant the difference between a healthy baby or not, I'd find some way to choke it down."

Phoebe put down her book and picked up the phone. The succulent draw of a new crime story would have to wait while she tended to mysteries closer to home. "Hello, Stinky," she said when she heard the machine click on. "Don't you think it's time we spent some quality sibling time together? I was thinking tomorrow we might take a drive to the Big Sur house, check it out. Come fetch me as soon as Sally goes to school. We'll have lunch at that restaurant with the dog on the roof. My treat. Lovies to you and Nancy. Bye-bye."

Ness lay down next to her in bed. "What a day."

"Did you sell all the things you wanted to?" Phoebe asked.

"Most of them," Ness answered. "Made a couple grand. I'm going to give the money to the AIDS hospice. I'd feel awful keeping it."

"Then that's the right thing to do. Are you going to put the house on the market right away?"

Ness turned over so she was facing Phoebe. "Not yet. It's like I can't let everything go all at once, you know?"

"I know," Phoebe said, patting her friend on the arm. "Believe me, I know. Don't let anybody hurry you, and don't give away all his clothes. Sometimes I put on Juan's shirt, just so I can remember him. "

"Phoebe?"

"Yes?"

"Can I stay here with you tonight?"

"You bet. Let me scooch over so there's room."

"Okay, spill it," Phoebe said to James as soon as they drove past Bayborough Highlands, the private estates barely visible behind crooked Monterey pines and elaborate gates just south of the farm.

"Spill what?" James said. "Am I supposed to know what you're talking about?"

Phoebe narrowed her eyes. "For God's sake, James. Don't play stupid with me. I know Nance is pregnant, I know you're freaking out over it, and I know that you, my brother, eat yourself alive when you don't get your way."

James kept his eyes fixed on the twisting two-lane highway, the yellow Mercedes passing through low-lying fog as it headed south. He frowned, and took his time responding to Phoebe's command. "So if you know all that, why talk to me about it? Why not have a baby shower, or call a meeting of the coven like you girls are always doing? After all, I'm just the father. Nance is the one who's pregnant. It's her body, and according to her, I don't have the right to stick needles in it even if I do have my progeny's best interests at heart."

Phoebe laughed. "Come on, James. This is a child we're talking about!"

"No, it's a fetus."

"A fetus? What the hell does that mean? A fetus also happens to be a baby, James."

"Don't you think I know that? Jesus Christ, I want her to have a test to find out if the baby's retarded or has spina bifida or whatever else they can get that makes their lives not worth living! Who wouldn't want to spare a child that kind of life . . ."

While James unloaded, Phoebe traced the wear pattern on her blue jeans. Why was it the second a pair got perfectly broken in, they weren't considered proper street clothes? Science could unravel DNA and clone sheep; surely someone could make denim feel as good as it looked. She said nothing while James ranted about congenital defects, how modern medicine couldn't cure everything, and the prejudice with which handicapped people were met. When he finally ran out of gas, she waited for him to come to the realization that what he'd said was offensive to her, with her crooked spine and inability to keep up with the rest of the world. It took him from the last Highlands estate to the Big Sur lighthouse, when he pulled into a scenic overview and put his face in his hands and began to weep.

Phoebe rubbed small circles against his heaving back. She'd

seen Stinky cry only a few times. There was something about men crying that felt unbearable to her. Not that men shouldn't be *allowed* to cry, but that whatever it took to get them there had to be pretty horrible. When Sally cried it was usually because she hadn't gotten her way or she was overtired. Phoebe knew that her child's sorrow wouldn't last or harm her in any memorable way, but not so with James. She felt a knot form in her own throat just listening to him. "She's almost at the halfway mark with the pregnancy," she pointed out. "Just a few more months."

"Unless she loses it," he said from behind his fingers. "Phoebe, I can't go through that again. It damn near tore me up when she lost the last one. But it killed something inside her. You girls don't even know the half of it."

Phoebe understood that Nance cut loose with her husband, that the things she told the girls were probably tidied up a little. She also knew that the miscarriages were the breaks of the game, just like losing your fiancé to a car wreck, or your beloved aunt to cancer, or having a heart that didn't work like everyone else's. She saw life and death in her garden on a daily basis. "Go with her to the doctor," she said.

"Midwife," he mumbled. Then, louder, "Midwife! For God's sake, with all her problems, she decides to use someone who didn't even go to med school!"

"Fine, go with her to the midwife. Listen to the baby's heartbeat. Make yourself an integral part of the checkups. Buy yourself a stethoscope and listen to the baby's heartbeat every day. I guarantee you won't be able to stick a needle in her after you hear that."

"But what if it's a Down's syndrome baby? Or that spina bifida—"

"James! Look at me!"

"I am looking at you. I'm—"

"Excuse me, I'm your sister, and I happen to be a what-if. Now I realize your life would have been much easier without me, you probably would have gotten way cooler Christmas gifts and an Ivy League education, but look me in the eyes and tell me it wasn't fun sometimes, that you didn't enjoy gluing all my dolls' eyes shut, or me cutting up your model airplanes and flushing them down the toilet. Who else would have thought to put salt in the sugar bowl on April Fool's Day? If Mother'd aborted me, you would have probably grown up to be a chubby librarian instead of married to a knockout and having all kinds of fun being an indulgent uncle to Sally. I still want to kill you for getting the pony, but look at how much fun Sally is having. Would you really rather have missed that just because my legs don't work?"

He shook his head. "I'm sorry about my colossal insensitivity. It never occurs to me that you're handicapped. Mostly I just think you're annoying. And I'm sorry about getting the pony."

"You are not. It's all right. I'll get your kid one, too."

He tried to laugh, but it came out tears. After wiping his eyes, he said, "The thing is, Phoebe, I don't know if I'd be any good to a Down's kid."

"Well, I don't know a soul on earth who thinks he is until it happens to him. You'd learn. And besides, it hasn't happened yet. Stop worrying this instant. Think positive. Go to the midwife. Get Ness to invoke the Baptist prayer circle. Now drive me to my daughter's inheritance, okay?"

"All right already," he said, just as he'd done when they were kids and he'd lost the argument. He pointed at her. "But just so you understand, I'm still not a hundred percent on the amnio thing."

Phoebe opened his glove box, inside which she found an unopened box of red licorice. "The minute you're a hundred percent on anything where kids are concerned, the game changes, my friend. I can't believe I'm giving you advice. Okay if I eat this?"

"Go right ahead. It isn't mine. It belongs to my wife. My junk-food-craving, pigheaded, absolutely gorgeous, and stubborn wife."

Phoebe broke the seal and pulled out a red twist. "Mmm, I haven't had red licorice in a long time. And just think, if things go well, I'm going to finally be an aunt. And Sally will have a cousin to beat up."

James shook his head. "Please, I can take no more. Where's the map? I don't want to end up in Esalen."

"Things look fairly flat down this way," he called up to Phoebe as she sat in her wheelchair, the brake set, peering down from the crumbly tarmac driveway to the house David Snow had left her daughter. Maybe "house" wasn't the right word. "Dwelling," or "cottage," or "This is like nothing you've ever seen before"—would be more apt. A big gray wooden box featuring rectangular boxy windows was what this place was, and while thirty years ago it was probably a source of much neighborhood controversy, right now it just looked shabby. The box looked to be about twelve hundred square feet, did not have a garage, and the roof—that flat expanse of patchy tarpaper, looked as if when the next high wind blew through it would take flight. She half wished James would come up and say they'd made the turn too soon, that this was the wrong place.

James walked back into Phoebe's view and unlatched the wooden gate that had turned gray and furry from years of exposure to the elements. There was a slight decline in the hill, so Phoebe waited until he'd come around to her side before she proceeded forward in her chair. "The patio has a few loose stones," he said. "Nothing that can't be fixed. I didn't go inside, but it looks like there's only the one threshold out onto the deck that might prove a problem. You won't even need a contractor for that. Still, it isn't the Tickle Pink Inn. It's rustic."

"Thanks for coming with me, Stinky." Phoebe rolled along the property, noticing where pampas grass, that gorgeous, plume-tailed invader, grew in bunches, overtaking the smaller, indigenous plants and grasses. Maybe it didn't belong, but it sure was pretty. And the view—once again, she tried to take it in, and once again, she failed at the larger picture and could only assimilate fragments. Her new place—to be held in trust until Sally came of age—sat tucked into the craggy hills along the most beautiful stretch of coastline California had to offer. Its only neighbor within view was the Pacific Ocean. A funky beach cottage with a clear shot of the Pacific was an impossible notion anymore. Every year Big Sur passed more stringent building regulations. Unless grandfathered from family member to family member, a person didn't get in except to rent. And forget about building improvements when new paint required committee meetings and applications and a whole lot of nonsense. But who could think about that when she looked at the water? Holy moly, mother of all! This deep blue water beat sunsets on her farm hands down. Turquoise near the rocks, the water was clear enough to see down to the sand. Farther out the pale blue muted as it deepened into layers of gray to steel to what seemed to Phoebe's eyes like endlessly deep liquid midnight. A person had to applaud the inaccessible shoreline simply because it took such Herculean effort for anyone to get down there and screw it up. The wind blew against her neck, so she pulled her coat close. Someday Sally would stand here and think her own thoughts, and right then it hurt to think that the little munchkin would grow up and think things she wouldn't tell her mother.

"This is why Nance didn't want to come along, isn't it?" James said. "So you could knock some sense into me?"

"I never said a word to her," Phoebe answered. "Ness told me Nance was pregnant. You and I really haven't spent much time together lately. I miss that. Not that I'd ever want to go back to the way things were, just you and me, but you are my favorite brother. It's just that you're so damn busy. Every time I turn around you're in Texas or San Francisco. "

"I'm your favorite brother? I'm your *only* brother."

"Oh, don't split hairs. Seriously, we talk about the farm, about money, but I miss the old days, just talking about nothing. Arguing, even. We've come a long way since Sadie died, haven't we, James? Did you ever imagine our lives would turn out like this?"

He shook his head no. "Some days I wake up in my house and look over at Nance and I think this must be someone else's life, because it sure can't have happened to me."

Phoebe smiled. "She adores you, James. You are one lucky duck."

"Don't I know it. Okay, then. Ready to look inside?"

"Lead the way."

James unlocked the front door and it creaked open, releasing the scent of salt and old wood, and a faint hint of the ever present mildew Central Coasters endured because it was such a small inconvenience compared to everything else.

"Is Nance—you know, eating?" Phoebe asked tensely. The word "anorexia" hovered close in the air, but she wasn't going to say it unless she had to. Again, Phoebe marveled at how reticent her brother was, how different from her who could never hold her tongue, and how differently she acted around him as a result.

"That she is," James said, dusting his fingers off on his blue jeans. "The morning sickness gets her down, but now that she's into this vegetarian thing full force it seems to be better." He looked at his sister. "I guess we'll never stop worrying, will we?"

"Probably that's a good thing."

"Yeah." He felt around the wall for a light switch, but the power wasn't turned on, and his fingers came away covered with dust. "Need a posse of Merry Maids to get this place in order," he said. "Look at the ceiling."

The ceiling was at least sixteen feet high, supported by exposed beams, and in every corner a gold-medal cobweb clung fast. Phoebe parked herself in front of the plate glass windows. Like everything else in the cabin, they needed attention. Salt spray had left them pockmarked and gritty. She wheeled herself to the makeshift desk—a door set on sawhorses—and wondered what David had written here, which movies he'd had produced, what his failures were, and how he'd dealt with them. The place would make anyone want to write. It had that feel to it—nothing but you and the water and the paper in front of you, permission to fill it any way you liked. In a way it also reminded her of Andrew's studio, spare and masculine, but permeated by something deeply sad. There was a red coffee can of pens and pencils on top of the desk-door. She tipped it until they all spilled out. Most were hotel pens, cheap and out of ink, not worth saving. The pencils were all mechanical, so old their eraser tips had turned brittle. There were some sea-polished rocks, too. Why had David ever left the place? Why had it been ignored when he took such good care of his home in the Valley? Maybe he couldn't bear the beauty of the water when he himself was so sick, she thought. Maybe he couldn't bear to let it go, either, so he just kind of abandoned it.

Maybe he wanted to surprise them all, which he'd certainly done.

"The chimney flue looks clean," James said, leaning back to stick his head into the fieldstone fireplace. "I wonder what the fire regulations are here. Got to be pretty stringent."

Big Sur had had more than its share of wildfires, acreage lost to heavy rains, and highway closures that panicked Phoebe even to think about. In summertime the traffic was one endless stream of honking automobiles. Tourist income kept the town solvent. Campers at the state park, honeymooners at the inns, leftover hippies searching for Jack Kerouac's ghost—as annoying as it might be, that kind of thing kept the winter residents flush enough to stay on until tourist season started again. Phoebe rarely visited Big Sur. It made her nervous. Early on she'd learned that wherever she went, she'd better scope out the exits, because they were different for people in wheelchairs than for the rest of the world. Suddenly it struck her that while she had that exit-plan thing down in just about every other part of her life, maybe it wasn't such a good thing, looking at everything new place as potential for disaster. For one thing it would either make Sally paranoid or a rebel. For another it was time she admitted to herself there really was no safe place, particularly now that her bedroom had transformed into the scariest place of all, thanks to Andrew lying down in her bed and kissing her a few short weeks ago. *Ha, ha, funny as a crutch,* she used to say when she was a kid, just to make the able-bodied nervous. But the memory of the kiss gave her insides a tiny shudder. Nice thoughts for a mother to be thinking, she told herself. So why hadn't Andrew called her since the kiss? She had the answers all lined up:

1. She was a dry run, a safe woman to try his moves out on before he returned to the world of able-bodied women.

2. He was going to marry one of the women from James's dinner party, she reminded herself. A man that handsome can get by without legs just fine.

3. Phoebe who? He said to himself every morning while he waited for the coffee to perk. Did I really kiss that woman? What the hell was I thinking?

James wobbled the sliding glass doors in their track, finally freeing one, letting in a blast of sea wind that smelled of summer. He stood on the patio and stretched his arms above his head and sighed. In front of him sunlight dappled the water until it looked like hammered copper. Phoebe inventoried the changes in her brother since marrying Nance. James had learned to listen—not just talk over a person and bulldoze his way. He'd found a workout that helped him shed the extra twenty he'd carried since high school, and as a result he'd started dressing more carefully, so that even in his jeans and a pullover shirt he looked crisp and stylish, and—she didn't know what—important, maybe, like he believed in himself. She'd always compared his looks to John Kennedy Jr. Now that the poor fellow was dead, it wasn't her favorite analogy. Now she decided, he looked like a Kennedy carrying a moral compass. He'd pulled most of his high-risk investments out of the stock market before losing his shorts, but he'd taken a hit nonetheless. Against James's counsel, Phoebe'd kept her money in the bank. So what if she hadn't earned a ton in interest? At least every penny was there and accounted for. Now James was investing in long-term, lower-yield ventures. Phoebe had seen his P&L; he had trust funds, one for Sally and one unnamed, which she suspected was for his own potential child. She looked at him standing there and said, "You know, if I didn't have such a crappy heart, I'd have a second baby and give it to you."

He wheeled around and looked at her, shamefaced, as if he had been thinking the very same thing. "For God's sake don't even say something like that. Maybe I wasn't meant to be a father. Maybe it just isn't in the cards for Nance and me. We're getting older, you know. Pretty soon I'll start using a golf cart rather than walk the back nine."

"That's ridiculous," Phoebe said. "Nance loves you too much to let you get old. When you're eighty, you two are going to look like Andrew's parents, all in shape, silver hair stylishly done, nice clothes, and give great parties. And I bet you'll have this child and a couple of grandkids."

"One can only hope."

"Hope hard, is what I say." Phoebe looked left and saw the roof of another house, hidden in the side of the hill like hers, peeking out from a twisted cypress tree that looked as if it belonged in a British mystery. She didn't tell James what she really felt, which was that hope was the one element that should have been let out of Pandora's box.

"My, my," James said. "What's that look on your face mean? Something's got your undies in a knot. Could it be Andrew Callahan?"

"No, it most certainly could not. I just think that age creeps up on a person, fakes them into doing stupid things, and it pisses me off. I want you to have me arrested if I start wearing those Bayborough-by-the-Sea sweater sets. Or pastel-colored sweats."

James sat down on the rock wall that enclosed the patio. Bright green succulents grew up the hillside, their purple blooms the exact hue of sea urchins. "I'll arrest you myself. So. You going to renovate this place or sell it? Something has to be done, or it will probably fall down."

Phoebe had already felt the atmosphere enter her heart and take up residence. "It would make the most wonderful getaway, wouldn't it? I mean, say you were sick and tired of yourself, you could come here and do nothing at all except look at the water. I think I'll fix it up a little, James. I can afford the taxes, and we're in no giant hurry here."

"Maybe Nance would like to take it on as a project," he said. "She's really great at getting contractors to show up and fix their mistakes. And a dynamite decorator."

"And she's going to make a terrific mom, and be uncommonly busy for the rest of her life. Hey, you want to go to lunch? I'm starving, and it's been years since I've eaten at the place near the Big Sur library. You remember—the cook's dog sat on the roof. How cool was that?"

"Pretty cool." James began locking the doors. "I was thinking of getting Nance a puppy for Easter. A lapdog she could take places. I know she misses Duchess like crazy. What do you think?"

Phoebe let her brother push her chair up the driveway so she didn't have to struggle over the bumpy places where the tarmac had worn to gravel. "I think a dog's a great idea. Although why not a pony?"

"Har-de-har-har, Phoebe. You can stop punishing me for Penelope. Sally is turning into a crackerjack little equestrienne. That pony is a champ."

"Yeah, but only because I have the worry lines to prove it. Don't go buying a puppy," she said. "They pee all over the carpet and dig in the garden. There're tons of dogs in the Valley that need homes. Put the word out you're looking and somebody will no doubt have a spare, or better yet, go to the shelter. It's spring. People move and dogs get left behind like ugly furniture. God, I love warm weather. It feels so promising. Sex and love and all things fecund, you know?"

"Speaking of fecund," James said to her back. "You never did elaborate on Andrew Callahan."

Phoebe didn't reply until she'd settled herself in the yellow Mercedes and thought about the days when her aunt drove the car, and how much fun they'd had before cancer claimed her and she had shrugged off her earthly bonds in favor of wings. "I hadn't planned to. He's a charmer," she said. "Southern as molasses."

"Yeah, but is he a good kisser?" James said.

Phoebe gave him double fish-eyes. "Shut up and drive, will you?"

"Herb tea, the house dressing on the house salad, and could I have some more rolls?" Phoebe said. "These are so good I'm ready to cram a few in my purse."

The waitress nodded. "Everyone says that. For you?" she asked James.

"Bowl of the vegetable minestrone, ditto on the rolls, and do not let me order that chocolate bombe cake, okay? I'm serious. We're talking DA."

"Excuse me?"

"Desserts Anonymous."

When the waitress walked away, clearly not finding this funny, Phoebe felt compelled to explain. "It must be harder for hippies to get old than it is for us, don't you think? Birkenstocks were never that comfortable, no matter what everyone said. Personally I think they give you bunions. And we've just witnessed what happens when a woman skips wearing a bra for twenty years. Not a pretty sight."

"Stop," James said, breaking the last roll in half and handing the larger portion to Phoebe. "Now I'm going to focus on that poor woman's bosom all through lunch, thank you very much. Why do you always have to talk about things like that in public? Why can't you just pretend that you didn't see it?"

"Because they practically smacked me in the face." Phoebe scanned the slanting roof of the café, and there it was, an old black dog, lying on the shingles, catching the sun. "That has to be a replacement roof dog," she said. "Unless he's in the *Guinness Book of World Records* for world's oldest roof pet."

"Probably a hippie dog," James said. "Vegetarian, like you, so he'll live longer."

"And your wife," she reminded him. And your baby, she thought, but kept to herself. What would it take to have that child make it, she wondered? Or were Nance's chances for a pregnancy lasting until term random? Oh, this town, Phoebe thought as they ate their food. Henry Miller's cabin and the miniscule museum. So scathing once upon a time, his legendary parties and the explicit sex in his books. What would he think of MTV? she wondered. The library next door to the restaurant so tiny it couldn't hold a thousand books. The general-delivery post office had burned down. Gift shops came and went, and Phoebe hadn't been inside a single one. How could she explore when her chair was always bumping into things, in everyone's way? I suppose I could have sued, she thought, and ruined the businesses so I could have those few extra inches, the ramps and wider bathroom stall, and so on. But it seemed so much easier to make my haunts other places. What have I missed?

"What are you thinking about, Wingnut?"

She set down her fork. "Sally's at gymnastics as we sit here idling. She's never seen Big Sur. But she will, and then she'll want to float down the river on an inner tube, hike to the falls, and buy a hundred-and-eighty-dollar wet suit and try to stand up on a surfboard in an ocean where great white sharks cruise by and the undertow can break a person's neck." She picked up her fork and stabbed a miniature corncob. "I guess the house thing is really making me take stock. It's as if David left it in trust to me to make me think about my life, to remind me I am at yet another crossroads, that I have a tiny little window of time to have a sex life, or throw a party, or—I don't know—go places that aren't safe. If he were here with us I'd probably have to slap him."

"Come on," James said. "He probably thought nothing of the kind. He left the house to Sally in lieu of a monetary gift. He was thinking of land as a stable investment. Same as Sadie, I suppose. Of course, she knew investments. The portfolio she left was top shelf."

"Listen to you, will you?" Phoebe said. "All of the sudden you're talking like a legal document. David was a lot of things, but he wasn't dry and unemotional. He loved Sally, and he wanted her to have that view."

"I'm sorry, I just don't see it that way."

"James? Will you try this little experiment for me? Suppose you could leave Sally one thing, only one, and it can't be money. What would you want her to have most?"

"Sound business sense."

"You're hopeless."

"Then tell me what you'd leave her. Besides a hopeless romantic nature that will break her heart repeatedly."

"It's easy for me," Phoebe said. "I'd leave her the flowers. She can learn everything she needs to by growing flowers. Which is why I submit that David left her a view she can learn from. Voilà! once again, I'm correct."

James signaled the waitress. "Chocolate bombe cake?" he said.

"I'm sorry, sir. I just sold the last piece."

"That's all I wanted to hear." He handed her his credit card and she took off to process the transaction. "Well, Pheebs," he said. "The way I look at it, David left the house to Sally because it was practical. If she owned a part of the coast, she'd have some say in what happened to it after he was gone. If you sense a message in all that, that's a bonus."

"No, James, it's not like that at all. He did it to remind her that just when you think you have your life running nice and smooth, and you relax, something else comes along to make you rearrange things. That's what he wanted her to have, James."

"Do you see your life that way?"

"James," she said. "Some mornings I wake up and think there's been a mistake. I wasn't meant to have this big a life."

He reached across the table and took hold of her wrists. "Me, too, Wingnut. It is the luckiest goddamn thing, and we have to make the most of it." The waitress returned with his credit-card slip, and he signed it and tucked a ten-dollar bill inside her receipt. "So, sister of mine. Where to next?"

She folded her napkin and set it alongside her plate. "I guess you better drop me off at Andrew's. Might as well face this thing head on. Will you pick the princess up from gymnastics?"

James looked at her, red faced, shocked, and a little embarrassed. "You're not going to—you wouldn't—oh, why do you tell me these things? Of course I will pick up my niece. But I expect you to call me later."

"You know what, Stinky? You are starting to sound like a farm girl. There is too much estrogen in your life. You need to make sure that puppy is a male. Let's go before I lose my nerve."

The driveway to the front door felt like a roller-coaster ride. Through the glass panes she saw Andrew working out with his trainer, a muscled guy with a shaved head and tattoos. Andrew could handle heavy weights with his arms. His chest was well defined. But all that stopped at his legs. She realized she'd never seen them. Today he was wearing shorts, and every other time she'd been near him he was wearing blue jeans or slacks. But then he'd never seen hers, either. Just like her, his shoes didn't get scuffed on the soles. Just like her, he needed someone to help him go through range-of-motion exercises. And watch what he ate. And deal with occasional bowel concerns no one wanted to hear about. And probably the catheter. Lord. Her body had taken a long time to get this way, but Andrew's had simply broken.

This isn't going to be easy, she decided. Not one minute of it. Sex won't be like it was with Juan. There will be accommodations. Rationalizations. Disappointments on both sides. I can't do it. She placed her hands on her wheels, and backed up, making it almost to the street corner, where she made the mistake of looking up. Everywhere she turned, there were the trees Robinson Jeffers had planted and carried water to. They were the symbol of Bayborough-by-the-sea, tall green giants, sentries guarding the coast, standing there accusing her of being a coward and a fool and of not allowing poetry into her life. Once Sadie had told her, *Without that poet these trees wouldn't be here. The coast wouldn't look like this, the deer wouldn't wander through neighborhoods, and probably Sierra Grove would be the hotspot. Imagine him carrying fresh water to them. It must have been a full-time job. Bless his heart, I think we need to go buy some more of his books.* The books were in the great room at the farm. Well-thumbed pages testified to their timelessness. Phoebe looked up at the poet's work and turned her chair around.

Phoebe wanted to imagine what she was heading into was easy, but first she had to look for the exits. Her money was safe. Sally would go to college. Sally had mothers to spare, a pony, cats, and soon a dog and, hopefully, a cousin. Should anything happen to me, Phoebe thought, James and Nance would take my daughter in and give her the moon. I have to try, she thought. I think Juan would want me to. She wheeled back and rapped on the glass pane in the door, and when Andrew looked out at her she smiled.

Butter-and-eggs grows wild anywhere it can find a space, and thrives in damp areas where trash is dumped. Its flowers are a warm yellow and pale orange and would look right at home in a country kitchen. Also known as toadflax, *Linaria vulgaris* is not native to Alaska, but rather has become naturalized due to its hardy constitution and ability to deeply root itself. Look for it in July and August, its favorite months, a bright yellow spot among the fuchsia of fireweed.

Beryl Anne

12
Old Horses

"COVER MY SHIFT?" Thomas Jack had asked her the first Monday in April, most unfairly, in the middle of the night, right after they had finished making love. "I have to fly to Fairbanks for a few days."

"No," Beryl said. "Alma hates me."

"Come on, Red, you can do this in your sleep. It's only four hours. Half the time she'll be on the phone."

"I just don't understand what I've done to make that woman so nasty."

"Welcome to the club," he said. "She's like that to everybody. Just say you'll do it—if not for me, then for the birds. Okay?"

And Beryl had caved in, mostly out of curiosity. But rather than a nondescript day spend scrubbing guano off mats and charting birds' progress, her four-hour stint turned out to coincide with the blessing of the new eagle mew, a fifty-foot-long structure built as a high school kid's yearlong shop project. When she made her way through the crowds at the door, Alma took her aside and handed her a smock. "Don't get used to this," she said, her hand gripped around Beryl's upper arm. "Most days we're shorthanded, ten birds come in the space of an hour, and the most glamorous task you'll have is folding laundry. Today you can hand out these brochures, but if you come back next week you'll be scrubbing mats and sanitizing cages."

"Thanks for letting me know," Beryl said, shaking Alma's hand off her arm as discreetly as possible. No wonder they called her Bitch and Game—the woman went out of her way to be off-putting, even at a party. Jeez. Beryl gathered the brochures and spread them in a fan on the display table and stood behind it, feeling huffy. Maybe it was proof of her need to be in control, like Thomas said, but she didn't like the structure of the place. She didn't mind scrubbing eagle poop from Astroturf when she could have been doing medical procedures, that was part of the job, but she minded plenty being told she had to pay her dues no matter what her experience. Likewise they didn't need anyone to hand out the brochures. The minute another volunteer came by to spell her, she hightailed it outside to watch the blessing ceremony.

The Tlingit elder was dressed in a button-blanket robe, but there was nothing extravagant about it. He asked everyone to gather near the eagle mew. For a spring day this one felt chilly enough to confuse with fall. Gray clouds overhead threatened rain, and what snow was left looked rotten and pitiful shoved to the side of the enclosure and spotted with bird droppings. Beryl was glad she'd brought her jacket. She hoped the elder could make it through the ceremony without running for cover. She liked his looks, this man with the black-plastic-rimmed eyeglasses and long graying hair falling down his back. Without the blanket robe he could have been anyone—an insurance salesman, someone she'd never met or would notice—but with it, she couldn't take her eyes off him. It struck her then how Earl's Buckethead getup—the chicken bucket and face mask—heightened his music while creating the mystery of who he was, and why did he have to hide in order to play? A child bumped against her, trying to get a better view, and Beryl gently pushed him through the crowd to the front row. Each pearly button on the elder's black wool swirled into the trademark graphic depiction of a Tlingit eagle. When he lit a sage bundle and blessed himself, she closed her eyes and thought of Maddy Caringella and the time she'd spent in New Mexico, where sage grew wild and the wind was perfume. The elder spoke about the mew being a wonderful structure, built with loving care, and how the birds—two longtime rehab eagles named One Foot and Baba Yaga—knew that, and appreciated it—which made Beryl think of Thomas Jack, her "bird whisperer" lover/friend, and how when he turned to her and said what he believed the bird was thinking it was as if an arrow had pierced her heart, his words came out so eerie. The high school kid looked embarrassed at having attention called to himself. When the Channel Thirteen news crew arrived, they shoved their way past the spectators to get a sound bite, and Beryl took advantage of that time to slip away, back into the depths of the building.

In the baby-bird room, a quail occupied one of the cage enclosures, and in a cardboard box atop a heating pad, an injured duckling looked up hopefully, his downy fuzz slowly giving way to feathers. The snowy owl in the crate on the counter was the same one from the week before, and she hissed at Beryl and then spread her wing protectively. Three dead mice bloated with Ringers lay on the edge of her Astroturf. "Don't worry," Beryl said quietly. "Nobody's after your lunch."

If she shut her eyes, the sounds and smells weren't much different from Bayborough Bird Rehab, where she'd worked in California even before she lived at the farm with Phoebe and the girls. Over the years she'd tried hard to keep herself from thinking about it, so as not to fall prey to homesickness. Of course it hadn't all been jolly; every volunteer effort had its share of politics and jostling for position. But most days when she left work to ride her bike home, she was counting the hours until she could go back. Each time she opened the door, it was to something new—shorebirds, a pelican, Steller's jays, migrating geese, and once, there had been an owl, and oh yes, Marty and his bats. She remembered the day they released them, and how the old man had bawled like a baby. A person couldn't help what they loved, and love, rarely logical, called the shots. She wished she could love Thomas Jack, for example—a nice, simple man who liked his work and knew his heart. But despite their sexual chemistry, something was missing, not just from her feelings but his, too.

They didn't talk about it, but it just wasn't there, and someday, she knew, it would be their undoing. She hoped that they could stay friends, but anytime two people made love, going back to friends was hard if not impossible.

She changed the duck's water and covered all but one corner of his box. The quail's food had a sizable dent in it; he wasn't in any danger of starving. She neatened up the rag pile, stacked more newspapers, swept and mopped the floor, and let herself out. People were standing in line to buy the calendars and books the center sold to raise money. In the center of a large group of people, Alma was showing her goshawk, trained to the fist. He was a beautiful bird with intelligent eyes, and Beryl had to admit that Alma knew how to handle him. In the front room, visitors viewed an eagle-release video taken at Fort Richardson. Even on film the moment the bird took flight caused a lump in her throat. Damn Thomas Jack for sending her here. Did she really want to have her heart broken all over again when one of these feathered beauties, despite all efforts, failed to thrive? She could have kicked him; he knew what it would do to her—sending down the thickest of roots—the more attached she became to the birds, the harder it would be to leave him.

And why should she change anything about her life? Their nights were grand. Sex was the perfect reminder that life was worth living. So why by morning was she was ashamed of herself for sleeping with him? Because they were taking advantage of each other, treating intimacy as if it were no more precious than dancing? They should stop now, before someone got hurt. Of course to stop that meant he had to come back, and have a breakup talk, and the last time she'd initiated something like that Earl had disappeared.

Earl.

The house is yours, Beryl. Free and clear. Something you own, something of value. Decorate it any way you want, babe.

When the crowds thinned out, she began clearing away the trash without being asked. Alma put the education birds into their enclosures, and within an hour meds had been dispensed, and it was time to lock the door. "So, will we see you next week?" she asked Beryl in the parking lot.

"I'll have to let you know," Beryl said as she walked toward the taxi she'd called. Just before she closed the car door she was sure she heard Alma say, "It figures."

Forget pissy Alma, forget Earl, his credit-card bill, whether he was alive someplace, happily going about his day, making love to other women, and while she was at it, forget Thomas Jack, too, who still wasn't back from Juneau. Today Beryl was taking her driver's test. Zoë had promised her if she passed, they were going to Wayne's BBQ for a pulled-pork sandwich and some "Southern Exposure" coleslaw—a meal in itself, with the cabbage, corn, pickled carrots, and slices of jicama. When the doorbell rang, Verde whistled, and Beryl ran to open it. Instead of Zoë, there stood a girl no older than nineteen, dressed in those impossibly tiny blue jeans that looked like they'd been run over by a truck. They showed more midriff than seemed humanly possible. Beryl gawked at them and wondered just where was it that the bird's nest began or—oh God, was she one of those women who shaved things down to a closely cropped landing strip? "What happened to Zoë?" Beryl asked.

"Fired," the girl said. In her spandex shirt and push-up bra, her perky breasts were unavoidable.

"Fired? Why?"

"Who knows? Maybe she called in sick too many times. I'm Tish. Let's get going. You're not my only lesson, you know."

Okay, then. So this was how it was going to be.

At the DMV Tish got out of the car and held the door for Beryl. Beryl stalled, playing with her seat belt, looking for Carmex in her purse, anything to delay the moment when she had to slip behind the wheel and prove herself cured of a lifelong phobia to a complete stranger. Tish got tired of waiting, tossed the keys in, and started to walk away. "Hey?" Beryl called out to her. "Don't I get any last words of encouragement?"

Tish, busy now lighting a cigarette she didn't look old enough to buy, frowned. "Oh, you mean the money-back thing. Believe me, you might as well pass this test. The owners of the school will drag out refunding your money for as long as they can. It's a family business, you know. My dad always told me never work for a family business unless it was my own family. Too bad he didn't stick around long enough to help me find a better job."

Beryl sat behind the wheel now and inched the car forward in the testing line. The air smelled of exhaust, cigarettes, and sweat. All the sand and ashes scattered on the ice during winter came back in the form of wind-driven grit as soon as the snow began to melt. Her skin felt dry and gritty. A person couldn't even slather on lotion, because that simply gave the dust something to stick to, and attracted mosquitoes besides.

She gave herself a buck-up speech. "If you flunk the test, you're only letting one person down. No one cares, Beryl. It has to be about you wanting it." She drew a nice-looking middle-aged test examiner who was wearing a very cheap white shirt that looked like it was going to fall apart if he so much as sneezed. He shook her hand, motioned for her to go, and she pulled away from the curb into traffic.

At seventeen she'd driven a few times but had only her learner's permit. Sometimes, rather than drive her, Bette told her to take the Chevy Malibu to the horse stables where she worked after school and on weekends. Her stepmother was waitressing on weekends, still paying off Moose's lawyer from the rape conviction. Not Beryl's rape; that one hadn't been reported. This was the *next* rape, the one he'd committed on a complete stranger, a fourteen-year-old girl who lived three blocks over and had never even kissed a boy. This time he'd gotten caught, and the girl's family had pressed charges. His sentence was five years in a Youth Authority Camp, and you would have thought it was the end of the world so far as Moose was concerned. There Beryl was trying to reassemble her life postdelivery of the son she'd never held, and Moose was the one crying and moaning about having his education interrupted. The fact that Moose was doing easy time was hardly consolation. Rape wasn't murder, Bette said, but Beryl knew that with good behavior, Moose would be out in three years, and he'd do it again. The brief time out was a mere hiccup, in her opinion. She and this poor girl would relive the memories, like Bette's soap opera said, "all the days of their lives."

As often as she could Beryl stayed late at her job tending the horses at Mickey's Stables. Mickey, a tough-as-nails divorcée with a passion for riding began asking Beryl to exercise the school horses, and "spot" the developmentally disabled kids who came for a group lesson on Saturdays. Beryl walked alongside their quiet horses and told them what brave riders they were. There in the sandy arena, with the smells of horse and hay thick in the air, time seemed to stop. For the longest time after the baby was born she couldn't daydream, but when she spent time with the horses, that wondering without boundaries seemed to come back to her. There could be worse things than working for Mickey forever. Who knew? Someday, if her training was good enough, she could start her own riding school and get to watch kids who couldn't manage on the ground feel powerful on the back of a horse.

She'd been driving home in the Malibu, with its oxidizing metallic blue paint and retread tires, when a truck overshot an intersection and T-boned her. Beryl broke her arm; the car was totaled. The driver of the other car, drunk, died without regaining consciousness. Bette's insurance paid for the car and the hospital bill, and then they received a letter informing them that the dead man's family was filing a lawsuit against Beryl as an unlicensed motorist. "What right do they have when it's his fault?" Bette said over and over.

"This is California," the insurance agent said. "People are lawsuit happy. Just wait it out. They'll settle."

Beryl tore up her driver's permit and flushed it down the toilet. Bette purchased a used Toyota with the insurance money. Every day when she brought the mail in, Beryl saw in her stepmother's face that moment when she expected more bad news. Bette began drinking a glass of wine with dinner. A year and a half later, when the lawsuit dust settled—out of court, a thousand dollars over what the insurance company wanted to pay in the first place—Beryl was nineteen years old, Moose was still in Youth Authority, and her stepmother had a serious drinking problem.

"Make a left turn here," the test examiner said.

Beryl came to a stop, checked the traffic on either side, and tried to judge when it was safe to go. She knew she'd let one perfectly reasonable opportunity pass by, and that the man would mark her test down. She let up on the brake and gave the car gas. Her forehead was creased, her shoulders tense, and she felt a drop of sweat roll down her back. Amazingly she was safely in the proper lane and there was no sound of bleating car horns or crunching glass. She let out a breath, and tried to quell the shaking in her hands by gripping the steering wheel even tighter.

They drove through Spenard, Anchorage's middle-class-with-attitude neighborhood. There was plenty to do there—Chilkoot Charlie's bar for music, drinks, and dancing; various hotels just far enough from the airport so you could sleep without hearing jets; Gwennie's Restaurant, where a person could get cherry pie à la mode and a lively chat with a waitress, or so Thomas Jack had told Beryl. So far as she was concerned, this part of Anchorage was archaeological. Only the ruts she frequented were real. They drove down Old Seward, exited, made a left, changed lanes, turned into a subdivision Zoë had once taken her to, and Beryl executed a perfect three-point turn in a neighborhood where kids and dogs ran rampant. A school bus pulled to a stop. The second the little stop sign opened its wing on a school bus, Beryl remembered that a driver had to stop, no matter where she was. Through a surreptitious glance she saw the examiner smile. "Take us back to the DMV," he said. Then it was over, and Beryl sat there speechless while her instructor signed the test and handed it to her under the eaves of the DMV. "Congratulations," he said. "You passed with an eighty-nine."

"Zoë and I were going to lunch," she told Tish on the drive back to Bohemian Waxwing.

"Huh. Well, I guess you'll have to go by yourself."

"Do you have her phone number?"

Tish blinked, her eyelashes so caked with mascara they looked like perching spiders. "No."

"Could you get it? I'd like to call her and tell her I passed."

"It's probably somewhere around the office," Tish said, speeding up the hill and startling two magpies that were having trash for lunch. "Call and ask the payroll lady. I have to go right now or I'll miss my lessons. And I need this job, even if it does suck."

Beryl stood in the driveway watching the Subaru head down the hill for the last time. Another relationship had run its course. Overhead a raven croaked, and she looked up, trying to find him, but wherever he was hiding was a good place. When the snow melted, the ravens seemed to leave town. In their place gulls arrived. She looked at the Bohemian Waxwing, trying to see it as others did, as the Nuthatch, but she failed. To her the house was an eccentric Valentine, the place the lumber baron had built for his bird-crazy, cancer-stricken wife—a structure of love for as long as it lasted. She went inside, fed Verde a red grape, and let him peck at her earrings. "You are a good bird," she told him, and he nuzzled her with his beak.

"I got my license," she told him. "Do you know what this means? It means I can drive anywhere in the world I want to, and even better, you get to come with me. Want to take a trip, Verde? If you could go anywhere in the world, where would it be?"

His top feathers lifted, he swore a few halfhearted curses, and then wanted on top of his cage, where his parrot gym awaited. The sunlight that poured in the window reflected enticingly off his various bells and chimes.

Beryl called information. There was a Z. Pratt on M Street. She wrote the number and address down, fed Verde a second grape, and noticed Mike Stokes's cat atop the fridge. She was intently watching a mouse race from one chunk of baseboard heating to another across the room. Beryl sighed, took pity on the cat, and poured her a bowl of kibble. She locked Verde in his cage, paced the living room, tried the phone number for Zoë, and got the "out of service" recording.

She took a load of laundry downstairs but dropped it on the floor and opened the door to the garage. There stood Earl's truck. His precious machine. The vehicle that had moved her from California to Alaska. Most of the fingerprint dust came away with a rag and some glass cleaner. She slid behind the wheel clutching the damp rag and studying the instrument panel. How hard could it be? She started the truck, pressed the garage door opener, and backed out, scattering a few logs from the woodpile that was showing itself since the snow level had receded. "Oh, no!" she cried, then, thinking a moment, added, "What the hell do I care? It's my fucking woodpile!" and she hit it again, and logs scattered, making a wonderfully satisfying noise and mess.

Zoë lived near the cemetery, with its fenced-in graves and well-trimmed green grass. People left artificial bouquets, toys, and balloons on the markers. On holidays it was crowded with visitors, but most of the time it was empty of the living. The few trees that managed to root had leafed out. It was raining, but Alaskan rain wasn't like the blinding sheets of rain they got in California. Here you didn't think to take an umbrella. Anchorage's skyline was so brief that Beryl couldn't help but compare it to New York City, the buildings so dense and tall and crowded together that a whole day could pass by without seeing the sun. But somehow it didn't matter there. So many people, museums, places to explore, a person just didn't notice. In Zoë's neighborhood too many of the apartment houses were painted a lifeless gray. Not even the addition of the comical bridge supports fashioned to look like red fishing rods and reels could provide the necessary cheer to make this part of town a happy place. Beryl parked the truck behind a Honda, pulled on her jacket, and stepped carefully through the puddles. At the correct apartment number, she rang the buzzer with "Pratt" written next to it in shaky block letters. A woman looked out an upper-story window, but it wasn't Zoë. To Beryl's surprise the door clicked open, so she went inside to the airless foyer.

The carpet smelled of mildew. The walls had been freshly painted, but the paint was flat, and the same shade as the building's exterior. She knocked on Zoë's apartment door and waited for an answer. She knocked a second time, louder. "Zoë? It's Beryl. Can you come to the door?"

She heard a shuffling and the door lock turn. Zoë opened the door a fraction and stared out of the crack just above the safety chain. "What are you doing here?"

Beryl held up her temporary license. "I thought I'd take you to lunch."

Zoë groaned. "I'm sorry. I totally forgot. Maybe we can do it some other time."

"What's wrong? Are you sick?"

"Yeah, I'm sick."

"You sound all right to me."

"It's just starting. You know, scratchy throat, cough. Take NyQuil and wait it out. That kind of cold."

"Is it okay if I use your bathroom before I drive home?"

"Beryl! You drove all the way here by yourself?"

"Well, they did give me the license."

Zoë made a noise that could have been a laugh but didn't quite shake loose. "I never really thought you'd use it. I don't know why—"

"Can't I come in for just a second? I really need to pee, Zoë."

"Well—I guess for a minute."

Zoë pushed her finger against the chain and eased the door open just enough for Beryl to slide through. When she caught sight of Zoë's living space, she knew something was up. The sagging couch covered with bedding was her only furniture. Cardboard boxes packed to the brim with kitchen stuff, clothes, and shoes lay in a jumble on the floor. Either she was in the process of moving in or trying to make a getaway. "Did any of my neighbors see you?" she whispered.

"Why?"

"I'm trying to hide from the landlord."

"Why would you have to hide from him if you live here?"

Zoë looked down. "Because he wants rent money I don't have, that's why."

"Why don't you have it? Because you lost your job at the driving school?"

"No. Because Cleveland 'borrowed' it to pay the mother of his child, that's why, and Beryl, don't ask any more questions, please. I'm barely holding things together as it is. I think I might have bounced a couple of checks, too."

Beryl touched Zoë's shoulder and felt how nervous she was. "How much do you need to cover the rent?"

Zoë began folding the sheets on the couch. "Nothing, if I can get my butt out of here in the next half hour."

Beryl sat down on the couch, suddenly feeling dizzy.

"You okay?" Zoë asked. "Need a glass of water or something?"

Beryl shook her head. "No, it's just been a long day. Zoë, I've been there, trying to outrun something that will eventually catch up with you no matter how fast you run. Do me a favor. Come stay with me a while. Get yourself settled before you make your next move."

"Please," Zoë said in a small voice. "It's my fault for leaving the money out. I don't want Cleveland to go to jail. It'll mess up his military record."

"But it's okay for you to flake out on your rent and ruin your credit? You remind me of myself, Zoë, just taking it and taking it. You can't do that indefinitely. Trust me, it'll escalate. By the time I got up the courage to say no and tried to defend myself, I ended up killing the man. It didn't matter to the judge what led up to it. Grab your purse, and let's get these boxes into the truck."

All along the drive to the Nuthatch, Zoë was quiet, not even a pop from her chewing gum. The weather turned overcast, and suddenly there were flakes of snow falling, collecting on the wipers of the truck, each one a miniature star before it melted.

"Freaking endless winter," Zoë said disgustedly.

Beryl smiled. She was driving the truck in the snow, legally, and Zoë hadn't said a word. " I keep expecting you to comment on my driving," she said. "That's how we've always been. You the teacher, me the impossibly slow learner. It's very weird to be the one in charge of our destination."

"Tell me about it," Zoë mumbled. "I still don't think this is such a great idea."

"Why not?" Beryl asked. "I'm offering you some time to get your plans together. There's nothing I want in return. Well, maybe there is something."

"What?"

"A little companionship. Think you're up to it?"

Zoë frowned, but the expression began to mutate the moment it was on her face. "Jesus Christ, Beryl. You talk like you're this lonely old spinster living in a mausoleum."

Beryl completed her right turn onto her street, and Bohemian Waxwing loomed into view, its strange angles and rust-colored decking always a surprise, but exceptionally stark against the falling snow. "My point exactly," Beryl said, and Zoë shook her head.

When the cat jumped up onto the hood of the truck Beryl thought of Detective Stokes. *Tell me about the last day you saw him. Take me through the day.* I won't do that, Beryl thought. I'll put Zoë to bed, feed her dinner when she wakes up, and listen if she wants to talk. I'll do all those things Nance, Phoebe, and Ness did with me six years ago. I've never forgotten how that linen napkin felt in my hand, the softness and the weight against my fingers. That was the moment I knew I'd come to a better place. When I knew I could keep going.

All Beryl's promises to keep life simple enough to fit in a suitcase had unraveled since she'd been with Earl. Her linen closet held a lilac-and-spring-green patchwork quilt in the sawtooth pattern, down pillows, embroidered pillowcases she'd found in antique stores while Earl searched for books. She made up the antique bed she'd bought in Sierra Grove and had shipped here, cost be damned, so she would have a guest room for her friends when they came to visit. She snapped the crisp sheets and folded them down, handed Zoë a nightgown Phoebe had sent her that she'd never worn. "Bath's right next door. Towels on the rack are fresh. If you need a razor or deodorant or dental floss or a toothbrush, just look in the cabinet."

Zoë nodded, staring out the window into space. "Thanks," she said, a beat too late, and Beryl could tell she was thinking about jumping out the window to run back to her old life.

"Zoë," she said, smoothing a wrinkle from the quilt top. "Guess who slept here last?"

Zoë looked up. "I don't know. The nut that built the house?"

"Nope. Eric Clapton."

"For God's sake, Beryl, you don't have to lie to me to get me to spend the night," she answered. "This is a nice quilt," she said, fingering the patchwork. "It's so soft, it's like baby's skin. Did your grandmother make it or something?"

"Somebody's grandma did. Why don't you take a nap, Zoë?"

"I haven't taken a nap since I was an infant."

"Naps are wonderful," Beryl said. "I highly recommend them. Sweet dreams. Holler when you want company."

Mike Stokes himself answered the phone when Beryl called. "Detective Stokes," she said. "I thought you'd be in a meeting or gone for the day. I was going to leave a message."

"If you like I can beep and then be quiet."

"Is that a stupid cop joke?"

He laughed—his short, staccato laugh that rubbed her the wrong way. "Cop jokes are always stupid. What's up, Mrs. O'Reilly? How's that cat working out?"

Beryl pulled the phone closer, keeping the cord from Verde's reach. He grumbled and returned to his parrot toys. "It's Reilly, and not Mrs., as I keep trying to tell you. Your cat doesn't like it here," she said. "Not that I blame her for being afraid of parrots, but she appears to have the same aversion to mice. I think you should come and get her and take her back to your place, but I'm betting you won't. I'm almost certain you're the kind of guy who wants what's best for himself, not the cat."

"Ouch. Now you're making me wish I were at lunch. I wouldn't be taking this kind of sass from a Subway sandwich."

Beryl sighed. "I didn't mean it to come out sassy. Let's forget I said anything, okay, Mike? The reason I'm calling is that a friend of mine is involved with a guy who sort of took her for a ride, financially. She doesn't want to file a report. She's bounced a few checks, too, and I'd like to help her get back on her feet. I was wondering if you could look her boyfriend up and maybe have a chat with him, see if he could be convinced to generously return her rent money."

"Now, Mrs. Reilly," he said. "You know a cop can't go into the system for the hell of it. That's against the rules. However, if the name rings a bell, if I have my own suspicions, that's a different story. He smack her around?"

"No, thank God."

"Just wondering. That I have to report. You would, too."

"I know," Beryl said. "She's a good kid. Smart enough to walk away from domestic abuse."

"Be careful," he said. "There's all kinds of weirdos up here, you know. I don't want you to get taken advantage of by some pyramid scheme. She staying at your place?"

"Yes."

Mike Stokes sighed. "Spell his name for me. Now hers. Okay. Consider yourself chaperoned. I'll come by tomorrow. I'd like to talk to you anyway."

Beryl felt her heart flutter. Was there news? Had he found Earl? "About what?"

"The cat, of course. Beryl?"

She looked out the window at the light snow falling in earnest, certain it wouldn't stick. The world was already set for spring. Her head hurt, and her left eye felt gritty. A squirrel perched upside down on the feeder, attacking the corncob she'd put out. Birds chattered high and flutelike from the tallest of the birches. She could throw a shoe at a magpie, squirt it with a hose, or scream to high heaven, but the most the magpie would do was fly upward for as long as it took for the shoe or water or sound to land elsewhere. The squirrel moved in little bursts, like Michael Jackson dancing in one of his videos. Zoë slept in her guest room, and somewhere around here was a cat that would no doubt suffer emotional damage from one detective's well-intended gesture. "Yes, Detective Stokes?"

"What you need right now is a friend you can count on, someone to trust."

"Is that so?"

"Yes. It's most definitely so. And this is why I have to remind you to be careful. You could get yourself in deep with a girl and her money problems."

"I'm careful."

"Are you?"

"What's that supposed to mean?"

"Well, first off there's the disappearing boyfriend. And the Native guy you let spend the night. Now this girl—"

Beryl felt the heat rise to her cheeks. "Who told you about that? And what difference does it make whether he's Native or not?"

"It doesn't make any difference to me, that's for sure. I'm a cop. I describe people like that. A Native guy. A white girl. Don't have a cow over it."

"Well, it sounds racist. Who told you I was with him?"

"Everything a white person says these days sounds racist. The Native guy told me. I came by one day, and you were in the shower. We shot the breeze. He didn't say, 'Hey, I'm a Native guy'; he told me he was Tlingit. You like long showers, don't you? I could hear you singing. Don't quit your day job."

"Thomas Jack is a bird trainer."

"Oh, I see. That explains why his car's there all night most of the week."

"You're spying on me, Detective Stokes. I find that very creepy."

"Around here we call it working a case that remains open."

"I don't have to explain my personal life to you."

"Nobody said you did."

"I only called you for Zoë's sake. And now I'm sorry I did."

He was quiet a moment. When he spoke again, he sounded amused. "I think you did call to talk to me, Beryl. I also think you got your heart kicked in by this Earl character, and you don't want to see that happening to your new housemate, so that's part of why you called me, and I admire that. I admire you, too. You're a strong woman. None of this 'Oh, poor me' crap. You're steady, and you make me laugh, and you certainly don't crack mirrors."

"Well, thanks, I guess."

"You guess? Then I guess you're welcome."

She watched the squirrel free several kernels and snap his tail around like at any moment an army of invisible squirrels would be moving in and taking him hostage. She figured he had to suffer from a squirrel-size ulcer, or at the very least, irritable bowel. "I have to hang up now," she said.

"I'll keep an eye out," he said. "No charge."

"I have to go." She hung up the phone and tapped on the glass, and the squirrel exploded, racing up the tree as if his life depended on it.

Beryl was just about to go upstairs and take a long bath when she heard the door to Zoë's room open and the light switch on in the bathroom. The toilet flushed, the water ran, and then she heard Zoë in the kitchen. "You want something to eat?" she asked. "I made spaghetti."

"Just a glass of water."

"Glasses are in the cupboard to the right of the sink."

Zoë filled and drank one glass, then another. "Your water is so cold here."

"We're on a community well." Beryl switched on a lamp. "Come sit with me," she said. "You have to meet Verde. Also, there's a cat around here someplace."

"There's a cat around here, all right," Zoë said. "She's in my bed. That has to be the most wonderful feeling in the world, sleeping with a cat on your feet. What's her name?"

"She doesn't have one yet. A detective gave her to me. He said I had mice. Now I have a cat *and* mice. I'm trying to get him to take her back. I have a feeling I'll probably end up keeping her, though. You can name her if you want to."

Zoë sat down on the couch and pulled her nightgown over her ankles. "If I name her, I'll want to keep her. I can't be responsible for a pet right now. I have to get myself taken care of. Find a place to live. Talk ADD into giving me my job back."

"You can stay at the Nuthatch as long as you want. I can use the company. As you can see, there's a ridiculous amount of room."

Zoë looked at her. "I don't have any money to pay you rent."

"Then you can do some chores in trade for it. How's that sound?"

"Too good to be true," Zoë said, and a tear squeezed out of her swollen eye and trickled down her cheek.

Beryl held out her arms, and Zoë came into them. She held her while she cried. "It's going to be okay," she said. "You'll get your life back in gear. It's just going to take time."

Zoë was in the sniffling stage now. "I've had a job since I was twelve years old. I shut my eyes and I see Cleveland's hand slipping my money into his pocket, and him walking away without thinking he did anything wrong. I thought he loved me. How could he steal from me? How could he—"

"Shh, Zoë. Listen. I want you to do something for me. Close your eyes and picture a bird, the prettiest bird you can imagine. A peacock, a wren, whatever you want it to be. Now picture her on a branch of a tree, just sitting there, resting her wings, and watching the sky grow dark, watching the sunset. Now feel her gather her strength and take off, begin to fly until she's just a speck in the sky. It's so quiet. Her wings open and there she goes."

It was a trick Thomas Jack had taught her for those times he was gone, when insomnia plagued her. Thomas Jack—the lover Mike Stokes knew about because despite its population of 260,000, Anchorage was at heart a small town, and people talked. People donated money when someone's house burned down, planted flowers when the mayor canceled the beautification budget because he was well intentioned but not terribly visionary. Oh, who cared? The bird story had worked. She gently laid Zoë down on the couch, squeezing herself into a corner, her feet tucked beneath her. She covered the girl with a quilt, and Verde watched the entire business with great solemnity, while the nameless cat jumped up and tucked itself into the fold of Zoë's legs as if to say, *This is my spot*. Beryl remembered the first night she'd slept at Phoebe's farm, how the quiet there had weight to it, and provided the first feeling of permanence she'd known since her mother died. How well she'd slept that night, and so many nights since. The women had quarreled and laughed and worked so hard growing the damn poinsettias that some nights her bones ached and her fingers were raw. She had to admit it wasn't just the tediousness of summer, and the hassle of waiting for the sunsets to return, or the idea of facing fall, acknowledging that Earl had been gone one whole year, that made her homesick for California. It was her friends. She missed the girls so intensely that at that very moment she wished she'd told Earl no, never dated him, and had stayed in her room reading books. Was loving a man something she needed to try one last time, just to say she could do it and get it right? Or had her relationship with Earl been, like so many other times before that, just another poor choice?

JW drove the flatbed delivery truck that brought hay, grain, and vitamins to Mickey's barn. Once a week he pulled to a stop in the parking lot, honked the horn twice, which spooked all the horses, and caused Mickey to yell "Beryl!" at the same time that Beryl dropped whatever she was doing, covered her head with her hands, and swore under her breath, knowing she was lucky she hadn't gotten stomped to death. In addition to her teaching duties, she also bucked hay bales into the covered storage and moved by dolly fifty-pound sacks of Sweet Feed and Senior Horse and pellets for those animals so old they couldn't manage hay. She was twenty-one now, working as Mickey's assistant trainer, which meant that she got paid twice what she had cleaning stalls, and she gave beginning lessons to awestruck little girls and the occasional boy who possessed enough self-esteem that being around all that estrogen didn't threaten his masculinity. Mickey concentrated on helping the talented riders place in shows, and pushed the few who could potentially be great riders into jumping higher and higher fences. Of JW Mickey said, "You stay away from that character. He's too good looking for his own good."

Beryl'd dated two guys in what was left of her postpartum youth. One was a baseball player at the community college, and the other a clerk from the convenience store where she sometimes stopped for a Coke on the way home. On their first date, some scary movie where women screamed a lot, the baseball player had placed his hand on Beryl's breast. She'd bolted out of her movie seat and run to the lobby, and when he came after her, she backed herself up against the glass booth where the ticket seller sat. "Don't you come near me," she said, upon which he called her a lesbian and people buying tickets for the late show stared. The store clerk was nice enough, but confessed he was gay on their second date, and that he wanted to continue to see her to keep his parents from finding out his sexual preference.

Otherwise, for Beryl, the days after the baby was born she spent in continuation school until it was time to go to the stables. Each day began with low light filtering in through the cracks in the stall doors, the haze of dust motes, a gentle nickering of hungry horses, the clatter of sweet feed falling into feed bins, and all around, the pleasant, commingled, earthy smell of alfalfa and horse manure. Once the horses were fed, turned out to exercise, and returned to their stalls, she headed over to the community college where she was taking two classes a semester, making her way through general education requirements. It was Mickey's doing that she was even going to college. She had watched Beryl work with the disabled kids, encouraging the tiny tots to leg old Bess into a makeshift trot. "Go earn your teaching certificate, Beryl," Mickey said as she tore her a check for the first semester. "Children adore you, and clearly the feeling is mutual. I'll pay your tuition. Hurry now, go register before I change my mind."

Beryl sat rapt in her seat while various professors explained geography, and who wanted what chunk of land, resulting in wars that seemed never to end. She learned how to tell the wiggly amoeba from the magical cell, and whether it belonged to a weed or a human being or the tiniest creature, life wanted to live. Sometimes she thought of her son growing up somewhere, with parents who loved and wanted him, and she prayed he'd never find out the circumstances of his conception. She managed work and classes on a schedule that deliberately left no time for campus social events. How could she miss what she'd never had? Moose was out of the Youth Camp. Bette had driven him to Arizona so he could work on a cousin's dude ranch, and sometimes Beryl would look up from whatever horse's hoof she was cleaning and wonder if at that moment her stepbrother was doing the very same thing.

JW drove up, honked the damn horn, Beryl tried to yell, "I got it," before Mickey told her to go shut him up. She pulled her hair up into a ponytail and brushed the dust from her legs. Out front of the barn she planted her feet in the dirt and lit into him. "How many times does someone have to tell you not to honk around horses? If you don't stop, someone is going to have a wreck, and we'll get sued, lose our jobs, and then you won't have a client. Why in hell can't you remember not to honk?"

He smiled a grin full of handsome teeth he didn't take care of and that stayed white anyway. His jeans were tight with an ironed-in crease, his T-shirt always bleached white, and showing off his muscles. If it was raining he might sport a flannel shirt worn like a jacket, but mostly JW was in that T-shirt, the definition of his chest and arms clearly the result of much working-out. "The horses are used to it," he teased. "If I didn't honk, they'd think I was sneaking up on them."

Beryl shook her head. "No, they would not. And I want you to stop it."

"Are all girls like you?"

"I really couldn't speak for all girls. Are all men like you?"

"Like me how? Good looking? The most fun a girl can have? I surely doubt that. You know what they say, 'Lightning doesn't strike twice.'"

"Jesus." She grabbed hold of her end of a bale and waited for him to pick up his. He took it away from her, snagged the bale with a hook, and lifted all 110 pounds by himself. "I hope you're not sacrificing your back to impress me," she said. "I don't give a rat's behind how much you can lift, or whether you end up with a slipped disc." She loaded the wheelbarrow with bags of grain so sweet the smell of molasses was in her nose and on her hands until she went home at night.

"Hey," JW said when she checked over the invoice and signed for the delivery. "Wanna get a burger after work?"

"No," Beryl said. "I have to study for my biology test."

"Oh, honey," he said, winking. "I can teach you anything you want to know about biology."

"Really?" she answered. "Then how come you can't teach yourself to lay off the damn horn?"

He smiled at her, flashing the teeth, and with his right hand, he made a gun and aimed it at her. "Sooner or later," he said. "You know you want me."

Beryl passed the bio test, not with an A but a C, and she fought tears until she was safe in a stall of the women's rest room. Everyone did poorly. The professor liked to give complex multiple-choice questions, so that if a student got any one part of the answer wrong, the whole question was marked incorrect. She knew he was trying to weed out the less serious students, but what if a student was serious, and still had to work to make money? She fell asleep in her geography class after staying up half the night with old Bess, who was trying to decide whether or not she wanted to colic. When she woke up the classroom was empty. She looked out the window and saw JW walking with a girl, his arm around her shoulders, their hips touching. Despite everything—the rape and Bette's drinking and all the classes adding up to an Associate of Arts degree in the spring—jealousy stirred in her. The girl knew how to wear makeup. She had straight hair and no stretch marks, Beryl felt certain. She dressed right. All the same, when Beryl walked outside to go to the bus stop, JW looked up at her, smiled in recognition, and made his finger into a gun again, mouthing "Pop" as she passed by.

The education theory classes were boring—schools of thought, no live kids in sight. The class met from eleven to two, and midway through the teacher allowed the class to take a break. This time, instead of stopping at the hot-dog cart and buying a chili dog and a coffee, she kept walking. At the stable Mickey squinted at her. "Aren't you supposed to be in class until five?"

"Teacher called in sick," she lied. "I feel like riding. Anyone need schooling?"

"Gunnar, if you feel up to it. Otherwise I'll ride him later." She looked down at her ledger sheets, and Beryl went to get the Arab gelding that was long on good looks and short on manners.

"Come on, you little crotch rocket," she crooned as she tacked him up. "Let's go learn some manners."

She wasn't a graceful rider and wouldn't have done a hunt coat any favors, but Beryl had balance and strength in her legs. She cued the horse to walk in serpentines, then cross the arena in an X shape, first at a walk, then a trot. The second time she changed directions, she came down on the trot wrong and had to sit a beat to find her posting rhythm, which was all Gunnar needed to push his long neck forward and tear the reins from her hands. He lowered his body and shot into a gallop, turning sharply and trying to leave Beryl in the sand. She took hold of his mane, stood up in her stirrups, and lay down on his neck until she could grab hold of the leather, reel it in, and make the horse listen to her. His sides moved like bellows, and she could feel the great drafts of air pumping from her own nostrils as well as his.

"You okay?" Mickey called.

"I've got things under control," she said.

They began again from the walk. Beryl kept Gunnar in hand, changing gaits every few paces, executing flying lead changes, tucking the stirrups up and over the pommel, using her calf muscles to show Gunnar she wasn't going to fall for his nonsense a second time. After an hour she was soaking wet, and he was cooled down enough to deserve a little alone time. She stripped his tack and left him in the arena, set the saddle and bridles down to clean, and stuck her head under the hose outside Mickey's office.

When she looked up JW was there. "You'll notice I didn't honk," he said. He stank of pot, and he was wearing the T-shirt. He reached over and wiped a smear of dirt from her cheek. Three weeks later Beryl was in his bed, getting no sleep, and missing classes.

A man touches you and your skin sings, and you're certain this has to be true love, Beryl thought. It means you and he will live together happily and make money and buy a nice home and fill it with children and grow old together like it says in books and movies and songs, even. "I want to get married," she said, one morning after they'd drunk so much she couldn't remember the sex until she tried to move her legs and felt the sore places aching.

JW laughed. "Come on. It's the seventies, Beryl. We don't need the piece of paper, et cetera," he sang.

She pushed his hands away. "I don't care. I still want to get married. Maybe I want the paper."

"Okay, we'll go to Vegas this weekend."

She had pictured her wedding differently. Wearing a peasant dress, standing together somewhere beautiful, say on the coastline at Point Reyes, or maybe in a redwood grove, but not here, with a rented bouquet and half-carat rings purchased on time. The JP promised that the ceremony between the gentleman and the lady was indeed binding. "That's no lady, that's my *wife,*" JW said, and Beryl felt her heart leap up.

Beryl learned it wasn't just pot that JW liked. His first arrest was for possession of speed, and he finagled his way out of a sentence by doing community service and an outpatient treatment program. Then he got into trouble with a coke dealer and had his face rearranged, and he lost his delivery job. Beryl called Mickey, who said she knew someone at the racetrack hiring drivers for horse transport, so JW got on there, and Beryl worked at the bank counting out money and cashing paychecks. Paper money was filthy dirty to the touch. She missed school and the horses at Mickey's. She registered for classes, but missed the first one when JW got thrown in jail in Reno and she had to drive down and bail him out. When he promised he'd go to NA meetings, Beryl felt sure things were finally going to be okay. But pretty soon he was gone all day and half the night, and then he lost another job, selling used cars, and then came the job selling furniture, and then the night she tried to find him at an NA meeting, when he wasn't there at all and came home three days later with his eyes so bloodshot they looked as if they'd been painted with watercolors. "Where have you been?" she said, a little too shrilly, and he lost his temper and hit her. She fell down hard enough to pass out.

She woke up in a heap on the floor while JW cried, explaining how sorry he was and how it would never happen again. Beryl's head rang with dizziness so deep she couldn't feel the pain. It was six months before he hit her again. She explained how she worked with horses—though in truth Mickey had fired her—while the ER doctor set her arm and said, "You can't be too careful around horses." The next time she made sure to go to another hospital, even though it meant driving herself.

Oddly enough JW's other women didn't faze her. She was happy they kept him occupied, out of her way long enough for her to try to get things in order. Part-time jobs, a loan from Bette, and as soon as she had room in her schedule, she'd go back to school and study twice as hard. It would take three years, she figured, to get a degree and a teaching credential. She heard people complain about teaching—it paid lousy, there was so much work to do outside the classroom—but it sounded good to her.

Then JW started gambling in Reno, and by the time she realized he'd emptied the bank account they'd lost the apartment. Through a friend of a friend, they rented a double-wide trailer twenty miles from the college. Every day when Beryl drove by she asked herself, how could I go in to school today, when I have a black eye, or a limp? Maybe next semester. She worked as a teacher's aide at a kindergarten, but sometimes she missed work as well. JW doled his rage out to her, a pinch here, a deliberate trip there, and then came the night he held on to her wrist and bent her pinky back until he heard it snap. "You want me to do the others, Beryl Anne? You want me to make it so you can't hold a goddamn piece of chalk in your hand? I will. You watch." He'd run over the neighbor's dog and didn't tell them. Beryl felt so bad when she heard them calling night after night that she wrote them a note, told them of the accident, and offered to buy them a puppy. Somehow her confession had brought out JW's demons. "I can run you over, too, bitch. You're no saint. Look at you. You already had one baby, and where's that baby now? Living with strangers. What kind of mother gives her baby away?"

Beryl sat in the living room of the Nuthatch remembering how at night she'd lain in that state between wakefulness and dreaming, imagining how if he'd only die in his sleep or get hit by a meteor—anything to end all this, to get her out of the trailer—erase the cheap and secondhand things that broke so often it set JW off, wash away the smell of hamburger clinging to her clothing because she had taken a job at a fast-food place in the afternoons so she could at least have a free lunch. Just have it happen so she could step around him and make her way to a normal life. She knew if she left he would find her and make her sorry. He knew where Bette lived. He'd make a scene or he'd find a gun, and something terrible would happen, so she stayed.

JW got arrested one more time before he died. He told the cops it was Beryl's dope. They knew he was lying, but they questioned her and fingerprinted her anyway. When he was released on bail he talked his cousin into posting, he came home and sat in the corner drinking beer all day. Beryl was slicing onions and making tuna salad with sweet pickles, the way she liked it for once. JW started in on her, little things at first. Her hair was too wild, and it made her look slutty. The trailer was a mess. When was the last time she'd lifted a finger to clean? He came to the kitchen counter and saw the jar of sweet pickles and tried to shove it to the floor, but instead he dropped the beer, and while that was a mess, Beryl minded it less than she would have the pickle juice. "Your own mother," he said, and the next thing Beryl knew, he was lying on the floor in the beer with the knife sticking out of him, the Ginsu knife she'd bought at the county fair because the salesman said it was the last knife she'd ever need, that it was good for everything from slicing tomatoes to tin cans, and would never, ever wear out.

Despite the snow falling outside, summer was on its way to Anchorage. Summer meant Alaskans playing softball at midnight. So much light that geraniums grew as big as dahlias. In the Valley farmers tended cabbages as if they were capons, urging them to grow bigger, fatter, more ridiculous, so they would win a blue ribbon at the fair. It was too much, all this light. Bulbs and green shoots on the cottonwoods and willows. And the birds would come—cranes, geese, gulls, and redpolls. Where *did* the ravens go? Where was that knife? What did police do with evidence once a trial had ended and the criminal had served her time? Surely that knife was still intact. Hadn't the salesman promised? She wondered whose hand was on its hilt now.

Phoebe

13

Braxton-Hicks

SPRING, PHOEBE THOUGHT, as she leafed through Sadie's journal, stopping to touch a pressed tiger lily that had become desiccated and as thin as parchment. You gotta love it. Saint Paddy's, Passover, and Easter, which means dollars for the farm coffers. And the weather was magic—sunny and seventy degrees in the fields, sixty on the coastal beaches, which brought in tourists, lovers, newlyweds, and business. Yes, things were percolating along. Well, almost everything. Sally had gotten in trouble at school. But Phoebe didn't plan on making too big a deal out of it. Even a six-year-old deserved to mess up now and then.

She dialed Beryl Anne, and the phone went directly to the machine. Rather than rattle off some boring message, she hung up, deciding damn it all, she would send her flowers. She'd order up a bouquet so springlike and scented that it would cause Beryl to pick up the telephone the moment she read the card. And so long as she was going to this much effort, she might as well use her womanly powers of guilt. That was bound to make a dent in the silence.

She called one of her florist partners in Anchorage. "How's the weather up there?" she asked.

"Snowing and dreary. Please don't tell me how nice yours is," the gentleman taking her order said.

"My lips are sealed on the topic. Listen, I want to send a friend something special. What have you got that's out of the ordinary?"

"Sunflowers, dianthus, iris, and just today we got in the first lilacs of the season."

"Oh, lilacs," Phoebe said. "Make this baby all purples and white and really special."

As she recited what she wanted written on the card, the clerk balked. "Log onto our website and type it in directly, why don't you?"

Phoebe did. She clicked the mouse, and letters began to appear in the window marked Message:

Dear Beryl Anne,

I'm writing this letter on a balmy spring day to catch you up on what's happened since we last heard from you, which was, ahem, *October*. Since you won't answer the phone, and you don't have email, I'm resorting to the oldest fashioned, most arcane of epistles, a letter and flowers. If the weight of this page in your hands makes you feel weary, imagine what it took for me to write it! Nance is six months pregnant. James is bringing home a new doggie for Nance's Easter gift—a surprise. Ness is having a hard time, really missing David. He left Sally a cabin in Big Sur. It's this crazy box that hangs out over a cliff. We're talking drop-dead romantic getaway. Mimi seems to be the only one living a simple life these days—working and pitching in with chores, no real drama in her life since Dayle left. Did Dayle come see you when she moved back to Anchorage? Sally's still mad about horses. You knew James bought her the pony, right? And I have a new beau who is Southern and loaded with do-re-mi. Who knew? The thing is, nothing's any fun without you, B. We all miss you. I hope reading this letter will make you miss us enough to get in contact again. Better still, come for a visit.

Love, Phoebe.

Way back in the fall DeThomas Farms had already planned for springtime. Not the few weeks of blustery warm days filled with farm business that began at dawn and didn't end until they started finding mistakes in their work. No, the girls had progressed to the point that they held actual meetings, brainstormed new product lines like those genius screenplay writers lying around somebody's pool in Beverly Hills, thinking up the next filmic blockbuster. Spring bulbs and flower arrangements—the staples they'd counted on for several years, selling to repeat customers and specialty florists—but as the farm became more solvent, these only pointed out that they had to continue expanding, explore ways to push the flowers into other areas, all in pursuit of the almighty collective profit.

"Our spring line," Nance—who came up with the idea—had said, "should be Easter baskets!" She pitched it to Ness and Phoebe while holding a glass of sparkling water in one hand and a candy bar in the other. Phoebe remembered thinking that for someone who'd not so long ago been the poster child for anorexia, the failed Southern belle had certainly swung to the other end of the spectrum. And that she wouldn't have minded a bite of the candy bar herself.

"For the yuppie parents who can afford to go all out, Sadie's Farm offers the following: for the perfectly reasonable price of forty-nine ninety-five, a custom Easter basket, handmade of all natural materials by a women's collective in South America. This angle's great because it appeals to those yuppie parents who vote Democrat, as well as your wealthier hippies. Think of it. None of that plastic bunny shit from the grocery store—a basket as individual as the kid it's going to. We fill it with high-end girly stuff for the feminine child—you know, ceramic ponies, petits fours, and beaded hair clips in a bed of Jelly Bellies. And we offer a tomboy option for the tomboy girls—Gummi Worms, for example, and a kit to make a kite, but either way we aim the main contents of the basket toward a gardening theme. Now comes the brilliant part. Clever little trowels, tiny gardening gloves, plus I've designed seed-packet graphics that conveniently feature our address on the flip side, and voilà, the parents are so impressed they come to us for all their flower and gardening needs! We give the kids easy-to-grow stuff—radishes, sunflowers, mint—you know, the things that will seem like a total triumph to a child's eyes."

Ness, being a traditional holiday fanatic, was quick to point out the flaw. "No spun-sugar eggs? No chocolate bunnies?"

Nance cleared her throat. "One organic chocolate Peter Rabbit per basket, and I've already found a source that has a model in a farmer's outfit, which is great because it crosses the gender line. But best of all—tell me this isn't brilliant—we *deliver* early Easter Sunday morning to each child's house. Maybe for an extra twenty, we can stamp out bunny footprints in cornstarch on the porch steps. What do you think?"

At this point Ness took the candy bar away from Nance, and said, "I think you're frightening when you're creative."

Phoebe watched the presentation somewhat distractedly, unable to pin down exactly what was bothering her, but her radar was buzzing.

"Pheebs?" Nance said, a hurt expression on her perfect face. "Don't you love it even a little bit?"

"Hand me that candy bar," she told her, and took a bite. It was Cadbury Fruit & Nut, her favorite, but the good thing about chocolate was that your mouth automatically adjusted. "Seems like you've covered the girl market fairly well, but what about the boys? If we don't wow them, this idea will tank due to sibling rivalry. Do they have to make do with hardboiled eggs or what?"

Phoebe leaned back in her chair and watched Nance dive into the challenge. She so admired the girl, not just as a friend and a sister-in-law but also for her head for business. An unenlightened person might say, "She thinks like a man," but the truth of the matter was that Nance's ideas were beyond gender comparisons. For the first time in a long while Phoebe understood how their fellowship made it easier for Nance to come up with innovations. It had taken living together communally, everyone lifting a trowel, so to speak, for their success to come about. And the weight that had been pressing on her shoulders seemed to lift away.

She could applaud the idea without feeling jealous, without feeling she should have been the one to come up with it. And that was a good thing where the farm was concerned. Between Sally's after-school activities and her very own love life—yes, things with Andrew were definitely heating up; he called her twice a day to flirt—she did not have a single brain cell to spare. "Okay," she'd told Nance when she was finished presenting. "I adore the ecology angle, and the science experiment is genius. How much capital do we need for setting it up?"

That was then, when plans were ideas, abstract as clouds. Now it was the week before Easter, and Phoebe found herself stunned at just how many local children of the wealthy needed a DeThomas Farms Spring Holiday basket. It reminded her of that first year with the poinsettias; they realized early on they were going to have to pull a couple of all-nighters to fill the orders. They'd hired Bayborough High School seniors to help, but one by one, they'd flaked out in favor of Mexico vacations, Fort Lauderdale trips, and good surfing.

Today they set the assembly line up outdoors because the day was nice, and Nance, who rubbed her rounded tummy so often that Phoebe expected it to shine, was waxing obsessive about fresh air and exercise. "Stand sideways and let us look," Mimi said. When Nance pulled her T-shirt tight, it looked as if she had tucked a small melon in there. Phoebe wondered if she was the only one who felt jealous. "It's a boy," Mimi said. "You're carrying it high."

"I thought that meant girl," Ness countered.

"So long as it means healthy baby, I don't care," Nance said, and Phoebe rushed in to break the uncomfortable silence.

"Ladies, we have to hustle to get these things done. Let's have belly show-and-tell at lunchtime, okay?"

After the first hour, Phoebe wished she were observing

everything from the rocking chair on the porch. And of course, now that she couldn't afford to, her hands ached to get back to the clay. This was partly due to Andrew. Just being around him made her want to spend her energy on art. If he could throw pots that tall, why couldn't she? Wheel-driven work didn't require her foot—she could use the electric model with the knee pedal. But she shook herself free of such thoughts, mustered up the spirit to work fast, get the job done, and earn her time in the studio later.

Phoebe manned station one, which was the placement of the bed of Easter grass, long strands of some kind of thinly shredded wood product instead of the plastic green stuff. She curled it into a nest, tucked a Farmer Rabbit in to anchor the stuff, added Jelly Bellies, and then in the custom-custom baskets, scattered a few foil-wrapped chocolate baby bunnies here and there, as if Farmer Rabbit were a stay-at-home dad. Then she separated the baskets according to gender and slid the girls' baskets along to Nance. Girls younger than age seven received a package of flowerpot stickers, nice-quality plastic gardening tools, as well as a packet of sunflower seeds and one of radishes. The seven-and-up crowd received gardening gloves, metal tools, and a six-pack of preplanted peat pots of herbs that only needed water and sun. In addition to the sunflower seeds, they got a packet of pansy seeds. And for a custom-custom-custom price of seventy-nine ninety-five, DeThomas Farms added a darling hardcover book on the legends of various flowers that just fitted a young girl's hands and was loaded with beautiful illustrations.

Ness and Mimi handled the boys' baskets, and had two tables' worth of the orders already waiting for wrap. The youngest boys' received a plastic tractor and digging tools. Older boys received all that but a packaged science experiment instead of the tractor, and manly looking work gloves. Once they had the tables filled, Nance pushed each basket down to Ness, the only one among them who'd figured out how to work the cellophane contraption to wrap the basket in. It mystified Phoebe that such a simple-looking machine had more moods than all four of them put together. When it cut, wrapped, and sealed properly, which it barely managed five times out of ten, from there the basket made its way to Mimi. She stuck on delivery labels that Phoebe checked against the master list.

"What's it feel like to be pregnant, Nance?" Mimi asked, straightening a label on one of the high-dollar baskets.

She smiled. "I have to pee a lot. I'm hungry. But I love lying still and watching the baby move inside me. It's kind of like the way ripples move across a creek. Nothing spectacular until I think, Holy Mother of God, that's a real little person in there making all that ruckus."

"How about going vegetarian?" Ness said, smirking a little and winking at Phoebe.

"Oh, my gosh. I can't believe how much better I feel. Lighter, like I used to when I'd starve myself, but at the same time calm, and grounded. Giving up meat has changed my life."

Ness and Phoebe high-fived each other. "We knew you'd come around," she said. "Didn't I say that all she needed was time?"

"Six years is a lot of time," Ness said.

Nance looked at them both solemnly. "I'd eat grubs if it meant the baby would make it."

"Isn't it nice you don't have to?" Mimi said. "The baby's going to be fine. Think happy thoughts. Tell us the names you've picked out."

Ness stopped the cellophane machine and carried finished baskets to the refrigerated truck Segundo had gotten for a rental price so low it seemed too good to be true. On Easter morning he would drive the truck around Bayborough and Sierra Grove and behave like a springtime Santa. "Don't," she said. "That's private between you and God. Just know that there are more prayers flying around this valley for you than there are birds in the sky."

Phoebe agreed. It was almost as if she might jinx herself were she to go that far. "Why don't you take a break? If I were you, I'd milk this pregnancy thing for as long as you can." Phoebe was thrilled and shocked to see the original Type A do exactly as was suggested.

"You know," Nance said, her feet up on a throw pillow, "next year I think we should include a tiny bottle of sunscreen. It's never too early to start taking care of your skin."

"Listen to you," Mimi said. "Slow down already. Live in the moment, Nancy."

"I'm trying," Nance said.

"You are not," Phoebe argued. "You're lying there thinking of all the money we're going to make on the Easter baskets, and you're planning May Day. You're like Donald Trump, when you should try being a little more like Ivana."

"Well, for Pete's sake, what does that mean?" Nance asked. "Divorced and doing car commercials?"

"Girls," Mimi put in.

Nance picked up a packet of Gummi Worms and threw it at Phoebe. Ness intercepted it, tore the bag open, and popped a long green one in her mouth. Phoebe held out her hand. "Give me the red ones." She stuck two in her upper lip so they hung down like fangs, made a face at Ness, and growled.

"Do you all see how far we've come?" Nance told Mimi. "Our first few months we were so scared that it would all flop, and we'd all be homeless. Now we can comfortably indulge in childish behavior when we should be working. That's real progress."

"I don't know," Mimi said. "It's good to blow off steam some way other than shopping."

"Oh, that reminds me," Nance said. "You should have seen my poor credit card in those days. It was so maxed out the magnetic stripe was worn through. Thought I'd end up in debtor's prison."

"Still could," Ness said, stealing a jellybean from the bowl in front of her. "Mimi, you should see this girl's closet."

"Ahem?" Nance said. "You're the one eating the profits. Phoebe, take those things out of your mouth this instant. You are making me ill."

Phoebe pushed the Gummi Worms into her mouth. "Why is it nobody complains when you do it?"

"When I'm *eating,*" Nance answered, "nobody is allowed to complain."

Mimi shook her head as if dazed. "Is there no subject too sacred?"

"No," everyone said in unison, and suddenly Nance started to cry.

"There really isn't, Mimi. And thank God for that, or I'd probably be dead by now." The tears were streaming down her cheeks.

"Dang it all stupid machine!" Ness said, sitting back to wait for the cellophane machine to cool down and to suck on her burned finger. "Once upon a time there was a girl in our midst who had a teeny tiny eating disorder. Now she's got a hormonal problem."

"Have you tried herb tea?" Mimi said. "Yerba Buena always cheers me up. I don't think it does anything specific—"

Ness interrupted. "Oh, that's like my granny's blackberry tea. The whole ritual she went through to make it took so long and had so many steps that by the time she handed me the cup I'd forgotten what I was sad about."

"Who says we have to be polite and calm all the time?" Phoebe asked. "Isn't family where you let it all hang out? Nance, you want me to go get some Kleenex?"

Nance shook her head. "I'll be okay in a minute, I think."

Mimi shrugged. "You see this is why I love being Mexican. We *chicas* have permission to cry over anything! PMS, burned cake, breakups, favorite television program preempted . . . *qué lástima!*"

While she ticked off more reasons to cry, Phoebe thought about impending menopause. Since she had had Sally, her cycles had been erratic. Lester said it was perimenopause, which sounded like a good name for a bad fairy. For someone who wasn't supposed to live past adolescence, she'd come a long way to make it to impending menopause. She glanced at her watch. It was ten to four, which meant that Sally's preschool group was ending, and soon the school bus would deliver her to the driveway. Even though she knew she was spoiling her daughter rotten, she liked to have milk and freshly baked cookies waiting.

Nance peeled the foil off a baby bunny and popped it in her mouth. Around the chocolate she said, "I sure miss Beryl Anne. I wonder why she doesn't call anymore. Too busy traveling with Earl, I guess. Remember when Verde would get going? That parrot was the life of the party. He knew more cuss words than Andrew Dice Clay."

The wind perked up and blew across their worktable, and Ness and Mimi quickly began to weight down items that were in danger of blowing away. Phoebe closed her eyes. This strange feeling came over like it sometimes did—she couldn't describe it any more than she could have spoken Portuguese. Maybe it was the scent of all the flowers, or a little mishap in the brain of a mother who was often stressed. But it was as if all around her she could feel the spring flowers blooming and the trees working hard to turn out new leaves. Penny whinnied from the arena because this was about the time of day when Sally came flying up the driveway with the leftover apple slices from her lunch. Off in a far section of the farm, she could hear Segundo's tractor. When the women were together, working collectively, she felt like singing with joy over the easy ways they joked with one another, pushed ahead through the boring tasks because in the end there was a tremendous payoff. At times like these she felt that if she could just turn quickly enough, she'd catch sight of her aunt standing in the sunflowers, holding a glass of iced tea to the space between her breasts. And that Juan was alive, and this was years down the road, and she was a grandma, even, waiting for the grandchildren to come up to the porch for cookies. Then, inside the house, the phone rang, but no one got up to answer it. No amount of telephone drama could compete with the sisterhood taking place in the side yard of Sadie's Farm.

Everyone turned to look at her, and then Ness began laughing. "Pheebs? Where were you just now? I must have called your name five times!"

"Oh, woolgathering. You know."

"That much wool, you could make a sweater," Ness kidded. "Make me one while you're at it. And some bootees for the new baby."

Nance was no longer crying, but it was only inside the refrigerated truck where the Easter baskets were waiting for delivery that things stayed cool and collected. Everybody bore down on their tasks, and only looked up when Sally was among them, a macaroni art project in one hand and her Hello Kitty lunch pail in the other. She was wearing tennis shoes that blinked with lights when she tapped her feet, and she did so now, an impatient pint-size tyrant dressed in a plaid skirt and a camel's hair blazer.

She struck a pose that reminded Phoebe of some forty-year-old burned-out case finding out she'd lost a role to a younger actress. "Hi, honey," she said. "What's the pout for?"

"My teacher gave me this damn note to give to you," she said, scowling.

"Another note? Well, better let me see it." Phoebe unfolded it and read aloud:

> Dear Ms. DeThomas:
>
> We are having a little trouble with Sally's tendency to boss the other children around. We're working on her ability to be part of the team, but I wanted you to be aware that her iron will is both her strength and her weakness. In addition, if you could counsel Sally about her vocabulary, that would be a help. It isn't just the swear words, which I fear are endemic these days, but the precocious nature of her vocabulary tends to intimidate the other children. In all other ways she is a delightful child.
>
> Sincerely,
> Victoria Shiasaka

"Well, that's a lovely little bit of news," Phoebe said. "Sally? Have you checked on your pony yet? I think Penelope needs to be groomed."

Sally tapped her foot. "Aren't you going to give me a time-out?"

"I wasn't planning on it."

Sally perked up. "Where's my trainer? Isn't someone supposed to supervise me?"

Here it came—the tyrannical language. "I expect she's probably off training horses," Phoebe said, "since that is her job. She isn't your personal slave. Now go see to the pony. Look at her; she's waiting for you."

Sally ran off clutching her bag of apple slices. Phoebe passed the note around. "She's only six," she said. "What can I expect when she's a teenager?"

"This is hilarious," Ness said, handing the note to Nance.

"It is not," Phoebe countered. "It makes my daughter sound like a despot!"

"Oh, I wonder where she got that," Ness said, smiling.

Mimi laughed. "Intimidating vocabulary. What do you suppose she says to them?"

Nance was still repairing her face, but she finally volunteered her view. "Oh, she probably kicks their little tushes at Scrabble and they cry like sore losers. There's nothing the matter with my niece except she's bored stiff. Phoebe, I think you should yank her from that silly school and take her on a tour of Europe. She'll learn more from traveling in other countries than she ever will from cheap, biased American textbooks. Either that or home-school her."

"Oh, that would be wonderful," Phoebe said, sarcastically. "I can just see her listening to me for longer than ten minutes when I can't even get her to eat a lettuce leaf. Are you going to home-school when yours is ready for kindergarten?"

Nance turned to face her, and Phoebe could see that her waterproof mascara had failed. "If I am that lucky," she said, "I probably won't be able to let loose of the baby long enough to let it learn anything."

Phoebe felt bad—it was hard to joke even the tiniest bit with Nance. "What does James think?"

She looked up, and Phoebe could see her blinking back tears again. "Oh, you know your brother. He won't talk about anything until he's certain the baby is going to make it. So mostly we don't talk about it. Or decorate the nursery. Or buy books on childhood. We act so civilized it's just plain crazy."

"That doesn't sound very supportive," Mimi said.

Nance sniffed. "It's okay, really. I know he didn't want me to take this chance, and I ticked him off not having the amnio, but I have you guys to talk to. My sacred bond of sisterhood. And God's in control of it all anyway. There. I feel better. Let's hustle and finish the baskets and have us a banner Easter."

Ness looked at Phoebe and shrugged her shoulders. The cellophane machine was back on track, so she continued wrapping baskets. Phoebe knew that once Nance had her mind made up, there was no backing her down. "Why don't you do the stickers?" she said. "That way you can lie down."

Phoebe packed bunnies and science experiments, wondering whether Beryl had received her flowers, and if so, why hadn't she called to say thanks? What would Beryl do for Easter? With no kids to share the holiday, maybe she and Earl had gone off someplace special, enjoying room service and each other. Maybe he was in between gigs, and they were spending a quiet day at home, watching the snowmelt and Alaska begin to turn green. She wondered if Beryl knew that all of them were a little jealous of that lasting partnership they seemed to have figured out, when it remained a mystery to the rest of the world.

"Well, I have to go to work," Mimi said. "See you guys tonight."

Sally came stomping over from the corral. "Okay, I groomed Penny and I gave her some apples and I raked up the horse buns and I put them in the Dumpster except for the ones that are too gooey and wouldn't stay on the damn rake. Now can I go inside and watch TV?"

"I think no damn TV today," Phoebe said. "You can read a damn book, though. How does that damn sound?"

"Mama," Sally said. "Quit talking like that. It sounds dumb!"

"Really?" Phoebe said. "Ness, does it sound damn dumb when I say damn all the damn time? I thought it made me sound damn cool."

"I get it," Sally said. "All right already!" She ran up the ramp and into the house.

"Crisis very neatly averted," Ness said. "I have to give it to you, girlfriend. You come up with some good ones. But it's still seven quarters in the swear jar."

"Sally curses because she needs attention," Nance said. "The child is of superior intelligence."

"Criminy," Phoebe answered. "That child is about to gag to death on attention. She already thinks she's the center of the universe."

Ness and Nance looked at her, surprised.

"Oh, for God's sake," Phoebe said. "I know she's smart. But does that mean we need to let her know?"

When Mimi finished her shift she came home to find everyone lying around the living room, a fire blazing in the fireplace, a pot of cocoa on the hearth, and a veritable smorgasbord of what Phoebe referred to as the "comfort dinner": English digestive biscuits, which by any other name were cookies; cheeses, from extra-sharp cheddar to that almond soy goop only Ness would eat; strawberries, which a person could find pretty much year-round in California; fat-free popcorn, and crusty French bread with a pesto dipping oil that made up for the fat-free popcorn. Sally was styling Phoebe's hair, inserting miniature clippies wherever the whim struck her. Phoebe was explaining to her that her teacher was "not a bitch. She simply doesn't like it when you terrorize the other children with big words."

"You know what they say in town about us ladies?" Mimi said, picking up a cup and pouring herself some cocoa. "That we are *brujas,* living up here all together and cooking up potions."

"What's a *bruja,* Auntie Mimi?"

"Any woman who is stronger than a man," Mimi answered.

Ness laughed. "Really? I thought it meant 'witch.'"

"Like Halloween?" Sally said. "We're really witches? Does that mean we can ride brooms?"

"No, sweetie," Mimi soothed. "There's no such thing as witches. There are only strong women, and unfortunately, a few silly men who get scared by that who made up the word to make themselves feel superior."

Ness gave Sally a squeeze. "You're going to be a cousin very soon, Sally. Aren't you excited?"

Sally looked unimpressed. "All I can say is Auntie Nance better not have a damn boy."

"Will you stop with the 'damns'?" Phoebe said. "Some people, like your teacher and me, think 'damn' is a bad word. Since you've gotten home I've heard you say it at least five times. Give 'damn' a damn rest, please?"

Sally started to pout, but one look at her mother's face put her in her place. Still, she just had to get the last word in. "But I really, really, really hope Auntie Nance has a girl and that she isn't a whiny brat."

Phoebe snorted. "Because you sure never were, is that right?"

Sally put the brush down and set her last clippie in place. She held up the mirror for Phoebe to look. "You're so pretty, Mama," she said. "Let's call Andrew and show him."

Before Phoebe could launch into why it was perfectly reasonable to want to look good for yourself, Sally stuck her finger in her nose, rooted around, wiped what she found on her jeans, and tore off down the hallway to her next adventure.

Easter Sunday Phoebe woke up with a start, realizing that with all the farm Easter baskets to fret over, *she'd forgotten her own daughter*. She hurried into her sweats, used her cane to get to her wheelchair, and sped down the hallway to the front door so she could see if there were any leftover basket goodies. When she opened the door, there sat Andrew Callahan, dressed in a bunny suit. Her mouth dropped open. "The gesture is commendable," she said, "even if your ears do look like they need a dose of Viagra."

He smiled. "Have mercy, woman. This was all I could find on such short notice. He held up a wicker basket that put the farm creations to shame. Phoebe checked for a label to make sure it hadn't come from their competitor, Dolores Doheny. "The things a man will do in the name of love," he said. "I'm afraid I didn't make the most spectacular bow."

Love. He'd said it first. And he sounded humble about it, toned down, like he'd deliberately excised the cracker accent and the usual ebullience. She rolled forward to meet him until their knees touched, and she felt a spark of pleasure so fierce it went straight to her girl parts. "Andrew, can you feel that?"

"In my heart I can," he said.

It sounded corny, but she fell for it anyway. She took hold of the arms of her chair, leaned forward, and transferred herself (sweats and bed hair and all) to his lap. When she was settled, she leaned down to kiss him, and then realized she hadn't brushed her teeth yet. "Oh, my God, wait. I haven't brushed my teeth," Phoebe said. "I can't kiss you on Easter Sunday with morning breath."

He found a peppermint patty in the basket, bit off half, fed the other half to her, and they kissed until Sally came flying out in her Hello Kitty nightgown and grabbed the basket. "Mama!" she screamed. "Look what the Easter Bunny brought me! A new Barbie, and dresses. They're black! Oh, I hope he got me a Palm Pilot, too. Hi, Andrew."

"Hi, Sally. Happy Easter."

She raced to the other end of the porch, where she had her own set of wicker furniture, and began to catalog her riches on the pint-size table. "You didn't have to do that," Phoebe said to Andrew, her mouth sweet with chocolate and mint and Andrew.

"Yes, I did," he said. "If I hadn't, I wouldn't be here getting all these kisses. Now get inside and put on your Sunday best, darlin.' Sally's, too. We're going to church."

"Andrew, I'm not real big on believing all that Higher Power stuff. And I sure don't want Sally laboring under the fear of hell-fire and damnation just because she's a strong girl with an iron will and a few bad words in her overly large vocabulary."

He put his hands on her shoulders. She definitely felt that. In fact, she felt things every time he touched her and everywhere he touched her, as well as the places he hadn't touched because little pitchers who were present also had big eyes, that Phoebe wished he would touch and lately found herself thinking about way too much. The thing was, she couldn't want him without feeling the pain of losing Juan all over again, and that was part of it, too, the bitter with the sweet, so that in her heart she wasn't sure of anything, not even the chocolate souring on her tongue.

Andrew held on. He didn't flinch. He barely touched her breast with his finger and said, "Aw, come anyway, won't you? Nobody's going to check your passport. Just come along and listen to the music and celebrate Christ's miracle. Then we'll go to brunch, drink champagne, and eat ourselves sick. What d'you say to that?"

Phoebe said yes.

Sally said, "Are you going to wear the bunny suit to church?"

"If you want me to."

So they went to church, and Sally promised to keep her cell phone turned off and in her purse, but kept peeking inside to check on the pearlescent pink phone anyway. Andrew's church turned out to be the mission in Bayborough-by-the-Sea, in the part of town where any able-bodied person would chop off a leg to have a handicapped-parking permit. The exterior of the church was that wonderful old California stucco imbedded with bits of hay, the roof clay tiles and exposed beams. Inside the floors were polished Saltillo and brick, and the wall plaster a foot thick. The wooden pews had worn smooth over the years of worship, and up front on the altar the aging statuary exuded peace. Once it had probably seemed garish with colors and gold leaf. Now it was covered in flowers. There were so many lilies—white in bouquets, yellow in potted plants, pink tied into ribbon around the pulpit, lilies everywhere—that Phoebe felt intoxicated by the sight and scent of them, and just the tiniest bit sick when she saw a gold Doheny Nursery sticker on one of the pots. It made her remember Nance bringing lilies when she was in the hospital, about to have Sally. And it made her recall reading about the history of the lily in Sadie's journal. *Trumpet-shaped, pendant, flat faced, or bowl-shaped, there are over two hundred varieties in the U.S. alone. They grow best in well-drained soil.* She reviewed the first year they'd begun to resurrect the farm, and how they lost so many bulbs to that flood that she had to shut herself in her room and cry lest everyone see her so scared. No, I don't believe in God, but hadn't the first words out of my mouth been God help us? And how in our second year they overplanted the same area with annuals and a few perennials, and the lilies did better. And how the third year they covered the field like uniformly folded napkins in the fanciest restaurant Bayborough-by-the-Sea had to offer, and just like that, they'd mastered another species. Lilies liked a tablespoon of bonemeal, but unfortunately, Duchess, Nance's old retriever had liked bonemeal well enough to uproot bulbs. She missed that old dog. James said he was bringing home the new dog today. *Let them keep this baby,* I say every night as I lie in bed. Please let this last time be the charm, Phoebe thought. Do you suppose that's praying?

As for her favorite lily, Phoebe had to say that nothing on earth could beat the orange tiger lily, its petals unfurled like a cancan dancer, its freckles pure sass. Sadie's journal said that way back in the early 1800s a flower enthusiast named William Kerr carried back from Korea the first tiger lily bulbs. She tried to imagine it, flowers traveling via the bravest individuals, all these flowers from a cutting wrapped in newspaper, an envelope of seeds, one seemingly ugly bulb, and pretty soon, the whole planet was one huge garden, and maybe that was the whole point.

Beside her the Easter Bunny sang hymns.

The day after Easter, the girls were gathered in the kitchen drinking coffee and making breakfast. Phoebe picked up the phone and dialed Alaska. When someone said hello, she assumed it was Beryl, and said, "You're welcome for the flowers. What's so important you can't call your girlfriends once in a while?"

After a short silence, the hello voice spoke. "Who's calling?'

"Who's this?"

"You first. How do I know you're not a burglar, trying to see if I'm home so you can rob me?"

Phoebe took the receiver from her ear and looked at it. "Listen," she said. "This is Phoebe DeThomas calling for Beryl Reilly. Is she there or not? And how do I know *you're* not a burglar, robbing Beryl?"

"This is Zoë. I'm staying with Beryl. She's not here, though. She went to work at the birdcage or something. She'll be back in a couple of hours. Wanna leave a message?"

"Did she get my flowers?"

"You sent the flowers? Yeah, they got here fine."

"Well, did they come out nice?"

"Are you kidding? It looks like something from a magazine."

"Thanks for letting me know. Would you tell her Phoebe called?"

"Yeah, I sure will. Bye."

Phoebe hung up the phone and turned to Ness and Mimi. "I think it's time we took away her membership in the coven. Either that, or descend on her en masse, cameras around our necks, begging to see moose, and buying up hideous tourist T-shirts and asking where the penguins are."

Mimi dragged her finger through the edge of the icing on the leftover coconut lamb cake they'd had for Easter dinner. "I have Dayle's cell number. I could call her and ask her to drive by and check."

"Not a good idea," Ness said, eating her icing from a fork. "You've been doing really well about not calling her. Helping her make a clean break."

"Well, at some point calling her has to be an option."

Nance came in the side door dressed in a red jogging suit. It was so tight on her middle she looked like she'd swallowed a balloon. "How's my niece or nephew?" Phoebe said.

"Really moving today. Actually, I came over here to ask you what contractions feel like."

Phoebe dropped her fork. "I don't know. I had a C-section, remember?"

"Why?" Ness said. "Do you think you're having them? It's too early."

"Cálmate," Mimi said. "It's probably Braxton-Hicks. Happens in the last month usually. But I'd go to bed and call the midwife anyway. Where's James?"

Nance's face was pale. "Downtown. He was meeting someone from the city council for breakfast. Oh, my Lord. Do you think I should call him?"

"Phoebe, get out of your wheelchair," Mimi said. "Nance, you get in. Let's get you back to bed."

She went out the door and Ness trailed after her.

"Hey," Phoebe said. "Remember to bring my chair back. It's not like I have a spare!"

Sally was off at vacation school, the bus having arrived at seven-thirty to take everyone to Salinas for the day. The kids were going to visit a produce-packing plant, and would be home by four. Phoebe hesitated only a moment before she said out loud, "I'm calling Stinky, just to be safe."

"Hello?" James said.

"Stinky, it's me, Wingnut. Where are you?"

"I'm picking up the dog. Why?"

"How long will it take you to get home?"

"Twenty minutes. Why? What the hell is going on?"

"Nance thinks she's having some mild contractions. Mimi just put her to bed. Ness is with her. I think you should come back."

"What about this puppy?"

"Oh, bring the puppy. Hurry now. You wouldn't want to miss anything."

"How can this be happening? She isn't even in her third trimester."

"Relax, will you? She's almost seven months. And it could turn out to be nothing. Just come home and let's make sure." She hung up. Ness had come back and was absently touching her braids. "Let's go for a walk, Ness. Oh, wait. I forgot, I don't have my chair."

"I'll go get it."

"Don't forget me, okay? Don't you get over there and all caught up and forget I am basically stuck here in the kitchen sitting in this chair!"

Ness, with her long legs and longer stride, was already gone.

Ness

14

Taking Up Quilting

AS USUAL, APRIL BROUGHT RAIN, which generated a quickly spreading spring fever. "Staying in bed for three months can't hurt," Lester Ullman said as Ness related Nance's latest plan to keep from going into another round of premature labor.

"The ER doctor gave her medication to stop the contractions."

"As would I," Lester said. "But the medication to stop the contractions doesn't always work. If she stays off her feet, and that's one more day she keeps the baby inside, that means one more day of maturation for the lungs."

"James is all but sitting on her," Ness said. "And you should see that crazy little rat dog he brought her—she won't leave Nance's side. I've never seen anything like it."

"A rat dog?"

"Oh, it's a purebred rat terrier, black-and-white and with just this little nub of a tail. Cute in a manic kind of way, but it couldn't be further from Duchess. I guess she was returned to the breeder when she didn't live up to her show-dog bloodlines. Silly, if you ask me. A dog's a dog, not some piece of art to be carted around and awarded ribbons."

Lester smiled vaguely and began to page through her test

results. He was getting down to business, but Ness didn't need him to read them to her. The moment Lester had opened the door to the exam room, Ness knew her results were good. Lester had a medical degree, and like any able-bodied soldier in the healing ranks, he'd been trained to deliver somber news delicately, but she knew him so well she could read the set of his shoulders. Here was a man who could empathize without losing his objectivity. Over the last five years, she'd felt his compassion and restraint, but there was no way the poor fellow could temper good news. He set the chart down on the table and smiled.

"Sometimes," he said, "things go right for no reason at all, and let me tell you, those are the times a doctor lives for. Your labs are great. I'd be happy if they were my labs."

Ness looked down at her lap, where her hands were clasped so tightly that her knuckles throbbed. She eased her fingers apart and felt the blood return. Six years ago, when her lover, Jake, told her he had HIV, she thought life was over. Blind with panic, she'd stolen his horse, run away from her old life, ditched her responsibilities, camped out by Bad Girl Creek, and stared up at the night sky trying to believe there was an afterlife that would allow a sinner like her entrance. She'd bargained her way into Phoebe's house so that Leroy could have a place to stay, and entertained thoughts of suicide. Even after she'd moved in, she'd spent many a night lying awake, shaking with fear of the disease that had marked her. Then came Nance, and Beryl, and their friendship had pulled her to the surface—to the small world of the farm and her girlfriends. When David entered the picture, a wider window had opened, and the world seemed to pour in. He'd been sick a long time, but that didn't stop him from loving her, or her from loving him back. She figured they'd talked more in those few years than most couples did over a lifetime. David had been the one to get her into the new drug trial, and receive the medication—or maybe it was a miracle—that had impacted her test results so that only a trace of the virus remained in her system. She was asymptomatic two and a half years now, though there was no guarantee she'd stay that way. She tried not to think about it, and she prayed for strength. Every six months she had the tests repeated, and every single time they came up with normal values. She wanted to cry, but shoved her joy down to that small corner of her heart where she stored impossible wishes and let it rest. "So, Lester. Where do we go from here?"

Her doctor tapped her patient file against his hand. "I counsel all my patients to practice safe sex. So far as I'm concerned, that goes for you, too. There's a big world out there waiting, Preciousness. I'm sure you can find something interesting to do with yourself."

"Can I go back to working with horses?"

"If you don't let any of them bite you."

"So that's it? I don't have to come back?"

"If you don't mind, I'd like to keep track of this, document your progress. Maybe write an article about it to see if it's happened to anyone else. But if you get the flu, or sprain your ankle, or any number of ailments that require a doctor's care, I'll expect to see you. But as for this other matter, every six months is still—"

She couldn't help interrupting him. "Can I keep my lab slip?"

He opened the folder. "Why would you want that?"

"Call it a memento. A landmark day. My own personal touchstone."

He chuckled, handed it over, and opened the door to leave, then paused. "Now, everything else is going okay at the farm, right? The tribe is in harmony for once? Sally's behaving herself? Phoebe's taking care of herself instead of everyone else?"

She placed her hand over her heart. "Lester, I swear, the farm thrives, the tribe will increase, Sally is spoiled rotten, and Phoebe's falling in love with that Andrew Callahan fellow."

He groaned. "Here we go again."

"I know," Ness said. "Isn't it wonderful?"

That weekend Ness had the farm all to herself. Earlier in the day she'd dropped Mimi and Sally at the airport so they could spend the weekend at Disneyland. They were staying at the hotel across from the park, and Ness bet that the child would run Mimi ragged, but that time spent with Sally was a good fix for a woman who hadn't seen her grandchildren in going on six years. James and Nance were squirreled away in their bedroom, with James appearing every few hours to take the little rat dog out or to collect takeout food from Tillie Gort's. Nance had named the rat terrier Calpurnia, after her favorite character in *To Kill a Mockingbird,* so every now and then Ness heard "Calpurnia! Not there!" and figured that housebreaking was still an issue.

Phoebe, bless her brave heart, intended to spend two nights in the Big Sur house with Andrew. She and Ness were in the kitchen packing the cooler with food when they heard Andrew pull up and honk his car horn. "Granny Shirley would have said that's an impolite way for a suitor to come calling," Ness said, *tsk*-ing.

"Lighten up," Phoebe answered. "It's harder for him to get in and out of the car than it is for me. He's just trying to save time."

Ness shut the cooler. "Relax. I was only teasing. Let me carry this out for you. You sure you got everything?"

Phoebe looked around the kitchen frantically. "Oh, God. Do I have everything?"

Ness smiled at her friend. Her sleek brown hair was pulled back in a ponytail, and her face was glowing with anticipation. She looked adorable in a turquoise-and-lime-green tie-dyed shift and lime-green tennis shoes. "You do if you have birth control and a credit card," Ness answered. "That's what a girl needs these days. And maybe a cell phone."

"But what about—what should I do if—and if my cell phone doesn't get enough reception to—"

"I expect you'll find some way to muddle through. Go, Phoebe. Have a wild, wonderful, delicious time. Make me proud, and even a little jealous."

Phoebe smiled. "I can't believe I'm really doing this. I feel like such a hussy."

"Oh, honey. The only thing I can't believe is how long it took you."

As they made their way to the door, Ness noticed that Phoebe was looking at everything—paintings on the walls, potted palms, even the coatrack in that inventory kind of way she tended toward when she was missing her aunt Sadie. Ness saw the panicky look enter her eyes, and practically heard her thoughts, that ricocheting wonder whether there'd been a colossal screwup, and all this happiness had been intended for someone else. She loaded the cooler into the backseat and waved hi to Andrew.

"Will you be okay here by yourself?" Phoebe asked, but what she was really saying was, *Give me an out, please, I'll pay you fifty bucks if you ask me to stay.*

Ness shook her head as if to say, *Sorry, you'll get no reprieve from me.* "Segundo'll be by later. I have the animals for company. If I want drama I can go see Nance and James. Please, you two just go have some fun. You guys deserve it. Andrew, you take good care of my best friend."

"I will be the perfect gentleman," he said, and winked.

When the car pulled away, Ness took Leroy out of his stall, brushed his coat, picked his hooves clean, filed down a sharp edge on his left rear hoof, and tacked him up with a fleece bareback pad and a D-ring snaffle. Penny started in whinnying and kicking the stall because she wanted to come, too. When Ness offered her a bucket of oats and alfalfa to work on, she forgot about going anywhere.

"Come on," Ness said, leading her old horse through the farm, passing the greenhouses that now numbered three, making her way alongside the fields of flowers, where if one squinted, it looked as if the earth was an endless color wheel of pink pastels into a vivid fuchsia that melded into outright purple, and then on the downhill side, the blues against the yellows that ended in green. They'd tilled every possible inch, fed the ground, watered, and here was the return. *Reap and you shall sow.* Beauty is indistinguishable from profit. Life, as far as the eye could see and feast, and it seemed an embarrassment of riches. And yet once all this had seemed impossible. She pulled herself up onto Leroy's back and felt the strain of her slack muscles. Riding had been second nature to her. She'd stopped out of fear. Postponed her life. That was going to have to change.

Leroy had forgotten, too. She had to cluck to get him moving, and to reassure him when the trail led downhill to the creek. The day was warm, so she let him drop his head and drink, trying to recall where it was she had camped during the time she was homeless. Every time she thought she'd found the place, she knew she was wrong. A red-tailed hawk soared overhead, and a sweet-scented breeze came up, rattling the branches of the oak trees gently, like someone playing the brushes in a jazz band. This was one of those Central Coast days residents lived for: enough sun, a slight wind, and the feeling that beneath you the soil could grow whatever else a person needed. She wondered how long it would take Phoebe and Andrew to end up in bed together, and she hoped they had the sense to put the groceries away first.

That night she watched the sunset over the ocean, made herself some vegetarian chili and a small salad of freshly picked greens. She flopped on the couch and clicked on the TV, but every newscaster had a mopey face. The president was trying to justify sanctions on a third-world country while right here in America people were homeless, hungry, and dying, and she knew if she went down that trail she was done for, so she turned the blasted box off. She looked up at Sadie's portrait, her wiseacre smile, and came to the decision that when some people died, instead of fading from your memory they seemed to grow larger and more present, to live on in other ways, so that you felt their presence all the more deeply, and came to count on their company. She went to her room, knelt down on the floor and looked under her bed, where box after box of things begged to be taken out and explored. But there was one box that had waited long past time to deal with its contents.

She popped the rubber seal and inside saw the sights and scents of the past. Childhood photos, including a studio portrait of her mother that Granny Shirley had kept in a gold frame on the sideboard. She fingered the dizzying array of satin ribbons she'd won riding. She stopped long enough to try on Granny Shirley's Sunday gloves with the pearl buttons, and to marvel that they fitted her. She thumbed through the cards and letters she'd received from her mother—maybe a dozen in all—the woman who'd given her away like a coat that had gone out of style, and gone off to live an entirely new life back East, married well, eliminated her past. She still didn't want to see her, but she knew that someday she might, so she tied them with a silk ribbon and tucked them back into the box. They'd find a way to build a bridge or they wouldn't. It wasn't doing her any good to dwell on it.

Then she found the Baggie full of material she'd collected to sew her own square for the Names quilt. She'd gotten so far as to cut out shapes and pin them to the background. A few of the pins she'd used to anchor fabric had begun to rust, leaving a stain. She eased the pins out and dropped them to the bottom of the Baggie. The horse shape she'd planned to appliqué was black satin, and at the time that reminded her of Leroy. It no longer hurt her to think about it. She knew she should throw all this away, but somehow she couldn't bring herself to. Then it came to her like a slap in the face: She would sew David's block. She left the fabric spread across her bed and hurried out to the farm computer, which was always on. On screen the DeThomas farm logo, a wreath of flowers and two crossed spades, swirled and danced.

Nance was the on-line expert, but how hard could it be? She typed "AIDS Quilt" into a space that read "search engine," and in a flash, she was on the website, and there it was, or at least part of it. In the background the Washington Memorial looked about as substantial as a toothpick. There were so many blocks they had to split the quilt into portions in order for people to view it. A series of black-and-white faces flashed continuously above the color blocks, and Ness couldn't help but ache at their hopeful smiles. It was a cornucopia of people—men, women, and children, even babies. She did a site search for Bayborough, California, and on page 1 alone fifty names popped up. At least David wouldn't be alone.

"Thank you for your block for the Names Project Quilt. If you cannot hem it yourself, we will hem it for you. Please include with your block a letter with the name, background, and your relationship to the person it represents. If you are able to make a charitable monetary contribution, please know that your money contributes to the importance of AIDS education worldwide, and toward the cure."

All that night she sewed and embroidered and topstitched appliqués until her fingers throbbed, and under her hands, David's life began to take shape. She quilted six horses running, a bottle of wine, the outline of his hands arched over a typewriter, and last she used gold thread to spell out his name. She pressed it with the iron, gave it a hem, and then she stretched her arms above her head and heard vertebrae crack.

She set it aside to fill out the last part of the application.

Dear Names Quilt People,

Enclosed please find the finished block for my late husband, David Francis Snow. We were married for three months and twelve days, but we loved each other from the first day we met, really. David worked as a television writer for most of his life, and he won an award for one of his after-school specials. Even when he was sick, he continued to write, but so far I haven't been able to look at the pages he left behind. Soon, I hope. I'm sure there's gold there.

David loved a lot of things, including the ocean, which was the last thing he saw before he passed from this earth into God's hands. He had eclectic tastes. His house was filled up with majolica pottery, 1950s era wagon-wheel furniture, an abundance of cowboy kitsch, some beautiful rugs, and a signed Keith Haring print that I am going to auction off at the Roth Gallery this summer, and donate the proceeds to Project Angel Food. David loved to cook. He made a mean bruschetta, introduced me to mizithra cheese, favored aged cream sherry drunk from Austrian crystal glasses, but I never knew him to turn down an A&W hamburger or a root beer float. He loved horses, and kept them to the very end. He loved to stay up late and watch black-and-white movies, many of which he could recite the dialogue to and provide the voices, as well. He loved my friends, he loved their children, and he loved me. And I loved him, but I've already said that.

Some of my friends can't seem to understand why a straight woman such as myself would marry a gay man who had a death sentence hanging over his head. I used to get so angry, trying to explain to them that love is bigger than any obstacle in its way, but you know what? It's simply that they can't get past the sex part. I must admit I was like that, too, until I met David. He taught me what it meant to truly love somebody, and how little sex had to do with that. He used to say that we were like a pair of old swans, mated for life, a beautiful unit, even if all we did was swim in a small pond for a short time. His heart was enormous and very intelligent, because it managed to teach me by example, how to forgive, how to let go, and finally, how not to forget.

Please accept this check on behalf of David Snow, and may it help to educate people everywhere while we work toward a cure.

In His Love,
Preciousness Butler Snow

The next day, Ness drove to Sierra Grove to mail the envelope containing the block and the check, using one of those Mailboxes places that kept convenient hours and didn't have hellacious waiting lines. She watched the clerk stamp it and throw it into a postal bin with at least twenty other packages, and felt peace flood her veins that she'd done the right thing. It was funny that David had listed the names of charitable organizations he favored, but neither of them had considered the quilt. She thought of Granny Shirley's old quilts, the worn-to-softness red-and-white-schoolhouse quilt she used to let Ness snuggle under when she was sick, but had to be folded away in the cedar chest at all other times. There were others she'd kept hidden, the intricate double wedding ring she was probably saving for Ness's wedding day, but that had never come, or at least not what Granny Shirley would consider a wedding. There was the riotous pink-and-green-pickle-dish quilt with minute quilting stitches, and the frail crazy quilt in velvet and satin, webbed with gold turkey-track embroidery. When her grandmother died, she'd barely looked in the boxes. She'd stood in her living room crying and told the movers what to pack and what to leave for the church, while in her hands she held on to the Carnival glass candy dish and remembered the woman who'd raised her up and remained loyal even when Ness had screwed up so badly anyone else would have walked away. The woman who once had three changes of clothing and the tools of her trade now had enough worldly possessions to set up house—and she had the house to do it, too. So why didn't she want to live there?

She drove around Bayborough-by-the-Sea, gawking at tourists clogging the sidewalks, watching the eucalyptus trees sway, listening to the chatter of traffic, and the occasional conversation, and smelling the smoky smells of good cooking that emanated from the various cafés. The few times she caught a glimpse of the beach the waves were small but inviting. She loved living here. Loved living with Phoebe and Sally, and Mimi, though if she had to lay down money, she'd bet Mimi was going to move north and settle down with Dayle. At some point she'd have to do something with David's place, but there was no hurry, and who knew what the future held, because if she'd learned any lessons at all, it was that no one could predict what might happen.

In Sierra Grove she drove by what used to be Earl's On Ocean, and wondered what had become of Beryl and her true love. Maybe their friend was so involved in her new life that her old one seemed a bother, and that was why she didn't return phone calls, or send postcards, or come visit. Or, maybe the farm had been a way station for Beryl. Maybe it had done its job and now she was where she was supposed to be, learning other lessons. It didn't stop anyone from missing her.

Ness thought of Revelations, of God's promises tucked in between the judgments, and how it would always be hard for her to reconcile what she thought of as a chasm separating the two, but that was part of the mystery. She made a left and found herself on Antique Row, a short block in old Sierra Grove. The Antique Mall featured plate-glass windows, gold, Gothic-style lettering advertising estate items, antiquities, jewelry, and outright junk. She parked down the block and hiked back. Down the first aisle tourists wandered, looking for bargains. Clerks were busy unlocking cases so someone could have a closer look at things. Ness stopped in a booth filled with blue-and-white kitchen things. A Storm at Sea quilt covered a table with peeling aqua paint that was marked two hundred dollars. The quilt was one-fifty, and it would go perfectly in her bedroom at the farm, which she was now determined to redecorate in celebration of her new start. She tucked it under one arm and examined a set of graduated French enamel canisters: *Sucre* and *Café*. The essentials of life. She thought of the farm kitchen, and how many nights she and Phoebe had sat there talking until it was way past bedtime. A light shone down on a cobalt glass cake pedestal, a set of collectible art deco creamers, Staffordshire calico china that matched Aunt Sadie's pattern, and when Ness found a butter dish that wasn't priced too high, she added it to her pile.

She didn't really expect to see the antiques dealer who'd come to David's estate sale here, but she had wondered what kind of place he ran, and okay, maybe she did want to see him again, a little. She walked the aisles and stopped whenever something caught her eye—a clever basket, some old railroad sign announcing the town of Rainbow, a glass case filled with shiny pocket watches and commemorative coins. When she found things she wanted, she surprised herself by giving herself permission to spend the money. Midway through the store there was a coffee cart and a plate of butter cookies, and next to that, two chairs. She set her pile aside in one of the chairs and served herself, adding two sugars and cream. From here she could see the front of the store, and that there was a staircase leading upstairs to a balcony where several desks and phones made up the office end of the business. And there he was, the same handsome man from the estate sale, sitting on the edge of one of those desks, the phone in his hand. She lifted a hand and waved. He hung up the phone. She watched him come down the stairs, a spring in his step that said he wasn't afraid of losing his footing.

You can tell what's in a person's heart by his smile, Granny

Shirley had advised her since she was a tiny girl. She remembered playing bride with an old Barbie doll, a box of tissues, and a couple of newspaper rubber bands. It was possible to make a veil, a dress, and a dream out of the same stuff you blew your nose in. *God made man tall, so a woman could lean on him when she needs to,* she'd said. *There are good smiles and bad ones, Preciousness. It's up to you to learn to tell the difference.*

When he was ten feet away, she set down her coffee and stood up to meet him. "Welcome to the biggest antique mall on the Central Coast," he said, reaching out to shake her hand.

"Thanks. As you can see, I've found some things I liked."

He looked at her pile, and then into her eyes, his smile gone. "You know, I told myself if you came back, I'd tell you what I was too chicken to say at the estate sale. Otherwise I was going to let it go."

Her heart fluttered. Please don't let this be some cheesy pickup line. "Tell me what?"

He reached into his pocket, took out his wallet, and opened it to a photo. Ness hadn't seen her since she was a child, but she would have known the photo anywhere. It was the same one Granny Shirley had sitting on her sideboard for all the years Ness had lived with her. Her mother.

"Do you know this person?" he asked.

Ness felt a chill travel up her spine. "She's—she's my biological mother. What puzzles me is how you came by her picture?"

He pressed his lips together. "She's my mother, too. I believe I'm your half brother. My name's Willie. And you're Ness, am I right? "

Wild iris is an Alaskan staple. It blooms alongside railroad tracks and thrives in the most out-of-the-way ditches. On the route from Denali to Fairbanks, look out the train window, and you're sure to see the elegant iris, standing like royalty, no matter what its surroundings.

Beryl and Thomas Jack

15

Summer Work

BY LATE MAY, the tourists were arriving daily on discount flights and package deals, or via busses that took them from cruise ships to Anchorage proper, where they picked up the train and headed to Denali Park. Fishermen readied their boats to go to sea, and Thomas Jack was among those headed out to try their luck. He and Beryl took a drive up to Hatcher Pass on his last day in town, and wandered through the timeworn buildings at Independence Mine. Beryl felt a small shock finding a white stripe of snow still lingering in the lee of an abandoned building. She felt as if that bit of persistent winter was sending her a message. Whole seasons had passed, and now the hills were covered with vegetation. Berries formed, chocolate lilies bloomed, and yet inside Beryl's heart, something remained frozen solid. "I don't understand why you have to go away for the whole summer," she said. "Your job at Raptor Rehab pays well. You're selling masks at the museum gift shop. The sun's out, and there's so many things we could be doing together. Why go fishing when salmon's at its lowest price in years? Why not stay here with me?"

Thomas Jack listened to her and nodded as if he were weighing her words carefully and thoughtfully. For a moment she swore she could change his mind. Then he petted a passing tourist's dog, looked out toward the glacier, and she knew she'd lost him. "I fish in the summer," he said. "I meet up with my cousins and uncles, and we catch fish, then we spend some time at fish camp, and even if I don't make any money, it's still good, because I'm fishing."

Beryl noticed she didn't appear once in his reasons. And why should she? She kept him at arm's length. Their sex was deliberately recreational. She looked toward the nearby glacier, trying to remain open to Thomas's logic. The icy grime of the glacier gave off a bad first impression. She was sure some of the visitors thought, Where's the wonder in this? But if wonder wasn't convincing coming from the compressed ice, all they had to do was take the train to Seward and board a wildlife cruise where pairs of otters seemed to pose on the way out of the harbor and, midtour, the puffins made kamikaze landings. One bite of the box lunch of fried halibut, a sip of cocoa to take away the chill, and just when they thought it wouldn't happen and began to change a roll of film, a humpback whale would breach the water. Alaska was happy to function as a wonderland for visitors—Denali showed its purple shoulders when the sun came out just so, the sun cast a golden light across a pond where loons called and a bull moose stood drinking, the earth pulled back its cape of winter darkness to expose trumpeter swans, sandhill cranes, a fleck of gold in a sandy stream—but it did so only on its own terms. "I understand," Beryl said to Thomas Jack, even though she didn't.

He grinned. "Thanks, Beryl. Hey, you could come meet me when the season ends."

"I really don't like to leave Verde."

"Verde's all right with Zoë. Them two get on pretty good. We could stop by the Army-Navy store and get you some Carhartts."

She smiled but didn't answer. Zoë had just that week accepted a job teaching kayaking at a gourmet camp on Growler Island. She had been planning on telling him, but just then changed her mind. A clean break, Ness used to say whenever they talked about boyfriends.

In midtown Anchorage, a line of cars formed in front of *Behold I Make All Things New Laser Auto Wash*. At the head of the line, a tired woman in damp clothes collected five-dollar bills, and for five more, pushed the undercarriage cleaning and spray wax. Zoë told Beryl to decline both. "There's puddles everywhere," she said. "It's only a matter of time before we get splashed again. This is just so cops can read your license plate."

Beryl aimed Earl's truck into the tentacles of cloth. After they finished here they were grocery shopping for Zoë's upcoming summer job. She was leaving in the morning and would be gone for nearly three months. "Are you sure this won't scratch the paint job?"

"Who cares if it does?" Zoë asked. "Earl hauled ass and left you with it. In my book, that makes it your truck."

"Well, I'm not sure how legal that is."

"If you want legal, why don't you ask the cop," Zoë suggested. "He calls you every other day. You might as well give him something practical to do."

Beryl frowned and inched the truck forward. "I know. I think he's hitting on me. I don't have the heart to tell him to stop it."

Zoë laughed. "Are you kidding me? That old geezer? He acts like he's your dad. He gets that total basset hound look every time he shows up, and I can tell he wants to give you buckets of advice. Believe me, Beryl. That is not the way he'd hit on someone. Though I wish it would happen to me."

"Really?" she said, wondering how she could have gotten things so wrong.

"Yes, really! Has he asked you out? No. He calls you even when there's no news because he wants to make sure you're okay. Maybe his wife left him, or his daughter got her heart stomped real bad, and this is how he's making peace with not keeping her safe. Let me tell you, it's a pleasant change to have a cop calling where I live instead of the other way around."

"Do you miss Cleveland?"

She laughed. "I miss *sex* with Cleveland."

"Zoë, what about trying life without a man for a while? Is that such a difficult concept?"

Zoë unwrapped a candy bar and offered Beryl half, which she declined. "Do you realize the irony of what you just said?"

Beryl felt her face flush. "Thomas Jack is—"

"Pure sex," Zoë said through a mouthful of chocolate.

"I was going to say he's left for the summer."

"Good for him," Zoë said.

"Excuse me, how is it good for him when it feels so bad for me?"

Zoë crumpled up the candy wrapper and put it in the trash sack on the floor of the cab. "Maybe it feels bad for you because it's inconvenient. Thomas Jack knows the score, Beryl. Believe me, he knows you're not over Earl. He's your transitional guy, and that will never be enough for someone like him. You're using him to get to sleep at night. To you he's no different from flannel jammies and hugging a pillow."

Beryl's face went hot. "I am not using him! It's possible to have sex with yourself, you know."

Zoë gave her a look. "We're both going to forget you said that and never speak of it again."

Soapy water pumped down from hoses, foaming on the truck's windshield. Beryl thought about how long it was since she'd eaten a candy bar. Maybe as far back as the drive from California, when she and Earl had stocked up on sugar and soda so they could drive all night. Why didn't she eat a damn candy bar? Why was she never hungry enough to overcome the ennui that settled on her when she tried to make a meal? Thomas Jack was gone. She'd let him go. Since the weather had begun to warm up, he'd been traveling a lot, and she'd seen less of him, anyway, and had even wondered once or twice if he was maybe seeing someone else. Didn't she tell him all the time that she was too old for him? To her left the light indicating the wash cycle was over blinked, and here came the rinse, a brief, blinding torrent, and then nothing at all. She was angry and wanted to cry, but those two things did not mix with driving, so she simply drove through the other side of the carwash, emerging into sunlight.

Ahead of her a Subaru splashed through a puddle and the car wash was history.

"Isn't that just the luck," Zoë said.

But for a moment, Beryl had had a clean windshield. Trailer parks, budding trees, the metal *Aurora* sculpture that changed colors as a person drove by—it was nearly summer, and Beryl was still here. In the distance, ebony mountains sported a crust of snow, but it looked brittle and sugary, and Beryl thought if she could reach out and take hold of the mountaintop, it would break off in her hand, crisp but bitter, like the last cookie in the jar.

"You're right about Thomas," she said softly.

Zoë's hand crept over the seat and patted her arm. "You'll live. I am."

At Fred Meyer, Zoë wanted to stop and look at the diamond rings, and then she went straight to the pony packs of vegetables. "I don't think the yard gets enough sunlight to grow those," Beryl said.

Zoë pointed to a prefab greenhouse. "Let's buy one of these. It wouldn't take long to put it up, and this way you could grow stuff all summer. I'll go in half with you."

"I don't know," Beryl said. "You won't be here. What if I decide to take a trip?"

Zoë sighed. "Ever heard of asking the neighbor kid to see to things?"

"I'll think about it," Beryl said, but the truth was, if she were to go back to tending plants on a daily basis, it would remind her too much of Sadie's farm.

Zoë filled the cart with foods she loved that would keep well in her pack—trail mix, green apples, barbecue potato chips, *cotto* salami, and lemonade mix. Beryl picked up the half-gallon size of soymilk, noticed Zoë's expression, and exchanged it for the quart size she always bought. "It tastes fine," she said. "I can't even drink cow's milk anymore."

"I'll take your word for it," Zoë said, putting a container of instant cocoa into the basket. "Milk from beans? I don't get it."

Oh, wait until you're fifty, Beryl wanted to tell her as she stocked up on low-fat yogurt. *The world looks a lot different from that side of things. You think it won't happen, but there'll come a day when you'll be chugging soymilk and popping black cohosh and the words "edamame" and "primrose oil" will jump off your tongue like you were born saying them. Age happens to all of us, kid.*

When Zoë hit the candy aisle, Beryl stood back and watched. Abba Zabba, Good & Plenty, Super Hot Tamales, sugary Bubble Yum; Beryl knew if she were to take the tiniest bite of any of them she'd lose a filling.

"I think that should hold me until I get back," Zoë said, popping the top on a cola from the cooler at the end of the checkout aisle.

Or until you go into a diabetic coma, Beryl thought as she looked at her and wished she had the nerve to ask her to stay.

Since Zoë had come to stay in the Nuthatch, the phone actually rang. They returned home to a blinking message light, and while Zoë was checking her messages, the phone rang again. Zoë's mother, who lived in Muldoon, wanted her daughter to come home and move into her old room. "Thanks, but I'd rather volunteer myself as a lab rat," Zoë said. "No, Mom, I'm not giving you crap, I'm being realistic. Terry doesn't like me, and believe me, the feeling is mutual. This is a great summer job. No. No, Mom. I will. I promise I will call you when I can. Yeah, you take care, too. Talk to you in a few months." She hung up and sighed. "Whoever said your mother is always there for you should be forced to spend a half hour with mine," she said.

"Is she really that awful?"

"Well, she likes to tell me what to do from the kind of toothpaste I use and which direction to brush. And her taste in men! Ew. Talk about robbing the ragbag."

The phone rang again, and Zoë held up a finger as if to keep her place in the conversation. "Sure can," she said, holding the receiver out. "It's for you. Someone named Phoebe."

Beryl looked at the receiver, and shook her head no.

"Talk to her," Zoë insisted, not even covering the mouthpiece. "She's only called you like nine million times."

When Beryl wouldn't take the phone, Zoë placed it back on her ear. "Beryl is sitting right here, but she says to tell you that she's out. I'm good at lying, but not that good, so ask me anything you want to know and I'll tell you if I can."

Beryl grabbed the receiver from her and hung it up. "Don't you ever do something like that again."

"Or what?" Zoë said. "You'll kick me out so you can sit around and feel sorry for yourself some more? My God, Beryl, a guy left you! Big deal. You're so brokenhearted you've been sleeping with Thomas Jack for months. It's not like you're the only woman in the world this ever happened to. Is it really a good enough reason to be mean to your girlfriends?"

Beryl pointed her finger at Zoë as if daring her to answer her own question. When she couldn't think of anything wise to say, she went upstairs. Verde began calling, but she shut the door and stayed in her room.

Back at the farm she'd lived in what she thought was the nicest of the rooms—it had two windows, and outside one of them, an oak tree with an inviting V of branches. Occasionally a bird would perch there, hop down the length of the branch, and look in her window. Beryl knew how to keep still well enough that she was almost invisible. To make herself appear small enough that birds would begin to think of her as just another tree. "Act like a tree," Thomas Jack had said, the day they watched the eagles hunting. She was ashamed of herself for not talking to Phoebe. For not responding at Easter when she'd sent her the incredible bouquet. For putting all the girls off for so many months, as if they had stopped mattering to her when exactly the inverse was true. But they had all looked at her relationship with Earl as if it were Beryl's gift for having endured so many rotten breaks. As if she had earned and won this perfect happiness, as if a life such as hers had finally found its harmony. Then, when Earl went away, she'd had the opportunity to tell them the truth and acknowledge her own human failings, or to push them away and allow them to continue to think that not only was happiness possible for her but for all of them if they just hung in there.

By now Thomas Jack would be in Kodiak, meeting his cousins. After a day or two of loading in supplies, their boat would set out to fish, and Thomas Jack, with the hopelessly flat feet and the cleft palate scar, would spend his days hauling in fish and struggling to stay upright when the water was choppy. She envied him his life; he had pared things down to a fairly simple pattern. If a man could be as happy as Thomas Jack, he was lucky indeed. And despite what Zoë said, she cared for him as much as she could allow herself to, but it was a far cry from loving somebody and growing old with him.

She turned on her side and watched the sunlight stream through her window, dappling the wood floor in a leafy pattern. There was plenty of light here. Enough that she thought maybe she would buy the greenhouse for Zoë after all, so that when she came back from her job in August, she'd see the fruits of Beryl's labor and be proud of her for digging in.

"What are you cooking?" Zoë asked as Beryl stood at the counter grating cheese onto enchiladas.

"An old friend of mine's recipe," Beryl said. "It's vegetarian, but you'll like it, I promise."

"I'm sure I will," Zoë said, eyeing Beryl closely. "After I get over the shock of you actually cooking. Suddenly you're hungry?"

She gave her a look. "I eat on occasion."

"You could have fooled me the last few months."

Beryl sighed. "Zoë, I'm trying to give you a peace offering. Are you going to pester me to death or make a salad?"

"All right, I'll make a salad. I was just making conversation."

For a moment Beryl felt as if it were one of her early days at the farm. At first every alliance seemed temporary, and the comfort of the farmhouse too good to be true. Then we found our niches and didn't want to give up an inch of space, she remembered. For a while, it was like a perfect bubble, and always, deep down, we were afraid some guy was going to come along and let the air out. And what do you know, one by one, they did just that.

"This is good," Zoë said when they sat down to eat. "Probably the last authentic Mexican food I'll eat until fall. Thanks for making it for my last meal."

"You're welcome."

"Beryl?"

"Yes?"

"While you were taking your nap, I had an idea. How about before I go, you and I tackle the downstairs? Just a couple bags of his things. Only as much as you feel comfortable doing."

Beryl set down her fork and looked at Zoë. "I don't know."

Zoë reached across the table, and beneath the table, Beryl felt the cat rub against her ankle. "It's time, Beryl. Let me help you do this, okay?"

Beryl had been in this position before—she and Ness cleaning out Juan's things from Phoebe's room. She knew how it was—Phoebe wanted them to do it, but she also hated them for taking that step toward closure, the admitting that Juan was gone from their lives forever. One false move and you were committing girlfriendly treason. It was best not to think about it, simply to go along. But it seemed that once Zoë had knocked at that door, she had all kinds of things to say on the subject.

"You know, things weren't terrible with Earl. I probably could have gone along the way we were living for a long time. They had just turned, well, sort of beige. He was the same guy I fell in love with, and although he was always nice to me and generous, he got strange and distant. It was when his friend George died, and after the funeral that things seemed to kind of unravel. He went to Sweden a couple of times to work on Tom's CD, and when he came back, it was like something of him was still packed in his suitcase. I knew he was leaving even before he did. We talked about it, and there just wasn't anything else to say, I guess. But he said he was going to leave in a few days, not that night. It's just too odd to be part of the plan. He took off in the truck, and the next thing I knew there was the trooper at my door, and since then I've been in a holding pattern."

"Okay," Zoë said. "But the only truth that matters is that he's gone. He's not coming back. Men are strange, Beryl. You want romance, they call you needy. You try to give them a stable ride, they accuse you of being boring. I swear they should have all stayed in their forts, jerking off to Wonder Woman comic books."

Zoë went to the fridge to get a drink, and Beryl watched her go. "So what am I supposed to do with all his stuff? Give vintage guitars and recording equipment to Value Village?"

Zoë sat down at the table. "If he were really missing, you'd think you would have heard from one of his friends by now, worried over him not answering letters and phone calls, and so on. But have you? No. I bet you anything he's still around. He couldn't just disappear. Did he take his favorite guitars?"

Beryl shrugged. "How should I know? He had so many. What was to stop him from buying new ones?"

"I don't know," Zoë said. "Musicians are a quirky lot. Guitar players usually have one or two instruments they can't bear to live without. You want to find Earl, inventory the guitars. That's just a suggestion."

Beryl tried hard to think of Earl's guitars, his favorites, the ones he got nervous about when they traveled. She remembered a blue Collings archtop he liked for the color. She'd been with him when he bought it, in a small shop in downtown Sierra Grove. And she could hear the mellow tones the Ramirez classical guitar was capable of making—it had a wide ebony neck and on the high end, soft strings instead of metal. He called that guitar his "fifty-five," because that was the year it had been built. It was a pretty thing, made of rosewood and Spanish cedar, but he didn't play that one when he was writing a new song, no. The guitar he used when he was writing was the Martin D-28.

"Ready to go downstairs?" Zoë asked after she'd cleared the table and put the dishes in the dishwasher.

"As ready as I'll ever be."

"Whoa!" Zoë said as Beryl unlocked the studio, revealing the recording equipment and tape decks. "This place looks professional. Where'd he keep his guitars?"

Beryl opened closets and cupboards until finally she found the one that was insulated and padded to maintain an even temperature. Inside there were two black hard-shell guitar cases stacked atop one another, and a small brown gig bag. Zoë pulled them out and undid the latches. The first two held the Ramirez and the blue Collings, and there was the gig bag for the Martin, but its hard-shell case was missing, as was the guitar. "This doesn't make sense," Beryl said.

"Tell me one thing about that guy that did make sense," Zoë challenged.

Beryl ran her hand across the empty gig bag. "The Martin was the guitar he played when he did small performances," she said. "His favorite. A dead man would have left it behind. Earl's not dead, Zoë. He's in some other time zone being Buckethead. I'd bet my life on it."

Zoë folded her arms across her chest. "So now that you know, what are you going to do about it?"

Beryl paused. If she said this next thing, her house of cards would topple, and she'd have no choice but to act. "This one time I was in Bayborough visiting friends, and Earl was supposed to be here, in Alaska, I noticed an ad for Buckethead in concert in Santa Cruz. So I rode a bus three hours, stood in line, got my ticket, and under my jeans I was wearing my best black satin panties. I had this idea that it would be fun to sneak backstage and make passionate love to him in his dressing room like a groupie, but the guy who came out onstage was shorter, and his hands were different, and right away I could tell it wasn't Earl. They didn't play a thing alike. And—" her voice caught and she forced it out "—he even held his guitar differently. Up toward his face, like Tuck Andress does, of Tuck and Patti. Ever since then, I had this notion . . ."

Zoë helped Beryl pull the guitars from the cases. She stood them up against the wall and inspected them. "Didn't you ever just come out and ask?"

Beryl's throat ached from so much talking. "I'm not sure. Maybe I did. Maybe I didn't want to know."

Zoë motioned upstairs. "It's colder than hell down here. This place gives me the willies. Let's head back upstairs."

When they were sitting on the couch, and Zoë had fetched the television remote, clicked it on, surfed her way to MTV, then VH1, and turned the sound down so they could watch the videos in silence, Beryl said, "I thought Earl *was* Buckethead, Zoë. I was sure of it."

"But the guy in Santa Cruz?"

"I know. It seems so simple now. He was Buckethead, too. And so is Eric Clapton, from time to time, and Pat Metheny, too, because Buckethead is whoever needs to be Buckethead in order to try out new material on anonymous audiences. Shoot, if I could play the guitar, *I* could be Buckethead. It must just be something they all do from time to time. So who was Earl, really? Someone who got his kicks hanging out with famous musicians? Was it even his real name?"

Zoë tossed the remote aside and picked Verde up. At once he stepped up to her hand, and then lay down in her lap. She rubbed his belly, and he fluffed out his wings. He reached up with one foot, and she gave him a finger to hold on to. "Seems to me the real question is what are you planning to do about it?"

Beryl gently ruffled Verde's head until he fluffed out his feathers. She was still in the throes of understanding something she'd been stumbling over for a long while. "Do you suppose it's one of those guy bonding things? Those guys he hangs with—Eric, Steve, they're getting old. If they hadn't been guitar legends they'd be plain old grandfathers living on Medicare and dashed hopes. They don't want to get old and be forgotten. Age is everything in the music world. B. B. King would probably be greeting customers at the Indianola Wal-Mart if he couldn't do those commercials for diabetes. . . ."

On and on she talked. Verde pecked at Zoë's nail polish, became fascinated with her thin silver bangle bracelets, stacked twenty deep on her arm. Beryl sat there stinging, uncertain what bothered her most—the vanity men had about growing old or the secrets they kept from the women they were supposed to love. At ten, when the sun finally began to go down, she looked at her watch, startled. "It's late. You should go to bed, Zoë. You have to be at the train really early."

Zoë yawned. "I'm okay. We can keep talking."

Beryl transferred Verde back to his cage. "No. Go to bed. I'll drive you to the train station. See you in the morning. And Zoë?"

"Yeah?"

"Thanks."

That night Beryl sneaked downstairs and brought the two remaining guitars up to her room. She laid the cases on the floor, knelt and unsnapped them, and removed the instruments, holding them by the necks like children who needed to go sit in the corner. She laid them down on the bed, side by side, their necks on the pillows. The blue one reminded her of beach houses in Sierra Grove, that same weathered color that meant the wood had seen seasons come and go and still remained. The Ramirez was so light as to be nearly weightless. It smelled like the polish that made it gleam. She studied the curves in the wood and imagined a luthier steaming thin pieces of wood until he could bend them into the arc he wanted. She sat in the chair nearest the fireplace and watched the guitars for a long time. If Earl had done this to Zoë, she might have sold the guitars. Knowing her what-the-hell attitude, she might have burned them in the fireplace. But at her age Beryl didn't feel like the drama was worth getting all worked up. Some mornings she looked in the bathroom mirror and touched her face, the skin growing softer every year, her neck starting to have that corded look that made her realize how sometimes, for no reason at all, she'd find herself clenching her teeth. She'd gotten into the habit of holding her head high from five years in prison. My stewardship on earth is on the downhill slide, she thought. There is no going back, no do-overs. I loved a man, we shared an adventure, and now here are these relics, leftovers, which some budding musician too broke to afford a decent instrument would just appreciate the hell out of. I'll find him—or her—and make them a gift and these beauties will go on to have other lives, make other songs, and that will be the end of it, and I won't have to look at them anymore.

At the train the two women embraced. "Have fun," Beryl said. "And be sure you wear your life jacket."

"I'll be fine," Zoë said. "Probably get fat on all the fancy food they fix. You don't have to worry."

"Send postcards," Beryl said, knowing she wouldn't, and started to cry.

"Stop that," Zoë said, blinking away her own tears. "I am so not worth crying over that I think you need hormones."

Beryl watched the train pull away, its yellow-and-blue cars bright against the rocky cliffs behind it. Every so often a cataract of water fell down the rock, emptying into the earth. "Bye," she whispered.

"Restless," Beryl said into the telephone when Detective Stokes asked her how she was feeling. "But eager to talk to you. I think I've finally figured something out."

"Interesting," he said. "Feel like having lunch with me today?"

"I don't know," Beryl said, looking at the guitar cases on her bedroom floor. "You have yet to pick up your cat."

"Keep talking like that, I'll bring you a second one," he said.

Thomas Jack was fishing aboard the *Ellen Cole*. Zoë was kayaking tourists around the cold waters, showing them eagles' nests and brown bear from a safe distance. Why not? "Lunch sounds good," she said.

Thomas Jack stood out on deck after supper, chewing on a toothpick and looking at the water. It was a good year for fishing; he'd make enough money to see his grandmother at Christmas. He stuck his hands into his pockets and planted his feet. To his port side, a hundred yards away, a humpback whale breached the surface. It was a baby, full of energy, its fins and tail still smooth and gray, unmarked by scrimmages or barnacles. A moment later its mother's broad back broke the water, too, revealing a scarred hide that testified to her years. Though it had seemed like her calf was alone, she'd been nearby all the while.

Then she dived, her tail flukes sliding seamlessly into the water. Like that, Thomas Jack thought, realizing just how quickly people came into and exited each other's lives. You could race after them, or you could maintain your steady pace that had always worked for you. There was always a choice. And it was at that moment he felt Beryl take leave from his heart, as real as if he were releasing one of the rehab birds out at Fort Richardson. First came the tentative stretch of wings, as if testing the air to make sure it wasn't another cage. Then the lift, leaving his hands empty. Finally, the heartbreaking and wonderful moment she pushed through the air and moved on.

Trillium, also known as stinking Benjamin, is common to rich woods and blooms from March to May. The entire plant is only four to twelve inches in height, but the blooms are spectacular. Mottled green, deep purple, or brown, they grow nearly straight up from the stalk. American Indians used the trillium to ease the pain of childbirth, but also as an eye medicine, to clear cloudy vision. Women believed it to be a love potion and boiled the root so as to extract the juice, one drop of which was said to cause a man to fall in love with the first woman he saw. An old mountain myth says that if you pick a trillium, it will rain.

Phoebe

16
Afterglow

"PLEASE DON'T CRY," Andrew said, stroking Phoebe's damp cheek as she lay curled into the pillow. "I know that wasn't very good. I promise next time it'll be better."

Phoebe hiccupped and turned to face her new lover, the second man in her life to see her naked, discounting a myriad of doctors, of course. Maybe that was the reason she couldn't stop the tears. She'd loved Juan with all her heart, had shown him her secret self, and then he'd gone and died. Grief was the hardest task she'd ever undertaken—well, maybe it tied with motherhood—but making love with Andrew Callahan in the Big Sur cabin left to her by David Snow, hands down, was the scariest thing she'd ever done.

"You did fine," she said, sniffling. "You're a wonderful lover. I haven't yelled that loud since Sally tried to ride Penny out onto Valley Road. My gosh, Andrew, can't you tell that I'm crying because it was almost too wonderful?"

"Hush up with the compliments," he said, using his arms to shift the lower half of his body closer to her. "I always thought it was a bad sign when a woman cried after sex."

"What you don't know about women," Phoebe said, "is quite a lot."

He smiled, but rather than one of his ear-to-ear grins of Southern good manners, this was a quieter expression. "It's strange for me, you know. The last time I did this, I could still get—"

"Hold it right there," Phoebe interrupted. "I don't want to hate anyone ever again, so no past histories of other women, please. Like all the hippies used to say, let's just be here now, man. We did all right, Andrew. Really, we did."

They lay together in the new bed Phoebe'd had delivered a few days ago. It faced the plate-glass window that looked out onto the Pacific. This way they could snuggle together and watch the ocean roll on and on, and Phoebe thought she just might look at it forever. It was quiet here with only the sounds of their breathing and the cabin creaking when the sea breeze grew strong. They were going to spend three entire days and two entire nights together without anyone else. "That's where the rubber will hit the road," Mimi had said. "Andy's going to have to let you see him go through his routines, and maybe even ask for your help."

"Fat lot of good I'll be with a catheter," Phoebe had said. "And if he falls down, I'll have to call 911. I certainly can't lift him up."

"Which is why God invented cell phones," Nance said. "You all thought I was pretentious when I had one, now you all have one, even Sally has that darling pink model."

"That was your doing," Phoebe said. "The child does not need her own telephone."

Nance sniffed. "Life is full of surprises, some good, some bad. I'm certainly thankful for my phone now that I'm remanded to bed. Now, no more negative talk, it's bad for the baby."

Since the episode of premature labor, her sister-in-law had clung fiercely to the power of positive thinking. Phoebe hoped it worked. All she knew of cell phones was that Sally's teacher was going to blow a gasket the first time Sally whipped it out to call home. Nance had put Phoebe, herself, and James's cell on Sally's speed dial. Apparently Sally had asked for Chuck E. Cheese, too, but Nance told her she had to wait until she was old enough for a credit card for that.

Stop wondering what's happening at home, Phoebe admonished herself. *Think about this incredible hunk of man in bed next to you and how he just made your body sing.* She inhaled deeply and touched Andrew's chest, where springy red hair curled over his muscles. The moment should have been bliss, but she was bothered by the fact that Andrew's injury took away such a chunk of his own pleasure. While they were in the thick of things, she had watched his face, glimpsed the moments of tenderness therein, and heard him sigh when things felt good, but it was a stretch to imagine he got as much out of sex as she did.

"Come snuggle with me," he said, sounding tired. "It's chilly in here. Pull that blanket up, why don't you?"

Phoebe moved into the crook of his arm. He was tall, and there was a lot of room in that space. Shyly she hooked a leg over his, because even if he didn't feel it, she did. She kissed his chest and raked the chest hair, and then she kissed his nipple, causing him to say, "*Hmm,*" with some enthusiasm, and to give her a wicked idea. "Andrew? You ever watch that TV show *Boston Public*?"

"Mmm," Andrew said. "Maybe a couple of times. Why?"

"Well, in this one episode, the secretary got fired for writing an article for the school newspaper."

"Sounds like she needs herself a good lawyer."

"One of the characters *is* a lawyer! But that's not the point. Anyway, the article said it was possible for a girl to make herself climax simply by having her nipples stimulated."

"Well, sugar, that's a new one on me."

"Me, too. So what do you think?"

"Are you asking what I think you're asking?" he said, running his hand down her arm, and over toward her breast. "You are a tireless creature."

"Well, actually, I was wondering if you wanted to see if it worked on guys."

Andrew's hand stopped. He was quiet. She glanced up and saw that he was biting his lower lip, which was she noticed he did when he was trying not to get angry. I have ruined everything, Phoebe thought. He must feel twice as bad now. Dear God, what can I say to take it back?

Then he laughed. "Would it do any good if I said no?"

Phoebe called home at dinnertime. Ness answered the phone. "How's it going up there in the pit of passion?" she asked.

"Pretty well, actually."

"Where's Andrew? Did you drain him dry and leave him out to cure in the salt air?"

Phoebe looked out the window to the patio where Andrew sat in his chair, a Pendleton blanket wrapped around his shoulders. "Yeah, but I think he'll recover. Did Mimi and Sally get to Disneyland? Did they call?"

"They called and everything is fine. They were already checked into the hotel and planning a room-service dinner and watching the fireworks from the balcony. Tomorrow they're going to spend the entire day in the park."

Phoebe shuddered. She knew Sally would run Mimi ragged. "How's Nance?"

"No news from there. That dog your brother got her is sure wound tight. She can jump straight up in the air like a cricket. At least she isn't a digger."

"That sounds nice," Phoebe said dreamily.

"Listen to you," Ness teased. "You sound like you're on morphine. Clearly you need to do this more often."

"Get away? Is that an offer to baby-sit? Be careful, Preciousness, I might take you up on that."

"Erase, erase," Ness said. "I mean the other thing. Singing the Hallelujah Chorus with Colonel Sanders."

"Har-de-har-har," Phoebe said. "You know, Sally can be a bit of a brat. I hope Mimi can handle it. Is James around? Do you think I should call him, check in? I don't want him to think I'm not concerned."

"We're fine, Phoebe. Stop worrying. Get back to your new boyfriend. You deserve to be happy."

"So do you."

"Well, as a matter of fact, I met someone who I think is going to help in that area."

Phoebe yelped, and Andrew looked back at her from his place on the patio. She waved to let him know she was okay, and pointed to the phone. "Spill, Precious. I want all the details."

"It's not what you think. He's an antiques dealer I met at the garage sale at David's. He's six foot four, very polite, and he's my half brother."

"Excuse me?"

"You heard right. "He's ten years younger than me. His name's Will. So far all we've done is drink a cup of coffee and take a walk around Sierra Grove. But we're probably going to have lunch tomorrow. He thinks I should meet my mother."

"I can't believe you've had a brother all this time and no one told you. Didn't your granny know?"

"I'm not really clear on all of it, but I plan to find out."

Phoebe's phone beeped. "Oh, no! My damn battery's dying. I have to hang up in order to charge it."

"We'll talk later," Ness suggested. "Go kiss Andrew. Make him something to eat besides you."

"Very funny. Love you," Phoebe said, pressing the End Call button and plugging in the power supply cord. She laid the phone down on the kitchen counter and wheeled herself outside to where Andrew was seated, his smiling face tilted toward the sun. It was that golden hour when the sun began to turn a deep, fiery orange. It would be an hour yet before it descended into the Pacific, but right now it was as brilliant as autumn leaves, sort of a goldfish color that would eventually slide into the sea like quicksilver. My aunt lives there, Phoebe reminded herself. And Juan. So does my friend David, who gave me this house to keep safe for Sally. But the ocean didn't need to have a person's ashes to hold his spirit. She thought of all the people who'd passed through here, fallen in love with the coastline, felt its kindred spirit. Sure, famous names sprang to mind: Robinson Jeffers, Henry Miller, Jack Kerouac, Ansel Adams, but for every well-known name she imagined thousands of ordinary people who'd paused here and felt the most extraordinary feelings stir, and that counted.

"What are you thinking, sweet cheeks?" Andrew asked.

How could she answer honestly without sounding entirely morbid? "How much I L you."

"L?"

"The L word. Neither of us has said it directly yet, so I'm going to use the initial until you say it first."

"You already know I love you, Phoebe."

"And now you know I love you, too, Andrew. Do you get the feeling of impending doom?"

He looked over at her. "Why on earth would you say something like that?"

She buttoned the shirt she'd pulled on after leaving bed. "Because of feeling so happy. In the past, whenever things started to go right, God dropped a cowboy boot on my head, and I don't think I can stand it if that happens again."

"I guess when that shoe hit your head it knocked a few screws loose, darlin', because there is nothing ahead of us except blue skies and dusky nights and gravy and grits for breakfast."

Phoebe crossed her fingers. "Promise me you won't drive without a seat belt, let anyone interrupt your wedding, and that you'll take all the necessary care us crips have to."

"Cross my heart."

"I mean it, Andrew. My heart can't take another loss right now. I need to build up my strength for Sally's teenage years. So you have to promise me that if we stay together we'll live this boring, sensible life, okay?"

"Okay, it's bland and boring from here on in. Well, now that we've settled that, would you care to go out to dinner?"

Phoebe thought a while. All the effort it took to get their chairs into the car, the problems with crowds and seating at local restaurants, the way people would look at them—was it worth the effort? But did she really want to live her life under that kind of either-or crap anymore? She had a gorgeous blue sundress packed in her suitcase that dipped low at her cleavage. Strappy gold sandals for her feet. She might even slip on the thong panties Mimi had given her, the pink lacy teeny-tiny ornamental clothing that was basically designed to be taken off. "If you do," she said. "But I'd be content with a peanut-butter sandwich and trying that nipple thing again."

"Mercy, woman," Andrew said. "Give me time. I'm still recovering from what is supposed to be physically impossible."

"Who told you that?" Phoebe asked. "Some dorky doctor, I bet. You should switch to Lester. He believes in miracles, and even better, he makes them happen."

Phoebe did a bad thing at Nepenthe. It was something her girlfriends and her brother, James, would have called her on, but Andrew didn't know that—yet. When they were told they had to wait for a table, she fanned her face and pulled a drawn look. The maître d' came flying over with a glass of water. "Ma'am, are you ill? Do you need help?"

She looked up at him in his hip black clothes and brown hair with the bleached blond tips. The able-bodied were just plain terrified of people like her. Lawsuits could be filed over discrimination, bathroom accessibility, or just about anything, and they probably worried about that last category most of all. "Just famished," she said. "We've been told there's a two-hour wait for a table for two. I'll *probably* be fine. The thing is, I can never tell when I might become—you know—ill."

He snapped his fingers and summoned a waiter, and voilà! a table for two with a window view of the water suddenly became vacant. As he left to find them some bread and butter, Andrew gave her a smug smile. "You are something else," he said. "I wonder what you'll do next. Probably get our dinner comped, right?"

"What a great idea," she said. "I'll see what I can do. Meanwhile, look at the water, Andrew. Tell me, is there anything this beautiful in the South?"

"The low country is special in its own way," he said.

They stared out at the shimmering Pacific, darkening by the minute as night drew a curtain over their perfect day. He placed his hand atop hers and once again, she was struck by the differences she felt—Juan's hands were always warm and moist, and they were strong but not much bigger than hers. Andrew's were cool, and the skin tougher, probably from his working with clay, and they were flat-out enormous, almost like paws. For some reason he always smelled like cloves. "What's that mean, 'low country'?"

"Swampland. Bogs. Little rivers. We may not have waves to surf, but we have nutrias and Spanish moss and gorgeous birds. The South is like stepping back a hundred years, Phoebe. When I take you there I'll show you ancient woods and kudzu that advances by the hour, and pillared homes so ornately decorated they look like Christmas tree baubles. The Gulf Coast is awful damn pretty, with sand so fine it sticks to your skin. It's different, but I'm betting you'll like it. We'll do that, won't we? Travel places."

She sipped at her water. "It won't be easy."

Andrew peered at her over the top of the menu. "Nothing good ever is."

Phoebe decided on the roasted vegetable platter. Andrew said, "Please don't hate me if I order the salmon, honey. I need protein. How on earth does such a small girl manage to take so much out of a man?"

The waiter grinned and Phoebe flushed. "I guess I'm a late-blooming sex maniac. You can eat a fish if you want to. Just apologize to the fish, and brush your teeth before you kiss me, okay?"

He laughed. "Sir, I'll have the salmon. My lovely companion here will have the roasted vegetable platter, and if you would be so kind as to bring her a glass of champagne, but only one, because with two under her belt she turns wild."

They lingered over their dinners, ignoring the other patrons. Andrew doctored up his iced tea with lemon and sugar. Phoebe sipped her single glass of bubbles. With every fizzy pop she heard Lester Ullman *tsk*-ing at her, ordering her to stop right there and switch to water. But then she recognized there was another voice vying for her attention, and it wasn't even Andrew's. It was her aunt Sadie's, gone seven years now, and it had been such a long time since her last visit that Phoebe felt a chill travel up her spine, and pulled her wrap closer.

When Andrew excused himself to use the rest room, Phoebe turned to look at the water. It was fully dark now, and she cupped her hand over the candle at their table so she could just make out the ripples on the ocean. She shut her eyes and listened to the soft murmur of voices, and heard her aunt. *Now, this is more like the Phoebe DeThomas I remember. This is the girl who learned to climb a tree—okay, a very small tree, but a tree nonetheless—and took honors at college. This is the same niece who stayed up all night with roommates she barely knew in order to maintain heat and humidity for some old poinsettias. And this is the mother who gave her baby to people who could look after it properly while she made a fearless and searching inventory, but took back the baby she didn't intend to give away after all. Well, let me tell you, it's nice to have her back. Juan says hello. He's very pleased to see you all dressed up like this, and so am I. We applaud your courage.*

Phoebe smiled and looked down into the candle flame, floating in its pool of hot wax. Oh, Sadie, she thought. I have lived so much drama in the last seven years I expect Zeus to have about run out of thunderbolts to throw. And it's your fault, giving me the farm and James the money.

But her inheritance had worked miracles. Still, why she couldn't have split things fifty-fifty . . . she remembered her aunt's laugh—a sound like silver fish scales caught in fine netting. Sadie did things Sadie's way. Phoebe sat up straighter and arched her neck until she had struck the same pose as her aunt's portrait. She reached up and touched her necklace, lying warm against the skin Andrew had kissed hours ago, and minutes later, when she finally came back to herself, she turned and saw that Andrew was drawing on the back of the menu, his face tight with concentration. "Don't you dare move," he said. "If I stop now, I'll have lost this forever. If I'm ever going to paint again, I can't let go."

Phoebe held still. The thought came into her head that she might marry this man, and that if she did, it would last.

Sally laid her hunt coat and helmet so lovingly referred to as a "brain bucket" on Phoebe's lap as she ran to help Ness unload Penelope from the horse trailer. The palomino pony was shining from hooves to mane, and the determined look on her daughter's face was a little unnerving. This was Sally's first show competing with girls from outside the Valley at the Links Beach Horse Show. Phoebe was afraid she wouldn't place in any of her classes, and from there, next on the menu would be Armageddon.

All around her, horse-show mothers were chatting one another up, giving last-minute instructions to their daughters, brushing horsehair from their coats—and oh, the horses! Phoebe had chewed James out for the POA palomino, but now she saw the pony for what it was, a bargain among delicately featured, full-size horses that cost in the ten thousand dollar range. There were dapple grays, Arabians, Egyptians, Thoroughbreds, and only a few Shetlands with their pudgy bellies. Those beautiful white ones—what the hell were they called? Icelandic? They looked like unicorns that hadn't yet grown the requisite horn. In this crowd, Penny looked every inch a backyard horse that hadn't yet learned her p's and q's.

"Ness," Phoebe called, and her friend turned. "Isn't six years old too early to do this kind of thing?"

"No, six is fine," Ness said calmly. "These days riders start showing in halter classes as young as four. Sally's ready."

"But won't it break her heart if she loses?" she asked for the tenth time in as many minutes.

"Relax, Phoebe. Sally's a good rider. You'll see."

But does she know that it doesn't matter? Phoebe wanted to yell. *Does everyone here know that my little girl, who spends far too much time around indulgent adults, and still likes to dress her stuffed animals, will have her tiny heart trampled if she doesn't go home with a ribbon?*

Minutes later Penny was tacked and ready to go, her mane plaited and secured with tiny pink ribbons—Sally's black phase had blessedly passed as quickly as it had come. Sally drew her irons up through the stirrups and walked the horse to where Phoebe had parked her chair, alongside horse-show mothers in folding chairs replete with umbrellas and cup holders. Phoebe helped Sally on with the hunt coat, a trim navy blue with nearly invisible pink pinstriping. She straightened her collar and checked to make certain her collar pin was properly latched and her shirt tucked in. "Mom," Sally wheedled, "I hafta go now or I'll be DQed!"

Disqualified? My daughter? I will get right out of this chair and with a crutch beat to death the judge that dares to do that, she thought. "Good luck, honey," she said, when what she really wanted to say was, *It's only a horse show, please don't get your feelings hurt, don't grow up too fast, stay away from boys for as long as is possible, please learn to love Andrew so he can be your daddy, because every girl needs a daddy, and right now I'm missing mine something fierce, and I might just need to ask Andrew to marry me tonight in case I have a heart attack watching you out there.*

"Mom," Sally said. "Stop looking at me all goo-goo eyed!"

Phoebe nodded. "Sorry."

"And don't cry! I know how to ride Penny, so just relax, okay? Jeez!"

"Done," Phoebe said. She watched Juan's daughter flip her reins in her hand, and pull herself up on that miniature horse as if it were as easy as breathing. She jogged the horse around the parking lot, and then rode over to wait for her class to be called to enter the spotless arena. Oh, no. Her gloves were sticking out of the back of her pants. She'd forgotten to put them on! Instant DQ, Phoebe thought. Lord, at least let this be over with quickly. But I pity the gloves when she finds out what she's done.

The seven girls in the youth equitation class entered the riding ring just as Ness slid in next to Phoebe at the fence. She whispered, "Have I missed anything?"

Phoebe could hardly speak. "Her gloves—," she started to say, just as Sally rounded the end of the riding ring and headed toward them. Ness reached up and plucked them from her pants and handed them to Sally.

"Did the judge see that?" Ness asked.

"I don't know." Phoebe's heart was racing so hard she had to stop and count the beats to make it slow down. It was too much, having a child and then having to watch her compete in things she was bound to lose at least some of the time. "I guess we'll find out. Surely they wouldn't kick her from the class for that? Would they?"

Ness glared at her. "I refuse to answer that."

"You're worried, too," Phoebe said.

By now Sally had the gloves on, and the judges cued the girls to begin a trot. Immediately two girls fell off, and the trainers had to stop the girls' mothers from climbing the post-and-rail fence and going in after them. Over the loudspeaker a judge intoned, "Numbers one-oh-two and one-fifteen are disqualified. Please leave the ring immediately."

Number 102 was crying. Sally trotted along, a smile on her face.

"Is my child being smug?" Phoebe asked. "Is that a mean-spirited smile or am I overreacting?"

"She's a competitor," Ness said. "Competitors know when being a brat is called for. She's spirited."

"What a nice way to say 'brat.'"

"All I know," Ness said, "is she's the spitting image of her mother."

The girls were told to reverse their horses, and there was a small problem with an Appaloosa that decided he wasn't interested in reversing, only standing sideways and refusing to let the other horses pass. This necessitated a trainer entering the ring and leading the horse out so that others could pass by. More crying, and now the class was down to four girls dressed in expensive riding habits, their bookshelves at home full of Walter Farley stallion novels and Breyer horse statues.

This is good, Phoebe thought. She might win third. God, let her win something, even if it's honorable mention. "Do they have runner-up ribbons?" Phoebe whispered to Ness.

"Will you shut up?" Ness hissed back. "I'm trying to concentrate."

The sun beat down on Phoebe's head, and she took a sip from her Power water—Andrew bought it by the case because it contained electrolytes, and insisted Phoebe drink it. The girls were asked to canter their horses, and the little black Shetland refused to change gaits. He was trotting like a madman, and the poor child, number 135, was bouncing up and down so hard it made Phoebe's teeth rattle. Sally had picked up the incorrect lead, but somehow miraculously managed to execute a flying change, and sat square in her seat, enjoying the ride like it was something she did every day. It was frightening how much the child liked to canter. The Shetland interrupted his trotting long enough to buck, which with his stubby legs wasn't terribly impressive. The girl managed to stay on, even though a chorus of gasps erupted from the bleachers. The judge stopped the class again. "At this time all riders please line up in front of the judge's stand."

Ness refused to look at Phoebe, despite her pulling on her arm. "Do they have fourth-place ribbons?" she hissed. "Please tell me they have fourth-place or honorable mention." Ness wouldn't answer.

They did, because fourth went to the trotting/bucking girl, and there was a smattering of applause for her hanging in with the Shetland. Third went to the girl Phoebe expected would win the class; her horse was beautiful, she had the long legs that were mandatory for true equestriennes, and so far as Phoebe could tell, she hadn't made a single error.

"Let her win second," Phoebe begged. "Second would be incredible."

And Sally did. When the judge called her number, she and Penny walked forward to take the red ribbon, which she then tucked into Penny's bridle. She waited while the final girl received her blue ribbon, and then the girls solemnly exited the ring like exquisite little sports, when deep down Phoebe knew they had to hate one another's guts over a five-inch length of gold embossed fabric. "Honey, you won a ribbon!" Phoebe said, as Sally came up to her. "Congratulations! Let's go give Penny a carrot."

Sally huffed. "Well, I should have gotten first."

"Red is good," Ness said. "Now, you stop whining. Let me take Penny."

Ness helped Sally dismount and led Penny away. Sally pulled her cell phone out of the pocket of her riding pants, and began to press numbers. "Who on earth are you calling?" Phoebe asked.

"Andrew."

"Honey, Andrew is probably busy working in his studio. You can call him when we get home."

The pint-size National Velvet scowled. "Mama, Andrew made me promise to call. He made me rememberize his phone number: Five-five-five-three-one-four-two. He said I was s'posed to call and tell him the color of my ribbon and I was only doing what he told me to."

"Andrew is not your mother," Phoebe said. "Either you start minding me or that cell phone is going back to Uncle James tonight."

"Can I get a hamburger and an ice cream bar? They're only five dollars. Can I?"

Phoebe shook her head. "No hamburgers. They're filled with hormones, and the grazing of cattle is depleting the planet of the rain forests. You go help Ness get Penny ready to go home. You can have a sip of my water if you're thirsty."

She stamped her tiny foot. "I don't need electric water! One hamburger is all I want! You never let me go to McDonald's!" She dumped her hunt coat and helmet and then ran down to the sea of horse trailers.

"Well," a woman standing next to Phoebe said. "She certainly makes her point."

Phoebe sighed. Yes, that was her charming little daughter. Pretty soon she'd be eating hamburgers three times a day and letting boys feel her up. Then she reminded herself of how miserable she'd felt without her, and said, "Children are a treasure, nasty mouths and all. I admire her spirit."

When Ness returned to help Phoebe to the car, Phoebe told her about Sally calling Andrew. "Like I'm chopped liver," she said.

"Andrew's exotic," Ness said. "Sally doesn't deal with him on a day-to-day basis. He doesn't tell her to clean up her room or turn off the TV, does he?"

"Someday he might get to," Phoebe admitted. "If he plays his cards right."

Sally rode home with Segundo, who used the farm truck to pull the horse trailer. Phoebe knew he would stop and buy her ice cream, but she relished the time alone with Ness. The PT Cruiser always made Phoebe feel like a gangster, but she loved that, and asked Ness to take the long way home. "So tell me more about your brother," Phoebe said.

"Half brother," Ness corrected.

"Whatever. What's it feel like? Is he a nice guy? Is he one of those fussy antiques dealers or is he a good guy?"

Ness didn't answer right away, and when Phoebe looked up, she knew why. Though the long way home was scenic, it also featured the piece of road where most Bayborough car accidents happened—Juan's among them. She saw movement in the trees, and the back end of a deer, sprinting away from traffic. Was that what had distracted him? Or was it the fog settling in, giving the impression boundaries had shifted? She thought about that day, her almost wedding day, and how the accident had changed their lives forever. So much sorrow, so much rage that had to be worked through. But it had led them to this very day, Sally's first horse-show ribbon, and the possibility of more to come. Phoebe tried hard to believe in a new future but had to admit she still ached for the past.

"He's down-to-earth," Ness said.

"What's he look like?"

"Handsome," Ness said, "In a Tiger Woods kind of way. I'm thinking maybe I'll invite him over for dinner soon so you all can meet him."

"Sounds good to me. Ness?"

"Yes, my friend?"

"Are you okay? What I mean is, is it getting any easier, without David?"

Ness sighed. "I guess I'm as ready to live the rest of my life as I'll ever be."

Phoebe swallowed a sip of electric water. "Does that mean you're leaving the farm?"

"No, but I am redecorating my room."

"Not in cowboy furniture, hopefully?"

"Not in cowboy furniture, definitely."

Phoebe thought a minute. "I can't imagine living anywhere without you. I think it would feel entirely wrong. I really hated it when you were living with David. I suppose that makes me selfish."

Ness smiled and turned on her signal indicator to make the right onto Valley Road. "Oh, but you're tolerable selfish. You know what I think, Phoebe? We have to make a little room now and then. Nance and James are settled, and pretty soon the baby will be here. What's to stop us from stretching our arms out a little wider?"

Phoebe placed her hand on the armrest as Ness braked for a bicyclist. "Nance's had so many disappointments. I can't stand to even think of the baby until it's born. James is going to flip out, buy out the cigar stores, and probably take out space on a billboard."

"Me, too," Ness said. "We'll have a weeklong party. I only wish—"

"What?" Phoebe asked.

"Beryl were here to help us celebrate."

The sound of their friend's name hung in the air like perfume, lingering, dense, and suddenly worrisome. Phoebe pulled her cell phone out of her pocketbook and dialed the number. "I've had it with her not returning phone calls. What time is it in Alaska, anyway? Earlier or later? Damn this thing. The call didn't even go through."

Ness shrugged. "We're almost in the driveway. Call her from the regular phone."

Phoebe punched the End Call button and threw it back in her purse. "I have a bad feeling," she said.

"You and your bad feelings. You worry too much," Ness said. "Nine times out of ten, everything's fine."

"But that one percent," Phoebe said. "It's when I'm right, you know? Did she answer my calls? No. Write to say thanks for the flowers? No."

Ness shut the car off and bit her thumbnail. "I have to admit, I have that bad feeling, too, Pheebs. Call her right this second."

There was no answer at Beryl's house, and the machine announced that the message-taking mailbox was full. Maybe she and Earl had gone on a trip, Phoebe and Ness told each other. Earl flew around the globe on a whim, it seemed. But how long had it been since they'd spoken to her, really had a heart-to-heart girlfriend session, each of them on extensions and talking over one another in a rush to get all the news?

"My bad feeling is growing layers," Phoebe said as Segundo pulled up with Sally and the horse trailer.

Andrew showed up the next day. "I heard a rumor of a red ribbon," he said. "So don't think this visit is about unbridled lust. Though it could easily be diverted," he said, winking a big gray eye at her.

Phoebe opened the screen door to the warmest day, the scent of flowers filling the air, and Homer trailing Sumo through the herb garden. "You hush up," she said, borrowing his Southern idiom for the moment. "Sally is growing up way too fast. I have got to find a way to get that cell phone out of her hands."

"Good luck. Did you know there's a game on it? She showed me how to play it. I had no idea cell phones were so versatile." Andrew rolled himself over the threshold, kissing Phoebe as soon as their chairs were close enough to manage. "You taste like maple syrup," he said. "Any of those johnnycakes left?"

"Sorry. Kitchen's closed. We were all kind of hungry this morning."

"Well then, lead me to the princess."

"Sally!" Phoebe called. "Andrew is here to see you." There was a muffled answer. "Go on back," Phoebe said. "You know where her room is. I'll be next door."

She wheeled herself through the garden to James and Nance's house. The front door was ajar—for the puppy, she figured. She peered inside, and there was Nance, lying on the couch dressed in a Mexican dress heavily embroidered across the bodice and sleeves. It was so colorful and intricate that the eye was immediately drawn there to linger, and effectively minimized the thickening around her belly. Next to her was her laptop computer.

"Look at you," Phoebe said. "You look like a high-tech Diego Rivera painting."

Nance smiled. She instinctively touched her belly, and

Phoebe worried that she might look at the round of baby as fat. "Don't tell James I'm out of bed," she said. "But I was going crazy in there, looking at the four walls. I had to see the flowers. I just had to look out the windows. I took a rest on the way out here, and if I can figure out a way to actually see the screen of my computer, I thought I'd see to the farm mail."

"It's Sunday," Phoebe said. "The post office is closed. Where's James?"

"Oh, I sent him out for soy ice cream. I figured it would give me at least a half hour alone."

Phoebe laughed. "I wouldn't count on it. He's my brother, so he knows where they keep the soy ice cream. Actually I was kind of hoping to meet the new puppy. What's her name?"

"Calpurnia. She's with James. He's got some crazy notion that she can become one of those go-anywhere dogs, you know, just ride along in the Mercedes and stay put without tearing up the upholstery."

"Sounds like a midlife crisis to me. Can I get you anything while I'm here?"

"I'm fine. At least, I hope I am." Nance lifted her chin, but not before Phoebe could see it tremble.

"Of course you're fine. The medicine Lester gave you is working, isn't it?"

"So far."

"So it's working. How about I fix us some of that raspberry iced tea you love? Then you can help me figure out how to find Beryl. You're smart. I just know you will think of something utterly perfect and entirely devious, and maybe we can get her to come for a visit."

While Phoebe heated some croissants and set out butter, Nance stared at her belly and talked. "It's strange she hasn't called. Not like her. I suppose I could guilt-trip her over my pregnancy, but I hate to use the baby that way. It's very negative, and she's not even born yet."

"She?" Phoebe said. "I thought you didn't do the amnio. Did the doctor see something on the ultrasound?"

"No, and no. I just happen to prefer to refer to the baby as she."

"You know it's a girl," Phoebe said. "You've probably been dreaming about it, and have hordes of little party dresses squirreled away."

"Well, if I do, that is entirely my business, isn't it?"

Phoebe laughed. "Around here? You have to be kidding. May I present Sally as a case in point?"

She was pouring tea when James walked in, brown freezer bag and rat terrier in his arms. "Hey, Wingnut," he said. "Did you have a craving for marble mint, too?"

"Hey, James. No, I just dropped by to meet the new dog and to see how things were going."

The dog in question yipped, and James set her down. She immediately ran to Nance, leaped up, and curled by her side, staring at Phoebe. "Why is she looking at me like she wants to see my ID?" Phoebe said.

"Callie's devoted," Nance said.

"Ha. She likes the heat your belly gives off," James countered. "She's a heat-seeking missile, aren't you, girl? So? How many for ice cream?"

"I'm not hungry," Nance said. "Just put that in the freezer, won't you?"

"Of course," James said. "And I think I'll just totter up to the house and visit my niece now, won't I?"

"Great idea," Phoebe said.

When he was out of sight, Phoebe brought the tray of tea and croissants to Nance. "Okay," she said. "Your baby could come anytime in the next four weeks. How do we get Beryl down here in that amount of time? Start brainstorming."

They made a list, consulted the Internet, priced plane reservations, and then Nance admitted she needed to sleep. "Come back after dinner," she said. "By then I'll have something figured out."

Phoebe let herself out and went to her studio, opening the windows to let the warm air in. She threw on a smock, then took out some clay and began to work, using a tool with a loop on the end to carve away until she found the shape lurking inside. Naked lady—no surprise there. But there was something else coming, too.

While she subtracted, she thought about Sadie's best-known event, the day she dressed up as Lady Godiva and rode a horse in the Fourth of July parade. When she first saw the newspaper clipping, she called her aunt and asked her how in the hell did she find the nerve to do such at thing in stodgy old Bayborough? Chalk it up to Sadie's sheer force of personality.

Phoebe gave the figure in her hands long flowing hair that swept across her breasts and threaded between her strong legs. One of Sally's Breyer ponies sat on a shelf, so she secured the clay woman to its back, set it down, and regarded it from her chair. It wasn't her best work, but it had spirit. She'd save it, make a mold from it, and start a new line of clay ladies: Contemporary Godivas. They could ride toys—and why not? Wouldn't today's Lady Godiva be as apt to appear in a Humvee or on a tractor as she would horseback? Quickly she took down a notebook and made plans for the entire line. Their hair would be copper wire, varying thicknesses, and she could use Sculpey clay squeezed through a garlic press for pubic hair. And maybe a few of them could sit astride flowers. Why not? North-country Godiva could straddle a moose. She bent her head and worked on sketches for an hour. When she looked up she realized she'd been undisturbed, and wondered what she'd missed. She called up to the house, and Sally answered.

"Me and Andrew are watching *The Little Mermaid,*" she said. "He thinks it's a great movie. He likes the songs, too."

Wait until he hears them thirty times a day, Phoebe wanted to say but didn't. "What else is going on? Where's Auntie Ness?"

"In the kitchen making dinner."

"What's she making?"

"I don't know."

"That's okay, sweetie. Where's Aunt Mimi?"

"I don't know."

"Hmm. Why don't you call Auntie Ness to the phone so you can go back to your movie?"

"Okay."

"Hey," Phoebe said when Ness answered. "Sorry I kind of bailed out on you like that. I went to see Nance, then stopped in my studio and got sidetracked. But it turned out to be really productive. I started with this idea of Lady Godiva, and, oh, it's probably easier if I show you. I'm heading up to the house right—"

"Phoebe," Ness said. "Apparently Beryl called, and Sally took the message. She said it was important and to call her back no matter what time it is."

Beryl

17

The Truth About Buckethead

"HE'S DONE IT BEFORE," Detective Mike Stokes said to Beryl over her uneaten lunch special—the one slice, half salad, and her choice of beverage at Moose's Tooth Pizza Parlor. "More than once, as a matter of fact. New York, Houston, and California all report similar stories. Long period of mysterious courting—like the music thing you described—big love affair develops. Seems to have lavish amounts of money, buys the woman substantial things—homes, sailboats, and cars—but he continues to live fairly simply. Then he disappears under questionable circumstances, the woman files a report, police spend a while looking for him, a year or two goes by, and then he turns up as if nothing happened. Gets a slap on the wrist and does it again."

As soon as they had pulled into the parking lot, Beryl knew this was the wrong place for their talk. Everyone and his brother appeared to be in the rustic restaurant, holding pagers, waiting for the next free table, buying tie-dyed T-shirts for relatives back home, and sipping the various microbrews. She heard Mike's words clearly, and her brain processed them fine, but her heart was still hiding behind its tissue-paper wall of faith that the Earl she had loved wasn't capable of such deceit. She looked down at her slice of white pizza covered with artichoke hearts and slippery bits of red pepper. The cheese had congealed into an unappetizing sheet.

"Do I want to know how many other women?" she asked, squinting because she was suddenly developing a king-size headache over her left eye. Great, a migraine on top of everything else. "Won't that make me feel stupider than I already do?"

The detective clasped her hand and held on tight. "It's not like you're going to lose the house, Beryl. You're not an accessory to a capital crime, simply the victim of one very clever con man. He's a buckethead, all right. A head case with a bucketful of money inherited from some East Coast Rockefeller–type parents and a penchant for breaking decent ladies' hearts. Apparently what he does best besides play that guitar of his is make women fall in love with him. And why shouldn't they? He showers them with gifts, they live the high life for a while, and then—*boom!*—he disappears. That's not really against any law on the books, though morally it's the worst kind of fraud."

Beryl's temple throbbed and she felt her throat close up, as if she'd tried to swallow an aspirin without water. "But we were together five years! He said he loved me. We went to Europe, and we stayed with musicians, famous ones, and they treated him like he was one of their own ranks . . . Eric Clapton . . ." She let her voice trail off. How could any of that matter compared to this flipping headache that had come out of nowhere? "Do you have any aspirin on you?"

"Sorry." Detective Stokes released her hand. "I have some in the car. Let me finish, and then I'll go get it. He's a talented musician, Beryl. There's no doubt he could have made a living as one if he had aimed all his energy in that direction. The evidence shows he preferred to diversify."

Beryl's face felt hot from the pain behind her eyes. All around her she felt as if the world was beginning to melt. The wooden walls shimmied, and the painting of the salmon running began to move in tremors. Their waitperson's tie-dyed shirt whirred and spun until it was a spinning disk, something left over from the sixties. Every one of the diners grew haloes, and the room was suddenly filled with what seemed like the northern lights, busily competing with the hanging kayak and empty beer bottles and countless conversations shouted above the kitchen din. Her breath came shallow, and then it was as if she felt something in her head go pop, as if she'd somehow cracked her skull and her life force was leaking out. "I think I might faint," she said, or perhaps only thought, as if by telling Mike he would somehow know how to deal with it.

She woke up in the ER of Providence Hospital. "What happened?"

"Your blood pressure is elevated," the doctor informed her as he checked her pupils and made her turn her head to prove that her neck was okay. "This can't have been a total surprise to you. Surely there were symptoms. Why aren't you on medication?"

"Lester said," she began. "But I—"

"May I please have that second reading?" he barked at a nurse who moved in and out of Beryl's view so quickly she was merely a flash of blue scrubs asking questions she couldn't answer.

"Ma'am," the nurse said, "Who's your regular doctor, your internist?"

"I don't have one," she confessed.

The doctor, back in view once again, said, "You're lucky all you did was pass out. Numbers that high, you could have had a stroke. Where exactly is the headache located? Describe your pain on a one-to-ten scale, ten being the worst pain you've ever experienced."

They moved like blurry ghosts within the curtained area, touching, taking notes, and probing her body in various places. Beryl tried to get her bearings. She had a bad headache, which she sometimes got, no big deal there. She fainted. Out of the ordinary, maybe, but not so awful, considering. Someone had brought her to the hospital. Detective Stokes? And her blood pressure . . . Lester had told her years ago to get it checked, to refill the trial prescription he'd given her. Something-blockers. Name like a child's toy. She was never good at remembering to take pills on time.

Detective Stokes parted the curtains and smiled at her. "Well, one good thing is that this happened while you were with a cop. I got you here in record time. Ran my lights and everything."

"Mike," she said. "What happened?"

He held on to the chair to the left of the bed, an orange plastic molded affair. "You told me you were going to faint, and then you slumped over and your hands started to shake. Your face is the color of chalk. I'll come back later."

She clutched at his arm. "Don't go. Did I make a total fool out of myself at Moose's Tooth? Do a face-plant in my salad?"

"None of the above. You started to slide, and I caught you. Made me feel like a knight in shining armor, even if I did buy this jacket from the Sears summer sale. They were so eager to get us out of the restaurant we got a free lunch out of it. Your doc's most unhappy. He says you have the blood pressure of a ninety-year-old."

"I know. I heard."

"He says they want to do a CT scan and an EEG. The hand thing, that bothered him. I won't be surprised if he orders some tests. I guess the important thing is to take the stress out of your life."

Beryl felt close to tears, and her mouth was parched. "But I don't really do much of anything, Mike. What besides finding out my boyfriend was a con man could stress me? Learning to drive?"

He moved to the head of her bed and pressed his fingers to her cheek. Even that small gesture caused her pain to intensify. "I'm standing here beating the crap out of myself because I think me telling you about Earl is what probably sent you over the edge."

She didn't argue. Mike had delivered the final card to the carefully balanced house of her life, and it was the one that caused the collapse. "If I know, I can make some sense of it. God, my head! Do you think I could have an aspirin?" she asked the nurse, who was back behind the curtain, rustling something wrapped in paper.

"Sorry, ma'am. Not until after your tests."

"But my head is killing me. And I'm thirsty. Probably even dehydrated."

"The IV will get you hydrated in no time."

"What IV?"

"The one I'm about to put in your hand."

"I don't want an IV," she whispered, trying not to aggravate her head. "I want a sip of tap water. And maybe a Tylenol."

Mike tucked the thin cotton blanket around her feet. "Sometimes all it takes is thinking too hard and a person—well, they need a vacation, but they don't take one until they get a scare like this. I think you should go back to California, let your girlfriends take care of you until you get back on your feet."

"But Alaska—"

"Will be here when you get back. It's not going anywhere. We may be noncontiguous, Ms. Reilly, but we're part and parcel of America up here."

The nurse began to lay out an IV kit, and Beryl had to turn her head, because she knew if she watched the needle sink into her skin, she would faint again, which was how this trouble had started in the first place.

The CT scan involved her lying absolutely still while her entire head was encased in a white metal doughnut–like affair. Not only did it make a terrible scraping noise, like Beryl imagined a butcher's meat-slicing machine would make, rhythmic and sharp, but it had the unique ability to produce instantaneous claustrophobia, even though she was mostly uncovered. Beryl shut her eyes and felt the beads of sweat trickle down her scalp. She tried counting the minutes away, thinking of how back at the farm she and the other girls went row by row, planting. She thought of Verde when he was sleepy, tucking his head under his wing stub. Thomas Jack at the Raptor Rehab, eye to eye with a raven. She tried to reach down to find a prayer, something she hadn't done in so long she could only remember a few words: *Now I lay me . . . Our Father who art . . . Bless us O Lord, and these thy gifts* . . . What gifts? I'm lying here with a headache that would kill a draft horse. All this medical stuff being done to her—she could probably afford to pay the exorbitant bills, but wouldn't it be better for everyone in the long run if she just made a donation to the children's wing and got rid of Earl's money forever? She resumed counting down the minutes; with no idea how long she'd been in the terribly loud machine beyond too damn long.

Mike was waiting when she was wheeled out of the radiology department into the hallway. She gulped at the air, which smelled of disinfectant. "I want my mother," she said.

He patted her arm. "Give me her number, and I'll call her for you."

"You can't. She's dead," she said, and started to cry big noisy tears that made her head throb worse.

Detective Stokes took out a hankie and handed it to her. "Calm down. Here."

In between sobs she managed to eke out an entire sentence. "You have such good manners."

"My grandmother once told me that every ordinary man who carries a handkerchief automatically becomes handsome in the eyes of a lady."

Beryl squinted at him. "You're a lot of things, Detective Stokes, but you're not ordinary."

Mike put his hands in his pockets. "Of course I only carry one hankie, so if I run into any more damsels in distress today, they are shit out of luck."

"I don't think I've ever heard you swear before."

"I swear all the time, Ms. Reilly. I do a lot of things that would surprise you."

"Such as?"

"Hang in there on cases everyone else gives up on. Track down bad guys and tell them what I think of them. You stop worrying about anything besides getting better. That's an order from a cop, so you have to comply."

He bent down and kissed her forehead. His lips felt cool against her skin. An orderly arrived to wheel her back to the ER. "Nothing's broken," she said. "Why can't I just get up and walk?"

"It's a rule," he intoned, and began to whistle.

Once again the doctor met them, but this time they were behind a different curtain. "I found a bed for you, so you'll be taken upstairs soon. There's a question about something we saw on the CT scan. An ophthalmologist and a neurologist are going to review it, and we'll confer and get back to you." He held up a hand as Beryl began to gasp. "Please don't start in asking questions; it could be nothing."

"Except it probably isn't," Beryl said. "Otherwise my head would stop hurting and you'd let me go home and come back tomorrow."

"We'll be getting the radiologist's report in a matter of hours. The reason I'm not releasing you to go home is your blood pressure is still erratic, and I don't feel comfortable with the description of your headache. If there's something serious going on, wouldn't you rather be in a hospital where the appropriate action can be taken?"

When he left, and Beryl was alone with the detective, the possibilities began to sink in. If ever there was a time to rail and gnash her teeth, to fling bedpans hither and yon, this was it. But she was too tired, and her head hurt, and she was not surprised that her streak of bad luck was turning out to set a world's record. Mike pulled up a chair and sat next to her, saying nothing. Eventually he took hold of her hand, and until then Beryl hadn't realized how badly she was shaking. Nerves? Seizure disorder? Or was it a brain tumor, that "little something" that had shown up on the scan? Detective Stokes rubbed her hand like he would a cat, and through his skin, Beryl could feel the muscles working.

Her hospital room window looked out onto Providence Drive. Across the street was the university, classes already in summer session. A postmodern wing to the library was under construction. People in town said it resembled a cockeyed turret, but it reminded Beryl of the Guggenheim, the museum Earl had taken her to one spring on a stopover in New York. As she'd walked the spiraling floors and looked at Picasso's cubist portraits and Judy Chicago's famous *Dinner Party,* Beryl had a moment similar to the one in Moose's Tooth, minus the pain. It was as if her eyes simply weren't big enough to take in all this art, the breadth of genius inside a building that Frank Lloyd Wright had probably sketched on a cocktail napkin one night when he was bored with his dinner companions. With Earl the world expanded at too swift a pace, and sometimes she wondered if she might have been happier not knowing all that wonder existed. Once something was in your heart, there was no stopping wanting it. Crumbling castles in Scotland proved their own history; hash brownies could be bought over the counter in an Amsterdam deli; the actual Colosseum still stood, ravaged by time but enough remaining that Beryl wouldn't have been surprised if a toga-clad god stepped out from behind what was left of a pillar and threw down a curse. Earl had shown her a blue-green Norwegian fjord, French restaurants where they allowed dogs inside. He'd taken her to Germany, a land that on one side was forests and on the other, death camps. She'd kissed the Blarney Stone, walked up to the fence surrounding Stonehenge's impressively mysterious pillars, stood at the grave of Sylvia Plath, heard Big Ben toll, drunk dark ales in pubs dating back to a time when horses were as pricey as sports cars. That knowing—the sensation of knowing that all these things and more were part of the world—had caused her to seek out a bench in the Guggenheim and sit alone, staring down at her Bjorn clogs with the scuffed toes until she was able to come back to herself without feeling like her head was going to blow up.

And now she had to add to that the evidence Mike Stokes had found. Earl was a con man, a serial heartbreaker; she was nobody special. Just one of a long line of women he'd fooled into thinking she was his one true love, his unfenced Stonehenge.

Outside her window it was the height of Alaskan summer, the sun pasted up in the sky for a ridiculous amount of time. They'd taken away her wristwatch in the ER, so it could have been noon or three or eleven P.M., and she wouldn't know until a meal tray arrived. She'd used up precious hours of the day here in the hospital having her head photographed to no particular conclusion, and even Detective Stokes had gone home.

Had Zoë still been living with her, she could have picked up the bedside telephone and called, gotten her to bring a change of clothes or feed Verde. Had Thomas Jack not gone fishing, she could have called him, and he would have kept her company, even if their love affair was winding down to a natural end. But what bothered her most was that she had so distanced herself from Phoebe and her girlfriends there was no way she could call them and expect that any of them would hop a plane to come to her bedside. She had herself, just like when she'd given birth, gone to prison, and Earl had left. She was alone in the world and had to make her way somehow.

Beryl listened to her roommates' visitors. Someone switched on a television, and she could hear the five o'clock news. She shut her eyes and listened. Survivors of abuse did that. They got the self-esteem hammered out of them and from then on, figured they caused every problem. But what did self-esteem and standing up for one's self get a person, really? Particularly when inside the dark spaces of the human body, all kinds of evil could lurk. Though the ophthalmologist had yet to weigh in, and the neurologist was hung up in emergency surgery, Beryl had already diagnosed herself with a massive brain tumor coiled around her brain stem and a week to live.

She looked over at her sleeping roommate. I want whatever you're having, she thought, and fell asleep before she could call a nurse to get her something to help her sleep.

At seven P.M. she woke to see her meal tray by the bed. Juice, Jell-O, tea. Pre-op, read the menu card, which resembled a diner bill. Her head was throbbing less than before, she wasn't so thirsty, and Mike Stokes was sitting next to her doing the *New York Times* crossword puzzle in pen.

"Hello, Ms. Reilly. You feeling better?"

"As well as can be expected. I think they must have put something in my IV, because I feel pretty trippy."

"Yeah, they do that in here as a matter of course. Charge you for it, though."

"Good thing the con man left me lots of money."

He grinned. "Good thing."

"I need you to do something for me," she said. "Would you call my friend Phoebe in California? Tell her what's happened.

And Mike—if she doesn't want to come, tell her I understand."

He nodded. "What's her number?"

Beryl gave him the number without hesitation. After five years of being gone, she still remembered it.

"I'll go make the call now," he said, and got up to leave.

"Thank you," she said. "I'll reimburse you for the charges."

"I think I can handle a long-distance call. You rest. We'll have you home in no time if you do what the doctors tell you."

Even as he said the words, Beryl realized that the Bohemian Waxwing was the last place she wanted to be. Maybe she would sell it. Hire someone to pack her things. List it with a Realtor and never set foot in the place again.

When Mike returned, he said he'd left a message. "Anything I can get you from home?" he said.

"Feed Verde?" Beryl said, "and the cat." She went over Verde's feeding schedule while Mike took notes. She took the pad from him and read over what he'd written. She had to cover her left eye to focus clearly. Mike's printing was big and blocky. "This looks fine."

The nurses shooed Mike out at eight when the neurologist arrived, looking haggard and in need of a shower, but dressed up in a suit so nice she knew he couldn't have bought it in Alaska. "How long did the headache last before you fainted?"

"I don't know. A few minutes?"

"Had one like it before?"

"Not as bad as this one. I figured it was migraines, you know, since I'm going through menopause and all."

"Are your parents still living?"

"No."

"What did they die of?"

Here was the old question of family disclosure. Did she say suicide or leukemia? "Mom, leukemia. Dad, they guessed a heart attack. But he had high blood pressure."

"Anyone in your extended family have a history of aneurysm? Die of a stroke, anything like that?"

"Not that I know of."

He pulled a chair up to her bedside and began explaining his take on her CT. Ten minutes later Beryl, mesmerized by the terminology and terrified by his surgical plan to drill a hole in her head to fix the bad blood vessel, found she'd lost the power of speech.

He continued. "Since you're out of the acute phase, and the bleed was so small, I think we can safely plan on surgery for tomorrow afternoon. Is there anyone you want to call?"

Beryl looked out at the strangely lit evening sky, trying to absorb what he'd told her. "A permanent abnormal blood-filled dilation of a blood vessel resulting from disease of the vessel wall," was that "something" on the CT scan. Specifically, it was located on her ophthalmic artery, behind her left eye. "But my head doesn't hurt so much anymore. What happens if I take a pass on surgery?"

"Eventually it ruptures. Brain damage and/or death."

"Surgery?" She laughed nervously. "Come on. I feel just about as good as I ever do. Surely you're being overly cautious."

He shook his head. "It's a time bomb, is what it is. If we surgically intervene and successfully repair it, you go on to live your life, possibly losing the sight in that eye. Or you call in a faith healer, hope for a miracle. We're not dealing with a hernia here."

"Can I have a sleeping pill?" she asked, and the neurologist shook his head no. "What about waiting a few days, just so I can think about it?"

He turned over the menu card on her tray and drew a picture. "Think of the inner tube of a bicycle tire. A pinhole leak occurs, and it begins to lose air. The area where the pinhole is located is under tension. Pushed further, it can tear and cause a blowout. Same concept with aneurysms. However, one can always purchase another inner tube."

"I need to think about it before I can give you my answer," she said. "I'll let you know as soon as I do."

He left; Beryl thought, Here I lie worrying to death about my CT scan, and the one time I could use a sedative, I don't get one. Just when I think my life has taken a turn for the good and I land somewhere nice, I go and fall in love with a con man. And now there's something wrong in my head on top of all that? You're right, what in hell do I need a sleeping pill for? What I need is a plane ride to wherever it is a person has to go to be able to legally kill herself. Oregon or Washington? Call the travel agent. My only loose end is I need someone stable and kind to promise to look after my parrot. Bitch and Game might do it. But do I want Verde to have to be nice to that woman? Nope. The only people who love Verde as much as I do are Phoebe, Ness, and Nance. . . .

Ten minutes later, the nurse appeared with a woman dressed in a very ugly brown pantsuit. "I'm Dr. McLean from the ophthalmic department. I'd like to examine you."

Beryl folded her arms across her chest. "I want a sedative so I don't have to think anymore tonight. The other doctor wouldn't give me one. Will you?"

She smiled gently. "I'm afraid not. Have you ever tried guided imagery?"

Beryl stared at her as if she was the patient. "No, and I have no desire to. I want a first-class ticket to that perfect noplace only drugs can deliver."

"I'm afraid I can't help you there. Now, let's have a look at this aneurysm of yours."

When Detective Stokes showed up with maple-frosted doughnuts and Kaladi Brothers coffee the next morning, Beryl started to cry. "It's not you," she said. "I have to tell the doctor whether I want him to drill a hole in my skull or not, and I can't decide."

"Cheer up. At least it's not a brain tumor. I was up all night worrying." He set the coffee and paper bag down on the bedside stand. "The nurse said you slept well."

"Yeah, after I kind of lost it a little. I begged them for a sleeping pill, and they wouldn't give me one. I guess I must have fallen asleep because the next thing I knew it was morning. Why are you here, anyway? Shouldn't you be at work?"

"Can't do a shift without my doughnut fix. I'll go to work in a little while. Just wanted to see how you are. Talk to me about the surgery."

She ran her hand through her curly hair, knotted up in places from sleeping on it. "I'm okay with it one minute and not the next. Probably not good coffee-break company. Actually I'm not allowed any coffee or water or anything. You should leave, Mike. I'm not fit company for man or beast. Get out while you can."

He took a sip of his coffee. "Speaking of beasts—"

"How's Verde?"

"He's fine. I was wondering—what happened to the bird whisperer?"

Beryl shrugged. "Men leave me. I guess I'm just a leaveable kind of gal."

"Now, now," he clucked. "Self-pity doesn't become you. The Beryl I know and like is a straight shooter. Will the surgery make the problem go away? What if you don't have it?"

She looked him sipping his coffee, and at her roommate's tray, a congealed hunk of oatmeal, fruit sitting in what looked like antifreeze. Mike Stokes, deliverer of bad news, bringer of coffee, and under all that, he cared for her like a father. The coffee smelled wonderful. How could something so simple suddenly seem precious? Was that another one of life's tricks? To periodically make everything seem so entirely dear that whatever time you had left was impossibly bittersweet? She couldn't tilt her head back far enough to keep the tears in her eyes. They began to slide down her cheeks. Mike set the cup down on her tray and sat on her bed.

"If there isn't a doctor here that seems to your liking, you can fly to Seattle or California or Texas or Sloan Goddamn Kettering, if that is what it takes. Alaska is not the end of the world. We have some fine doctors here. I say have the surgery. That way you can go fishing with me next summer."

"I hate fish."

"So sit in the boat and take pictures of bears," he said, taking hold of her hand and gripping it tight. He rubbed her back, and his hand on her spine made her relax. "Here's how I look at it. The world needs more uppity women. Let the guys in the white coats fix you."

Mike Stokes could make her laugh, but could he make the sun set at a reasonable hour, or make sense of Earl, or the concept of love, or say why it was that even Thomas Jack, with whom she thought she enjoyed a real friendship, had left her for fish? Why it was some of the most well-intentioned people could not find love that lasted? Worry floated along behind her like a wake. Once fear took up residence inside a person's heart, it was there forever, growing like a rope around the chambers. She didn't want anything beyond hearing that the scans were a mistake, that all she needed to do was take stronger vitamins and she could go back to feeling normal—well, what passed as normal for her life. "I just want it all to go away," she said.

"I can understand that," Mike said.

When the doctor returned, Beryl was momentarily confused. When he didn't ask Mike to leave, she felt a breath of relief, and then when he smiled at her so kindly, as if he was terribly sorry for her, every crevice that had pooled with relief turned rancid and transformed to dread. "Three physicians are in agreement that you have an ophthalmic artery aneurysm, repairable by one of two options. Surgically, which I've already explained to you. There is a second option, which involves using a coil threaded through an artery. It's less invasive, but risks accompany each procedure. Either way you may lose your sight in the affected eye."

Beryl tried again. "What happens if I do nothing?"

"You'll probably succumb to bleeding if not in the immediate future, then somewhere down the line."

Mike interrupted. "The surgeon here, how many of these operations has he performed?"

"Dozens."

"And the coil? Has he done those, too?"

"It's a newer procedure, but yes, he's done them."

"And the outcomes?"

"Every surgery has its adverse outcomes, but the positive outcomes are still in the higher percentage."

"Is there someone better in Seattle? Do we have time for a second opinion?"

The doctor frowned. "We can perform either procedure here. You're not going to help the situation by postponing it to shop for doctors."

"Mike, help me decide," Beryl said. "I can't think."

The detective bristled. "Well, goddammit all to hell. Don't people live for years with goddamn aneurysms?"

When her bedside phone rang, Beryl picked it up and said hello, expecting the call to be for her roommates. Instead she heard a birdlike voice ring out. "Beryl?"

"Phoebe! Oh, Phoebe, thank you for calling back." She started to cry, and Mike leaned over and spoke words to the doctor that made him shake his head and stride out of the room.

"Ophthalmic artery," Beryl said into the phone. "My left eye. They want to repair it surgically, or do this thing with a coil."

"Hang on," Phoebe said. "Nance is doing a search on the Net. My God, Beryl, where have you been? We've been calling and writing, and there's never anyone home. Aside from the life-and-death thing, are you all right?"

"I will be," she said. "Just as soon as we get this aneurysm taken care of. Then I'll be fine, or I guess I'll be dead."

"Don't talk like that."

"Phoebe? I want to come back to the farm."

"So come back to the farm! You can recuperate here, and we'll wait on you hand and—"

"I mean for good."

"What does Earl say? Is he all right with this?"

Beryl looked out the window. It was still sunny. "I don't know and I don't care," she said. "It's a long story, but I am putting that god-awful mansion on the hill on the market the second I get out of here. Let someone buy it and turn it into a B&B. I want to come back to Sadie's farm. It's the only place I was ever truly, honestly happy. Please say my room isn't rented out."

She heard a squeal in the background, and then Phoebe was back on the phone. "Nance says the coil procedure has a higher rate for positive outcome. They can repair even, yes, it says it right here, ophthalmic aneurysms, and Providence has a good surgeon. He used to be at—U-Dub? Oh. She says that means University of Washington, and it's a good hospital. I'll email all this to you, but tell the doctor you want the coil. What's your email address?"

"I don't have one." Beryl handed the phone to Mike, who gave Phoebe his Palm Pilot email, thanked her, and Phoebe asked to speak to Beryl again. "This is going to work," she said. "You'll see. Now I'm going to make reservations for Ness, Mimi, and me, and we will see you tomorrow morning when all this is over."

"What about Nance?"

"Oh, my gosh. You don't even know. She's incredibly pregnant, Beryl. No way will I let her get on a plane. Now try not to worry. You're tough. We've been through so much worse. Remember staying up all night with the poinsettias? Compared to them you're a piece of cake."

In the doorway of the room Beryl saw that Mike was explaining things to the doctor. A few minutes later, the nurse came in with forms for her to sign, and told Beryl to press hard in order to get all three copies.

When they wheeled her into the procedure room, Mike bent close and said in her ear, "I have spent my lifetime finding and punishing bad guys," he said. "The man upstairs owes me. See you soon, Ms. Reilly. We'll finish that lunch."

Saxifrage, or foamflower, derives its name from tiny white flowers that resemble ocean foam. Its leaves are shaped like those of the maple tree, found at the base of the stem, and the flowers come in pink and white varieties. The Greeks referred to this plant as "little tiara," because its yellow pistils rise like a crown above the flowers. In Greece the foamflower is a token of love. Saxifrage spreads easily, producing underground "runners," and forms colonics. Though small, you must not underestimate its determination. Oftentimes, when planted in rock gardens, it will split the rock to make its chosen way.

Ness

18

Seeing the Light in the Last Frontier

JULY IN ALASKA WAS NOT a normal thing, in Ness's opinion. She sat on the deck at the rear of Beryl's house looking out at hundred-foot-tall spruce trees and papery birches separating her land from the neighbor's, an acre away. It was seven P.M., but from the location of the sun in the sky, it looked closer to high noon. Beryl was upstairs, Mimi was out, and Phoebe lounged nude in the Jacuzzi. Somewhere in among the thick green branches, one angry squirrel was delivering an earful, and Ness guessed she was in his territory. "Sorry, little guy," she said wearily. "My buns are tired, and I am not moving."

"Are you conversing with fauna?" Phoebe said from the Jacuzzi. "Sounds to me like my girlfriend needs a boyfriend. Should we go back to the airport and pick up some German tourists again?"

Ness took a sip of her Diet Coke and smiled. "Phoebe, my dear, t'ain't my fault European men in airports find me so darned fine they fall all over themselves trying to fetch my luggage. That plane ride just about did me in. How does anyone over five feet fit into coach seats? Felt like I was doing yoga the whole way from Seattle."

"Try walking on my legs and using crutches in the aisle,"

Phoebe answered, kicking her legs against the bubbles. "I wish German tourists thought *I* was worth fetching my bags. If I fell on the luggage carousel I'd go around ten times before anyone noticed. Seriously, I thought those men were going to kidnap you. Since when did you become the epitome of a sexpot?"

Ness laughed. "When we met, you were such a good girl. Now you're a middle-aged sex maniac with a mouth closing in on Verde's."

At the sound of his name, the parrot screeched from his outdoor perch, and Phoebe splashed Ness with a handful of water. "Nice talk coming from a Baptist. I'm telling God."

"Go ahead, I have no secrets from my Creator," Ness said. "My conscience is clear, and my soul is ready for whatever he sends my way. More siblings, a wealthy German bachelor, a moose sighting—"

"Oh, please," Phoebe said. "The mythical Alaskan moose. I think they're a fable, like Paul Bunyan or the Abominable Snowman. The only four-legged wildlife I've seen since we landed is that dachshund in the old lady's purse at the rental car counter." She moved to the other side of the tub, and put on her sunglasses. "Do you think Beryl will come downstairs today?"

"I surely hope so," Ness said, wondering why it was that for every blessed miracle on earth there seemed to be a price dearly paid. Yesterday, after they'd landed, they'd gotten the official word that the blindness in Beryl's left eye was permanent. The coil procedure had been a success, but she'd never regain her sight. So far Beryl had been a portrait of stoicism, nodding as if she expected this consequence, but as soon as she was released from the hospital, she'd taken to her bed and refused to come downstairs for anything, including meals.

Ness knew how she felt. She'd had the wind knocked out of her own self so many times that she was expert at maintaining a straight face while her legs turned to jelly. The trick was to fall apart in private, and not to get up until you knew you had hold of yourself. "She'll work it out, Pheebs. The shock of learning about Earl and now this—it's just too much for her to deal with right now. She'll be all right. A lot of folks are praying for her."

"I wish I could believe like you do," Phoebe said. "But I only get so far, and then I start asking how could God exist and allow little kids to get cancer? Or torture or rape or kidnapping or let teachers get paid the same ridiculous salary as a salesclerk? And what about Republicans?"

"And I keep on telling you," Ness said, "God is love. Start from there and you will build a relationship."

"Fine, God is love," Phoebe said. "But he really needs to take care of those things I just listed. Otherwise he loses all credibility in my book." A magpie darted down from a spruce and cocked his head, then tugged a sunflower seed from a potted plant not even a foot from the Jacuzzi, pulled it from the dirt, and flew away. "Jeez, don't forget to tip your waiter," she told him. "Man, the birds up here are so bold it's freaky. You think Alfred Hitchcock spent any time in Alaska?"

Mimi opened the sliding glass door and came out onto the deck. "Okay. I got organic peppers to make *rellenos* for dinner, two six-packs of beer, a chocolate cake, and six Abba Zabbas. I also bought this game called Alaskaopoly. Sort of like Monopoly, only if you win the pipeline, you can rule the world. And I rented three Marx Brothers DVDs. Now all we have to do is get Beryl to come out of her room. Ness, it's your turn to try."

"I don't mind," Ness said, getting up to go indoors.

"Hey," Phoebe said as her two roommates went through the door. "You guys better not forget me out here. You know I can't get out of the water by myself."

"Cálmate," Mimi said. "After I put the groceries away I'll be your lifeguard."

Beryl had drawn the shades in her bedroom, but against the summer light they didn't make much of a dent. The room felt warm and still, like a sickroom, and the tabby cat had claimed one of the bed pillows. Ness sat down and petted her, saying nothing. Beryl lay on her back, looking up at the ceiling. She was dressed in a pair of crisp pink-and-green-cotton Liz Claiborne pajamas, Nance's contribution to the effort of helping their old friend through the current crisis, since she was too pregnant to get on a plane. Not only did they fit Beryl perfectly but they gave her pasty face a healthy glow. "Leave it to Nance to know just the right colors to pick," Ness said. "No matter how you feel, you look great, even if you have lost weight."

Beryl's response was to close her eyes.

Earlier that morning Mimi had given her a backrub and polished her toenails a dazzling scarlet. Around lunchtime they'd piled on the bed to watch a *Sex and the City* DVD, and eat a dozen doughnuts. Tonight it was Mexican food, cold beer, and old comedies. Before leaving Bayborough, Ness had contacted her Baptist ladies' prayer group requesting extra prayers on Beryl's behalf. Ness picked up the cat and moved her to the floor, then lay down next to Beryl and stretched out. Her legs were so long they touched the footboard. "It's a shame what happened," she said softly, running her hand over Beryl's arm and then clasping her hand. "And a tough thing to accept. But you still have your sight in your right eye, honey. Some people don't get that much. And I hope you know that if you lost your sight entirely, we'd still be your friends and help you find your way in the world. That's what girlfriends are for. You take all the time you need. There's no hurry." Then she dangled a carrot. "Tomorrow morning we're going to Saturday Market. You can stay home or come with, either way. No pressure."

Beryl squeezed her hand; Ness smiled, and began to hum "Amazing Grace." Baby steps, she thought to herself.

Halfway through *Duck Soup,* Phoebe sighed and pressed pause on the remote. "Okay. I have a question. Why weren't there any Marx Sisters?"

"Oh, Lord," Ness said into Beryl's ear. "Gird yourself for some feminist ranting."

Mimi laughed. "But Ness, Phoebe makes a valid point. Who are the great women comics?"

"I have no idea, but I would like to see the end of this film."

"I'll tell you why you can't name any," Phoebe said. "Nobody knows the names of the women in vaudeville because back then they looked at women actors like interchangeable nobodies."

"It's not that bad—," Ness began, but Phoebe interrupted.

"Then along came Imogen Coca, Lucille Ball, and Carol Burnett. But not as funny girls per se, women in dysfunctional situations."

"Fine," Ness said. "It was the stone age of TV. They had to start somewhere."

"I don't know," Mimi said. "Lucy and Ricky, the racial stuff was a factor, right?"

"And Cher, when she was with Sonny," Phoebe said. "Though she didn't really do anything for American Indians, and Sonny—well, for once he was the lovable dope half of the duo."

"God rest his soul, Sonny Bono was as ugly as a pug dog," Ness said. "Can we postpone this discussion until after the movie?"

But Phoebe was on a roll. She drank her beer and said, "Roseanne, Sandra Bernhard, and maybe Margaret Cho. They're funny on television or in a sitcom, but put them on the stage and forget about it. Why? Can't women be just as funny? Remember *Nine to Five? Steel Magnolias? First Wives Club?*"

"*Nine to Five* was only funny insofar as it was retaliation," Mimi said. "Same goes for *First Wives*. *Steel Magnolias* was a "disease of the week" kind of movie. And I'm ticked you didn't list Ellen. My son's ex used to call her Ellen Degenerate. How I wish he'd never married that girl."

"Survivors!" Phoebe crowed. "Only women who survive are funny, is that it?"

Ness sighed. She pushed another beer Phoebe's way, hoping she would take the time to drink it and then Ness could grab hold of the remote. "Is this discussion really so earth-shattering we can't finish watching the—"

"Here's what I think," Phoebe said, pushing the beer aside and opening a bag of Kettle Corn. "Men can be buffoons, but women, deep down, no matter how hilarious they are, are supposed to be well-mannered ladies. We are trapped in sexist roles for time immemorial!"

"Towanda!" Mimi said. "Kathy Bates in *Fried Green Tomatoes*!"

"Okay," Ness said. "It's unfair and sexist and someone has

probably gone and written a book on all this. Can we go back to the movie now?"

"Did you ever notice how in Disney cartoons all the women are—," Phoebe began.

Ness groaned and took a pillow from behind her head and turned to place it over Phoebe's face. "Do I have to commit murder to see the end of the movie?"

Mimi pulled the pillow away from her, and put it under her head. "Clearly Phoebe is on to something important. *Chica,* you should write a book."

"And maybe if you're lucky, they'll make it into a movie," Ness said. "And some tipsy friend of yours will put it on pause and ruin the experience for everyone."

"I never liked the Marx Brothers," Beryl said softly, and the girls turned to look at her. Her eyes glittered with tears. Ness tried to discern a difference between them, but they looked like the same old Beryl so far as she could tell.

"Go on," Phoebe said. "Tell us why."

"I don't know. Maybe they were funny the first couple of times. But the jokes were so corny, and I really hated Laurel and Hardy. The big guy was such a bully to the little guy. I always wanted to take the little guy to the doctor and get him some antidepressants. Knock some sense into him."

"Amen," Phoebe said. "Do you see how this proves my point?"

Mimi smiled, and Ness leaned in close. "Welcome back, Beryl Anne," she said. "We sure missed you."

For a moment no one said anything, and Ness felt sure things were going to collapse into collective crying. Then Phoebe looked at her watch and saved the day. "For pity's sake," she said. "Do you realize it's after midnight? Doesn't it ever get dark in Alaska?"

Beryl propped herself up on her elbow and shut her right eye. "Really? Seems plenty dark to me."

Mimi gasped, and Ness grinned, and then Phoebe began to laugh. "Who says women aren't funny?" she said. "Come on, survivors. Group hug."

"Nance says shopping is perfectly legitimate therapy," Phoebe said as they began the circuit of Saturday Market, which was held every weekend from May to September in the Hilton parking lot. "Though I expect she'd be happier if we went to Nordstrom's. I want to get Sally a set of those Russian nesting dolls, so yell if you spy some."

Ness pushed Phoebe's chair while Beryl held on to Mimi's arm. She noticed that Beryl seemed a little off balance, but that if she had something to hold on to, she did fairly well. Here in the crowded open-air market they were simply part of the crowd, and she hoped that took the pressure off. The sky was blue, and though in Bayborough this would have been considered a chilly day, up here it felt balmy. To their left Ness could see the water, and beyond that, more mountains. It seemed to her that a body could spend a lifetime exploring Alaska and still not see everything. She'd looked out the airplane window as they were landing and known instantly why Beryl had wanted to move. Even in high tourist season the crowds were nothing compared to downtown Bayborough-by-the-Sea.

She tried to imagine Beryl's view of things. Here the man she'd loved had turned out to be a stranger, and to admit to her friends that she'd been taken in by him made her feel like a poor judge of character. Beryl couldn't imagine them empathizing with her, only belittling how small she already felt. Yet Beryl was the most compassionate of all of them. She was the quickest to forgive, and also the peacemaker. Ness guessed maybe it was a lesson that one kept on learning.

"What is that?" Mimi said, pointing to a twelve-foot length of black stuff with unraveling ends propped in front of a booth selling Ulu knives.

"Baleen," Beryl said. "Whale dental floss."

"What do you do with it?" Ness asked.

"Hang it on the wall like art," Beryl said. "Or it can be woven into baskets. Tears up the fingers, though."

Phoebe reached out and touched it. Next to the baleen was

what looked like a stick of ivory with a rounded tip. "And this?" she said. "Is it the whale's toothpick?"

"Hardly," Beryl said, smiling. "That's an *oosik*. More commonly known as the penis bone from a walrus."

"Oh, ick," Phoebe said. "And I touched it. Ness, do you have that hand sanitizer with you?"

"Somewhere in here," she said, placing her purse on Phoebe's lap.

They stopped at the produce stalls, marveling over the locally grown cabbages and flowers. "Get a load of that zucchini," Ness said. "Somebody take a picture so we can show Sally she hasn't got it so bad."

"Look at those lilacs," Phoebe said. "Oh, what I wouldn't give to grow those on the farm. But it just doesn't get cold enough to encourage them, really. Let me smell them one more time before we move on. And oh, look at the columbines. Tell you what, just leave me here and get me on the way back. I'm in heaven."

But heaven was also in the free samples of birch syrup, and the stand that sold salmon quesadillas and vegetarian tamales filled with sweet corn and pineapple chunks. Ness bought a hand-painted scarf, Mimi stopped at a booth advertising a women's collective and signed up for the mailing list, and Phoebe wanted to buy several bars of handmade soap to study so they could consider adding such items to their gift line. Only Beryl didn't seem to want anything. Ness knew she'd never been one for indulging herself that way. Beryl was plain, and she didn't wear jewelry besides her gold hoop earrings, and no one looking at her would suspect she owned that barn of a house on the Hillside. If Nance had been there, she might have been able to get Beryl enthused, but instead she was home, putting the last finishing touches on the baby she was growing.

Ness's brother, Will, had said there was an antique mall to check out. Old things needing a second chance, maybe that was more Beryl's cup of tea.

At *The Really Good Store* booth, Phoebe made everyone look at the silver jewelry they had for sale. There were buffalo nickels fashioned into bracelets, a concho belt with Mercury head dimes, drop earrings and post earrings, and pins. "Look," Mimi said. "These French wire earrings have little white flowers on them. They look like lilies of the valley. Oh, that's us. Lilies of the Valley. Let's each get a pair. Nance would love them, don't you think?"

Ness held a pair up in the sun. "I wonder what they're made of? Please tell me it's not ivory."

A silver-haired, ponytailed gentleman smiled at her. "Selling ivory's illegal. This is tagua nut, from the Philippines. I know, because I make them myself."

"What is that?" Mimi said. "Some kind of like vegetarian ivory?"

"Exactly," he told her, taking them out and laying them against black velvet, which made anything look wonderful.

"They are kind of cute," Phoebe said. "Beryl? What do you think?"

"Think about what?" Beryl said from behind her dark glasses.

"The earrings. Should we get a pair for Nance?"

Beryl looked at them without expression. "No, I don't think those are quite Nance's style. She's more the big-hairy-gold-nugget-with-a-two-carat-diamond-in-the-center type."

"Oh, you make her sound like Jackie Collins," Phoebe said. "She's not that bad. Did I tell you she's on a vegetarian diet?"

"Only about six hundred times," Beryl answered. "Mimi? What do you think of the earrings?"

"I like the kind on the wire instead of dangling. Those drive me insane."

"I know what you mean," Phoebe said. "Especially bad during sex, flapping against your face and all."

Ness shook her head. "How nice that you feel relaxed enough to talk that way in front of total strangers," she said. "Everyone should know your private business, don't you think?"

"Hush," Phoebe said. "I didn't name a single name. Sir, we love those earrings. By any chance do you have seven pair?"

He nodded, and his girlfriend laughed, and from below the cloth-covered table, a big black German shepherd began to wag her tail. Phoebe lifted the cloth and petted her. "Aren't you just the most wonderful Alaskan doggie?" she said. "You remind me of Duchess. Beryl, did I tell you James bought Nance a rat terrier?"

Beryl nodded. "She's going to have her hands full training it and tending a baby."

"Not to worry," Phoebe said. "If James can handle Sally all week he'll have no problems with a terrier."

When the earrings were boxed up, Phoebe whipped out cash. She wouldn't let anyone contribute, and as soon as the transaction was completed, she made Ness wheel her over to a shady spot so they could all put the earrings on. "They're so light," Ness said. "I can hardly feel them."

"They look completely great against your skin," Phoebe put in.

"They look all right on you white girls, too," Ness answered.

Mimi smiled and tucked her hair behind her ears. "But they look better on us ethnic types."

"Beryl Anne," Phoebe said, "You haven't bought anything. What do you want to look for?"

She looked toward the horse and carriage parked at the curbside. "Maybe a new Ginsu knife? How does the song go, 'Earl's gotta die'?"

While Ness and Phoebe struggled to stop laughing, Mimi looked at them blankly. "If it happened before Sally was born, I missed it, so you have to explain."

Ness turned to push Phoebe's chair down the aisle, and in the process, saw Dayle before Mimi did. There she was, Mimi's old flame, selling those Russian nesting doll sets, the graduated ones that fit inside one another. Dayle looked blond and tanned in her hiking clothes. While the girls were all wearing sweatshirts and jeans, here she was in a tank top and tight jean cutoffs, her arms a golden summer tan. "Don't look now," Ness whispered to Mimi. "You might turn into a pillar of salt."

But it seemed that the ladies noticed each other at the exact same time. They'd been so busy with Beryl that Mimi hadn't had time to call Dayle. Now she stood face-to-face with her. Dayle was the first to recover, only because she had a customer in front of her waving a credit card in her face. She took the card, looked away and gathered her composure, and then began to wrap the dolls that had just been purchased in bubble wrap. "I predict these will become a family heirloom," she said. "Years from now, your great-grandkids will play with them, and realize what a treasure you found here in Anchorage, Alaska."

Mimi just stood there listening.

"Aren't you going to talk to her?" Phoebe asked.

"Go talk to her," Ness said. "She realizes how much she missed you but she's too proud to say anything."

"All I can say is don't hold a grudge, Mimi," Beryl said. "Life's too short."

Mimi tucked her hands into her pockets. "I'll catch up with you all later," she said. "Call my cell number when you're ready to leave."

They moved along down the aisle of vendors, stopping to look at hand-painted pottery and fleece coats. They were chilly, but it was far from weather for heavy coats. Phoebe tugged Ness's sleeve. "I'm sorry, I can't stand it. Isn't there a place we can park and spy on them? It's distracting to think they're just over there spilling their guts to each other. I wanna know what happens."

Ness shook her head. "Eavesdropping isn't polite."

"How can it be eavesdropping if all we're doing is looking?"

"Ahem, isn't that spying?" Ness turned to Beryl. "Do we stop and gawk or move on?"

It took a minute for the words to sink in. Beryl seemed to come back to them from a faraway place. "When Phoebe went on her first date with Juan, we camped out in her bedroom and ate all the chocolate he'd brought her. And when she got home, we made her describe her goodnight kiss in painful detail. And Nance—well, we used to set things up so that she had to run into James at least five times a day. We were that determined to get them together."

"It takes the surprise out of things," Ness said. "If it's God's plan for those two then it'll happen without our tinkering."

"Come on," Phoebe said. "If it weren't for girlfriends pushing each other into trying new stuff, fate would go on a permanent holiday with its best friend, just rewards."

"It's not right," Ness said.

"Fine, you guys go on," Phoebe said. "But turn my wheelchair around so I can see."

Ness did as Phoebe asked, and from where she stood, Mimi and Dayle were just friends. They were looking at each other; their bodies were casual, nowhere near touching. "Show's over," she said. "I want to buy some of those beets from the produce stand before they sell out."

Mimi took off that afternoon just before dinner. Ness grilled corn and Beryl defrosted some seafood chowder. After the dishes were done, the Realtor came by with paperwork for Beryl to fill out. "You understand this contract allows my agency to list your house exclusively for three months," the woman said.

"I do," Beryl said.

When she tried to put pen to paper to sign the contract, her hand landed six inches from the page. Ness saw her falter, and quickly scooted the contract to Beryl's pen. "Who's up for Soy Delight Mint Marble Fudge?"

Phoebe's hand shot up. Beryl signed the last three pages and handed them to the Realtor. "How long do you think it will take to sell it?"

The Realtor fastened the latch on her briefcase. "I have no idea. Whoever buys it will have to love this place for its quirks and stories."

"I was thinking it would make a good bed-and-breakfast," Beryl said. "It has so many bathrooms."

"I'll sure put that in the listing," she said. "Now do I have your number in California? And your fax?"

Beryl repeated them. When the Realtor left, Ness sat a dish of soy "ice cream" in front of Beryl. "It will sell," she said. "Somebody is going to fall in love with this place and love it forever."

"I'm not worried," Beryl said.

But to Ness it certainly looked that way.

Phoebe wheeled over to Verde's cage and took him out. "Hello, Mr. Green Jeans," she said. "You're going to have to work on your vocabulary around Sally. The last thing I need is her learning more cuss words."

"Mimi must really be having fun," Phoebe said the next day, as Ness hustled the trash to the curb for pickup. Beryl had explained that up on the Hillside, it was best to wait until they heard the truck approach, or else the returning ravens would take advantage, flinging garbage every which way until they found an empty pizza box or chicken bones. "I can't believe she hasn't called."

"Give her time," Ness said.

"Why did she and Dayle break up?" Beryl asked.

Ness gestured at the tall trees that lined Beryl's street. "She missed Alaska. Our little tourist town wasn't enough for her."

"This place gets under your skin," Beryl said. "There's something compelling about the extremes. Darkness, light, snow so deep the world goes quiet. It'll be hard to leave all that, even for warm winters." She took a few steps to the right, where forget-me-nots had sprouted of their own volition in the ditch. A pile of moose nuggets was scattered nearby. "Be careful not to step in the moose poop," she said.

"I think you're making it up about the animals," Phoebe said. "We've been here three days now and I have yet to see anything that we don't have at home."

Beryl turned Phoebe's chair so that it pointed across the street to a neighbor's yard. There stood a spruce tree, its trunk trimmed of branches about five feet up from the ground. The bird feeder that hung from its branches was empty. "Just before they hibernate, bears show up, looking for whatever they can to fill their bellies. If you leave dog food out, or trash uncovered, pretty soon the bears come to expect it. Then you have a nuisance bear, and Fish and Game has to come out and shoot it."

Ness tried to imagine this place in winter, with snow piled two feet high, and frost turning the bare trees into white skeletons. She thought how David would have loved to see Alaska, and that for him the snow would be just another form of art. She felt the old familiar pang in her chest, bitter and sweet at the same time. She doubted she'd ever feel that kind of love again in her lifetime.

"Oh, a bird feeder and a tall tale," Phoebe said. "Be still my heart. This is probably as close as we're going to get to seeing a moose."

"If it's wildlife you want," Beryl said, "That can be arranged. Go pack your warmest clothes."

When the whales leaped from the waters of the Kenai Peninsula, everyone on board the cruise boat began making noise. It wasn't yelling, exactly, nor was it laughing, and to call it screaming would have been inaccurate. What it was was the simple sound of human joy, Ness realized. There were still some sights in the world capable of making people stand in awe. She put her arms around Beryl, and they stood on deck, waiting for the next surprise. Phoebe had opted to stay inside, sitting next to the window, but Ness knew it would take more than a mere pane of glass to dull the sights of glaciers, seabirds, and bears roaming the beaches.

Later, on the return trip, the girls sat around a table drinking cocoa, tired and windburned but happy. "This was great, Beryl," Phoebe said. "But nary a moose. Time to give it up. Admit you were lying."

Beryl sighed. "Dang it all! Why won't you believe me? They're everywhere."

Phoebe smiled. "In the words of my smart-aleck daughter, 'Prove it.'"

"Oh, Lordy," Phoebe said as the three of them bounced down the road to Eklutna Lake. "Hope I don't break a tooth."

"Keep your window up," Ness said. "We're raising so much dust I can hardly see out the windshield."

"Stop over there," Beryl said, pointing out a small thicket of cottonwood trees and a trailhead.

"Happily," Ness said, pulling the rental car over and shutting off the motor.

"This ground looks too bumpy for my chair," Phoebe said. "You guys go look for moose. I'll stay here."

Ness and Beryl got out and walked around the trees. The air smelled of spruce and lake water. Ahead of them a couple portaged a kayak toward the water. "Looks cold," Ness remarked.

Beryl agreed. "On a clear day you can see Denali from here," she said. "But today apparently the mountain is closed. That's what Alaskans say, that it's closed for the day, like a tourist shop that sets its own hours. I wish you could have seen it."

Ness put her arm around Beryl and pressed her cheek against hers. "It's still a pretty spectacular view."

Beryl looked down at her feet. "This is where they found his truck, you know."

"Earl's truck?"

She removed her sunglasses, revealing eyes puffy from tears, not just surgery. "I look at that lake, the steely blue water, I see people in a kayak that doesn't look strong enough to hold them paddling away. Across the water the mountains are blue-green and so lush they look like they could be in Peru for all I know. And no matter what's in front of me I know that just a few feet behind me the man I thought loved me stopped his truck and left, thinking I would be able to handle a ridiculous disappearance better than him telling me the truth, which was that he didn't love me anymore."

Ness hugged her friend. "But now you know the truth. You weren't the only one he fooled. That has to make it easier to let him go. You want my advice? Don't bother hating him. And don't pine after him, either. Just tell him goodbye and be done with it, and leave him here. Why don't I give you some time alone?"

She walked back to the car, leaving Beryl standing under the canopy of trees, which in winter, laden with snow and rimed with frost, made an entirely different landscape. Ness watched Beryl throw her left arm out to find her balance, and saw her mouth move, and wondered what words she let fly through the clean Alaskan air like perfectly aimed arrows.

In the car Phoebe was drinking a bottle of water and taking pictures with her disposable camera. "Where's Beryl?" she asked when Ness opened the car door.

"She needed a minute to say some things," Ness answered. "Spotted a moose?"

"As if," Phoebe scoffed. "Is this where it happened?"

Ness nodded. "It's a such a pretty lake."

"And such a lame-ass, thoughtless way for him to leave," Phoebe added. "I tried to call home on my cell phone," she said. "The reception out here is terrible."

"You're as impatient as Sally," Ness said. "Can't you sit and enjoy nature quietly for two minutes?"

"I could if there were a couple of moose in it."

Half an hour later, Beryl returned to the car. She was no longer wearing her sunglasses. "Hey," she said, opening the passenger door.

"You ready to go?" Ness asked.

Beryl nodded, her cheeks bright with color.

"Did you say goodbye to Earl?" Phoebe asked.

"Yes, I did."

"Good," Ness said. "Now, when you think of him, remember this place, and how beautiful it was, and your anger will be tempered."

"How did she get to be so smart?" Beryl said to Phoebe.

Phoebe shrugged. "I know for a fact she's been kicked in the head by a horse. Are you feeling better, Beryl?"

"Tons."

Phoebe smiled. "Good, because even though I couldn't get my cell phone to call California, it worked great when I called Detective Stokes. I invited him to dinner."

Fireweed begins as a leafy plant and then blooms a hot pink or fuchsia color. Folklore (and most Alaskans) says that when the fireweed tops out, when the blossoms change from pink to cottony floss, the first frost is only six weeks away.

Phoebe and Beryl

19

Second Sight

SAVANNAH ROSE MATTOX DETHOMAS was born at ten A.M., a perfectly reasonable hour, on the third Saturday in July. Nance's labor had begun around four in the morning, but she'd waited until six-thirty to wake James. "There's nothing wrong with wanting him to be rested," she'd said, and it seemed that the queen of organization had everything ready. The nursery was painted periwinkle blue and finished with ivory crown molding found in a salvage yard. The room had been furnished with an antique iron-and-brass cradle, a full-size crib, a hand-loomed rug featuring fat, sleepy sheep, a changing table, a velveteen chaise for Mother to lie on while she nursed Baby, and enough fine linen and diapers so Nance could go a month without doing the laundry. She'd pooh-poohed cute mobiles and instead hung a Museum of Modern Art Calder reproduction over the crib. Books on every aspect of childhood filled the pickled pine bookshelves, and a veritable Noah's ark of stuffed animals awaited curious little hands. Four hours after she'd checked into the hospital with her midwife and Lester Ullman in attendance, it took only two pushes for Nance to send her little girl into the world. Phoebe knew this because Nance had insisted she be there, and be first to hold the baby in her arms. "It's only fair," Nance had said,

"Since I was the first to hold Sally. Just keep it short, and whatever you do, don't drop her."

Phoebe was astonished at how difficult it had been to let go of that baby. While James whooped and snapped pictures, and Nance waited patiently, a peaceful smile on her face, Savannah had looked up at her aunt, and Phoebe had been struck dumb at the wonder of the tiny baby in her arms. "You're going to love it here," she'd whispered, ideas flooding her mind of the many ways she would spoil her niece. Then she'd handed her over to Nance and James and wheeled herself out of the birthing room to where Ness, Beryl, and Sally sat waiting for her to give them the good news.

"Is she all right?" Ness asked, and it had taken Phoebe a moment to remember what that question entailed: Nance's refusal to have the amnio, and her relatively advanced age to bear a first child. But Savannah had turned out perfect. No melon head, no ugly birthmarks, and her blond hair looked as if she had recently visited the José Eber Salon. She weighed in at a trim six pounds, had no unsightly fat rolls, and her little outfits looked like Versace originals.

That long and dreamlike day stayed with Phoebe for weeks. Sometimes she would be working in her studio and have to stop what she was doing in order to relive the birth in her mind. It puzzled her how Nance's makeup and hair had stayed nice throughout the whole ordeal. She managed to look cool and stylish even in a hospital johnny.

At first Sally had been thrilled at the idea of having her very own cousin. However, at Nance's baby shower, Sally was a little put out when there was nothing for her to open. Ness had let her win all the shower games, but then Sally was peeved to discover that the prizes were boring old gift certificates for hot-rock massages and pedicures. Then there was the little matter of her name not being on the cake. Phoebe explained to her, "Other people in the universe have babies every day, and while you're a great kid, you aren't the only one on the planet."

James had tried to get her to go with him and Andrew to Chuck E. Cheese's during the shower, but Sally wouldn't budge. That night Andrew promised to take Sally shopping at Toys "R"

Us. While Phoebe expected the worst out of that trip, it turned out that Andrew and Sally had bought toys to take to the women's shelter in Sierra Grove. Sally had shopped "sensibly," he said. "For every Breyer horse she put in the cart she also picked out a toy truck."

On the last Sunday in August, Phoebe wheeled herself into the kitchen to start lemon scones for breakfast. The house was quiet, but Verde flapped his wing stubs, trying to get her attention. She let him out of his cage and set out his morning meal, a cup of fresh fruit. In no time at all it seemed that the parrot had adjusted to his old routine. Mimi's cats had been shipped to Alaska, where she'd decided to stay with Dayle. Calpurnia the rat terrier spent much of the day playing ball with Sally, but come nightfall she slept on the threshold of Savannah's room, guarding the baby as if she'd been born to the task.

The doorbell rang, and Phoebe peeked out the window. "Ness," she called, on the way to the foyer. "Your brother's here."

Phoebe opened the door, and the tall man smiled as he handed over a shopping bag from Whole Foods. "Plums and peaches," he said. "I couldn't resist."

"Thanks, Will," Phoebe said. "How's tricks in the antiques biz?"

"Just fine," he said. "How are motherhood, flowers, and art?"

"Just nifty-galifty. Come sit in the kitchen and have a cup of coffee while you wait for your sister."

"I'd love to."

Nance walked in the side door with Savannah in her arms, struggling to balance the diaper bag hanging over her arm. Will jumped to his feet. "My goodness. Let me help you."

"Thanks, Will. Seen my rat terrier around?"

"Cal's in with Sally," Phoebe said. "You can leave Savannah here while you go check." But the terrier seemed to understand that she was needed, and ran down the hall into the kitchen, barking once at Verde, with whom she had an uneasy alliance. Phoebe wondered if there would come a time either she or Andrew would need a companion dog to do life's chores for them. She wanted more than anything to remain independent for as long as she could, and she knew Andrew was fanatic and overly proud about the subject. But it was a real possibility somewhere down the line, and it didn't seem so bad to have a dog around.

Ness walked in, dressed in her Sunday clothes. "Morning, everyone," she said. "Will, Nance, we'd better hurry or we'll be late for services."

"I'll mind the baby for you," Phoebe said.

"No, I want to take her along," Nance said. "I like her being around all the singing."

"Okay," Phoebe said, trying not to sound disappointed.

When they left, Phoebe fed Calpurnia, took the scones out of the oven, and set them on a tray to cool. She yawned and then decided to go back to bed. Sally was old enough to get herself a juice box. Besides, the odds of her letting Phoebe sleep were next to none. She hoped her little munchkin would remember to be quiet. These days Beryl slept so fitfully she might not get up until noon.

Phoebe slid into bed—beside Andrew.

He turned to look at her. "Morning already?"

"It's early. Go back to sleep," she whispered.

Phoebe was tired and fell immediately asleep in Andrew's arms. It was heaven to have him there in her bed, and she had grown as used to it as he had. On the nights they spent apart, she tossed and turned and woke up cranky. Right now, though, the Egyptian cotton sheets her aunt had bought years ago and that had softened so nicely over time felt like a nest of pure silk, as did his skin. The two lovers slept like spoons, curled into one another, as able-bodied as anyone else at that moment. Phoebe dreamed of hummingbirds. Their lacy wings buzzed and blurred as they hovered over the flowers on the farm, and she remembered Sadie telling her that the Aztecs believed hummingbirds were fallen warriors, reincarnated. In Native American lore, hummingbirds were the creators of the universe, and responsible for bringing rain to the desert. All those legends and stories aside, the remarkable bird could fly up, down, and backward, its heart beating fifty to seventy-five times a second. They aggressively protected food sources, and in addition to flower nectar ate ants, aphids, beetles, and gnats, making them a superb addition to any garden.

But had Phoebe gone out the back door instead of back to bed, she would have run across Beryl, sitting alone in the cedar swing, still dressed in the previous day's clothing. She'd sat there most of the night, wrapped in an afghan, nodded off a few times, and awakened roughly around the same time Phoebe had. Had Beryl not been entirely consumed with her own thoughts, she would have heard the clink of dishes in the kitchen, smelled the coffee as it brewed, caught the faint scent of lemon from the baking scones, or at least heard the doorbell when Will arrived. But Beryl had her eyes and her ears closed. The natural world could have been a million miles away.

Meanwhile, in a time zone that made things an hour earlier, Thomas Jack made interesting the life of a caged blue jay by hiding pine nuts around his cage. While the damaged bird searched for his food, Thomas thought about the woman with red hair who had for a brief time been his friend and lover. He missed her, but missing was a way of life for him, so he was able to step outside the emotion and take a fearless inventory. What else did he miss? His grandmother's gentle laugh, and snow so thick it lay like diamonds on the ground. He wondered how much it would cost to fly to California. He bet he could get just that amount if he sold the mask he'd nearly finished.

Detective Michael Francis Stokes sat at his desk at home looking through papers that explained the details of his pension. Twenty-eight years on the force was a good long stretch—enough, he figured. He thought of how comfortable it would feel to wear jeans and T-shirts every day instead of a suit. The Central Coast of California held a definite appeal. He fingered the brochure Beryl's friends had slipped him, that night they'd had him over for dinner. He might call, but then again maybe he would just show up.

Beryl, on the other hand, was exactly where she was supposed to be, which was sitting in the cedar swing facing the herb garden her friend Nance had planted—what—could it really be nearly eight years ago? The herbs were thriving. Rosemary, the herb for remembrance, grew in fragrant, lush bushes and spilled into the other plants, requiring careful trimming. Beryl could hardly walk by without pinching off a sprig. Purple sage, such a sun-loving fast grower, could easily overtake a garden. Maybe that was nature's intention, since sage possessed so many practical uses. Native Americans used it in ceremonies. Someone with a lingering cough might brew it in a tea to restore health or give a boost of energy to one who felt flattened down by life's trials. Just now, however, the sage had attracted the first Anna's hummingbird of the day. The tiny bird was hungry, and the sage had delectable flowers, as fuzzy as velvet, and the rich purple color of a child's crayon. Beryl knew from reading that the species was named for Anna de Belle Massena, someone the artist James Audubon had described as "a beautiful young woman, not more than twenty, graceful and polite." She wondered if Audubon had known that hummingbirds had the highest metabolic rate of any bird in the world. That most were not even as long as the middle toe of a bald eagle. Because things like that—comparisons, attributes, from the largest beak down to the tiniest feathers—mattered. One thing could exist without the other, sure, but the variety and their hardiness was what made all birds precious.

When Beryl closed her right eye, her world turned the color of mud. At first seeing nothing had been terrifying, but she'd discovered that if she relaxed into it, breathed her way out of the panic, scent began to creep in, layered and diverse, and then came sounds, from the quiet shuffling of horses to the whistle of leaves carried by the wind to faraway voices. Because she had the power of memory, her world still grew in dimension and clarity until it glittered like the metallic feathers of the hummingbird. She knew that in front of her crops of flowers waited to be harvested, and flagstones laid in a maze by her own two hands pointed a way to go, but she didn't need to see any of it to believe it. From far off she heard Verde tell his invisible foe yet again to perform what had to be a physically impossible task, and then Sally yanked her sleeve.

"Auntie Bee! Auntie Bee!"

Beryl opened her eyes, and it seemed that all around her the world had burst into color. "Good morning, Sallykins. What's got you up so early?"

She leaped into the swing and threw her arms around Beryl. "Can we walk down to the creek before breakfast and look for polliwogs? Can we take Calpurnia? Mama says I can't go to the creek without an adult, and Calpurnia is just a puppy so she couldn't save me if a mountain lion came along."

"I see." Beryl smiled. "Come on, then. But you have to hold my hand."

"I know," Sally said wearily. "Because it's not safe even where it's shallow."

"That's right."

Their feet grew damp with dew. Sally squished mud between her bare toes. The two of them stood at the edge of Bad Girl Creek while Calpurnia snapped at water bugs.

"Hmm. No polliwogs today, I'm afraid," Beryl said, bending down to pick up a leaf and fold it into a tiny boat. She handed it to Sally. "Can you set this down very gently on the water?"

"Of course I can."

She gave it a little push with her finger. "Look, Sally. There it goes."

They watched the leave twirl and drift out of sight in the current. In the distance Beryl saw two deer standing still, blending into the oak trees and scrub.

"Auntie Bee?"

"Yes?"

"Do you see her down there?"

"See who down where?"

Sally leaned out and pointed at the water. "That little girl in the water. She's looking at us."

Beryl leaned forward, and felt a lump form in her throat. "Yes, I see her," she said, knowing that while what she saw was a reflection, to Sally it was someone who wanted to play, and that this was probably the exact thing that had enticed Florencio's daughter to enter the creek and be swept away, crushing her parents' hearts. What was beautiful in the world was not always safe, but maybe that was part of what made it so beautiful. This land revived to breed flowers, a mistreated parrot finding the perfect owner, the song that issued forth from a troubled man's guitar and for a while meant love—there was a measure of sorrow to all of it, but at the same time that sorrow laid the groundwork for joy. The hell of things was that the human heart was able to hold both without coming apart. The hell and the heaven.

Sally tugged her hand.

"Ready for breakfast?" Beryl asked, and Sally nodded.

They walked up the flagstone path toward the farmhouse, passing the carefully planted rows of flowers where birds sang and insects buzzed. The hem of Sally's nightie was thoroughly damp, and Beryl's heart was full. Sally hurried, and Beryl went slowly, taking time to breathe deeply, to feast her eyes, and to commit each marvelous moment to memory. "I love this day!" Sally sang, beginning now to skip.

Beryl let go of Sally's hand, and watched her race up the path toward the house. The truest words in the world were those that came from a child's mouth. There was only one word she could think to add, and so she did, out loud, for the whole world to hear.

"Amen."

Acknowledgments

This writer is extraordinarily lucky to have both Deborah Schneider and Marysue Rucci in her life, professionally, personally, and creatively. During the writing of this book their calming assurances, steadfast belief, and continual challenges made my work a joy. Thank you, ladies, and may we continue making books together until we are old and gray.

To Sue Llewellyn, my copy editor and savior from bad grammar, thanks!

The Bird Treatment and Learning Center in Anchorage gave me the great honor of working briefly with raptors, during which time I researched some of this book for the fictional world in which Beryl and Thomas Jack bear witness to this important work. Thank you especially to Mary Bethe, Lisa, Kristen, Ferg, Lynn, and Elise for one of the peak experiences a human can have. Long live One Wing and the Old Witch.

Earlene Fowler, Judi Hendricks, Caroline Leavitt, and Jodi Picoult are some of the best friends a writer could have. Thank you, ladies, for reading my drafts, helping me find my way, and being kind to the core.

My extraordinary friend and colleague Sherry Simpson kept me in dolphins all the way through this book—what more can a woman ask? Sabrina Haverfield is an island of faith and calm in the often-stormy waters of CWLA, and her little girl, Sydney—who is (thankfully) nothing like Sally—helps me remember that with imagination, anything is possible. Gail Boerwinkle is perhaps the only Rolfer on the planet who can put me to sleep, and I thank her for helping me to keep carpal tunnel at bay. Among my writing students I wish to thank Pat O'Hara, Ernestine Hayes, Amy Meissner, and Nan Hallock in particular. Also writers and girlfriends Susan Morgan and Pam Cravez.

Thanks to my doctors for their care and creativity: Gerry Sagahun, Michele O'Fallon, Michael Armstrong, Ronald Feigin, and Susan LeMagie.

To my sister CJ, who has the interesting life and is kind enough to share her experiences with me in the name of story, thank you again for your spirit. To my mom, Mary, and brother John, who provide much needed humor and great company, even via AT&T, love and the door is always open. To my son, Jack, and my wonderful daughter-in-law, Olivia, thank you both for the phone calls and stories, and for your love for each other, which renews my heart.

Without the support and kindness of my husband, Stewart Allison, I would forever be stuck on page 1. Thank you, my love, for knowing the answers to impossible questions, for making every effort not to flinch at my non sequiturs, for creating dinners when I'm past cooking, for finding Diet Cherry Coke in Anchorage, for walking the insane clown posse, for vacuuming the posse's hair up, for your wonderful, magical paintings that show me your heart over and over, for being handsome and fascinating all these years, for your deep and abiding love, and for telling me it's perfectly all right to have another cookie. I love you always and forever. Amen.

Simon & Schuster Paperbacks
Reading Group Guide

Goodbye, Earl

1. In this story, setting is more than a backdrop. The depiction of Alaska and coastal California, where most of the novel takes place, goes deeper than just creating the mood. These places seem to actively reflect the characters' state of mind and emotional "landscape." As such, what significance does Beryl's moving to Alaska have in terms of the larger story? What did Alaska offer her that California did not? What tools does the author use to make the natural landscape such a vibrant part of this novel?

2. How are animals used to the same effect throughout this story? Often, as the lives of

these people unfold, their relationships with nonhuman characters reveal much about their personality. Think about Sally with her horse, Thomas Jack with birds, and Beryl with many different kinds of animals. Why is it that animals give us a window into the emotional worlds of these people?

3. Beryl religiously writes in her journal. As such, it is a key in understanding her as a character. At one point, we learn this about her writing: "What she'd written in California wasn't earth shattering, but here in Alaska she was digging down to the bedrock of her life, and it was a stony parcel of land to till." This metaphor not only sheds light on Beryl's relationship with Alaska but also alludes to the unresolved pain surrounding the rape that she suffered as a teenager. A few pages earlier, that rape, and Beryl's inability to move fully past the memory, is recounted hauntingly. To what extent do you think that experience and her subsequent stay at Saint Margaret's have shaped the person that Beryl is? What kinds of wounds remain?

4. Among other things, her time at Saint Margaret's turns Beryl somewhat sour on religion. The calloused nuns, and to some degree the

Church itself, come off as bitter and ignorant. But despite many negative depictions (including Phoebe's slightly critical attitude) of the Church, some characters seem to take great comfort in religion. Ness, especially, holds Christianity very close to her heart. Were you surprised that women as close as this hold such varied (and sometimes opposing) views on this topic? Although one might not call all of the women in this story religious, do you think they share a common sense of spirituality that binds them together and transcends organized religion?

5. Zoe is an interesting peripheral character, as she really brings out the caregiver in Beryl. When Beryl finds the girl broke and trying to quickly flee her apartment to avoid the landlord, she insists that she come to the nuthatch with her to get on her feet. While Beryl comforts Zoe, she is reminded of her first night on Phoebe's farm and the feelings of permanence and stability that it gave her. Why do you think those memories, long dormant, awaken at that moment? Why is it so important for Beryl to provide comfort for this girl? How might she be healing herself by helping Zoe? Is it simply man trouble that brings these women together, or is there something more?

6. Much is made in this novel of the choices and patterns with which individual characters struggle. Seeing Zoe come to grips with her own failed relationship, Beryl ponders this concept, asking herself, "Was loving a man something she needed to try one last time, just to say she could do it and get it right? Or had her relationship with Earl been, like so many other times before that, just another poor choice?" (229) Do you think any of these characters successfully break free from the patterns that plague them?

7. Early in the novel, Beryl writes in her journal, "I know that in a man's world problems exist to be solved. What if I don't know what the problem is? 'Just let me be sad.'" (5) What might she mean by this? Is there something about the nature of sadness that makes it a worthwhile state—in and of itself? Does sadness need a *reason* to exist, or can it just be? It is interesting that she describes this concept in terms of gender: in a "man's world" sadness must be overcome—it is only a matter of figuring out how one can achieve that. Which outlook seems healthier to you? Is there middle ground between Earl's inability to sit with sadness and Beryl's reveling in it? Which might serve these characters better?

8. In many ways, the real backbone of this novel is the relationships between women. While men float in and out of their lives, taken by tragedy or ordinary circumstance, the one thing that remains, the one constant that these women can rely on, is the love and support that they receive from one another. Talk about the way that this concept is treated in this story. What draws these women together? What keeps them together when times get tough?

9. Along similar lines, what is it about men and women (at least on an emotional level) that makes it so difficult for them to click? According to Thomas Jack, Beryl "did cry a lot, sometimes even during sex, but she was a natural redhead, so he chalked that up to excess passion. Though, there were times he wished he could push her off button." (163) Why is it that men and women often seem to occupy different emotional places? Could the women of this novel ever be totally fulfilled by their men? Do you think that the level to which they lean on their female friends for support exacerbates this problem? Why is it that most of these characters can't seem to find lasting happiness in their romantic lives?

10. It is interesting that Beryl hides from her friends that Earl has left. Late in the novel, we are given a glimpse of her thinking: "But they had all looked at her relationship with Earl as if it were Beryl's gift for having endured so many rotten breaks. . . . [S]he'd had the opportunity to tell them the truth and acknowledge her own human failings, or to push them away and allow them to continue to think that not only was happiness possible for her but for all of them if they just hung in there." (277) Why does Beryl think that Earl's leaving would somehow be emblematic for all of them?

11. At one point, Ness describes her relationship with David as "beyond sex, beyond friends, a kind of love I never dreamed I'd experience." (182) Talk about why Ness found such joy with David, despite the fact that they were not romantically involved. In what ways does this concept—that love can be strong without sex—get to the heart of the larger themes in this novel (themes like sisterhood and the power for friendship)? After David dies, why is the act of fashioning the AIDS quilt so significant for Ness?

12. Where do you see these characters in ten years? If you were the author, and you were to craft a

scene somewhere in the future with these folks, what might it look like?

13. Have you read other Bad Girl Creek novels? If so, how did you like the story as continued here? If you have not read any other Jo-Ann Mapson books, how did you find the experience of coming into the story at this point in time? Did you find yourself wanting to go back and read the others? Did you get a strong sense of Sadie's character, despite the fact that she is only present in this novel through memories?